HONOR IN WAR

By the light of torches I saw Kallijas Itrean rush back towards the breach, his men following; he was coming to me.

Around us his people and mine drew back a little. I learned why he had his name instantly. His skill was perfect, impeccable in form and speed, made of water and steel whether his teachers had called it that or not. I ceased to think of the battle, or see or feel anything but him, and his sword. Yet I began to feel all his spirit was not in it; his fire was muted somehow by his heart, as if with some trouble. I wished I could see his eyes better.

Just about then I made a bad parry, and felt his sword glance my sword arm hard enough to part my mail. Not to do much else; I felt only a trickle of blood. But he jumped back, and froze, and spoke something in Arkan. Startled, I didn't press him; though it was melee it felt like a duel of honor. I saw his lips pressed tight under the nasal of his helmet, as if sealing out bad air. Then a man near him shouted with joy, as if he had beaten me. An absent thought, as the God-In-Ourselves often sends, made me look at the edges of his sword. Hard to see by night, they were both evenly stained their full length with

I know q⬜⬜⬜⬜⬜⬜⬜⬜⬜⬜. But in the end ⬜⬜⬜⬜⬜⬜⬜⬜⬜⬜⬜eart: "I heard so⬜⬜⬜⬜⬜⬜⬜⬜⬜."

Novels of the Fifth Millennium:

The Cage by S.M. Stirling & Shirley Meier
Lion's Heart by Karen Wehrstein
Lion's Soul by Karen Wehrstein

LION'S SOUL

Karen Wehrstein

LION'S SOUL

Copyright © 1991 by Karen Wehrstein

A Baen Books Original

Baen Publishing Enterprises
P.O. Box 1403
Riverdale, N.Y. 10471

ISBN: 0-671-72071-6

Cover art by Larry Elmore

First printing, July 1991

Distributed by
SIMON & SCHUSTER
1230 Avenue of the Americas
New York, N.Y. 10020

Printed in the United States of America

**To S.M.M.,
of course**

Thanks to:

The Bunch of Seven: Shirley Meier, Steve (S.M.) Stirling, Louise Hypher, Tanya Huff, Fiona Patton, Mike Wallis, Terri Neal, Marian Hughes, Mandy Slater, Julie Fountain, Victor Raymond

R.S. (Bob) Hadji, Terri Windling, Steven K. Zoltan Brust, Guy Gavriel Kay, Dave Kirby, Mary Goodall (nee Farrell), Helen Anderson, Jeff Hayes, Kristi Magraw, all those at Unicamp for whom this story is a childhood or adolescent memory, plus everyone else who encouraged me

Jim Baen, Toni Weisskopf, Ralph Vicinanza, Chris Lotts and Larry Elmore, for treating me with undue respect for a first novelist

Olive Shaw (1926–1991) and everyone else in my family who was supportive

Bill Chong, Way Lem, Robert Hayes, Thom Gardiner and the late Robert Lombardo, my karate teachers

Anderson, Bruford, Wakeman and Howe, who somehow predicted this, plus far too many other musicians to list

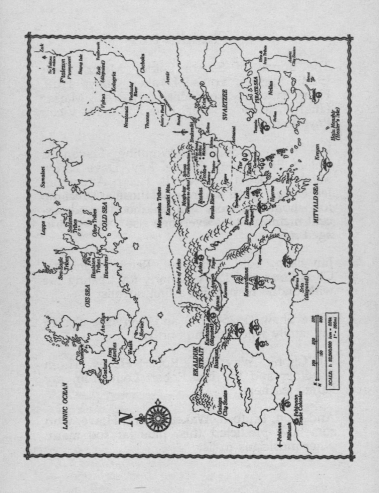

I

I am standing in the silence of night, beside a great circular pool whose bank rotates with time, like the Earthsphere. Distant on the opposite bank is the black silhouette of a cloaked woman, standing still as a stele, but moving as the bank moves; I see her black head creep across the face of a blade-silver moon. Her name is Vora, "scythe." Like the marker of any clock, she frightens me; but she is far away.

I busy myself with administrative tasks; somehow their monotony becomes engrossing, changing the unbroken thread of time into a shuffle of moments. Then suddenly I feel a presence at my shoulder. Vora is beside me, close enough to touch me if she willed, her face like living white stone. Panic seizes me; I realize how much time has crept by, wasted on trifling things I could have delegated, that much of my life gone without my living it. I want to strike myself, repent, beg it back; but it has no more soul to answer than a river, flowing one way, only more time to rush by while I waste it begging, gone forever. Vora waits.

Memories. A voice, close, solas-accent, "So-o-o, horse. Celestialis, lad, that your mother should see you, like this . . ." Wet leaves slapping, thorns raking, horse-stall smell, deck heaving, rain slashing out of black night, "All-spirit, ro-o-o-o-o-ocks!" Fighting, muscle-flesh clenching around my

1

sword, the big man, blond, falling, blood splashing free through air, muscle-flesh clenching around his sword, a thread like a string of spittle stretching between me and the right ear of the one in the pool of blood below, Merchoser leaning. The inside of my own skull. A standing stone in the Shrine of Vae Arahi, from my childish height, I can barely tell Kaninden the memory. "The books, history; the war; daddy riding me on his shoulders; nothing; nothing; grium, that's grium I know that feeling—" Emerald, sapphire and ruby fish, swimming over fingers of fire-orange, pink, gold.

A swishing and clacking of long dry reed tongues, above me. Brightness. Distant rushing thunder, but too steady for thunder; sun, white hot, hotter than sun is, on my skin. Sky; blue; brilliant; against it, an impossible tree, its trunk smooth and grey as an elephant's, a single burst of branches flaring out from the top, each shaped like a single great leaf longer than a man, but formed of green spear-heads spaced as perfectly as by a bridge-builder, sun flickering burning-bright between them; Alchaen's hand on my brow, seeing my eyes open. "Chivinga." *His Haian accent. His flat round face searching nine closer, as if newly intrigued.*

How can I know his name, I thought, when I've never seen him in my life? I was on a beach wider than I thought could exist, of white sand fine as flour. As its edge lapped a brilliant turquoise sea; the thunder was far-off surf. The air was both sweet and salty, fresh in the lungs.

I sat up. My body barely felt my own, weak, sore, delicate as tatters. I saw the scars I knew, the demarchic brand, Second Amitzas's monogram; but there were new, sword-cuts, deep and still a flaming pink against the brown of my tan, on my arm, my leg, my side. I was wearing a loin-cloth, a black arm-ring, a crystal and a leaf-green ribbon tied around my wrist. I ran my hand through my hair, found it cropped short but even.

"Do you remember where you are, Chivinga?" I signed charcoal, then shook my head. "Haiu Menshir. The House of Integrity."

"Haiu Menshir?" I cried. "Saint Mother accept me, I made it here?" My life came crashing back into my head then, so many faceted it was dizzying. I was on Haiu Menshir; I'd planned to get here; I'd got here. They'd made their slip and I'd escaped—hadn't I? "Ask all you need to," he said, reading my mind.

One question pushed aside all the rest. When waking up, one can feel, roughly, how long one has slept. What I sensed of that now broke me into a sweat, like Vora's hand near my shoulder in my recurring dream. "How long is it since I was in Arko?" He answered, "Five months."

While I sat trembling, he explained everything, his hand on my shoulder. Artira had, as I'd suggested, demanded to see me alive. But on the journey I'd ground one of my chain links through, won free from the carriage bearing me, got onto a Yeoli ship in Fispur. We'd been shipwrecked, and got into a fight with pirates on an island, hence my new wounds; they'd been healed by the Haian they'd held captive, Merchoser, who'd been driven to drink—a Haian—by what he'd seen there. I'd been cured of the *grium*, by surgery; Alchaen guided my fingers to the scar, a pentagonal ridge in my skull. I've never remembered these things well enough to give a proper account, or I would. In the war, though Vae Arahi had been taken, my people held out still; my family were coming here.

Now I was, and had been for the last three moons, a patient of the House of Integrity, in the University of Haiuroru, the green ribbon the sigil of such, and he was my psyche-healer.

My head filled with calculations, and I knew again what it was to think with a mind clean of *grium*, joy beyond joy. I was free to seek our alliances. Brahvniki, Tardengk, Curlionaiz; I counted off days in my head. Five moons: I was twenty-two and a half; it must be midsummer, fighting season. Four moons before snow closed the high passes in Yeola-e; plenty of time to win back ground, and winter was on our side. Remembering the name of our ambassador here, Denaina Kotelai, I sprang up, which was much harder than it should be—I'd have to work myself back into training too—and asked Alchaen which way to her.

He blinked, surprised; then said, "You aren't well enough yet, Chivinga." I got the impression, as I argued, that he wasn't used to that from me. Finally he laid his hands on my shoulders, fixed my eyes with his, and said, "Describe the table." I found myself wanting to shake him off, too violently for a Haian, and had to restrain myself. "What table?"

"The table in the oubliette."

Integrity. The first meaning of the word, older than the ethical tone it carries now, is "wholeness." Wholeness, as is needed by those torn asunder. So easily, signs in his words had slipped through my mind, like oil through grasping fingers.

I'd been trained in the ways of mastering fear. I took the first long breath, told myself *I am a warrior*, and felt how out of practice I was in this too. The thoughts that brought on terror kept getting their black paws through the bars; somehow I couldn't put them aside, as I had been able to before. Suddenly it came to me that nothing in my mind felt right.

But that's just it. The thought was laughing and smug, its voice not belonging in me. I heard myself gasp. From then on the wrong thoughts came like sparks, each setting off a fire in my mind as across a tinder-dry city. I could do nothing to stop them; whatever self-mastery I had ever learned was ashes; I felt dragged, helpless as a slave in chains, to a pit I knew would destroy me. The worst of it was that it was all familiar; I'd fallen this way a thousand times before. *He succeeded*, I thought, *I'm insane, All-spirit help me, he did it, All-spirit, I am*, and Kurkas's laughter echoing from high above me mixed with my words in flames, licking me all around with searing truth, drawing me to the pit's brink.

"*Chivinga.*" Hands gripped mine hard enough to hurt: earthly pain, something familiar. I saw Alchaen's face, still calm. The sand, the sea, the sky, the sun's warmth; it was all around me, and yet was not; I had forgotten it. I would swear I smelled smoke. Now I understood the line in the play, "My mind is in darkness." "Take strength from my hands," he said. He had a steadiness about him, like a sage, knowing how to be one's rock in the storm. "Can you hear me, Chivinga?"

Yes. The word formed my mind—it was the truth and all my intent was to say it—but somehow my tongue was cut off from my will, as with truth-drug, but the other way round: I wanted to speak and could not. My throat closed, my lungs were stone. The Mezem was child's play, I thought; *this* is madness.

"You fear for your sanity with good reason," he said. "But you are thinking of this state as permanent, as people do, and it is not. In time you will heal entirely, you will be as capable as you ever were, or more so. You are a very strong soul, and you've already come far, much faster than I thought was possible. This is the first day, for instance, I have ever seen Chivinga as described to me, bright-eyed, quick-tongued, brave, stubborn. . . . This is the first day you have been sane enough to fear for your sanity.

"They had you for a month," he said gently, when I was calm enough. "They left no marks on your body. He meant it to be permanent, but failed, as you see. When you first came here, even after your body had healed, you could not speak, nor truly move of your own will, except, apparently, when your life was threatened; then you'd go berserk. You would not eat or drink unless urged; you never truly slept, for nightmares. That was three months ago."

I will never know all Kurkas had done, or did himself, to me, though others do. A full account is on file, but I will never read it.

Drugs, all-spirit knows what. Hallucinogens, weakeners, purgatives, drugs that blind and deafen, Mahid's Obedience; any substance Arkans have that can be used to hurt has probably been through me. Smothering, rape, humiliation of a hundred kinds; these are only words, yet though I can write them, if you asked me I would not be able to say them smoothly, even now.

They truth-drug-scraped me; Kurkas knew of my fore-knowledge, and the single-wing if he believed it. What they got out of me they used, convincing me Niku and the child were dead, that Yeola-e was defeated, all the circle-stones smashed, the sword of Saint Mother melted down, my children killed, my family all rendered barren. They'd had to convince me otherwise, here: Alchaen had Denaina tell me we were still holding, and show me the current Pages ("Ultimate Victory Over Barbarians Soon to Come"); for Niku it was a Niah trader who'd heard she had a child.

"He hated you," Alchaen said. "And feared you. He could

not know what he did, since he has never felt it. Yet you know all these things, and still cry, 'Why?'. For you there can be no answer that is enough, no reason that justifies to your heart what you have suffered, for all it might explain to your mind. You will have to accept that."

Now my healing was my work, half a day, every day, bitter and painstaking as war-training, in some ways harder. I was torn asunder a thousand ways; madness has as many branches as a tree. But, I learned, so does sanity; in a thousand ways I would knit. As the body will attempt to heal itself even without a healer's guidance, so will the soul; as Haians say, that is the way of the life-force. Yet I was lucky, being guided, and by one so good. Like a Teacher, seeming to read my mind often in the same way, saying, "Follow the threads, Chivinga," Alchaen led me along the black twisting path.

He drew out of me what information he must by putting me in trance, to question the deeper layers of my memory; there he found a sane and patient voice claiming to have been a fly on the wall, and so knew all that had happened to this other person, Chevenga. The fly even knew what I could and could not bear to remember when I woke. "No, don't tell him that," he said once to Alchaen—it was in his notes—"he'd jump in the fire-coral." Madness is devious, no less devious than the mind on which it feeds, but so is healing.

He was sense in the whirlwind, routine in the aimlessness, embracing arms in the terror. He made me take care of my looks in the morning, train, eat when I was hungry, swim when I was hot, nap when I was tired. He filled the missing patches; to my every question he had, or was, the answer, even if that were only his calm. He taught me to speak again, like a child, from nothing.

He set me laws to hold to: don't fight what I felt, but let it take and pass through me (hearing this, I thought immediately of what Iska had told me to do the night before my fight against Riji Kli-Jas); tell him so I need never face it alone; distinguish myself from my madness; be patient. He forbade me ever to curse or hurt myself, even so much as a smack on my own temple to clear my head. "You are hurt enough already," he would say. "You feel as if you are weak, childish, stupid, cowardly; but you aren't; these things are not you, but your madness." Always, look at my heart with the eyes of a scholar, question all I felt, ask why. I had never done that before, always knowing, or thinking I knew, and putting it aside by will if I had to. Now those faculties were gone; terror or sickness or pain or rage would seize and toss me at their leisure like sea-waves a leaf, and most of the time I had no idea why. I had to build it all up again, my understanding of myself (it's for that reason, apparently, the mad are so engrossed in themselves), slowly, painfully learning many things several times over. I would tell it in more detail; but in entire honesty, like a fight or a pain, I don't remember it well. Alchaen made his notes, but them too I will never read.

Yet in the end, I think, I came out better: certainly wiser, broader and quicker of mind than I had been before. I knew what I could survive. To understand insanity is to understand sanity.

Once when Alchaen and I had been speaking of the surgery, I found myself distracted; on a shelf near the bed stood a glass jar of liquid, with some grey tentacled mass the size of an eye suspended in it. I was never squeamish, but this somehow turned my stomach. I asked him what it was. "Your mind seeks out the strands," he said, smiling. "We brought it here, because you took comfort from seeing it was no longer in you. The *grium*."

All I had time to think was, *so big*; then it was out the door, while he dashed after me worried. Behind a bush I heaved up everything in my stomach. Feeling better, I excused myself, and took a good look. Turning the jar in my fingers, I marvelled that the thing had not affected me more. But it was out of me, as he'd said, harmless, captive in my hands, defeated, dead; on my shelf, it was not a haunt, but a trophy. I still have it, and bring it out every time I think someone needs a good shaking.

He showed me what I had written and drawn while I had not been able to speak. Truly they were the scrawlings of a lunatic, words and shapes in ragged shreds, broken swords, broken circles, smashed crystals, splashes of blood, the lines sometimes carven into the paper as if the pen in the writer's

hand had been to his mind a knife. One pattern I did not
understand that came over and over again, a twisting tree-
branch with one fork, turned out to be the crack in the
ceiling of the oubliette, that I had come to know far too
well. I remembered words on Jinai Oru, from five years
before. "The black lightning bolt with the forks, that never
goes away."

"Why," I asked Alchaen, "did they train me to make no
sound? I thought that's what I would want, and not they."
He answered, "Crying out in pain is a release, that sends it
outward. You've noticed, haven't you, how it eases?" I told
him honestly I'd thought it was the other way around, having
trained myself to keep silent and still because of my position. "That's for lesser pain. Pain this extreme, denied that
egress, turns inward and does worse."

It should be no surprise to anyone who understands
Arkans that Kurkas tried to render me impotent. I'll write
no more, than that they'd trained me to fear pain out of
pleasure. My last memory of sex seemed too beautiful to be
real, now, like a dream from which I'd been awakened by
the touch of a branding iron: the night before my execution,
when I had finally given Skorsas, my Mezem boy who had
done more than anyone to keep me alive there, my love in
body as well as soul. Now the brand burned all the deeper,
for that apparently having been my last.

This being something Alchaen felt he best not take into
his own hands, as it were, he sought a woman volunteer,
preferably a Yeoli, to be my sexual healer. Now and then
Yeoli privateers would come into port, bringing wounded;
one ship was here now. Alchaen sent to the captain; I can
imagine how it went. "*Chen*, line up! I want a volunteer for
a crucial secret mission, of national importance ..." He
chose a young woman by the name of Ronatora-e Ekaina,
whom I name because I am forever grateful. I have never
been the same in bed since; I can't abide any roughness at
all, for one thing, and sometimes go icy cold right afterwards; but I can please, and be pleased. Rona, with her
tenderness and patience—she lived with me, in effect, for
a month—is to be thanked for that.

∘   ∘   ∘

My mother, my shadow-father and Etana came, with Krero, Sachara (who was now married, to one of his fellow scholars in the University of Terera) and seventeen of the Elite. Alchaen had spoken to them carefully, told them what had passed and all the ways to be careful with me; yet their faces were still shocked at the sight of mine. Aside from the scars, I apparently looked ten years older.

Esora-e looked more careworn, but otherwise the same, the greatest joy; we flung ourselves into each other's arms, and he made the remarks I expected about my gold teeth when I smiled. I turned next to my mother. The world froze, and turned black and icy; I was done with healing, and there was nothing left but to die. By my memories, so long ago now, the knife in her hand, the darkening scarlet on her tricolor shirt, I knew; she had killed my father.

I fell in a faint, at least to my knees; then I got up and ran, planning to kill myself. Alchaen raised the House alarm; the strong-arms came; I would not strike them, since they were Haians, so they seized me and pinned me to the bed. Niku had spoken of A-niah captives biting through their tongues to commit suicide in bonds; I tried that, tasted the iron tang of blood, breathed some in and choked. Voices rose, a hand laid a sharp-smelling cloth over my face, and the world spun away like a leaf falling.

When I woke my mouth was full of linen; I was not restrained, but knew by the heaviness of my limbs that I was drugged, and could do nothing but weep. Alchaen questioned me; I answered with my hand, chalk or charcoal. I feel for him, trying to calm my parents, without knowing why I'd done this. "There were other lies," he said, when he knew. "Chivinga, how could you do this to yourself without finding out whether this was one or not?"

Encahun nenanhanun, the closest translation "empathy of memory," is Haian for the process whereby the recollections of one person are brought into the mind of another. A Yeoli might call it being the other, perfected. It requires three Haian psychics: two telepaths to make the bond, and an empath to sense whether matters are getting out of hand, as they often do. More specialists; I wondered helplessly how much of a bill the treasury of Yeola-e, which was probably flat broke, was running up for putting all my bits back together. My mother and I both agreed to it though. "Best for you, and her, that you know beyond a doubt," Alchaen said to me.

It was done at night, in a room lit by one small lamp-flame. The reading and sending telepaths sat together, almost embracing; to their shield-side they placed my mother, to their sword-side me, while the empath (Megiddan, who apparently had worked with me before) faced them, where she could reach both of us with her hands. They explained everything twice—the ways of breaking the bond three times—and handled me as if I were a glass statue cracked almost through.

In the silence of trance, I felt fingers on my temple, the sending telepath's, a touch as gentle as feathers. But when Megiddan guided my mother to begin remembering, my mind was suddenly stabbed full of brightness, as strong as my own thoughts but coming from my shield-side. *Sunlight, green, the smell of cedars; above their highest branches, the peak of Haranin against a blue sky. I was home, walking, a warm arm around my waist, a strong hard body in my own arm; my husband, my love, Tennunga.*

He smiles, his cheeks flushed a sweet pink between sun-gold curls; he was just sparring. We kiss; in that I can forget the sound of the wings of Shininao, that I am carrying a knife in Vae Arahi, that something terrible I cannot name will happen. We walk silently past the rock. A jolt, all through him. I look. On his face, the ultimate shock, the last horror—something on his chest, the steel tip of a knife, reddened, from inside him—the Enchian face behind him— the eyes I love look at me, anguished, knowing. Then they turn to glass

I tore away from Megiddan's hand, breaking the bond, hearing the echoes of my own scream. Alchaen caught me at the door; I fell at his feet, keening like a child. My mother had lived this, probably a thousand times; this had been my first. But the lie was slain; we flung ourselves into each other's arms.

The next morning when she came to see me, I started; it was as if her shoulders wore my head. She'd cropped her hair to warrior-cut. "I am going to fight the Arkans," she said, "long in the tooth or not. Stop looking so worried, my child; I *do* plan to train first. But I see no other way to free myself of this anger."

Alchaen arranged as best he could that nothing should be asked of me but healing; when not with him I swam or exercised or lay on the white sand and let the sun soothe me, by his orders. I wrote my sister to ask her consent to seek alliances in Ycola-e's name, which she granted me. I wrote Niku as well, and got an answer. She'd confessed to giving up the Niah secret as soon as she'd got home, and had been tried; after invoking their oracle, the Council of Elders absolved her. Then they'd heard the news of my execution; though she doubted it, she was in fear until my letter came. She'd given birth: a girl, who she named Vriah, which means "freedom."

Now she was proposing to her people that they send a wing, as the unit is called, of seventy-five crack fliers, to my army. It would take much convincing; though they had made agreements with kings and generals to work in armies on occasion before, it had never been known how they broke sieges, scouted and carried messages so well. In my reply to her I included a letter to them, proposing alliance as formally as I could, wearing the ribbon.

That was as much time as I thought I would spend on politics, on Haiu Menshir. I should know the shape of my life better.

The day after my family arrived, and the Elite had been set to guarding my cottage, a shift came on who were armed. "You know nothing about it," Krero said cheerily, when I called him in. "You're a patient of the House of Integrity, you're not responsible, don't worry your head."

I'd missed him, and his endearing habit of choosing for me. "I'm a patient of the House of Integrity who has weapon-sense," I said, "and who can make an appointment with Dinerer tomorrow. Shall it be I who tells her what's going on, or you?"

He sat down in his sulking way, with a snort. "We all thought it best you be kept out of this . . . well, I *tried*. We asked Speaking Elder Dinerer for a dispensation, to carry weapons. Yes, Cheng, all properly, through the ambassador. It struck us that the Mahid, or whatever Kurkas might send after you, are unlikely to extend the same courtesy. She didn't seem to see the truth of this." He railed on for a time about effete, cowardly Haians being blind and naive and having no care for the harsher world that protects them, ending with, "if *she* wants to die for her beliefs, fine—but I don't think *you* should!

"So we sneaked arms in. If they don't try anything, no one will ever know. If they do, we'll have been proven right."

"The demarch of Yeola-e is welcomed as guest and patient onto Haiu Menshir," I said, "and the first thing he does to show his gratitude is sneak on twenty swords— by their reckoning, an act of war. A well-considered move, Krero."

"That's why we thought it best you didn't know," he said, all blinking innocence. "You can appear not to. They don't know about weapon-sense, do they? If there's trouble, just play ignorant; they aren't going to call Haians out of Yeola- e for what a mere guard captain arranged. Shit, Cheng, you can't even talk straight; they can see that." I decided to speak to Dinerer myself.

I did not know quite what this entailed, though, having been too insane to notice the constraints of insanity on me. The reply to my note from the Hall of Elders came not to me but to Alchaen, saying it was understood I was still his patient, so how had I come to ask an appointment, as if I were competent to? Of course he asked me what it was about, and when I said as much as I was willing, that it was a guard matter, he suggested I let Krero deal with it. Krero slipped a sword under my bed. "I hid it there without your knowledge," he said with a broad wink. "If something happens, I yelled to you it was there, got it?" I resigned myself to hoping Kurkas would not find out I was here; in vain.

It was at night, in my fifth month there. Weapon-sense tore me out of sleep; both guards on the roof had fallen, without a sound.

I leapt out of bed, grabbing the sword and crying the alarm; it must have been blood-curdling, for it carried all the old terror I didn't even know I had left in me, for knowing Mahid were near. But I had forgotten: I was a patient of the House of Integrity, Merchoser, who was watching over me that night—I was never left alone—tried to push me back into bed. Outside my guard, two on each wall, didn't even move, let alone draw weapons; a blood-curdling scream in the night from me was a shrugging matter for them. The pair on the back wall went down, one of them Krero, just saying, "Easy, Cheng, go back to—" Then four Mahid, dart-guns in hand, were breaking through the palm-frond wall.

I hissed to Merchoser to take cover, and slapped the lamp out; under woods and roof on a dark night, it was pitch-black. Guessing they'd shoot low I sprang up onto a wall-beam, and heard two sharp huffs of air; one dart landed in my bed, the other skittered off the wall. "Light!" the leader hissed. Where Merchoser was, I could not know, only hope. I leapt for the one closest, who was reloading, and took his head off. Then I was back in the Mezem quarters, fighting them; it seemed Skorsas should be near, swearing quietly. The only difference was having sensed Krero fall, Krero, who'd wept with me for Mana, probably dead himself.

I heard my own laugh, long and ragged with blood-rage, a maniac's in the dark. They froze; I moved, Arkan words coming easily to my tongue as I let my hands fly. "You know this sword, black dogs! I will destroy you, my nightmares incarnate, I always have, I always will; send a hundred Mahid, a thousand Mahid!" In time my blade stopped finding men and found only air, tedious after the catch of flesh and bone, and blood spattering warm. Outside the Yeolis had finally figured out something was amiss. "He's up in a tree!" I heard, over moaning near my feet. "Inside! Krero! Demarch! Cheng!" Four came in, one with a bow.

"Where were you for the height of the party?" I said. Then, remembering myself, "Never mind me, I'm crazy, lend me your bow." The two Mahid climbing down from trees were easy shots; silence fell.

Someone got the lamp alight. To our astonishment, we'd lost no one, just one broken arm and an eye pierced by a dart; Krero was unconscious, but unharmed. They'd used stun-darts, intending, it seemed, to take me alive if they could, or kill me and themselves if my guards trapped them and would not let them take me. A choice from a guard's nightmares; all-spirit be thanked mine never had to make it. All the Mahid were dead, having used their poison teeth.

We found Merchoser curled under the bed, his face buried in his hands, saying mindlessly, "*Anamun anamun anamun ...*" After sixteen years in the midst of barbarity he had returned to the home of peace, thinking to escape bloodshed forever, and seen it follow him here.

It came to me then that we—no, *I*—had killed six, and they had killed none, on Haiu Menshir. Just then Alchaen came running, with four House strong-arms; they patrol the woods at night, and had heard. All five froze like stones at the sight of me, then shrank backwards, calm flat Haian faces gaping in horror. I hadn't had time to wash; I was coated with blood. My warriors, of course, were laughing in victory and slapping me on the back. I opened my mouth, and nothing came out; trust my tongue to fail me now.

Alchaen only stared at the corpses, with their onyxine and bound blond hair—I knew some of the faces—and then at me, as I had never imagined his face could look, as if a monster stood in my place. From him, it cut the heart out of me. "Go to the sea and wash, lad," my mother's voice said softly; someone had run for her.

Cool water brought calm. As I came back, I heard Anchera say, "Yes, he really did it all himself. All-spirit knows how, but break my crystal if I lie." So much for my playing innocent.

The next day, Dinerer called in Krero, who had barely woken up from the drug and needed hard convincing this was neither a dream nor a prank, Denaina, who had no idea anything had happened, and me. No mention of my competence now.

During Krero's meeting with her, I flinched, hearing through the door the young deep voice and the old high one raised through the door; I'd never heard a Haian even go curt in anger in my life. I could imagine what Krero was arguing, despite all my warnings: that he'd been right to sneak weapons in against her will. He came stamping out, livid and trembling, and called her something I shall not write. He'd got her in just the mood, I gathered, to see me.

Dinerer was elderly, looking over sixty, which in Haian meant she was likely over eighty, her hair bright white around a slender tawny face, the web-work of wrinkles carven in a kindly mien, but the black eyes all hardness now. I thought it best to let her speak first. As I listened, my heart went to water. By her reckoning, both Yeola-e and Arko had violated the trust of Haiu Menshir by sneaking his arms and then bringing our war here; she was considering calling all Haians out of both.

One could see her way: Haiu Menshir could not renounce its ways, and remain itself. Attack and defense are not truly different to the Haian mind. When I got a chance, I said, "My presence here is a danger to you. I will go."

To my surprise she answered, "No. You are not healed yet, and we will not forsake you. Whom we heal, need shall dictate, not Arka." I answered that if I could not protect myself my life was in danger; the Mahid always left one man back to report, and his pigeon would be halfway to the City itself now. (She had already called in the Arkan ambassador to give him the corpses, without telling him who had made them so; I can imagine his curiosity.)

Though it was a matter of only a few healers in the strips of Yeola-e that were still free, I went to my knees, asking what else could I have done, given my position. "It's been a noted trait of Yeoli rulers," she said, "to care for nothing but their country." I begged her forgiveness. At heart I yearned to be reconciled with the principle of Haiu Menshir itself; I remembered Alchaen's look, and Merchoser under the bed chanting *"anamun,"* and felt worse than nothing. As usual these days, I didn't know how shaken I was; my tongue locked; I knelt panting, straining for words, nearly weeping, and felt an utter fool, representing Yeola-e like this before the one who stood for Haiu Menshir. But she was Haian; she took my hands. That let me feel less like a diplomat shaming my nation and more like a child solaced by a grandmother, no matter if I showed my heart, and calmed me.

In the end she judged that they had done worse than us, coming as assassins while I had come as a patient; she gave me the dispensation for arms, dated back to when Krero had first asked, and tore up the paper declaring Haian withdrawal from Yeola-e, while sending the one for the City itself. She feared calling every Haian out of the Empire, it turned out, for that would leave her without any hold on Arko at all. There were other grievances, it seemed; Kurkas's personal healer had not been heard from far too long, all inquiries of him ignored, and another had died somewhere by Arkan hands. I asked after Persahis and Nemonden, since I'd been scraped; but she had heard nothing.

New fears in mind, I offered again to leave. I learned then that she held it was not for me to choose at all, until I was healed, and hence competent. No one had told me that, worried how I would take it, I suppose, with reason. "You are saying I can be kept here against my *will*?" I said, wondering vaguely how they proposed to do this, when I'd brought down six Mahid the night before; but of course I would never strike a Haian. It was up to the one considered my guardian, she said, which would have been my mother except for my position; that made it Denaina.

We called her in, and I argued. Would it not have been worse for my case, I would have beat my head on the desk, when Denaina patted my shoulder and said, "Easy, lad, they'd never attack Haiu Menshir; All-spirit, you've been through a lot." Alchaen's bare minimum to finish my healing, which he didn't like, was two moons. Using every grain of persuasion in me, my tongue seizing on every fourth word, I talked him down to one.

"You cold charm the bark off a tree," Krero said when I handed him the dispensation. Esora-e burst out laughing. "I know how he did it . . . speak to them in the tongue they understand, you always say. All Haians are dupes for tears, ha ha! Well done, my son."

Ten days went by, and I felt healthy enough to press Alchaen to let me go now. He said flatly no, a mere month was stinting enough. Twenty, and I pressed again, for the same answer. On the twenty-first day, Alaecha, on the roof, spied three red sails.

It was in my mind, when I took the decision I took, that the ship we had could not outrun theirs: they were fast frigates, not quinqueremes. Else I should have not chosen so much, for Haiu Menshir. I threw on Esora-e's armor, and led the full guard at a dead run down to the harbor.

There, a terrible silence had fallen; on the promontories and hillocks all around Haians were gathering, without even a whisper. It is the Haian belief that their passive way is too delicate to last forever; one day, inevitably, mainlanders

will come to destroy it; but they will resist the way of war
to the end, by not resisting. They will only gather around
the harbor in silent thousands, to bear witness. Seeing the
sails of Arko, they thought it was today.

There is a district of Haiuroru near the piers which, being
the domain of visiting sailors, is just the same as any port
town on the Miyatara, full of taverns and brothels and
brawls. Sailortown, as it is called, is walled off; the famed
gate at which one must relinquish one's weapons stands
there. Full-armed we ran out through it. On the streets and
piers people of all races were running back and forth, or
readying ships to fly, fearing whatever they feared from
Arko.

I jumped up on a bollard, and hailed in every language
I knew, "To arms! Arkans are coming, to take Haiu Menshir—but only three ships! We needn't let them; shall we?"
Soon I had a crowd, mostly with hooks and poles and sailor's
knives, but some besides mine in proper gear, all yelling
and waiting to be told what to do.

A plan came, brought to my mind by the sight of about
forty Srian archers, their ebony heads towering over the
rest; they had come here because of bad casualties on their
ship, I imagined, and would not flee without their laid-up
comrades; their captain, thank the die, didn't know what
the green ribbon meant. Without them, I wouldn't have had
much of a plan, I suspect, and we'd all have been cut to
pieces; as it was I just started giving orders, calling out of
long disuse my command-voice; to my delight they were
followed.

Two piers side by side were empty, but for one ship that
I got its people to heave off to another, a place where the
Arkans could land together, and would, seeing nothing but
a line of Haians, standing back. Dinerer was there now, in
full formal robes with the green stripe and the Haian poppy
on a golden chain, the sigil of state, under a canopy held
by four apprentices. I had everyone hide behind bales and
crates, the Elite night-shift around the head of one pier, the
day-shift at the other, the Srians, seventy or so at full
strength, on the next piers over, half on each side.

I would be lying, to say I wasn't afraid; I hadn't commanded for better than five years. As the Arkans made fast

hawsers, each ship bearing a scarlet-armored phalanx of sixty on the foredeck, a forest of spear-tips over their heads shining in the sun, I wondered what crucial thing I'd forgotten in haste or weakness of mind. No point running it all over again in my head though, now: it was too late.

More ready to impress than to fight, since this was Haiu Menshir, they marched down the piers three abreast, with the eagle standard and their commander in front, an *Aitzas* with armor made to fit his paunch, bearing a drawn sword in one hand and a set of polished shackles in the other: symbols. He looked pleased with himself for doing this, not troubled; seeing his huge audience he seemed to think, "All these people, turned out to see me." Of course, they'd had to send that kind; anyone decent would balk.

As he came close enough I called the signal, and charged him. He stood flat-footed, as did his men, entirely surprised. It needed to be a spectacular death, to unspirit the rest, so I faked him low and struck off his head. The standard-bearer was easy work, since, to his credit, in truth, he would not drop it; and the eagle ate dust, under our feet.

We held them on the piers, far enough out that the water was too deep for wading, little trouble for Demarchic Guard Elite against Arkan regulars; then I signalled the Srians. Strung out along the piers, the Arkans had nowhere to go to escape the arrow-rain, no bows to answer it, no enemy near to fight; they fell into disarray, some dashing back to the ships, some pressing their fellows ahead, all cursing and yelling. I drew out of the fighting, got up on a crate, signed cease shooting, and spoke in Arkan. "Do you think your Steel-armed God would let you do this thing without punishment?" Somehow I knew superior-to-inferior, from *Aitzas* speaking to me, I suppose. "It seems he put us here, instead. Give it up, or we'll send you all to Hayel!" It took another volley, and more of them to fall thrashing into the harbor to drown; then they surrendered.

We stripped them—two hundred sailors who'd hardly got near the fighting came away crowing with an Arkankilt or sword or breast-plate—and imprisoned them on their own ships. I remembered how they stared at my face, the news having run back through them who I looked uncommonly like. A Mezem with standing room filled had witnessed the death of Karas Raikas. Then, thinking of the wounded, and that there were plenty of healers here, cleared battle-haze out of my mind; I remembered where we were.

The Haians stood still as trees on the hillsides, ten thousand pairs of dark flat eyes fixed on us, even the children's unmoving. Even as Krero and Sachara lifted me up onto their shoulders and the sailors soaked me with wine, I felt myself shrunk down from the victorious general to a careless child who'd not only trespassed on temple land, but murdered. I looked for Dinerer, thinking, shall I cry at her feet this time? She was gone, the canopy disappeared.

I made them put me down and ran through the gate, leaving my sword, as if it mattered. Haians flinched back from me all the way, throwing up their hands as if I would strike them. The streets near the Hall of Elders were deserted. I was dripping with sweat and blood, I realized, as I stood at the threshold with its spotless white woollen carpet. There was a fountain near; I washed my face and hands, and took off my sandals.

In the austere bright open rooms, the ring of shell wind-chimes which one hears everywhere on Haiu Menshir still sounded, faint and fragile; aside from that I heard only my armor creaking as I walked. Dinerer's door stood open. My heart pounded.

She was sitting at her desk, flat-eyed. It was all cleared off, but for one thing: the gold-chained poppy, which lay before her. "I was expecting you," she said softly, holding it out to me in her hand. "You have conquered us; this is yours."

This was far worse than her anger. "Dinerer, Speaking Elder, I didn't fight them for that! It was to keep you free, and myself too, I won't lie. What was I to do, for my people, for myself? I wanted to leave; you wouldn't let me! What was I to do?"

She stood and stepped close to me. For all her age, she moved fast enough to hang it around my neck before I could back away. "Whatever you want, or think you want, you choose what ways are to be followed on the island; that is proven. So it is yours; I hope, Fourth Chevenga Shae-Arano-e, what you do with it is to the good."

I was speechless, not from madness, but from truly having

to answer. The cursed tears, *they* were from madness. No, I thought, there has to be an answer to this. I could always find them before; somewhere in me I must still know how, somewhere the God and the path unconceived still lives. I touched the lacquered petals; nothing in the world could look more wrong, more sick, more mad, than this against blood-soiled armor.

"I may do what I wish with this?" I said. "Then come with me." She came like a prisoner, but with a Haian's passive pride.

In the harbor, the crowd had barely moved, except for those near the fight, who tended the wounded, or helped lifting corpses out of the sea. Some raised a grief-chant, rising and falling like wind through a crack; others stood waiting for word, for her. I saw the other elders, green-striped, circled. As the people saw her without the poppy and me with it in my hand—I could not wear it—they fell silent again, even the triumphant sailors.

I've probably never made a speech less smooth. In front of all Haiu Menshir, that had just seen me do what I had done, nothing pat or grand was possible; as well I feared every moment my tongue would lock. I said only, "People of Haiu Menshir; your Speaking Elder gave this to me, since to her mind I am Haiu Menshir's conqueror. She says it is mine to do with what I think best, so that I will do. I didn't fight to conquer, but to defend; I want Haiu Menshir to remain as it is forever; I am nothing but a patient of the House of Integrity,"—I held up the green ribbon—"who came here for healing only Haiu Menshir could give me." Then I went to my knees, and held the poppy out to her in two hands. With my head bowed, I could hide the tears then. After a moment's pause, she took it, and put it on, and began speaking to them in Haian. I crept away, to the knot of Yeolis.

The gist of her speech, I understand, was that it seemed Haiu Menshir's time was not at hand after all, but it must heal itself of the wound done here. Krero said, "She should thank you. She should call you back and kiss your hands." I shushed him. Whatever my act had spared them, to their mind I carried its stain; I agreed she should keep me at a distance.

The Arkans I let go on one of their ships, though many argued it should be sunk. I'd have no more of killing even near here. We took the pigeons, though, to send a message to Arko saying the mission had succeeded; it would buy me time to get off the island, after which it would be in no danger from Arko—I prayed.

To get the message right we had to use their own truth-drug on the second-in-command. I'd seen a syringe used often enough to do it myself. Thus I learned Kurkas's orders, and felt chills spread out from my heart, as if his hand could touch me here. If they missed me, they were to find my healers, and bring them to Arko. Haians, for the crime of healing, saving life and sanity, who would do the same for him, should he need it.

I showed the transcript to Dinerer, who spoke her anger at my using truth-drug, which Haians believe rightly to be violation, and hence violence. I wanted to call in the priva-teers, have ships here, but I knew better than to suggest that, to do any more than say, "If there is anything you wish of me, anything at all in my power as demarch . . ." She said only, "Heal." And go away; that went without saying.

I dreamed of bedding Shininao again, as I had in the Mezem. This time when he stabbed his beak into my ear, I fought. He struck my head back and thrust one hand into my mouth and down my throat, pressing deeper finger-width by finger-width with slow surges like a worm through earth, or a frog in a snake's throat; with the stopping of my breath, my eyes closed, and my limbs relaxed and would not move; his fingers, warm with my life now, laced around my heart. Afterwards I said, "I no longer want you, but I accept your power." He said, "You're more sane now."

"You are ready," Alchaen said the next day, "for the last, and the worst." The day they'd told me Yeola-e was de-feated, his foot on my neck, superior-to-inferior Arkan, no more the language of equals; the same day they'd told me they'd killed my children. "That wasn't all. Set your teeth. Give me your hands."

The name of Fourth Chevenga Shae-Arano-e, Kurkas had said, had been effaced from every record, stone or paper, and was unlawful to speak in Arko or the province once called Yeola-e. Soon I would be forgotten entirely except as Karas Raikas, and eventually as him too. I will keep you secretly as my slave, my toy, until the eve of your thirtieth birthday, he said, then put you down; but preserve your corpse, to be buried with its head under my feet when my great God claims me.

So well I knew the feel of more hidden darkness, beginning a steady whipping and clawing from the pit of my soul. So familiar, fear-sweat, scalding and freezing at once.

" 'Cease fighting and it will cease hurting,' he told you," Alchaen said. " 'Let your mind die.' "

"No! No, All-spirit, I didn't! All-spirit, tell me I didn't!" I cried. What was I, if I had chosen this willingly, if I'd given myself up to him, if I'd killed myself?

Alchaen's fingers tightened. "The ultimate lesson," he said. "Learn this, and you will not only be sane, but wise. And don't think yourself weak for it; it is the same with all people. The torturer never wreaks the worst on us; expert torturers, such as these, know that. We only wreak it on ourselves."

"Yet what Kurkas did to you," he answered, when I could hear, "even a Mahid could think beyond the pale." Amitzas, I thought. The Pharmacist. Somewhere in me I remembered all.

He had come in after Kurkas had gone, looked over me lying on the table. What thought passed through his mind, no one could know; but he had laid his hand on my brow, then taken my head in his arms. When my tears had come, he'd let me weep them. Alchaen thought that one mercy had drawn me back from the cliff's edge.

"Then I . . . did not . . . save myself," I said: I could only speak haltingly. "He did. Amitzas."

"Yet think of it this way, Chivinga. You moved him to do it. Even helpless, wordless, on the table, you somehow moved him to do it. To whose credit is that?"

I lay thinking for a moment; then I heard the voice of the harmonic singer, and the wind, the first time I had since before this tear in my life that divided it in two. Understanding unfolds like the opening of a rose, petal by petal; now

I saw another petal stripped back, in the thing I must understand the most.

My grandmother had told me, "Power is not a trait; it's an agreement. No one person has it, for you cannot have it while alone." I'd understood this in skeleton, as I did my demarchic work; now I saw it fleshed out.

Power is between two people. That I'd not had the strength to save myself was no matter; I need never stand on my own, while my people claimed me; they would be there. For an instant, Amitzas Mahid, whatever he intended, had been one of my people. "True power comes only from the love of the people," the ancient philosopher wrote—or sympathy, in this case, yet what is sympathy but love?—and now I truly understood.

We were on the beach; as I often did there at twilight after a hard session, I dozed. But my mind was still coursing ahead along this trail even as the shades of sleep, which sometimes bring clarity, fell across it; I murmured something, in future tense.

I woke in the morning, as Alchaen sometimes did, he'd had me carried to bed, something which would only fail to wake me on Haiu Monshir. When he came, I said, from my heart, "Alchaen, that was the last; I'm sane. I may be a little thin around the edges but I'm solid in the middle. Let me go."

He said, "I want to talk about what you said last night." Being reminded brought the words back clear: *I will go home, and win back Yeola-e, and conquer Arko.* "Is that a sane intention?"

Haians think any fighting is madness; it was a running joke in the guard that if Alchaen really knew what I planned to do at home he'd never let me go, and in fact tie green ribbons on all the rest of us as well. But that was not what he saw wrong. From my heart, I said, "it's not intention. I can't choose that, only my people can."

"You said, 'I will conquer Arko.'"

I thought for a time. The spirit of those words was gone; I had only them to go on. "It depends on a thousand things," I said. "How the war goes, the alliances, above all, if my people ask it of me. It's against our custom to cross our border. But they might rescind that, temporarily. They will ask me, 'Is it possible?' If it is, I will say so; I must give an honest answer. Then they'll send me. It's not intention. It might have been foreknowledge."

He said, "Give me your hand," and untied the ribbon.

I threw myself into his arms, kissing and pressing my brow to his hands. "Thank you, Alchaen, thank you—so many people in the world would take that for madness."

"They do not understand sanity," he said. "I won't say I wouldn't keep you longer, if I could, for I would. But perhaps that is the Haian in me, and I do you disservice to forget your circumstances. You come from a different world than I know. You are very well suited to it."

All my healers recommended I hire a personal physician, for the war; Alchaen felt he or she should know some psyche-healing. I chose instead one I knew. All through my healing Merchoser's nephew Kaninjer had tended me as well, gratitude making him devoted; he'd passed with honors in healing, and studied things Yeoli, in preparation to go there on his mainland service. I took him on.

I sailed as soon as I could. Alchaen and I stood by the gangplank, reluctant in the end to part; it occurred to me no one knew me as well except perhaps my mother, and maybe not even her. But some chill haunted his face, in the hot sun; I played psyche-healer, urging him to speak it. "An oath sworn in insanity," he said finally, "is not binding. To my mind when you swore to sack Arko—not conquer, *sack*—you were insane."

We hadn't spoken of that for two or three moons; I think he'd put it out of mind, ascribing it to grief and anger that would fade. Now he'd been reminded.

"I forgot a few things," I said. "My people's will, for one."

A good psyche-healer never fails to catch one being evasive. "Yet they might leave it up to you. Tell me true, Chivinga: if you ever find the city of Arko at your mercy, what will you do?"

"As you once said to me, Alchaen," I answered, "to some questions, there is no answer."

I read the thought on his face, as I turned away to cross the gangplank; I didn't turn quick enough to escape it. From the world I took a madman who was helpless, he was thinking. Have I given it back one who is capable?

II

We came into Brahvniki in the dead of night. The privateers had a way into the back of the Benai Island, for dealing with Ivahn. It was raining, a dead-straight hard fall like dark curtains hiding us, and soaking us all to the bones.

At the door I told the sleepy-eyed Vra in his red robe, "Tell the Benatat his long-lost grandson Vik is visiting again. He'll get up for that." In a short time we were shown in.

He embraced me as if I were his long-lost grandson. Things were going hard in Brahvniki, with Arko controlling Selina; they never had less than five ships in harbor, fully manned, and the marines walked the streets freely with unbonded weapons. Two Arkans had worked their way onto the Praetanu, acting with typical arrogance, and it was no secret that they'd had Imperial backing. I saw what a fine line Ivahn was running, aiding us.

He looked older, wearier, limbs thinned, motions slower and more careful. He coughed wetly, too often. When I asked after his health he said, "It's well enough," and wouldn't tell me more.

"I know you are not just here to pass through," he said, once we'd shared the salt. "How much do you need?"

"All I have, you see," I answered, smiling. I was wearing borrowed standard-issue armor and sword; I didn't have the demarchic signet. No point in hiding what he knew. "It's a

25

good harvest this year, but the Arkans hold the great grana-
ries and herds. I need every mercenary I can get, and then
I have to feed and supply them for the winter. How much
can you spare?"

He'd just had a large sum deposited, luckily, by some
adventurers who'd crossed the great western ocean. Twelve
thousand gold ankaryel and five thousand sword-blanks, at
five per cent yearly, we agreed. As I needed him, he needed
me; still, it put heart into me, to be trusted so much. I
kissed his hands and we drank Saekrberk on it, his toast,
"May the taste be slightly steely." His practice was to hide
sword-blanks in Saekrberk casks.

Sharing the bottle he gave me with my guard, I appointed
Esora-e as mercenary recruiter. He would not have been
my first choice in all Yeola-e, but of the twenty people here
he was the best judge of warriors, and hardest dealer. I told
him the best places for hiring, the Kghghnota Voorm and
others, laughing to myself to imagine him in a taproom full
of foreigners. But he didn't complain; it was necessary.

For some reason we'd been housed in a cellar, which I
think had been used for tanning hides. But, as I told my
people, if we wanted to complain to the innkeeper, we'd
better move to paid lodgings. In the way of foreigners, of
course, Ivahn offered me a bed upstairs; in the way of Yeolis
I refused. I must learn to be one, again.

The next day, as Ivahn and I did the paperwork—I had
to draw the demarchic sigil—he said, "It struck me, I might
not be the only Brahvnikian willing to help you." Just as he
was about to say more, his assistant, Stevahn, rushed into
the office. "Benaiat, the inspector's on the ferry."

His hands moved faster than I thought they could, seizing
up on papers, locking them away in walnut chests. "Honey-
giving one, why now? You must be hidden, Shchevenga; go
with her."

I didn't move, feeling my stomach creep. "The inspector?"

He made a brush-off gesture, saying, "It's no trouble, lad,
but you must go." There was more annoyance in his brown
eyes than fear; but perhaps he was hiding it. "If I and my
people are in some danger, my friend," I said, as Stevahn
pulled on my arm, "I think I should know."

Ivahn let out a rushing sigh, his mouth pursed as if something sour were in it. "Yes, yes, of course you should. Stevahn, tell him as you're going."

She hurried me through the onion-arched corridors with their sweet air. "The Arkan embassy demands the right to come into the precinct, to see, as they say, that nothing is amiss." I felt my back stiffen and my teeth set. My heart had known. "You see how it is, *semanakraseye*. We have mercenaries—but Arko could have twenty ships here in three days. Don't worry, they suspect nothing; they haven't a hope of not being outwitted by the Benaiat, as you can imagine."

No wonder we're sleeping in the cellar, I thought. But why hide this from me? It wasn't to get the better of me in the bargaining; he wouldn't do that. He must not have wanted to weaken my own hope, I thought. My sword wrist still felt odd to wear a wristlet, not a green ribbon. But he can't think so little of me, and still lend me twelve thousand gold ankaryel at five per cent. I thought of his deep-wrinkled face, the joy dimmed in those peaked bird-eyes. No: it was *his* hope needed strengthening.

I asked Stevahn where in the Benai the inspector went. "Oh, it's fairly random," she answered. "Always through the barrels, though; he finds our distillate growing on him." She laughed, a welcome sight. Even to Arkans, the monks of the Bear are generous. The liqueur is a sacrament, to be proselytised, and do its good work whatever way.

I don't think she thought about the favor I asked—to lend us a store of red robes—being in too much of a hurry. Such an Arkan would never descend to visit our cellar, if Ivahn even let him know it existed, else he'd never have put us there. I put one on. From my month away here I still knew the corridors well enough to find the main barrel-store; there I set to sweeping the floor with monkish devotion.

I knew they were coming by weapon-sense: the Arkan wore a sword, two daggers and full armor, as if someone were going to attack him in the Benaiat, and none of it was peace-bonded, sure enough. Ivahn and Stevahn were conducting him personally.

I saw the nature of the deception right away. In a reedy obsequious drone, Ivahn prattled on endlessly about every trivial Benai detail as if it were all-important, forgetting

things and losing his train of thought now and then (with
Stevahn reminding him in a long-suffering tone), and laying
on flattery with a trowel whenever the Arkan seemed near
to getting annoyed enough to wake up. The blue eyes glazed
over, the mouth yawned; I could see him thinking, "If you
say 'Excuse me for being tedious' one more time . . ." His
fill of Saekrberk he clearly considered his fair payment for
wasting his time with this dotard who couldn't find his
behind with both hands and a map, let alone pose any sort
of threat to Arko. Stevahn was right; the Arkan didn't stand
a chance.

But it wasn't without price. Ivahn had to bear the
remarks, the contemptuous angle of the nose, the spitting
on the floor. Here is some of the weight, I thought, that's
bent those shoulders. While the Arkan was upending his
flask, his back to me, Ivahn took a quick glance, to see who
this Vra was who wasn't staying clear as he ought to be. I
lifted my head just enough to show him my face under my
hood, and winked. The string of unctuous words broke for
a moment, adroitly changed into a clearing of the throat.
The *solas* must have had a boot-leather throat, for he drank
more, and I did the Arkan prayer gesture, two hands to the
temples, and turned it into wiggling ass-ears. Ivahn sput-
tered and had a coughing-fit.

"You peach-chinned pup!" he snapped, when all was clear
and I was back in his office, chuckling. "No wonder the
things that befall you do. And I just quartered my bank to
you . . ."

"Did I get caught?" I said, shrugging. "I know how not
to."

He gave me a dark look, but said, "Well, it's good to see
the boy still in you after all you've been through, anyway."
The smile in his voice brought back old days; just what I'd
hoped for.

He'd been thinking of a particular Brahvnikian who might
help me. Annike, called Lady Gar; she had been on the
Praetanu, but was no longer, it seemed, having been ruined
by pirates burning her ships. Pirates under red sails, flying
the eagle; an Arkan had taken her place. "She has little to
lend," Ivahn told me. "But she is better connected among

those antipathetic to Arkans than I. I mean to invite her to tea tonight."

He gave me a once-over, making me suddenly aware I wore one of Esora-e's old black shirts, thread-bare at the elbows, and a raw cotton kilt. "Dealing with these people, you'd better look like a king," he said crisply, "not a reformed gladiator, with nothing shining but your teeth. I'll send someone into the city with your measurements." I remembered how long ago it had been, that I had last been a diplomat, wondering vaguely where my peace-sigil was; in Skorsas's strongbox, no doubt. I needed some brushing-up.

They got me a good satin suit, black embroidered with gold roses, and the Benai barber shaved me and trimmed my hair. Ivahn got a Zak stone-carver who didn't know a word of Enchian, let alone what a demarchic signet might signify, to make me another one; that would take three days, though, so I'd have to put off signing anything. Some part of me felt like an actor, rushed on-stage with quickly-done face paint and hardly knowing my lines, to play the lead on which the whole production depends. Before I went to be introduced to Annike, I got in front of a mirror, unclasped the shirt to bare the brand over my heart and remembered who I was.

Annike had been a self-made clawprince; even with sparse jewelry, and satin Brahvniki pantaloons that looked old-style, she had the presence of great wealth, without the foppishness. Her eyes were hard and measuring, the kind that miss nothing, being too honest with herself; her handclasp was firm and cool. Her manners were polished as an ancient sword, of course. When we had shared the salt and were alone, though, she said, "So, here you are, young Shchevenga: a king without a country."

"Who means to take it back," I answered, quick but not too quick, drawing myself up just a little, "as I hardly need say."

She smiled. "And here am I, a clawprince without a fortune. Whatever were we introduced for, except pleasant conversation?"

I laughed. If bitter humor has any purpose, it is to draw the aggrieved together. "Ivahn was struck, I think," I said, "by what we have in common: having lost by the same agency."

That opened the way for an exchange of stories. Though I knew better than to play for pity with mine, I took my time; it wouldn't do to get too hastily to the point, and make her think I had no use for her presence but to get into other peoples'. Those who have gone down in the world feel that very keenly. I liked her, anyway, so could be sincere.

She patted my hand like a mother when I was done, and said, "Your whole heart is in this war; it truly will be all or nothing for you." Then, her eyes turning back into the clawprince's: "Which makes you a good bet."

She would speak with her son Vyasiv, who had more means, she said, and warned me away from three people who could no longer be trusted, and spoke of others who hated Arko. "If you wish," she said, "I shall write on your behalf to Mikhail, called Farsight." That name I recalled clearly. He was as close as the Praetanu had to a leader, one of the wealthiest people in the city. The door was open.

I asked what he had against Arkans. "The same all Brahvnikians down to the house-mice do, which you know; and a personal matter, recently. Zingas Mikhail has four beautiful daughters, of whom he is immensely proud, and dearly fond, in the strict way of old-house Zak, you understand. Are you familiar with the Thanish goatherd song?" I had to say no. "There is a verse . . . well, you aren't faint of heart, I need not paraphrase. 'Your daughter's run away to Yeola-e/Was her father's love too close?' "

I understood. One who rapes not only a child, but his own blood. "Nothing to an Arkan, of course; but to a Zak, words that can only be overstruck in red. Well, Edremmas Forin, one of our Arkan members, sang it to Mikhail, in *council.*"

I could imagine it: the stunned silence falling over the ancient oaken chamber, the Zak lord, who'd had civility bred into his family for a millennium, freezing as if run through. How do Arkans expect to stay in the world, I thought, behaving that way?

"Knowing what I know of Brahvnikian custom," I said, "I would have thought that would bring a challenge."

"It did. Edremmas, who's soft and fat, designated a cham-

pion, one of his guard. Mikhail would accept only Edremmas himself. He called him a coward to his face; but the
Arkan just shrugged it off. Stalemate." The Zak must be
seething; frustrated of revenge by that course, I thought,
he'll be looking for another.

Our appointment was made for two days hence; people
seemed to understand I was in a hurry, as the precious
warm days passed. I felt every one turn in the pit of my
stomach. The recruiting was going well, though; Brahvniki
being a port, what had happened on Haiu Menshir was
common knowledge, and had awakened shock, and anger.
It was also what I was best known for. Not anything that
had taken time or pain, that Lakan war or my forty-nine
chains but a tenth-bead's skirmish won without a scratch.
No matter; it brought in sharp-toothed warriors by the
hundred.

Mikhail's house was next to the Kreml. It was almost a
palace in itself, with walls and sentries and stonework carved
F'talezonian style, like lace. At the main gate, which had
brass hinges with spars a forearm long and polished to a
fire-gleam, I spoke the password I'd been given; we were
let in, my guard shown to the guest house while I went on
alone, speaking the password three more times at various
torchlit gates and portals.

Deep inside the house, I was met by a dark-eyed long-
haired girl who by her height I would have thought was ten,
but by her shape and manner seemed thirteen or fourteen.
She led me in by the hand, which I saw was a formal gesture, through a maze of ornate wood-carved passages and
stairways, the touch of her tiny fingers elegantly tender on
mine. They'd never had a king visit before, she told me, but
in a way that showed it was nothing untoward. Deeper in—
the innermost rooms seemed to be underground—everything become subtly smaller, as if built for a short race, and
I understood. Old Zak are a short race. She was one of the
beloved daughters.

Finally we came to a door made of tiny glass panes, sparkling like crystals, in the pattern of a phoenix rising from
flames. I had to bend to get under the lintel. Beyond, in a
room full of books and curios lit by a bright fire, waited
Mikhail.

I remembered his face, vaguely. He was sitting, in a velvet chair, but I guessed his head would come up to my collarbone. Edremmas, being *Aitzas*, was probably tall; such a challenge takes a certain courage. But there was that in the Zak's wide jaw and piercing eyes, that one would not want to cross. "Welcome, young *semanakraseye*, let me look at you!" he said, and I found myself feeling like a child in front of a visiting great uncle, being measured, only I was too big and gawky instead of too small.

He was not one for long pleasantries; he shared the salt almost as soon as I'd sat down, and said, "So. Your nation's in ruins, your people nine out of ten in chains, you have nothing but loans and need more; I have money, want more, and hate Arkans; I am clear on where we both stand, yes?" I reminded myself that I had always admired bluntness.

"I should have not even loans, Teik Mikhail, had I nothing else." The Zak style for addressing an equal seemed right here. "Not things you can count in your ledger-book, but they win wars. The allies I will unite, my ability, and my people's faith in it." Sometimes modesty doesn't serve.

"Weren't you in the House of Integrity in Haiuroru for half a year, rather recently?" he said, his bright black eyes unwavering.

"I was," I said, gazing back. "Now, as you can see, I'm out."

That was only the beginning. He grilled me, like a tutor examining a student; I told my whole story in point form answers, curt and impassive as the student does. He had done his homework, too; he knew the names of my Teachers, even Daisas. He showed nothing, smiled or frown, to let me know how I was doing.

Finally he said, "The Benai has loaned you twelve thousand at five per cent, and Vyasiv Gar's Child fifteen hundred at seven. I generally do joint ventures, not loans, and once swore I'd never loan for under ten; but this is a special matter. I'll give you five thousand at seven. But that is predicated on your signing alliance treaties with Laka and Tor Ench. I am a businessman, not a politician like the Benaiat, nor impulsive like Vyasiv; I haven't got where I am by foolish risks. As well, I want a favor for it. I know you are not above this, *semanakraseye*; arranging an assassination, that is, for the benefit of Yeola-e."

I hardly needed to ask who. Yes, he would have his revenge.

"The daughter of yours I met seems thriving," I said, running one finger along the arm of my chair to show him my hands weren't shaking. "Indeed that is too precious a bond, for anyone to blaspheme." I saw the first trace of feeling yet in his eyes. Part of it was resentment that I should know at all; that had been the worst of it, the publicity. "Five at seven contingent on alliances is certainly a fair loan," I said. "But assassinations are generally done for flat fees, not loans."

"Take it or leave it," he said, just like that.

I sat back to think, smoothing ruffled inward feathers, reminding myself that he had said nothing untrue or insulting, and even pronounced my title well. No reason not to consider aloud; he would think me a fool if I did not ask him, a serious enemy of the man, for intelligence. "I know nothing of this Arkan, except that he's one likely to guard himself well. Who's the best person to ask about his house, when he goes out, what places he frequents?"

No great surprise, he had a dossier, in Enchian, fortunately. As I sat poring over it, wondering whether the Voorm was the best place to hire assassins as well as mercenaries, he suddenly said, "You killed Inkrajen of Laka with your own hand, didn't you? That would prove something. . . . Eight thousand at seven, if you do it yourself."

I drew myself up, looking at him hard, and realizing I'd been hoping for a chance to. "I don't think so, Teik Mikhail."

"You doubt you could?" He leaned forward, a grin playing on his lips; dealing was his life, I saw, as fighting is a warrior's.

The opening I'd left purposely, as the warrior does. "No," I said, brisk and light, "I could. But when I killed Inkrajen I was not yet *semanakraseye*." Let him think it would be a relinquishment of my pride, as a foreigner would, though it was not; pride was the last thing I could afford these days, and I'd been well-trained out of it anyway. "Besides, it's a matter of personal risk; and, if you will excuse me, I'm worth more than three thousand gold ankaryel at seven per cent to my people." I left that to sink in for a bit, then said, "For three as a flat fee, I'll do it."

We sat considering each other. Then, three thousand gold *ankaryel* could buy a castle and lands to maintain it near Brahvniki. "It would have to be done where I could witness it myself," he said. "Not that I don't trust you, *semanakraseye* . . ."

We had a deal, it seemed, so I smiled and said, "No, not at all, I understand. You want to see him die." It needed only the handclasp and the Saekrberk.

As agreed I stayed the night, and read the file from end to end. It came to me how rusty I was at dark-work, or any killing not in front of fifty thousand spectators. Idea after idea was too difficult or too risky or didn't allow for him to witness. I strained until my mind was running in circles and my eyes closing of themselves, and sleep dragged my head to the pillow. At cocklight when I woke, the plan came fully-formed, and I saw I'd been a fool to panic. I was out of practice at this too.

I got a wig and false beard, straight blond *solas*-cut, black shoe-wax to coat the teeth, and a low-brimmed straw hat I showed Mikhail so he would know me. Under a short cloak I hid my sword.

It was a pastime of Edremmas to go every day to the slave market; as there are dog- and horse-fanciers, he was a human-fancier, and dreaded missing choice items. He travelled in a hammock chair borne by four, with four guards (Arkans, of course), two on each side. All around were alleyways where one could go in a hatted Arkan and come out a hooded Yeoli; I learned three routes.

I got Krero, Sachara, Kunarda and Alaecha to wander near me, pretending not to know each other, in case I had trouble with the guards. Mikhail need only position himself right. We waited till the market closed; they'd be slower and perhaps leading slaves.

The day was hot and dusty, sun-swirls rising from the buildings, the people in a mood to push and curse. I ambled to the designated fountain; there was Mikhail, with his entourage all liveried in silver and black. We exchanged a glance. Four dark-haired young women stood close around him; it seemed his daughters all wanted to see Edremmas die, too.

Suddenly I thought, I am this man's servant; I am about to kill for his sport, just like in the Mezem. The feeling came back so strongly it was dizzying; I almost heard oddsmakers barking, and Skorsas's piping death-words at my shoulder. My fake beard itched, my brand burned; it took strength I had only recently found again to keep steady. Yes, I am his servant, I thought; but I chose it. It's well-paid and for my people. The demarch of a country all but conquered is all but a beggar.

Edremmas was coming. Brahvnikians gave him a wide berth, as I'd expected. As I'd hoped, two of his guards had their hands full of rope; the slave was spectacular, a woman a full head taller than me, colored and muscled like a bronze statue, with flame-red hair, and still fighting though they whipped her. He meant to enjoy breaking her, it seemed. I forgot I had no grudge against him.

She was pulling the pair back and apart from the fluttering retinue; Edremmas, who was indeed soft and fat under his jewels, swung slightly in his hammock, his side wide open. He saw Mikhail, and gave a smug smile. Mikhail gave an even more smug one back.

I took two steps and a long leap between two of the servants, drawing in mid-air straight into a two-hand downstroke, just hard enough to go half through him.

He couldn't scream—I'd cut the bottom of his lungs off—but everyone else did, as they saw his blood. The vanguard pair of guards were too close to run from, but they were standard stock, as I'd expected, easy work if you did not fear them. The rearguard stood still, torn between coming too late to defend their master, and holding the slave, who saw this as a chance and struggled with new strength. The bearer's froze with the hammock poles still on their shoulders, a dead weight swinging now, while the servants backed off, setting up a mourning wail. And all around, Brahvnikians looked from the dripping corpse to me, smiling, and slowly began snapping their fingers, in applause.

I bowed, like a dancer. It seemed the thing to do. I saw Mikhail throw back his head in laughter. Then I ran, with heels on fire; the watch was coming.

The crowd let me through out of sympathy, them out of duty. I dashed around the first corner of my route. There I found, and all should have gone well but for this, a fence all the way across, beyond which the road was dug out too wide to leap over and too deep to ford. Brahvniki has sewers, at least in the rich quarters; where they were being repaired today had not been on my map.

I almost fell trying to stop, my boot heels scraping on the cobbles. The watch were at the corner, long whistles shrieking, fast, well-trained. I dashed down a side alley, leaping over a garbage heap and two five-year-olds playing with knives. More watch ahead of me; I couldn't shed my disguise; I heard whistles all around, using a code. Soon I found myself in an alley with them at both ends. Sheathing the sword, I sprang for the rougher wall, which was too smooth to climb fast. Two man-heights up, as my fingers were finding an edge, something hooked around my foot and yanked it off the wall. I fell sliding, clawing for holds; hands trapped me against the wall; then a billhook blade half-circled my throat, and a voice barked, "We have you, assassin." There was nothing to do but stop moving and say, "I surrender."

As they locked my hands behind my back in ironwood rings and unfastened my sword from my shoulder, I thought, now what? They were friends; it didn't feel the same as being captive of Arkans. I'd murdered, and they had taken me; it was just.

They would lead me to the Benaiat—or so I hoped. Just as I was wondering what words, said without a Yeoli accent, might ensure this, the captain unfastened some device from his belt, and seized me by the ear. Brahvnikian law is careful to ensure fair trials, the measure to prevent one incriminating oneself by one's own words simple and effective. All I could get out was, "No, wait, you don't need to—" before he sealed the clasp of the gag with something like a peacebond, the court's assurance that no confession had been beaten or drugged out of me.

They did take me to the Benai, leaving me in a monk's cloister fitted with a thick door. There I sat cooling, cursing myself, and running over all the ways it could have gone differently, while the gag got heavier and stickier on my tongue. I felt best when I didn't think about what would happen, or imagine what a fool I must look, a demarch in false beard, wig and hat, bound and gagged in a cell of the Benai Saekrberk.

After a time they led me to his office. My sword lay across his desk. The watch captain suggested it would be safest if he bind me by the neck to the chair; Ivahn agreed and it was done.

When we were alone, the door well-closed, I relaxed; now he need not worry about underlings, he would free me. Instead, as I peered at him, he said, "No, I think I will leave you like that for now. I don't want to hear any of your golden words." I hate even writing what he said, but under the Oath of the Scrivener I must.

"So. You think this is the wilds, here, where you can hunt as you please. You think we have no laws, or at least you are above them. No, I didn't like Edremmas, and spoke ill of him; but he was still a citizen of Brahvniki and I still his Benaiat." He tapped the sword. "This I waived the peace-bonding for, in trust that I did not need to ask it of you, whom I thought a friend. Should I ever trust you again, Fourth Shchevenga?"

How helpless one feels, gagged in the face of such, is hard to describe. I could only nod or shake my head wildly; I knew as I did it what wrong meanings I was giving, and what a fool I was making of myself. On my head the hat felt like ass's ears. "But that's the least of it, Shchevenga. Would that we lived in a time when principle could be our only concern. You think you can do anything, and anyone in any danger, no matter what they entrust you with: if they are not your precious Yeola-e, they can go to the dogs!" I remember Dinerer, saying as much. "The Arkans would leap on any excuse to truth-drug me, can't you see? And then what? I hope you had cursed good reason to do this, good enough to be worth the end of me and Brahvniki, as it might be."

The world seemed to slow down to death-silence as he spoke, so that there was nothing in it but his words. "This fortune I've loaned you comes with my trust in your ability, too, Shchevenga," he said. "When I think, your record isn't so long, the deeds that distinguish you, not so many. You give an impression; but perhaps it is wrong. Will you lead your war, that I've invested so much in, the same way? How many more mistakes do you plan to make?"

Like a child being shown how the evil he's done is far worse than he knew to imagine, I found I was not what I thought I was, and felt my soul's faith in itself being torn away, something I should have long finished with, at twenty-two and a demarch. No wonder Alchaen didn't want to release me, I thought. It took all my strength to swallow my tears.

When he finally freed me, I thought all the answers building up inside me would burst out; but it all died on my tongue. As I bared my head, it came to me what I must say. I saw the news coming to every mercenary in Brahvniki, "Chevenga goes back on his promises," us, too few without them, starving in the mountains, and all Yeola-e, slaves forevermore, swearing to remember for all time who had failed them, and how. But I must say it. "Ivahn, if there is a disaster, we should suffer it. The loan's off, if you wish. And if the Arkan strike at Brahvniki because of this, I will do for you what I would do for my own people." Yeolis might doubt my loyalties, on hearing this; but for Yeola-e's sake I had to say it.

His eyes fixed mine, measuring whether I meant it; judging I did, they softened. He got up from the desk to pace; remembering his health I gave myself another inward lash. A craving seized me that I didn't recognize at first: for a *katzerik.* "Well," he said. "You made a mistake; it can be cleaned up. Perhaps it's better you made it here instead of in some battle at home. It seems Brahvniki stands or falls with Yeola-e anyway. Grant me just one thing: learn from this so you don't fail us." I swore, Second Fire come.

A corpse had to be found in the city morgue; the story, that the prisoner had broken free of his guards and leapt out a high window, to avoid being given to the Arkans. It worked well enough.

In the cellar my people, once they knew I was all right, leapt on me. They'd seen me led off. Then Esora-e began: irresponsible, I was, reckless, too long in the Mezem, he feared for Yeola-e.

I had never seen my mother give anyone such a look. I

pray I am never in the path of it. It shut him up; I heard Sachara later hauled him aside, pointed out my pallor and said, "You know he's still all we've got! Shake his faith in himself, and we lose that too."

I looked all around, at the crowded faces, the smiles fading, and said what was in my heart. "Do you trust me? Do you all still trust me?" Hands seized my shoulders, arms closed around me. "Yes, we trust you," they answered. "Of course we do, if we didn't, we'd be counting votes, not saying this. Chevenga, our lives are in your hands, and we'd have it no other way." It was then I wept.

I couldn't sleep that night. *High stakes, no mistakes* kept running through my head. So terrible, the consequences could have been, but so easily avoidable, by nothing more than a stroll along my getaway route beforehand; how, I kept asking myself, can I call myself a tactician if I didn't think of that? It was carelessness brought on by being out of practice, I suppose, or thinking because of my victory on Haiu Menshir that my mind had knit more than it had.

I must make no more mistakes, whatever the cause, not one, ever; but how many people in history have said "never again, after this one," several times? I lay sweating in the cool foul darkness, yearning for arms around me, Niku's or anyone's, my thoughts eating my heart; then near wakingtime, it finally came into my head to remember childhood knowledge. Shy at first, thinking disuse might have withered it, or Arko burned it away, I closed my eyes, and clutched my crystal. "Of course I am still here," it said, and it was as if no time had passed at all. "Where would I go? You've just snubbed me, that's all." I saw my weak point plain, and easy to solve: insufficient reconnaissance. My bed turned warm again. On retrospect, the shaking Ivahn gave me was what I needed most to steady me for the war.

We were five more days there, for a total of thirty-one thousand five hundred gold at various rates, most on condition I made alliances with Lake and Tor Ench. I spoke again with Ivahn. "You might have difficulty persuading Astalaz," he said. "Considering the treaty he signed with Kurkas— didn't you know?"

"When?" I gasped. "And *why*?" I felt my feet cut out

from under me, again. Astalaz was the key to everything. Insufficient reconnaissance, indeed.

"Three months ago," he said. When I'd been in the House of Integrity, of course, too riven in mind to be told. "I don't think he knew you were alive. Between you and me, I think it was in fear. It's a ten-year pact." My skin crawled. Az didn't know Kurkas, he'd never met Kurkas; I could see those big dark honest eyes, reasonable and just, thinking "It's only right to give the man a fair chance," as I had myself. An awful thought came; did that treaty extend to extraditions? I had already sent a pigeon to Tardengk to say I was coming.

No, I told myself, he wouldn't do that, not without listening to my side first. Then he will know Kurkas. I'd seen no word of the treaty in the Pages, which didn't bode well for Kurkas honoring it. As for proof of treachery, I had it graven on me.

"Why not Segiddis?" Ivahn said.

"Segiddis of Hyerne?" I said, staring. "She's dead."

"She is?" His peaked eyebrows shot up. "When?"

"A year ago—how could you not know?"

Now it was his turn to look puzzled. Only for a moment; then a smile tweaked his lips. "Well, I can hardly blame you for not running spies, from the Mezem. I guess you got all your news from the Pages." As he told the story, my jaw dropped wider and wider.

"The garrison of Kreyen has been under Milforas Tatthen, *Aitzas* for nearly thirty years, and reports to Arko on his order and discipline have always been gleaming. The inspectors were always bribed or drugged. . . . While he feathered his own nest the citadel walls crumbled, the ships rotted, the equipment rusted; the good officers quit in disgust, the bad fattened, the men went to drink or herb, or married women of the island and moved into straw huts. When the order came to take Hyerne, he was apparently at about fifth strength in warriors, and tenth strength in gear.

"He sent the Marble Palace for money, citing storm damage, plague, mutiny. . . . But the Imperial patience has limits; he could only delay the conquest within reason. So he had it happen on paper. That Pages fellow made the living of his dreams, with all those heroic battles; maybe he'll go on to novels. Kurkas didn't know Segiddis's head from any other Hyerne woman's. . . .

"They've taken maybe three or four villages, at most; with warriors all soft and contemptuous of women, the Hyerne have made hash of them. Poor Milforas, having to sell off his paintings and gilt chairs and toy-boys; it's a hard life, the military. What will be interesting is when Kurkas begins sending tax collectors."

So, I must visit Segiddis too. Artira must not have mentioned this or the Lakan treaty in her letters, I thought, because she thought I knew.

We were finished, and it was time to go. I pleaded with him to take care of his health, having wormed the truth out of Stevahn: he'd had this cough for a year, and was steadily weakening. "There is so much needs doing," I said, clasping his hands at the door, "and you know so well how. The world needs you, old fox; don't die on us yet." Blunt, but honest; he laughed, said he'd see a Haian, and now would I be a good lad and get out of this city before I caused more trouble.

With half the guard I sailed upriver to Tardengk in a small *cormarenc*, the ship used for the hunting of the giant cormorant, fastest type on the Miyatara, leaving Esora-e with the other half to lead our mercenaries into Yeola-e.

Astalaz welcomed me with all the honors, brass gongs and *zinarh* and ribboned dancers. He looked unchanged, reminding me how little time had passed, in truth. Though he took my hands, and spoke delight that I was alive, there was a certain awkwardness in his eyes and stiffness in his smile, as if at least part of him wished I hadn't arrived. You didn't expect me to, I thought, and you acted accordingly.

So I was as warm as I could be without seeming false or favor-seeking; when we were alone I pulled him into an embrace, and reminded him of our old jokes. If it hurt him, let him learn.

When we were done with dinner, being shown to our chambers, and all the Lakan formalities, he took me to his formal office; it seemed I was no longer privy to his personal mess. I asked him how it went in Laka, and he spoke in his slightly pedantic way at some length, wanting to avoid asking me likewise. It was all still in formal Lakan circumlocution, though I'd dropped it as soon as we were alone. He didn't mention the treaty.

"We've got a great many fresh troops now," I said when he finally asked, "and loans enough for us to fight down into the plains before winter, if we fight well." Let it get fixed in his mind, even though it would not happen without his aid. "As for how I've been, better to ask where: Arko." I fingered my scar, as if absently.

"So I was informed." He stood up suddenly, and began pacing, the tassels of his robe trailing on the floor." "J'vengka—I know what you are here for. You must ask, I know. But you can appreciate the circumstance I am in, surely, why I must refuse. I put my name to an agreement. Don't persuade me, J'vengka; I know how cursed persuasive you can be; don't make it difficult for me. When a king signs to an oath, in particular, the gods keep record."

I tried not to let my knuckles go white on my chair arms, and swallowed the words, "You idiot!" He'd dropped the obfuscation and was sweating more than I was, at least; that was comfort.

I said, "What do they make of the oath of a king who laughs the gods off as the comforting fancies of fools?"

He whirled and stared at me frozen, not knowing whether to take mortal offense in the high Lakan style, or be curious, since he didn't know who I meant.

"I am *athye*," I said, "but you know my way of praying. Kurkas is an atheist in the truest sense of the word: one who believes in the sacredness of nothing whatsoever." I gripped my crystal. "Second Fire come if I lie. He and I had a number of philosophical discussions. Are we in total privacy here?" I began undoing the glass clasps of my shirt. "You probably still have a copy of his oath to me, in a heap somewhere. By that he should have set me free from the Mezem. Instead: well, see for yourself." I'd had my back to him, stripping to the waist; now I turned and faced him, naked.

He gasped, and sat down silent. I told him all of it. "Why wouldn't he betray you, as well?" I said. "He's using treaties to take us all one at a time. It's a game: whoever breaks it first wins."

He got up and paced, more violently this time. "*Liz Kazh,*

I knew it would be this way, that you would come and put me in the wrong, with my oath; yet I've still sworn it, my honor still rests on it. Curse you, J'vengka! You have more Lakan blood on your hands than he." (More than he knew; I was glad now I'd never confessed about the ten thousand.) "You know, my Arkan ambassador, an honest man for a diplomat, just now begged to speak with me. The sum he offered for you would feed my cavalry for a year."

My *kri*-spiced dinner turned cold in my stomach, and prickles went all up and down my arms and legs. With Ivahn or Mikhail or Kranaj, one would know this was a test; but Astalaz often thought aloud. He would never trust my strength if I showed fear, though; so hoping my nakedness had betrayed nothing, I said, "Why are you telling me that, Az? Do you want my opinion on whether you should give me to them? Well, speaking utterly free of bias or prejudice, I'd say no, don't, it's an awful idea, just terrible, unthinkable." He broke into laughter. "It tells you, anyway," I added, "how much stomach Kurkas has, for a face-to-face fight against me."

He started to look a little convinced, so I worked on him, making maps with my finger on his table, telling him more of Kurkas's ways, of the attack on Haiu Menshir. "Is Kranaj in on this?" he asked under his brows. "I'd be much more inclined to do this if he did too. I don't want him slipping the knife in my back while I'm looking Arko's way . . ."

"My impression is that he feels likewise," I said, with no grounds whatsoever but my own guess, "though we've made no firm agreement yet. But everyone knows, many are stronger as one."

Then suddenly he looked at me quizzically, and said, "J'vengka . . . how are you?"

"Fine, thank you, how are you?" I replied, puzzled.

"I mean . . . how *are* you?" Understanding came, just as he was saying, "Your letter said you'd been in Haiu Menshir, but not why. I investigated, and learned."

I felt my fingers start to clench. It was like one of those dreams, in which one throws all one's strength into running, but can't move a finger-width, one's feet bound to the ground. This is going to go on, I thought, until I carve out proof of my sanity.

But him I couldn't fight; not that way. "Do you still have time for *mrik*, these days?" I said. "It's been a long time, what do you say to a game?" He looked relieved to be offered an escape from this unpleasant business. "Come upstairs," he said. "You perverse Yeoli, just sitting there like that; get your clothes on."

His office was the mess I remembered, though heaped higher and mustier in two years, like a dead city sinking slowly into the dust. Apologizing for it as usual, he dug up the *mrik* board and in another long while the stones, called for incense and musicians.

When we had stones in hand to start, I said, "What do you say we put a stake on it? If I win you must join me in an alliance; if you win, I go without another word, or grudge."

He gazed at me blinking, wanting to laugh, I think, but knowing me just well enough to worry that I might be serious. "I'm serious," I said. "The issue is my mental competence, isn't it? What better test of it? If I win, you'll know I'm all here, and making good arguments; if I lose, I'm no good to ally with."

I saw his cheeks go ruddy, under the brown. There was no arguing with the logic; yet he might lose. He didn't want to face it, that was all; I'd come to him out of nowhere, like a meteor out of the night. Sometimes, Az, I wanted to say, life does that.

He looked at the board, with my two stones already set on it; one for my handicap from before, one for lack of practice. Friendly, he'd offered me two for that, business-like, I'd accepted only one. Now he knew why. I wish you'd been to war, I thought. All you have to lose is an oath sworn to someone dishonorable; think of what I have to lose. I wanted to urge him; but it might make him think I had some trick. Silence was stronger.

Finally, suddenly, he sat down at the board. His eyes were lighter, now thinking, *I might win.* "Very well, J'ven-gka. Without another word, or grudge." I nodded; he ordered no disturbances, and placed his first stone.

So it was, in sweating darkness full of the Lakan smells of spice and bougainvillaea, to the soft weaving strains of the *zinarh*, I played *mrik*, for my people, my freedom, my life. I was out of practice indeed, as he showed me very well at the beginning; but in time the feel came back. It was a long game; we both played hard; fatigue entered into it. In the end, it was so even we had to count up. I'd beaten him by four stones.

He sprang up out of his chair, almost throwing it over, and paced, his heels ringing on the floor. "Well, there you are, J'vengka. You have it, may it benefit you. Only the gods can see the ending; may it be to their taste."

"Astalaz," I said, "I absolve you of it." He spun around, stunned. "You are thinking the fate of nations should not rest on a game, and you are right. It should be your choice alone, to reconcile with your gods as you see fit. I just wanted to show you my wits were well enough to win, when our fate did rest on it."

He came to me, arms crossed, and just looked into my face for a long time. "Kazh rule your soul," he said finally, "with what you are capable of. And so young; so much life you have left, to do with. What terms were you thinking of?" He called for the wine.

We agreed he would take back the Diradic Tongue, with the help of what was left of my fleet; that would either draw Arkan strength out of Yeola-e, or be an easy win, his reward; meanwhile he would send seven thousand infantry to my army, under Arzaktaj, seven hundred of the best cavalry once we reached the plains, and fifteen thousand more infantry if my people chose to invade Arko. He wanted Kreyen if we won, but I haggled him back to the smaller island of Ro. I would rather have seen Ro free, in truth, not trading one master for another; but I had to promise something. All of this was contingent on my allying with Kranaj.

I left the next day. I'd wanted to see Klaimera; but Astalaz said, "She asked me to convey her regards, which are the fondest. To look upon you would pain her heart too much." Fair enough.

Thenai, the closest that far-flung Hyerne has to a capital, is a great rock with a citadel over a plain that was a great city before the Fire; the soil is still full of its dust. The Hyerne say their walls are built on ones from twice as long ago as the Fire. They are ruled by women as much as Arko by men, so that my escort must be all women; Segiddis, I saw, had to make herself overlook my gender to remember I had a mind. She had a certain way of patting my shoulder. When we'd done laughing over Milforas's deceit, and dealing—she could spare a thousand warriors, sending her worst rival to command them—she made it clear she wanted me for the night. She was authoritative there too; but from a dark, hard-built woman who sought my pleasure, I found I could bear it. "You are beautiful, in your pale white way," she said afterward. "And so delicate. Even if you have scars—how strange, on a man! When the war is over, may I take you as my fifth husband?" I answered, "Certainly, as long as I may take you as my third wife."

Next it was Curlionaiz, and Kranaj's old lyesian-style sitting room, with the velvet curtains and embossed table maps. He had thought it over already, clearly, for his first question was, "What about your old friend Astalaz? He's signed no treaty with *me.*" I told how I'd talked him out of the Arkan pact, and rattled off the numbers, leaving out the condition. He agreed, though not getting as good a deal out of me as Astalaz had, just the island of Tuzgolu if we won Yeola-e back; he'd wait and see if it went beyond that, in his cautious way. Then he said, "One other condition: you must accept my son as your apprentice in generalship."

I was about to agree smiling, wondering why he should feel it necessary to make such a small matter a condition, when it came to me who his son was: Reknarja, who'd sneered at my size when I was twelve and been kicked by his father for it. He'd had no reason to gain any love for me since, as far as I knew, and nothing would improve when he, two years my elder, found himself my student. When I asked whether he'd agreed, Kranaj said laughing, "He doesn't even know yet. But he's going." A fine start, I thought; we'll get along like cats and water. But I was not in a position to kiss off ten thousand warriors for that; I would have to trust in my own forbearance.

With that, my outside dealing was done. "Steer by the star we call Vara-imayen, Exile's Hope," I said to the captain of my *cormarenc.* "Take me home."

III

The Yeoli camp was high on the pass near Ossotyeya, in the sparse country far north of Vae Arahi. We came in at midnight. Emao-e was commanding; guessing that my arrival was excuse enough to wake her up I got her guards to let me in, knelt beside her where she lay in her bed-roll and barked, as I had once before, "Fourth Chevenga reporting for duty, General!" She bounced about two hands-pans straight up, seized me in a bear-hug and roared, "Shit-britches, boy, I never know when you're going to appear!"

The command council was only seven people, and I saw some missing who should be here, which meant the worst. Looking those who were left over I saw a deeper fatigue than from having been shaken awake, as well as a bandage here and there. We've all aged a decade, I thought; losing despite one's ultimate effort will do that. Their smiles at me were desperate, as at their last hope. In Hurai's eyes I saw the thought: *I hope I taught him well enough.* Jinai Oru, who looked the same—nothing could age him—gave me a rib-cracking hug, and said, "I told them all you'd be back."

So I stayed light and laughing, broke out my gift-flasks from Astalaz, and rattled off all the help that was coming. The smiles became amazed, and heartfelt. We were beyond shame, now, that we could not stand alone.

Artira was a day further north, in Kefara, with the family;

the Assembly met and stayed where it could these days, in stubble-fields and on hearthstones. The New Mountains were mostly free, too, Renaina Chaer holding there with her usual ghost and lightning tactics. My heart went weak, when I heard our number, and I had to fight to keep my grin. Of all the warriors who'd faced the Arkans on land, each the fruit of ten years toil in sword-schools, only eight thousand remained. The Arkans, in the way of an empire subduing a land, killed or crippled every one they could lay their hands on; such people make bad slaves.

Four thousand five hundred Yeolis were here. I thought long about them that night, to know them, since soon I would speak to them. The survivors, I thought, by luck or by skill, not cowardice, else they wouldn't be here; the disciplined, for they have stuck together despite the recriminations of defeat; they must be like siblings. Those who have sworn, whether they spoke the oath aloud or only in their hearts, to fight to the end; so, though they carry the weight of defeat on their shoulders, they must be near the end of fear. The speech began to take shape in my mind.

Yet other matters remained, before I could lead with a free hand. The summit-person of Ikal came to debrief me; with horror I watched her bring out an Arkan syringe, with a crisp smell I knew too well. Fighting Arkans, it was natural enough, I suppose, to borrow their weapons; it aids the memory. I bared my arm. I had to tell my foreknowledge, since Kurkas knew, but begged off the A-niah secret. To tell is to relive; when I came off the drug I wept on her arm.

When that was done, I asked where the Arch-Arbitrate was sitting: Kefara, also. Next morning I rose at dawn, and did the courier's route there. Hard: I'd got unused to thin mountain air, breathing the easy heavy stuff to Arko and Haiu Menshir. The scribe of the Arbitrate kept her desk in the temple; sweated and flushed as I was, I took off the Brahvnikian-made signet and knelt before her. "I have done what warrants impeachment without vote," I said, "but plead extenuating circumstances. To judgment I submit myself." She stared speechless, then dashed inside.

"This is a story you should only tell once," the Arch-Arbiter said, hearing the gist. She had the bailiff take me to a monk's cell. While I knelt there alone, fears settled on my skin like mosquitoes. Perhaps I should have kept quiet, I thought, let them stay missing in action forever, as the Mezem Yeolis, all dead now, probably, intended. If I were impeached I would still serve as First General First if Artira asked me; but how much store had they set by my being demarch, and how would this touch morale?

No, I thought, I had to do this. It would have haunted me to live in the dark, turned all my strokes, weakened my spirit, muddled all my plans. The God-in-Myself demands clean face and open heart, else it does not speak; and without that we are lost.

A voice came faint through the heavy door. "Chevenga?" It was Artira; they'd sent word to her first. We threw ourselves into each other's arms, laughing like fifteen years ago, before she'd known trouble. Her whole term and adulthood, so far, had been losing this war. I told her why I was here. "We have all done what we must," was all she said.

We caught up; she had sent me a last letter in Arko, that never got to me. I told her my intention, that whatever happened I would accept whatever appointment I was given if I were impeached, so they need not fear losing me as a general. "Better I'd never left in the first place, though," I said, "and put all this mess on your shoulders. Ardi, for my part I'm sorry."

She had never much come to me with her troubles; this time, perhaps, she saw I was the only one she could let see the strain. She wasn't yet married. "Everyone's been praying for your return," she said. "You can save us, and I couldn't, we all know that. How can I feel I haven't failed?" She'd been flung into an avalanche, not called it down; I said so, but the heart won't always listen to words addressed to the mind. So I just said, "You can rest now, love." In time she let me take her in my arms, and wept on my shoulder, telling me between sobs of Arkan atrocities.

I was tried before Assembly, in a field under Merahin. So the Servants got their first sight of me in two years, as the charges were read. I was the only witness, being the only survivor.

I told it as impassively as I could; when the tears came, at the end, I kept my head up and dashed them away. The prosecutor asked me few questions, mostly on why, when I'd held to the Yeolis' will for nine fights, and that justified my deeds, I had defied it on the tenth, defeating the purpose of the nine; that was where my case least favored me. I told the truth: that my strength had run out, that I'd felt I should be as good as dead if I killed Mana, that I still believed it. I asked clemency, as I must, for having acted as demarch under false pretenses, to seek allies.

The judges went away to confer. Alone in the witness's spot, I heard my name called over the buzz of the crowd. As is edge were my parents, my sibs, my grandmother, my aunts and uncles, my spouses, all blowing me kisses. Shaina lifted over her head a toddler with a thick thatch of black hair: Kima Imaye. My eyes brimmed again. Fifth wasn't there, though; soon it came to me why. He was old enough to understand this.

The judges returned, decided. I stood, and silence fell.

In the circumstances, they ruled, I had acted with the good of my people foremost in mind, as best I could, throughout. In keeping with the Yeoli Mezem custom, I should have nine marks branded on my face, and I should see to the informing of the families myself; and they recommended that I be reinstated as demarch. It was then, I wept with abandon.

They voted me back right there, Artira giving me her signet, new-made after I'd left, and Chirel, with a kiss and a blessing. As I had asked, Skorsas had found a way to send the sword to her, though not the wisdom teeth of the dead Yeolis; I'd have to write. I made my first war speech to Assembly, holding the Crystal of the Speaker; then submitted to the branding. It was far lighter than I'd given in the Mezem, done with wire rather than a rod; the nine stripes fit in a space on my cheek two finger-widths wide, as everyone who has met me ever since has seen.

I spent the evening with my family. Now I saw Fifth, a strapping six-year-old, his face lengthened so that he looked, at least to my eyes, like a little man, and dark hair past his shoulders. No one doubted now that he was bright, for he could read and write. He remembered me, to my delight, and everything he didn't remember he'd heard. He'd gripped the sword of Saint Mother, which the Teachers held in hiding now, though he hadn't lifted it; still, he was determined to be as great a warrior as I.

I remembered speaking to Azaila, three years ago when I'd brought Fifth home. "You know the odds," he'd said. "It's almost certain your child won't be as good as you. To expect it of him is to do him wrong." I'd answered that I'd expect his best, no more, no less, and thought to myself, I won't see the end of it anyway.

Now here he was, taking on that ambition himself. I did wrong to him too, I thought, by being gone. Who put him up to it? Esora-e, if not all the rest of Vae Arahi; people will look for missing parents in children.

"Will you train with me tomorrow, Daddy, pleeeeease?" Fifth was saying; I wouldn't have time, I said, but I could for a little now. Out onto the dark mountain we went, and I challenged him to blind man's bluff. When the cloth was tied across his eyes, I drew Chirel, and cut to within a finger-width of his head, a stroke that would have made me leap my own length sideways at that age. There wasn't even a break in his chatter.

Fifth, I thought, as he stumbled blind over the meadow, laughing, I took you from your mother, then abandoned you myself, will abandon you again, tomorrow, and then again for the last time, before you are in your teens. Did I do you wrong by claiming you? I looked ahead, through the years of his life. With a child's resolve, all or nothing, he'd started a futile quest; he who would be called on to match me, even his name begging comparison, was defeated from the start; his highest lesson of warcraft would be to abandon his aspiration. He was quick and sensitive, too, the kind to know and feel it hard, and when the shadow fell strongest, at sixteen, I would not be there. If anything, I would be a curse to him, my memory the summit he failed to reach.

I sat him down under my arm on the mountain, and said, "I'm going to tell you a story, Chevenga—only I can call you that because I'm not going to mix you up with someone else—which is a secret between you and me. You have to swear silence." Eyes wide and solemn, he did, gripping his crystal. "I've never told anyone this, because it wasn't their business; but it is yours, because it has to do with why you're Ascendant. Has anyone told you about that?"

He signed chalk, and said, "It's 'cause I'm your eldest child, and you chose for me to."

"Why do you think I did, when I could have left you with your Mama? I thought you'd be a good demarch: has anyone told you why?"

He signed charcoal, staring mystified as only a child can, with a question he'd never before thought to ask. I remembered myself, under my father's arm after his Renewal; I must have looked the same. "Why do you think it might be?" I asked him.

He gave me the answer I'd feared, and hoped. " 'Cause you thought I'd be a great warrior, and throw off the 'pressors?" Already, in that little face with my lines, was tension and doubt I cannot recall ever feeling, so young. I'd been raised in peacetime.

"No," I said. "That wasn't it at all. I didn't choose you for anything I thought you might be; I wouldn't do that. Only for what you were. You think you were too young then to prove yourself in any way, my child, don't you? But you did prove yourself, very well.

"I didn't choose for you, Fifth Chevenga. That's the secret. You chose. As always." And I told him about the toad, on Leyere mountain. For a moment, a memory seemed to spark in his eyes.

"If in your life people say you aren't good enough, or as good as me, or strong enough, remember this, always: that you won my approval for justice and for kindness. And if while I'm not here, anyone says *I* wouldn't think you were good enough, tell them what I tell you now: From the day I met you, you were good enough for me, and you always will be."

In an eerily adult manner, he said, "Thank you," then gave me a neck-crushing hug. As we went back down, he was silent in thought. I doubted he would forget; but he might. It was about that time, when the business of the war and the demarchy left time, I began writing letters to my children.

That night I met the new one, Kima, too. Her face was more Shaina's, but her hair was mine. She was at the shy age, and turned away from me at first, though she'd been taught the word "Daddy"; my face had become something of a harsh sight for a young child, even beardless, with the scars and the furrow between my brows and the short hair. But with careful courtship, a feeding of baby-gruel and two diaper changes, I won her over, and she started saying "Daddy" with meaning.

For that night, Shaina and Etana welcomed me onto the mat they were sharing. She was carrying his child; though by our agreement she need not, she offered me herself. I declined. I was still full of fear, knew it would show and feared what they would feel; here it could not be impersonal, as with Segiddis. Or perhaps it was vanity making me shrink from showing myself as one to be pitied, now, in bed. Segiddis had not known me as I was before. But Shaina said, "Chevenga, that's not like you at all," and it all came out anyway. Saying I should waste no time facing the chasm, she had her way with me. "Yes, you are tenderer," she said afterwards. "But that makes you no less a lover. You are still full of caring." It struck me that just this night I'd said a similar thing to Fifth.

The next day I kissed them goodbye again. Gathering the army in Ossotyeya around a place where the stream runs slow and deep, I made my speech. I remember the day, a shining one as they get in the high mountains sometimes, the sun seeming more silver than gold, as if being closer to it brought it brighter, the ripples of the stream dancing over the pebbles, clear as if all the love of All-spirit were in every line.

As with the command, I told them first how many more warriors should be joining us presently. From then on they were in my hands. It is your names that will be graven in history, I said, since all the world remembers those who ceased to give up ground, who were present at the turning-point of defeat into victory. Forgive me for not being with you when this began, I told them, but I am now, and I will make it up. The singing wind was in my ears the whole way through, and my tongue never faltered; like a spark my spirit caught them, grew like fire in trees, came roaring back to me in their voices. At the finish, wearing my wristlets as the sign of the demarch bound to war, I did the Kiss of the

Lake in the stream. It was a year and some before I was
due, but now was the time for Renewal of all things, and
especially the time to show my people I could still die for
them, whatever Kurkas had done to me, that a thousand
smotherings could not make fear my master. It was the
hardest time ever. When I woke in the monks' arms, the
fire-dish leaping with flame, the army was chanting my
name.

In council, Hurai commended me for making what had
been the slimmest, most naive hope before seem inevitable.
I said, "As it seems, so shall it be." Later Emao-e drew me
aside, and said, "You certainly set your stakes high enough,
don't you, lad? After that, if we lose ground ..." I just
shrugged, and answered, "Are they any higher than they
already were?" Then we went to work.

The Arkan land victories had been mostly the work of
one Triadas Teleken, who commanded the force facing us.
From the start, I wanted to get rid of him; he would almost
certainly be replaced by someone inferior. One can count
on that, fighting a people who promote by bloodline instead
of merit. By all accounts, though, he guarded himself
extremely well by night, having already survived all manner
of attempts, and, if he knew the stories of me, would double
his guard if anything. But a plan came to me when it was
noted that he had kept his command-post well back in past
attacks on this pass, the land to either side being impass-
able—or seeming so to Arkan eyes.

I sent for someone born here. Yes, the mountainsides, a
third talus, a third steep forest, a third cliff, were difficult;
but local hotheads made a game of climbing them, and knew
the ways. Twenty hotheads, I called for, as well as fifty
Demarchic guard regulars and thirty Elite, all good cliff
people. Of course the council tried to talk me out of going,
but I stood on rank. Jinai foresaw nothing, but my own
feeling was lucky; and I made sure my reconnaissance was
very detailed, as I did all the rest of the war. That night, in
the dark before dawn, we climbed down, and crouched in
the trees, a long arrow's flight from where his command-
post had been last time.

At dawn, Emao-e did as I'd commanded; began a charge
down from the pass, five thousand odd on fifteen. Triadas

had no doubt heard my name as rash, and his spies had no doubt told him how my speech had fired up my people. I'd said enough times, how with enough spirit the wasp can sting the bear to death, and we would have to, how it would be all or nothing in one toss.

So when Emao-e turned tail and fell back to the pass, apparently losing nerve, Triadas sent his force after. Even the greatest general will sometimes forget the things he learned first; habit or complacency or stiff-mindedness creep in like bedbugs. He did what he had not intended, at a time I, not he, chose; and he set his command-post in the same place as before.

As soon as the battle was well-locked, we broke out in a wedge. He had some seventy guards, but they were regulars; his elite were in the pass. No fool to pride, he didn't try to play hero, but ran for the nearest safety, his army's rear, in the hopes his guard could hold us off long enough; it was easy to pick him out over their rank, by the scarlet mantle bordered in gold billowing out behind him. Two aides flanked him; the rest scattered, arms full of maps. I'd called wedge-form and tempered its tip with my Elite to break through, though; soon we did. "Well, Triadas!" I hailed him in Arkan as I sprinted after him. "Wondering where I was, were you?"

So he was the rabbit fleeing for his life and I the fox chasing for my dinner, then; but he was middle-aged, out of training, an Arkan breathing thin air, and it was uphill. As well the fox knew he could become dinner if he were too slow; already Arkans ahead in the fight were seeing, and turning to come to their general's aid. Clever to the end, he pulled his mantle in around him so I couldn't grab it as I drew close. I caught him by his long streaming *Aitzas* hair.

He turned then, drawing a dagger, and almost hurt me, in truth, but he was too tired to have a firm arm and my breastplate turned it. There was the stern square face I'd seen in the Pages' engravings, flushed with exhaustion now, and angry at himself. It had come into my mind to take him alive, but I could hardly bind him and lead him away now. So I struck off his head. For a time I held it high, for the Arkans to see, while his body lay at my feet, the legs trying to run for an instant longer. Then we fled, the hotheads laughing as they led us. The Arkans fell back from the pass; nothing remained but to celebrate.

One day later the Hyerne came, a thousand in number, a day after that the Lakans, seven thousand. They were led by Arzaktaj, who had thumbed Emao-e, Esora-e and Denaina, and captured me in the Lakan war. All laughed over it now, but my shadow-father. He just kept silent, under my orders. Our mercenaries were up to two thousand now, trickling in all the time: that made fourteen thousand five hundred, enough to fight fifteen thousand. It was odd, though, to command an army half dark-skinned. The officers I could speak to in Enchian; whether the men laughed behind their hands at my bad Lakan I will never know.

I remember once later in the war I was sitting at a Lakan campfire, when I felt one man staring at me, as if he knew me from before; his face was familiar to me as well. With time, and wine, he came over. "*Shaikakdan,*" he addressed me bowing, as they did, "seven years ago you were shorter and slenderer, no? Did you not give me freedom, in Kantila?" He was one of the twenty-two wounded Lakans I'd saved from the massacre. We became brothers then, arm in arm and toasting each other for the rest of the night. I did not get so close, though, as to admit I'd conceived it. One can ask forgiveness to stretch only so far. At another fire I happened into Klajen. "My quicklime boy never had a dull life," he said. "Imagine, those straw-haired infidels making a *slave* of you!" The interest he took in my accomplishments after that was not unlike an uncle's.

Triadas was replaced by Abatzas Kallen, who had the name of a fool, promoted only through Kurkas's favor. He began to prove it right away. Just before battle, the Arkans were called to assembly, and one was flogged and made to kneel for him; I smiled, to see them given that sort of inspiration. In the battle, he made a thousand blunders, not the least of which was underestimating our number, though being on open ground we could do nothing to hide it. They fought with even less spirit than I'd expected, showing faces implausibly hopeless for warriors who had all but conquered a nation. It was a rout; we chased those we did not strike down all the way to Chegra, where they found a strong position at the pass. If the rest of the war goes like this, I thought, we'll be in the plains by leaf-turn, let alone snow-fall, and have them out of Yeola-e in a year.

The village welcomed us, even the Lakans, with shirts and kisses. As we stood on the cenotaph, showering in wine, a report came to me. The Arkan who'd been flogged was, as my people called him, Kalicha Ityirian, a champion even people in the Elite were in awe of, and who had above all a name for honor in battle. It had been for verbal insubordination; probably trying to talk sense into Abatzas, I thought. Everyone in earshot gaped, wondering what sort of a general would do that to one of his best, then; no wonder they'd fought so miserably. It was better even than I'd hoped.

Later it came to me that I'd heard of the man. In the Mezem: he was Kallijas Itrean, whose father had forbidden him to enter it. If the chance comes, I remember thinking, I shall have to tell him what he missed.

Two days later the Enchians came in, bringing us to twenty thousand odd. An honor guard of some thirty, and dressed in pomp that made me feel up-country, came; in their midst, like a crow among peacocks, stood a stocky young man dressed all in black. I remembered his slouching carriage, and his face, with its pinch of resentment; though bearded and moustached now, it was just the same, the ill-temper if anything worn deeper in. When I stood to greet him I saw he was still taller than me by three finger-widths; he always would be. "Welcome, Reknarja," I said.

He was itching for a scrap right from the start, but tense as a board as well, as if somehow by teaching him I held his fate in my hands. Truly, my diplomacy would be tested. For now, I took him straight up the mountain, gave him the numbers, and said, "I want one brilliant battle plan, as comprehensive and detailed as you should have to give if you were me, practicable and inspired in all its aspects, overlooking nothing, sure beyond a doubt to bring us a massive victory at negligible cost—in short, an example of perfection in the strategic art—and I want it by the time the sun is two fists over that peak tomorrow."

All through this time, I learned, in fits and starts, what things the Arkans had done in the land of my people. We'd been overrun quickly only because they had great numbers,

and gone on fighting afterwards. That always makes for the
worst, with Arkans.

No one wanted to tell me such things, at first; I had to
urge them to come forward, saying it would fire our spirit.
Then they came, in terrible numbers. Arkans have a way of
torturing people in village squares; or they'd seize a child,
and cut off and cauterize some part of him every day until
someone who knew where the resisters were came forward
for truth-drugging. The couple or four who'd seen their
children raped to death before their eyes came to me a
hundred times, as well as the man with his eyes, tongue
and hands cut away, or the woman with her face burned so
that she had only the slightest opening left for a mouth,
who signed to me that the same had been done between
her legs. Many a warrior whose wristlets had been taken
came wearing manacles with the chains struck off, saying
they'd do, until Arko was conquered. I would listen gravely,
give them heartening words and a grin, then weep my heart
empty when I was alone. That is enough to write, I think.
There was plenty more.

IV

We chose the night of the next day to attack the pass. Reknarja, the book-learned general, wanted to charge straight up the valley; "Go sprint up that hill," I told him, pointing out one of similar incline, "and see if you feel like fighting at the top." For the sake of peace, seeing his scowl, I let him concede without doing it. By moonlight, we climbed the side of the mountain out of arrow-range, and charged level along the slope.

It was a hard battle; for one thing, they had mountain-people. Bitter to see the black shirts of the Schvait, whom we had always considered friendly neighbors, side by side with scarlet Arkan armor, shedding our blood on our land. But they hold with the mercenary's highest ethic, to fight for who pays them. It put me in mind to hire some myself, now I had the money. Schvait will not fight other Schvait; both sides will sit down in the field. As often as not that means they draw high mercenary pay for being spectators, sweet work if you can get it. I would send to the head of their clan council if I lived tonight, I decided.

We were beating them back; Abatzas had left an opening on his flank that we could stab into, perhaps through. By the light of torches I saw Kallijas Itrean rush back towards the breach, his men following; he was easy to know, for the red of his armor was scalloped with gold, and he was left-handed. He was coming to me.

Around us his people and mine drew back a little. I learned why he had his name instantly. His skill was perfect, like Riji's or Tyirian's, my old war-teacher; impeccable in form and speed, made of water and steel whether his teachers had called it that or not. I ceased to think of the battle, or see or feel anything but him, and his sword. Yet I began to feel all his spirit was not in it; his fire was muted somehow by his heart, as if with some trouble. I wished I could see his eyes better.

Just about then I made a bad parry, and felt his sword glance my sword arm hard enough to part my mail. Not to do much else; I felt only a trickle of blood. But he jumped back, and froze, and spoke something in Arkan. Startled, I didn't press him; though it was melee it felt like a duel of honor. I saw his lips pressed tight under the nasal of his helmet, as if seeing out bad air. Then a man near him shouted with joy, as if he had beaten me. An absent thought, as the God-in-Ourselves often sends, made me look at the edges of his sword. Hard to see by night, they were both evenly stained their full length with some dark substance.

I know quite a few Arkan death-insults. But in the end all I said was what was in my heart: "I heard so much of you, and your honor." Probably that was far worse. I saw his mouth flinch; then he flung down the sword and ran back through the lines.

I felt weak, and the pain, tingling and wet and cold like a stun-drug spreading through the veins, almost immediately. I called second, then help. By the time I was out of the mill, I was staggering. Quality stuff, fast-acting, only the best for a demarch. There was nothing more to do but lie still on the litter to save my strength, and breathe deeply; I didn't even feel it when they cut my arm open and tried to suck the poison out. I told them what I'd seen of it, and the symptoms, so they could tell Kaninjer if I fell unconscious. After a time of dreamy raggedness, in which I saw the stars flow to and fro like a gossamer cape on a woman's arm, and the flashing black shadows of little wings, I did.

* * *

I first tried to shut out the words, wanting peace. "Chivinga, you'll be all right, wake up, wake up, Cheng, the people wills." Kaninjer said, "It may be he can't hear, but can feel." Hands stroked my brow and gripped my shield hand; one touch I knew from as far back as I'd been alive, my mother's. When I turned my head the world spun, making me sick. "It's too soon to move," Kaninjer said. "Just lie still. Good, he's still; he heard me."

I was in the infirmary, and it was morning. The pain came back, sharp on my sword arm, dull and throbbing everywhere else. Mana's arm-ring was on my shield arm, my sword arm swollen thick. The poison had almost killed me; it was only because I'd been brought fast that Kaninjer had been able to save me. Later when my mind was quicker, I knew he was being modest; he'd had to discern the poison just as fast. That is why I hired a healer, I thought, who was highest in his class.

When I could, I heard the reports of the command. If Abatzas had thought to unspirit us by this, he had timed it wrongly. It just made my Yeolis angry, to fear they might lose me again, so soon. The outlanders, three quarters of my army, hardly knew me. They'd kept on as they'd started, and soon the pass was ours; the Arkans fell back to the valley. Vae Arahi had been walled, made into a proper Arkan fortress, with a sun-clasping eagle two man-heights tall over the gate. Now at the first smudge of dawn, while I'd lain slowly waking, they'd slunk inside it.

I gave Emao-e words of my own, both rousing and loving, to speak to the army when she announced I would live, and heard the roar and clashing of wristlets, all around the infirmary; they must have stayed awake, waiting, having time now, as the warmth of fighting cooled, to worry for me. I took it in like medicine. Then, though Kaninjer had forbidden me to command, I called Emao-e back in, and whispered, "Break camp, and march. Nothing's stopping us; tonight we'll sleep in soft beds, in Terera."

So it was I came home, in a wounded-cart, weak as a lamb, and not even allowed to see; it had been decided that sight of Vae Arahi walled would be too much for me in my state. I could smell the pine wind off Hetharin, though, and hear the roar of the falls; finally I shed the tears that had waited so long.

The Arkan civilians in Terera had run away; the Yeolis poured out on the streets and roofs. Against Kaninjer's protests, Krero and Sachara put me on an open litter, with pillows to hold me half-sitting. I couldn't do much more than smile, but that was enough. Soon my bedclothes were speckled with flowers, and pink with wine. From up ahead came a crash and a rumble. The Arkans had walled the town hall and converted it into a governor's mansion; now he and his guards had fled, the people were tearing the wall down.

I had them carry me down to the shore, where later this fall I should have done my first Renewal, had I not already done it. I dipped my fingers in the water, and brought them to my lips. The people's cheer was thunder; let it be heard all the way to Arko.

They were willing to billet even Lakans, and no one in the market would take money for food; so we stocked up and settled in. Ankarye Chermena came to see me; apparently the Workfast Proclamatory had been secretly running news out of Terera into all Yeola-e all through the war. People died for it. "A hot-bed of underground work, you've heard?" she said laughing. "This nest of ex-scribblers and bureaucrats? We'd die of boredom otherwise." So I made a speech of inspiration to all my people, in a whisper. The leaven works in the bread, I said, and the flame spreads silently beneath the ground; soon the time will be right for it to roar upwards, burn away our chains and cleanse us of this long sickness. A bit overdone, perhaps, but right for the task.

Then Kaninjer buried me in a back room of the hall—the signs of Arkans, beef-smell and a brass oil-lamp, were still there—and cut off my visitors. Probably he was right that I had done too much; as well I had thought too much. In the midst of celebration, I had smelled trouble. Never besiege, the old rule says; all the advantages are to the besieged. No doubt they were well-stocked, certainly long enough for reinforcements to arrive, as I'd be a fool to imagine wouldn't. I didn't have the numbers to waste fighting walls. At the very best, we'd be stopped here, in the position I'd done everything to avoid, trapped in the mountains for winter. But we must retake it; it was Vae Arahi.

It needed the path unconceived, and the flash didn't come. I would have been best off leaving it alone, and sleeping, as Kaninjer wanted me to. But bothered by my pain and wanting to make up for my weakness, I strained and fretted. He couldn't give me sedative; too many other foreign substances had polluted my blood lately. Soon the fever he'd feared came.

By midafternoon I was burning, by sundown raving. I recall conceiving several brilliant plans, which somehow were accompanied by the music of Ilesias Janiscn; but each time I came to myself enough to think of dictating one to Chinisa, both details and gist went out of my head like a puff of smoke, making me want to bang it against the wall. They'd built Arkan-style baths, and when they laid me in a cool one, I thought I was back in the Mezem and started yammering in Arkan, offending everyone in earshot.

Finally, near midnight, it broke. "Kaninjer," I said, when I'd lain quiet for a while. "Send for someone who was there when Kallijas cut me, who saw. I won't sleep until I've spoken with one." I knew this was true; the beginnings of an idea had finally come, and I feared losing it. He argued, but fetched Sachara.

"Well!" Sach hadn't had a chance yet, to voice his opinion to me. "So much for the great Kalicha Ityirian! We all knew he couldn't take you honestly; I guess it shouldn't be a surprise, that he agrees."

I said, "Sach, you're starting to sound like Krero. Tell me, what expression was on Kallijas's face, right after he wounded me?"

"His face? I thought he was sure he'd succeeded. I'd love to see it when he finds out he didn't!" But seeing I was serious, he said, "Well . . . he looked a bit as if he'd swallowed a peach pit."

"He said something to me. It was Arkan, but if I repeated it, do you think you would know it?" He signed a hesitant chalk. I did the *solas* accent as best I could. "*Maen ipelatzis.*"

"Something very much like that," he said. I tried it in inferior-to-superior, instead of equal-to-equal. "Yes!" he said. "That's it, that brings it back clear. What does it mean?"

" 'I'm sorry.' No, he didn't agree with you that I could take him, Sach. His commander did. Had it been his plan, had his heart been in it, he wouldn't have apologized, or thrown down the sword and fled." It all came together in my mind. "He's Abatzas's better, and both know it. But Kallijas is *solas*, and Abatzas *Aitzas*, and in his petty soul he can't stand to see a born inferior do so well. We've already seen him flog and shame the man; but if he *really* wanted to bring him down, what better way to than this? While someone suited for it wouldn't have regretted and given it away, so I would have got to Kaninjer too late . . . the idiocy boggles the mind." I saw the path, and chuckled. "Trying to break him, he'll have killed him—his best warrior." Sach squinted, and said, "You've lost me," but I said no more; I'd have to be firm on my feet before I sprang this on the command council. I slept.

Next day I was well enough to sit up, eat and walk a little, and take visitors. Sachara brought his new wife, Tera Azachira, and they gushed and cooed at each other so much I almost offered to lend them my bed. Reknarja came, looking pleased to see me hurt, so I made a gift to him of my one copy of *The Book of Five Rings.* The worse he was to me, I had resolved, the better I would be to him; if he didn't come to my side, everyone else would. The former mayor of Terera was dead, beheaded by Arkans; now the eldest of the surviving council, the best they could do for an official, came to greet and thank me formally. Best of all, Azaila came.

If he looked even slightly different, I couldn't see it. We spoke of training, and the Mezem, and he bade me get well, so he could spar with me and find out what tricks I'd picked up among these barbarians. After a time we came to what I'd been shy to ask him. I'd heard the Arkans had burned down the School of the Sword, as they had the Senaheri Dependent and much of the shrine when they had first come; but the School they'd tried to occupy first.

"Yes," he said, smiling his moon-faced smile, "they did. But they had quite some trouble, I understand, with a ghost. Walking through walls, laying traps, killing pairs of sentries

All-spirit knows how ... something every day. They had to fire it; they were losing too many. When the officer came back to check, he found a spectral message written in the ashes: 'You are fled; I win.'"

I looked at him under my brows. "I've never known the School to be haunted; nor ghosts to be so daring or consistent."

"No," he said, looking down his wrinkled old arm, in his way. "Nor did I ever think to be one until I died."

"Then you're done here, for now," I said. "Master, we'll rebuild the School; but until the war is over, the warriors who need you to keep them awake the most are with me. May I beg you to join us?" He told me smiling that his armor had rusted away forty years ago; no matter, he was too valuable to send through an arrow-rain anyway. In the end he agreed to train us. I told no one; let them find him when they needed his teaching, as they would.

The Oath of the Scrivener requires me to add that sometime later, when after one of my plans had succeeded better than even I had expected, I was strutting past a tent very impressed with myself when a force and a yell like wind struck my feet out from under me, pinned me down and ground my face in the dirt until I yielded. "I could have killed you!" I said when he let me up; I was wearing three blades, he none at all. "Oh?" he grinned back. "You didn't, did you? You won't next time, either; I'll bet my life on it. Because I'll strike when you can't." Nor was that the last time; I got my cheeks smudged with the earth of a number of places before that war was over.

Soon after his first visit I was on my feet firm enough; time was passing. I spoke my plan to council: to challenge Kallijas Itrean to a duel, under the agreement that if I won, Vae Arahi would be surrendered to us, and if I lost my life would be forfeit.

Naturally they thought I was out of my mind. Emao-e reminded me of Brahvniki, again; Hurai said, "We haven't fought well enough for you, you must do it all by yourself, now?" I felt the unspoken thought in the air, of my time on Haiu Menshir. They even called in Kaninjer, for his medical opinion. Not wanting to explain that it mostly rested on a look and a word, I reminded them of my forty-nine duels in Arko, and that I'd fought Kallijas enough to know something of him as well as myself. In the end I stood on rank.

It had been the last thing to discuss; the generals gathered their things from the mat to go, in a thick silence, oppressive to my ears. I remembered how close they'd come to losing me, only two days ago. But they were veteran leaders, not peach-faced youth who could be reassured by a few sure words. "Listen," I said. "The God-in-Me spoke; need I say more? You are happy that I'm back, aren't you, because you know when it speaks you can trust it? When are you going to start trusting, then?"

They all stared, halted in the motion of lifting waxboards and papers. I savored seeing Hurai speechless, not expecting another chance soon. Putting my hands on my hips like a mother, I said, "Oh, come on! Has this war made you all twenty years older? Here we are, the dwarf planning to drive the giant off our farm, and we *will*, too—and you're all afraid of an even fight?" I remembered the Mezem, where on pain of torture I had learned to fear no one in single combat; never before had I thought of it as part of my training. "Cheer up, you circle-collared sheep-turds; anyone over the rank of millenion caught worrying does latrine pushups with me on their shoulders, until I say stop." Silence cracked into laughter.

I wrote the challenge with my own hand, mentioning the poison blade—I wanted to remind Kallijas of it at every chance—and invited Abatzas to parley.

It felt strange beyond strange to ride up beside the falls of Vae Arahi armed to the teeth and guarded. The white water danced in the sun, I found the rainbow in the same place I always had as a child, the rocks and roots I knew with my eyes closed. It seemed I was coming home from a month-away; at the top of the hill I would find a warm bowl of stew, my mother's kiss and the mob of my little sibs, then after I'd eaten, and thrown off these stifling clothes, I'd run on the mountain with Sach, Krero and Mana.

The wall around Vae Arahi might indeed have set me back had I seen it while weak, a monstrosity of black stone in the massive Arkan style, purposely imposing. They'd cut down every tree with arrow-range, too; the stream ran naked, the fragrant cedar grove a patch of stumps, the mountainside a hacked waste. Over thick crenels like a giant's square black teeth, fringed now with red helmets and spearheads, I saw the tower of Assembly Palace, and the peaked slate roof of the Hearthstone.

Abatzas came out with five more guards than I had, nervous, I think, about what had become of another Arkan general, though I was under the ivy branch. He was a paunchy man, bald on top with the *Aitzas* hair down to his waist behind, and plenty of jewelry; about fifty, like Kurkas; perhaps they'd met young. He'd once been handsome, but now the lines of his face all pointed to the middle in a suspicious, petulant shape; his nose seemed made for looking down. One sensed his family had believed only its own blood good enough to breed with, for generations. His squire looked brighter.

He was taken aback by my proposal, but warmed to it soon, eager to see the end of me, and sure his man was my better for no other reason, I think, than he was Arkan and I was Yeoli. I began to wonder whether he would even give Kallijas any choice. Not that I meant to myself: everywhere in my letter, I'd penned his name in yellow ink, an insult answerable only with steel, for an Arkan. Keeping in mind Abatzas could forbid it, though, I acted less sure of myself than I had before my command, and made as if my honor required the duel, without thought to my chances. I could see him taking me for a reckless boy. He didn't even question the terms.

He sent my letter in through the gate, with a message of his own; soon the answer came back, yes, though Kallijas did not come out to give it. I invited him to choose the weapons: sword and shield. Kaninjer had promised me, if I slept well and did not overwork, I'd be in good form in two days; so we set it for then.

I took light exercise, did little work except sending my letter to Bitha Szten, *Lynto Johtaja*, or clan head, of the Schvait, and widening my contacts with the underground. Its work, sabotage, assassinations, kidnapping, breaking into dungeons to free its own, and passing information—in Athali, the short-hand my writing-tutors had frowned on my learning—had been ceaseless all through the occupation.

Only women commanded or knew anything; Arkans being Arkans, they would truth-drug every man in a village, find nothing and so think nothing was going on.

Whenever I went out, Yeolis would touch my shoulder, and say, "My strength infuse your hand." Not that they were afraid; the lightness from the command council has spread, so that it seemed the only one in town who wasn't entirely certain of my victory was me. And Kaninjer; he didn't succeed in hiding his nervousness. I tried to comfort him, but he felt too shamed to take it.

The day dawned bright and turned cloudless, the trees the ripe green of late summer. We'd agreed the duel would take place on the Palace side of the bridge. My army lined up in the plain at the foot of Haranin, still cheery and confident—I heard warriors laugh together—and Abatzas's beneath the heavy black walls. They did their noon observance, to the call of an Arkan bell inside. It came without thinking to do the Mezem warm-up; only the intrigued looks made me realize. Remembering how the same stretches had felt there, I knew my body was weaker; but here, fighting for the only reason I should, my spirit was stronger.

Their party came out, with a full ten eagle-standards, and Kallijas in his red and gold armor riding a blood bay. It made me wish I could have been better turned out; I'd been fitted for a good suit of armor in black with blue and green, but though the Algra smiths were working day and night, it would be another month.

We crossed the bridge, our horses' hooves clattering on the cobbles above the hiss of talk from both armies. Just beyond I dismounted and walked out alone, my helmet under my arm. Kallijas did the same, pulling off his gauntlets as he did, since I wore none. That is honor, from an Arkan. He was built much like me, but a little taller, longer-legged. His hair was pulled back in a fighting-braid. I had seen the type for his face in Arkan war paintings, but never thought to see it in person; of course, I thought, he must have modelled. The painters had left out the tan, though, that made his eyes stand out ice-chip blue. In them I read resolution; but more worn-in was the grimness of one fighting his circumstances. There was more to it than I knew, it seemed.

Behind him one of his party called out, in sing-song Arkan like the selling-boys in the Mezem stands. "Peanuts, sausages, wine, candy! Take your bets, gentlemen, for today a slave shall die! Mourning dye, for Karas Raikas!" The Arkan army within earshot heard, and roared with laughter. I just gave him a grin that said, "I will remember you," though likely I wouldn't.

I halted, and Kallijas did likewise, ten paces away; the buzz suddenly fell to silence. I drew Chirel. Making the gestures wide for all to see, I ran its edge along the palm of my shield hand, just deep enough to draw a thin streak of blood. With a sword so sharp, one hardly feels it, at least at first. I held the hand palm out to him. The Arkans went silent. Behind me my army let out their jeers.

I saw him stiffen, and his lips thin as they had on Chegra. It was a bitter weak point to use against him; he did not deserve to die for it. But this was war. He drew his sword, a straight narrow two-edged blade in the Arkan style, curled his hand around it and drew it through slowly, then showed me two scarlet cuts.

I sent an open kiss to the Hearthstone, and a fisted one to the place where the School of the Sword had been. Let them see, who truly belonged in this place. We put on our helmets. The armies burst out in a roar of exhorting, and we closed.

I had known from the start how to fight him: gently, kindly with perfect form and honor, to make him feel what kind he had almost murdered. A sly or petty stroke might make him forgive himself, and fight unhindered. No surprise, he fought me the same way, as if to say, "This is how I really am." In fact I soon knew it was his only way. His sword seemed lighter in his hand, for being clean, and thus his beautiful skill that much greater.

I suddenly knew what I had hungered for, fighting Riji: to feel such harmony without malice. Nor had I ever touched it with Koree or Azalia, since that was only sparring. Kallijas lifted me out of myself, forcing moves I had not known I could do, making me know I'd never fought better in my life; I saw by his face I did likewise for him. The roar of the people and the clangor of steel on steel and lacquer faded from my ears; I heard only the singing wind, and knew he heard only the voice, whatever it sounded like, of his god. As we circled reaching for each other's lives we understood each other, admired each other, were bound, our souls one; we made peace for what he had done before, something I had not intended to do, for in his shame lay my advantage. But I saw now how petty it was to hold it over him; I almost felt petty myself to have conceived it. We needed no words, speaking through our bodies and eyes like a pair making love.

Perhaps this is something only another warrior can understand. Tell a pacifist of beauty in fighting and he will call you perverse, tell a Haian we could intend to cut each other down and love each other, both at once, and he will commend you to the House of Integrity. What I felt is only possible dancing with death—how many have given their lives just to feel it?—and I would give it up without a thought in return for peace. But for some reason, it feels good; perhaps the die was just for once, and wove into our nature some recompense for our suffering. Or perhaps it is just that the doing is joyful; tragedy and ugliness comes with the end.

I yearned to spring back, sheathe Chirel and say, "Kallijas, forget all this. Your commander doesn't deserve you, you're too good and you know it. Come over to our side, talk with me, spar with me, forget about being my enemy, and I will treat you as the world should." But whatever his dispute with Abatzas, treason was not in him. No, it was too late; he was Arkan; that die, rolled before we were born, had been unjust, decreeing that we should never meet, except here.

There was one mercy we could grant each other, though; in a glance between strokes, we agreed on it. I would not kill him, for I could win without; and while if he won, he could not save me without treason, I would know his wish was not in it. We had fought in a dream; it had gone a long time, perhaps because our hearts had shied from ending it; I was not tired, and felt I never would be, though my breath was coming hard and sweat poured off me everywhere. But it must end; I must end it. The people willed.

The wise strategist learns from what he has lived; let him not remember the past incompletely. In the Mezem, where

I'd trained for this fight, they smoothe the golden sand between every fight, raking out any object or irregularity. No one does that on the plain of Vae Arahi. My foot found a pebble, slipped and threw my weight sideways. Not enough to upend me; but too much.

I had a moment in which the air turned to amber, freezing all motion, long enough to see my error's full meaning, to know the extent of my failure. It was not I who would end it, but him; I had lost; in the same instant that I knew where his sword should come at my head, to defeat me, it was there. His stern face, the black walls and the friendly roof-peaks beyond them, the gold-green slope of Hetharin and the blue sky, all crashed away in a lightning flash, to darkness.

Then the world was a howling din, splitting my skull; *shake it off*, I told myself. No relief came, only searing pain. A sword floated near; where was mine? Near, on the ground; but I couldn't find my legs or arms. *Up. He's coming*. I thought I was in the Mezem; I could hear a crowd roar, some *Aitzas* bellowing, *"Kellin!"*

Light came streaking back with my next breath. I saw green, the pine forest sideways, and red: greaved legs. Kallijas Itrean, facing away from me, arguing, while two crowds howled out their lungs in the distance. Chirel lay just beyond my fingers. Then my mind made sense of the world and I remembered everything. It was the duel; he'd struck me on the head.

Up, I commanded myself, for whatever reason I still can. I got my hands under me, but my arms were weak as a baby's. Kallijas turned. Too slow, I thought; now he's seen me move, I'm done. I waited for him to slit my throat; instead he knelt near me, and looked into my face with his clear blue eyes. "Honored Enemy," he said, inferior-to-superior. "Fourth Shefen-kas. You stepped on a stone, as could have happened to either of us, by chance. I struck you only by reflex; I am sorry. It proves nothing. When you are recovered, let us continue."

My heart wanted to fall out of my chest. *Come to my side*, the words grew on my tongue. *You are too good for Arko*. Beyond him I heard the *Aitzas* voice again: Abatzas's.

"Kill him!" he was shouting, "kill him, you son of a whore, kill him or I'll run you in for active insubordination!" That carried the penalty of death. Perhaps he is even too good for me, I thought; had it been the other way around, I'm not sure I would have been so merciful. Remembering how the fight had been, I felt smaller than a worm; tears came. I should admit it to him and concede the win, I thought; a warrior with honor would do that. But I was demarch.

I turned my face to my people. The dark column was seething; whether they knew what had happened or not, they leapt and reached and waved fists; now and then I could pick out words from the din. "*Get up! Chevenga, get up!*" Kill your conscience, that voice, the voice of All-spirit, said to me; kill your honor. You have none, you are nothing, but our will.

So I lifted myself up, raising Chirel out of the dirt, and heard the shouting from my side double. It took time; the dizziness clung to my head and the weakness to my body. Kallijas was patient. I paced a little, and shook off the trembling; the pain I'd have to live with. Ready as I would be in decent time, when the crowd noise had eased, I called him.

I could see him easily outstaying me now; so in the first exchange, as he struck, I gave up my parry to thrust for the artery in the underside of his sword arm, as it came forward. The tip of Chirel bit through chain mail, then found the clench of flesh; his sword fell behind him; I twisted mine hard, and yanked it out. He staggered back, his arm spurting bright inner blood. His eyes did not change, still resolute; he knelt by where his sword had fallen, flung away his shield and tried to seize it. I leapt in and stunned him with a kick, and touched Chirel to his throat.

The Arkan host went silent, as if they were all dead, while mine made an ecstasy-roar. His eyes opened, and rose silently to me, made bluer by the sky. He looked younger, the grimness gone. I understood; he saw his fight with fate ended. "The duel is yours, Honored Enemy," he said. With the hand that would move, he pulled up his braid, and offered it to me.

I knelt to cut it, just the end, with my dagger, then pressed my hand to his wound to staunch the bleeding. One of his men, the one who I remembered congratulating him before, looked eager to run out and aid him, so I beckoned him to take my place, and stood. Abatzas sat trembling with anger on his horse, which shied and fidgeted. "It is done, as all have witnessed," I said. "You have until sundown to be out of Vae Arahi."

"You cheating barbarian!" he cried. "He had you, and you know it! That's no victory."

"He let me up, though he could have killed me," I answered, then for the benefit of those who had not seen, "because that was mischance. Now he concedes: you saw. It's done, Abatzas; but with a healer you will still save him."

In a moment I regretted the last words. Abatzas was in a mood to do the precise opposite of what I said, whatever it was, like a child. Yet if I'd never said it, perhaps, all would be different now. "Save him!" he cried. "To Hayel with him! He shall die, I command it! *Solas*, let go! Yes, you! Let him bleed to death."

I felt my body whirl around, almost without my mind willing it. The friend still knelt, staring at the general with his jaw hanging. Kallijas's eyes were closed now; whether he'd heard I couldn't tell. I signed my party, by the bridge, to bring a litter double-time. "I defeated him," I said. "He is my captive."

Abatzas only laughed. "Have him then! Enjoy him! And your hillside heap of poor-quarter stone, you can have that too. By sundown, yes." He turned his horse, and rode away, ordering his party to follow. The friend looked from him to me, and back again, his eyes desolate; I was the demon he didn't know, but the demon he did had abandoned him. Finally he begged me to let him come, giving his oath as an observer. I agreed, if he left all weapons and armor behind. Right then and there he stripped, in front of ten thousand pairs of Arkan eyes, and twenty thousand foreign. No surprise, that Kallijas's friends would stand by him. I had time only to hear Kaninjer say that he would live, then I was swept up onto joyful shoulders.

Abatzas took the time I'd granted him, and enough more to stretch my patience. They had been well settled in, all right, with enough food for months; all Terera looked on hungrily, as their supply wagons trundled past on the ring-road. But safe conduct was part of the agreement. By the time their army was through, leaving the way clear for me to go home, it was dark.

I should have seen the signs, I suppose—the wagons sent first, to have the army between us and them, the wait until dark, that would hide the first smoke, how he had complied suddenly after disputing, and spoken of a heap of stone. Truly, that had been what he'd intended to leave us. I suppose I was naive to trust him, knowing he felt cheated himself; but I was always naive in that way, thinking others would do as I did.

They must have done a good job of it, straw in the stairwells, oil on the beams. I heard the exclamations, and saw the first orange brightness above the walls, when I was at the foot of the falls; the smoke was too high to smell. By the time we'd got to the gate, flames had broken through the roofs, of both Palace and the Hearthstone, and all around me were cries of rage.

It had been a long day, full of feeling. Most of the army was still in Terera, able to see this already. I saw anger getting the better of them, making them chase the Arkans pell-mell, without order or thought, half-action since some would hold back; the Arkans ready, taking the charge like a thresher takes wheat. But I didn't even have the gong, to call them to me. I ended up running flat out back down while my home burned down behind me, until a runner met me. Blessed is the general with a good command council. They'd held the army back, and were sending them up.

When I went back inside the walls, both buildings were full of flame, sheets of it wreathing around pillars, great tongues licking from windows. Such a common thing, smoke rising from the kitchen chimney; such a wrong thing, pouring out so thick and fast.

We made bucket-lines; but one might just as well spit into the inferno of Hayel. It became all but unbearable to stand within the walls, for the heat; seeing it was too much to ask, I called them off, and from under the gate eagle watched the roof over my old room, the black beams carven centuries ago whose running patterns I had followed with my eyes before I understood words, break like a spine and crash down. "This war has been like this," a voice said behind me; my mother. "Right from the start, when you weren't here." When I didn't answer, Krero signed Kunarda, and they took a grip on my wrists. The day had been longest for me; I suppose I did feel some inclination to run into the fire. I watched with them holding me, since this was my last chance to see it all standing, until everything had fallen but the black Arkan walls.

At midnight or so we went back to the town hall of Terera. I tried the door of the room I'd borrowed, found it locked. "Password!" a voice rasped, Kaninjer's; but he let me in.

He was white and sweating, his hands trembling on me. "Come in, sit down. I never checked you, after the fight." I started; Kallijas Itrean was lying, with his friend sitting beside him, on my bed. "Here was the only safe place to hide them," Kaninjer stammered. "The Yeolis went berserk, would have killed them."

Kallijas's friend stared at me, transfixed; he would have dashed out the door, I'm sure, if it didn't mean leaving Kallijas. The champion himself looked tired, and in pain from his wound; but still younger, and at peace. "He shouldn't be moved again," Kaninjer said. "You must bathe, and let me check you, then sleep." I called my squires to move my things to the room next door.

"Honored Enemy, now my master." Kallijas had a deep voice; I'd heard it ring on the field. He spoke inferior-to-superior twice removed, now. "Your healer is to be commended. He saved our lives, standing over us and facing down warriors with swords, nine times." Because you are his patient, I thought. No wonder Kaninjer was so pale. When I took him in my arms, he clung hard, shaking. "It's when you don't feel brave, you're being the bravest," I said, something he might not know. I kissed his hand, and commended him formally. Then, though he wanted me into bed, I asked him and the friend, whose name was Minakis, to go. It seemed even longer a time than it had been, that I'd wanted this.

Now we were alone, I found myself shy for words. I sat on the healer's stool beside him and leaned my face in my palms; the skin was tender from heat, like a sunburn. My hands were black with soot; no doubt my face was too, but

tear-streaked as well; suddenly I was aware of what a sight
I must be. I sent for a water bowl.

The first words were his. "Your healer's seen to me, master. Has he seen to you?"

"There's been no time," I said. "Kallijas, call me, Chevenga, please; you know me well enough."

"As you will. Shefen-kas. I would make the proper
respects if I could. You are a warrior in whose presence it
is the highest honor to be."

"As are you," I said. It was the truth from my heart. "It
could have gone either way, I think, stones underfoot or
not."

He smiled. That I had never seen before. It was like the
first flash of gold sun and blue sky after a month of rains,
warm on the skin, lifting the heart. "So the gracious victor
will say. You are too kind, Shefen-kas."

"It's one thing to give a second chance to someone
you know you will beat," I said. "Me, you didn't. That is
courage."

"I could not do dishonor. Not again." My squire came
with the water; excusing myself, I began washing. "But you
won," he added, "and proved I am all you called me."

I stared at him blinking through a face full of water, trying
to remember what I had called him. "Kallijas. I don't think
of you, I never did when I wrote; I . . ." Truly he and I
were at peace, for he could shame me. "I wanted to make
sure you'd accept. How you felt, I did not care, then. They
were the lies of war. Now I care, I'm sorry. Will you forgive
me?"

He stared at me, confused; I went on, throwing out words
to show my heart, as if we were lovers who'd had a misunderstanding. "Kallijas, you are no coward, I'm not sure you
aren't braver than I; I don't know that I would have done
the same. I know it was Abatzas who commanded you to
strike me with a poison blade, and left you no choice, I
know you'd never choose it. All-spirit knows why, but he
was trying to bring you down, I could see that, and no one
can do that better than a commander to a loyal warrior. I
would never—" I cut myself off for a moment; how much
it would hurt him, to hear this? Yet better he know the
worst of his betrayal, than take it on himself. "It would be

too risky, for a high commander, to fight you alone. I did knowing I had Abatzas fighting with me."

Again on his face, I saw I was speaking truer than I knew. But he said no more, and we turned to speaking of wounds; he'd never got one before and didn't know what to expect. He let me look at it, a short gash, on the surface, rough-edged from the twist and with a slight forking on one end from when I'd pulled Chirel out, all closed with Kaninjer's fine, even stitching. Taking off my shirt to wash, I showed him my scars, which made him gasp. "I'd heard you were tortured," he whispered. "I'd also heard it was just a story, to besmirch us. But the proof is written on you. Who is A.M.?" I told him; he flinched, and whispered, "Celestialis, Arko." We went on to the duel, asking about each other's training, commending each other's skill. He'd been taught the classic Arkan style by Adamas Nizen in the City Itself; the strict honor had been bred into him, mostly, I gathered, by his late grandfather. The Mezem came up; he had indeed been forbidden by his father to enter. I fulfilled my old hope, to tell him what he'd missed, but in a friendly way instead of ironic.

You have suffered, I wanted to tell him, for being honest in a land of corruption. But how to say that to someone who was Arkan to the ends of his blond hair? He loved his people as I loved mine; and though his family, faithful *solas*, were clear-eyed about rot in the military and by extension in the nobility, he still thought without question that whatever the Imperator commanded was good and right. "But who *appointed* Abatzas Kallen?" I kept wanting to say.

He saw the general through a warrior's and an officer's eyes; I told him how it looked through another general's. "Every warrior has his nature, and you don't assign him to things against it, any more than you'd use a saw to drive a nail or a hammer to cut; it doesn't only fail, but might ruin the tool. Perhaps he did want you to fail, in some part. . . . But you know the ones who taught me never even *said*, you shouldn't bring personal grudges into it, when the fate of the people is at stake. They didn't *have* to; it went without saying! So for no gain he lost his best warrior. At least until we agree on your ransom, *if* we do."

His eyes went still and quiet. "He won't pay ransom for

me," he said softly. "He was going to let me die on the field."

"You were awake," I said. "You did hear that." I felt pain in my palms: the clenching of my hands pressing my nails into them.

"It was the last thing. Everything else was a muddle, but I heard that clearly."

"Tempers can cool and sense return; perhaps even to Abatzas."

He shook his head. "Once he's said such a thing, he feels bound to it. Especially if anyone tries to beg him to change his mind, as they will for my sake. Shefen-kas ..." He looked me in the eyes, but gently. "You will have to kill me. I ask only one thing: that it be by your hand."

I must have looked a blinking fool. "I'll have to kill you?"

He had thought further ahead than I, having more time. "By your customs, it's the only choice. I won't be ransomed, you don't keep prisoners, and between thumbing and death, I'd take death."

"I don't consider you a prisoner," I said. "The only reason I took you was what *he* intended. To me, you are a guest."

His blond brows flew up. "Then when I heal, you'll free me?"

It's not only Abatzas, I thought, who doesn't know what he's doing. Here's my half-action. "By the terms, only Vae Arahi was forfeit, not your life or your freedom. Everyone was just assuming I'd kill you. I was myself, I guess, in the beginning. . . . But I mean to try to get ransom for you. Even if Abatzas doesn't want to, you must have friends and admirers in the City itself who'd pay to free you. There are a thousand other choices, and I mean to try all of them. I didn't save you just to kill you."

He looked at me, suddenly marvelling. "You've just seen us burn down your birthplace," he said. "How can you be so forgiving?"

"*You* didn't do it. You weren't even in on the planning. I know you. You wouldn't do such a thing."

We gazed at each other, and I think our thoughts were the same: how can we understand each other so well? We don't share nationality, mother-tongue, nor a single opinion, probably, except of Abatzas; yet we somehow share the shape of our souls.

I bared mine then, about the one matter that shamed me before him: that since I might not have granted him such mercy, I should have, in all honor, conceded. Let him forgive me or condemn me; either way, I would feel clean. He said only, "It was all over your face, Shefen-kas. Then you looked back towards your army. I saw it was for them you got up, not for yourself. That is honor enough. We're fools, if we forget you are a king, who will do what a king must." I found myself weeping. Where a Yeoli would have given me his hand, he turned his head away so as not to shame me by seeing my tears, Arkan-style. It is no less sympathetic.

After a time he said, "You defeated me. I am yours."

It took me a moment to understand what he meant. When I did, I sprang up and away from him, tired though I was. It seemed to me more just to put out my own eyes.

"We who demand submission of those we've defeated," he said, "should we not submit when we are ourselves defeated?"

"That's an Arkan thing," I said. "I'm a Yeoli."

"No Arkan feels entirely defeated, until he suffers it."

"You don't feel defeated enough, thinking it's proven you're a coward? You think I want to make you feel *more* so?"

When I looked again, his eyes were straight on mine, even in the candlelight. "You must have seen, when Abatzas flogged me," he said; I nodded. "How I went to my knees willingly. If I didn't serve him, he might take me." At that his eyes creased, as with pain he meant to hide, but failed to. "My grandfather said the first time I gave myself, it should be to a man better than I." Somehow I was not surprised, that he was a virgin. "Abatzas was not. But you are."

At my age I should have known by now what it meant, my wanting to be near him, the sudden self-consciousness, the sparkling and shiver that spread over my skin now. I remembered the duel, and felt my heart leap. His hands were hidden under the linen, but I could see the shape of his sword hand, lying on his chest. An Arkan's is all nerves, as I'd found with Skorsas; he'll twitch if you even breathe on them, anywhere, fingers, palms, even knuckles.

But my mind froze my hand, and my heart, in time. I was a Yeoli, in the habit of taking such offers as love, whatever the trappings. But he was an Arkan. How he was offering, and would take it, was as he'd said; as subjection, in the Arkan way. I suspected he saw sex as unclean, and his strength in purity; certainly he did not see it as the highest expression of love, else he'd have done it by now, whatever his grandfather said; one considers lovers equals or better, and such a one as him had to have had them. No, this was by obligation, against his inclination; it would be pain to him, and fear too, since he was a virgin, but he would bear it, out of honor, because he'd lost. So I knew, I could never do it, no matter how gently; I wasn't sure I could even trust myself to be gentle, with an Arkan in my hands, and he would take anything I did to heart, and suffer as I knew too well myself. Better to die, than do such to one I loved.

So I told him that, while I towelled off. His blue eyes, already wide, flickered on the last word, as if it had hurt him. He whispered, "Loved?"

"Probably," I said, wrapping the towel around myself to go, "I'm a cursed idiot." He didn't laugh, but said only, "Then I am, too."

V

Next day at dawn, we began sifting the smoking ashes. There was nothing much to find, even the cellars gutted. The linden tree was black, its leaves burned off. Esora-e held back those who wanted to comfort me; I heard him say, when he thought he was out of earshot, "No, let him feel it all. It's good for us."

There was nothing to do but arrange the clean up, and the tearing down of the Arkan walls. It was felt by all that the complex should be rebuilt precisely as it had been. As well I sent a force of five hundred, all good at forest cut-and-run fighting, east. The Arkans had begun a road through the mountains from Akara to Vae Arahi; it must be halted.

Calling my army to assembly, I brought Kallijas out before them, in chains. It was his idea; whatever happened, he wanted to be seen as my prisoner, not my friend, for that might be taken out on his family at home. But I made him stand only for a moment, since he was still weak, and shamed my warriors out of jeering him.

I called parley with Abatzas, meeting him by the shore of the Lake. He was all smiles and full of taunts I won't bother to repeat. I hadn't been close enough before to see what he wore as a pendant: a golden Karas Raikas figure, hanging by its neck instead of its raised hands.

The amounts I had in mind were what any sane general

would: I would ask for six hundred gold chains, and let him bargain me down perhaps to four hundred fifty. There are some who would say a warrior as good as Kallijas is worth more than any amount of gold. He offered me fifty—"it's to court-martial him, barbarian, that's all," he said, and wouldn't go higher. "Fifty gold, that's the final offer?" I shouted, as if in anger, but in truth to make sure all his men heard, so it would get out in the Arkan camp.

Kallijas looked better, smiling his beautiful smile, when I came back. I told him only that he'd been right, Abatzas would not take him; no need to pass on the insult of the amount. He only nodded. Then he told me he'd thought for a time, and was against my seeking ransom by any other means. It would mean becoming a fugitive from his commanding officer, and therefore in effect in his own land. Yet somehow we did not decide what we would do.

In the evening, I found myself wanting no company but his. We spoke late into the night, mostly of politics. Like so many Arkans, he had a quick mind and remembered all he learned, but knew next to nothing. The Marble Palace chooses, and one bears it; that's as much as they think they need and ought to know.

I explained the demarchy, which he would barely believe was possible; as Arkans will, he'd thought I was a Yeoli Imperator. He went quiet, but listened, when I made my critique of Kurkas and his reign, the structure of state of the Empire, the policy of promotion by birthline instead of by merit. What shocked him most was my saying, "You'd make a better imperator than Kurkas"; in sheer astonishment, I think, he laughed so hard he nearly fell off the bed.

"What is the purpose of the Imperator?" I asked him.

"To do right by his God, and provide for the people." We'd spoken of matters divine before: as I heard wind and a voice with two notes when the God-in-Myself spoke, he felt a lifting, and heard a silvery note, half-breath, half-flute, which he took to be the voice of Aras Steel-armed, the *solas* god.

"Then you'd be better than him two ways, just by believing this. He holds no God, and provides only for himself." Telling him all I knew of Kurkas, I had to swear on my crystal a dozen times to make him believe everything.

By Arkan creed, it was blasphemy, and he was religious to the bone. But he neither denied nor justified any of it, listening in silence as if to a story he'd already known in his heart, slowly tracing the scars on my chest with his finger.

The next morning Minakis took his leave, by Kallijas's wish, I gathered. The tale he would carry there was that I had done the Arkan thing, excessively; bitter news but safer than the truth, for Kallijas's family.

We fought a battle against Abatzas by the Lake, defeated and routed them; they scattered almost to nothing, not even taking all their wounded, though we would have let them.

I had hoped Kallijas would spare himself watching. I didn't know him well enough. He praised us, as was civil, but his smile was forced; that night, he spoke wishfully of death.

I made my arguments, that he was no coward, that Arko's losses were not his fault, that by his own law he'd had no power to prevent any of it; that he'd broken the letter of his ethics to follow the spirit, and to let himself be destroyed between them was half-action. "The world deserves you," I said. "The world needs you. There are too few good people already; will you take away one more?" His stubbornness, and his wanting to be responsible for everything, reminded me of myself.

In time it came to me what he would have to do to live with himself: renounce the divinity of the imperator, the superiority of the *Aitzas*, fling away four-fifths of all that had been instilled in him. I was sure I had it in me to bring him through it; but now, here, I didn't have the time. Finally I said, "You hold yourself subject to me, yes?" and when he nodded, "then I forbid you to condemn yourself, or even judge yourself from now on, then, until I say so." He looked startled, but acknowledged it, as an order.

At Siriha we found the reinforcements Abatzas had sent for, ten thousand strong. (Twenty-five *rejins*, the Pages would say. Perhaps they did not lie, but one could see how the embellished measures of Arko's strength might have started. A *rejin* doesn't necessarily mean a thousand; in history, as I recalled from my studies in the Mezem, it has meant as few as two hundred seventy-five. This is why I

never counted Arkans in *rejins* myself.) I rested my army
for two days; on the second the Schvait came, six hundred,
the Clan Szten led by Bitha herself. The Schvait clans each
elect a leader, the *Johtaja*, for both home and abroad if the
clan hires itself out; from those at home one is elected
Lynto Johtaja. Should she leave, another is chosen; so Bitha
had given that up, for this.

She was some forty or forty-five, and Schvait to the bone:
short, stocky, practical-minded and sparing with words. I
asked her whether her coming might be taken by Arko as
a blow from Schvait itself, and gain its enmity; answering
with her rough Enchian she shrugged it off. "No longer am
I *Lynto Johtaja*; let them though take it as they please. We
are not worried of engagement with them." The Arkan
Schvait, I gathered, were there only for pay, as Schvait hold
for honor.

"So," I said casually as we did the papers, "how goes
it with Abatzas's Schvait anyway? That's three times we've
thrashed him now, good for a hefty raise." The standard
Schvait contract, which I was just signing myself, allows for
raises in pay if they are with a much larger force and get
defeated; compensation, shall we say, for foolhardy risks,
inferior comrades or poor generalship.

Bitha looked at me under her brows. Two opposed
Schvait units have friends and relatives on the other side,
exchange letters, meet in inns when on leave. This (and
their black shirts as well, I suspect) has often got them
suspected of spying, so that they've found it best to bind
themselves not to; my contract set it out clearly. "Would
have me break this so soon, you?" she said scoldingly.
"Handsome young men who lead are dangerous." I laughed,
and said I just wanted gossip, not intelligence. "You know
not of saying, 'intelligence is war leader's gossip'?" she said;
but added Abatzas's Schvait were satisfied.

Two days later an Arkan showed up at our camp gate
bearing the ivy branch. He was here to perform a vital
function for the public of Arko and the world at large, he
said, being a writer for the Pages; could he please accom-
pany us as we waged our war, to get the other side's view?
One of the sentries he spoke to wanted to turn him off right
there; the other thought they should report anything this

odd to officers. His centurion came to me. I ordered the
writer truth-drugged, but said, "Only ask him whether he
means to kill anyone, harm anything or cause any trouble
here; don't ask him whether he's a spy. It's unnecessary."
Passing that test, he begged an interview with me, to which
I consented.

I knew him; he'd been a Mezem man for a month or so.
"Seems you can't escape the surly Karas Raikas," I said
laughing. "Well, I'm much more amenable to questions
these days, so go ahead." He did, the first being what our
battle plan was.

"Well, since you ask so directly," I said, aware of Reknarja
turning green outside, where I'd posted him to listen, "we
mean to start straight on, with the usual crossfire, but hide
our strength behind the right flank—or was it the left? No,
no, the right."

"The right?" the writer said, his fingers going a little white
on his pen. "Are you *sure*?"

I dug through some papers on my lap-desk, pretended to
find it. "Yes, of course it's the right, *our* right, because that's
where the upward slope is as opposed to the plain, where
Abatzas would *expect* it, you see. . . . We mean to outflank
him and swing around behind, the Demarchic Guard Elite,
that is, led by myself."

He barely stayed to finish his tea, saying he must get his
pigeon back to Arko in time for deadline. Next day as we
readied for battle my mountain-scout reported that Abatzas
had put an archer behind every rock and bush on the slope.
I did as I'd said but on the left, over clean ground he'd left
unprotected; it was so easy I feared he'd put something over
on me. They were soon in confusion, and we killed at our
leisure until they scattered.

The next Pages would excoriate me on the front page for
a liar and a sneak who had done the unforgivable: broken
the ancient institution's sacred trust on truth in all things. I
looked at the author's name: it was indeed my credible
friend. "You've got to be joking," I said to him when he
came back later, for more. "You worked in the Mezem!"
He just sniffed, "You almost got me beheaded, Raikas."

In that battle we captured Abatzas himself and his command council as well; Krero led the column that did that.

Abatzas apparently made a good show, flinging himself down at the feet of the first Yeoli who came near and yelling, "I'm worth a lot in ransom, I am, a thousand gold chains or more, and you'll get all sorts of reward, throw away all that if you hit me with that thing!"

I'd ordered Kallijas to stay inside my tent, this time; again he'd disobeyed. I found him sitting on the bed, calm-faced, but red-eyed. "I need not judge myself," he said. "Judgment is laid on me every battle . . . Sheng. Forgive me. I shouldn't complain while you rejoice. You were brilliant again."

Ten days ago, Kall, I thought, I should have enacted the plan rattling in the bottom of my mind: sent you back to a safe place. However much I want you with me, however much like a child dragging on an adult's hand I want to show you my victories: while I put you through this, my love is a glass gem. You want to cling yourself, to suffer because you think you deserve it, but that will bring nothing but ill to anyone. I have been worse than selfish.

I took his face between my hands. "I love you," I said. "Perhaps when this is all over, fate will let us be friends. But for now you are going back from the front. I know someone who will put you up, in return for a few chores." He didn't give me much argument, seeing sense himself, perhaps.

"Many times you've told me what you'd tell or do to Abatzas, if the chance came," I said, as I towelled off. "It's here now."

He stared bright blue for a moment; I don't think he'd ever expected it would come, thinking in his Arkan way Arkan generals never get captured. After a time of thinking, he said, "No. I have no wish to see Abatzas Kallen." But his eyes stayed on mine for a moment, thinning with some thought I could not read. "Who are you sending me to? Sheng, don't let me impose." I didn't hear that; I was thinking of what Arkans do to captured leaders, and his words: "No Arkan feels entirely defeated, until he suffers it."

That will tell you what a heart Kallijas Itrean has, why I loved him, though he was Arkan. Here I had offered to his mercy the worm of a commander who had shamed him, betrayed him, tried to kill him, and he'd not only declined, but held off reminding me of what any Arkan would consider my due, to spare him that as well.

I did not consider it my due, though, and it slipped my mind. In the after-battle meeting of the command council, we argued over how much ransom we should ask for the Arkan generals, once we found someone on the other side qualified to negotiate for them. Then Krero said, "You know what you should do to them, Cheng." At my glance, he said, "What they would have done to you."

That debate went for a good bead. Arzaktaj and Misiali, the Enchian general, both favored it for the sake of unspiriting the enemy; the Yeolis favored it for rewarding and putting heart into our own. Horror spread like rot on my skin. "But what will they think *me*?" I said. "Do they want to see me turn Arkan?"

"You know, Chevenga, that's your weakness," Emao-e said. "The weakness that is the other edge of the strength, as always. You are so good you don't understand evil or anger or vengeance, you think all Yeolis are crystal-pure like you. In that way, you are out of touch with the warriors, as the general should never be. There's many won't admit it to you, fearing you'd look down on them for it; but they tell *us*. 'I'd love to see Chevenga make that Arkan suck him,' I've heard them say, a thousand times." The other Yeolis all signed chalk, that they'd heard the same. It was my duty, they argued.

I thought through the night, and in the end decided it was neither for me nor my command council to say what the people willed. The next morning I called Assembly, pulling Abatzas out with me before them, to the jeers and gestures. "Resolved," I said, once I'd finished my speech in praise of their deeds, "that I do the Arkan thing, as it is called, to the Arkan general. All who favor chalk . . ."

The council had been right. I looked down at Abatzas kneeling at my feet, his pinched-in face full of horror; he somehow understood what the thunder of wristlets clashing meant.

Some aspects of the act of war tend not to show themselves on a written page; it is a compact among warriors, as among healers or cremators, that the cruelest secrets of our work be spared those who need not live them. Yet war is a public undertaking; nothing of it should be hidden from those who vote on it. So I believe; yet my heart shrinks from writing this, as it shrank at the time from doing it.

The people wills, I had to chant to myself, to make my hands unclasp my belt, to seize his narrow patch of long hair; though he was defiant at first his fear soon made him so hungry and fawning I wanted to wipe his touch off me, like dung. But duty turned to pleasure, soon enough; his desperation I started to enjoy. A human body will feel as it will feel, and so will a human soul.

He was Abatzas; but he was also Arko, and the hand of Kurkas on the border, his minion, his representative, his friend. *You who forced me to my knees before you*, I thought, *I now force to yours before me. You serve me; it is I who am power, now.* Who can help but feel pleasure, to know his helplessness so ended? The army cheered, and chanted my name; when I threw back my head and raised Chirel to the sky, it rose to a shattering roar. *I am the people's will*, I thought, and felt their hate flash to my outstretched fingers like lightning to tree branches, and burn through me into him; on his agony and their ecstasy and my own power, I rode as on a wind, and could image no pure joy. "Even that," people would say to me after, "you can make grand with every motion; even doing the Arkan thing, Chevenga, you look like a perfect demarch. How?" Like the rest, I answered, my heart was in it, that's all.

But when I was finished, I ran into the darkness of my tent, ordered everyone away from me, threw up everything in my stomach and beat my head on the ground. Alchaen was right, I was thinking, to have wanted to keep me longer. Truly, Arko has forced itself into me, and remade me in its shape.

An arm reached down to stop me, and a deep voice spoke. "You did what you must. You hate yourself only for enjoying it, I think." Kallijas; he alone had felt free to disobey my order. "Sheng, don't pull away, don't make me wrestle you, it hurts my arm. Are you listening? Don't hate yourself, you are a good man, else you wouldn't be suffering now." Then why, I cried back to him, is *that* pleasure sweeter than any other? He said, "Is it?", and touched my shoulder.

I am willing, those gentle fingertips said. Abatzas was

compelled, by fear, but I would give myself to you, though it makes me suffer, because I love you. So he cleaned that stinking touch off me with just one shining instant of his own. This was sweeter; I'd just forgotten, that was all.

I just wept after that, and thought, and came to an understanding of decadence that made all I knew of Kurkas, and Arko, much clearer. It is, I think, to feel that black pleasure, but without revulsion afterward.

Yet that evening, Kallijas was overly silent, thinking; finally he gazed at me sharp, the blue of his eyes resolute, as if against fear. "I look at you," he said, "and see the death of my people."

While I was still blinking, thinking to myself, "We've barely got Vae Arahi back, three-quarters of Yeola-e is still occupied," he said, "Shefen-kas, take me. My life, my freedom, whatever you wish of me, in Arko's place, for Arko's punishment."

I stared until it sank in; it took me by surprise, I suppose, because it came now. "But I've got all I wish of you," I blurted; it was only afterwards the tactlessness of that came to me. "Kall, *you've* done us no more wrong than any other warrior, why should you suffer more? To pay for all I love that I've lost by Arko, you want me to lose one more I love? You think *I* want that?"

I read his eyes: *But what else have I to give?* he was thinking. *I've offered you everything.* Clear as air, another day came back to me; Mana's arm-ring, which I'd ceased feeling on my arm, seemed to clench. "What do I say to the man who offers me everything, and has nothing?" Shock and pain that I knew too well myself flooded his eyes. "Not my words, Kall. Kurkas's." And I told him how I'd thrown myself to the ground, trying to save Mana's life, to no avail.

He is doing what I would do in his place, I thought, as he knelt, and begged me. Even if I thought there was no hope, as perhaps he thinks now, I would try because I must try, and try hard, invoking our love, invoking the honor between us, invoking the virtue of mercy, as he is now, invoking everything I could think of. "Will it undo what has been done? Will it bring your friend back to life?" All arguments I'd have made myself, that I had made in other disputes in the past. It's a compliment, I thought, that he thinks I am forgiving enough to be moved. I lay seething, letting him lash me with the word "Please?", until words for what was in my heart finally came to me.

"Kallijas, I love you, and when you speak for yourself it always rings true. You don't do so well speaking for your people. They never chose you to, for one thing, else we wouldn't be having this whole trouble, would we?

"I went to Arko on a peace mission, trusting—not begging, mind you, trusting—Kurkas's oath. A hundred ways he betrayed me, and through me my people, then turned on my people themselves. A thousand times, Yeolis must have begged and pleaded; but the answer was always sword or arrow, rape or fire; I could tell you atrocities all day, and never repeat one, that *you* did to *us*. We are Arko, you would say, we are the conquerors, we don't listen to pleas, we have no use or need for kindness, we ask nothing, only take; thus we deal with the world because we are the strong.

"Now things are turned around, Arko's suddenly losing, and what do I hear? Oh, pity us, we beg you, be kind! Poor us, we never expected to lose, and didn't worry about being made to pay for it! Do you speak for your people, Kall? Will you say, we never meant to be so cruel, it was all a big mistake? Just because we sacked every Yeoli city we went through, surely we don't deserve to have our one city sacked? Just because we killed off a good quarter of Yeolae's people doesn't mean the other three-quarters shouldn't be understanding of our troubles?"

"My Imperator . . ." He had to set his teeth to say this, so much against the grain it was. "My Imperator is not a good man. Will you sink to his level?"

"No," I said. "I couldn't if I sacked Arko ten times over. He had nothing to avenge; it was only greed for himself, not greed for his people even, just for himself."

"Then should you punish all of us for *his* crimes? Did we who are his subjects choose them?" As I say, he had a quick mind, to learn from our talks what would move me.

"How many Arkans," I said, "do you think oppose what you've done here? Most? I think not. One in ten? I doubt even that."

His head was bowed now, so I could only see the two sheets of his unbound hair, shining gold in the candlelight, and trembling. When he looked up his eyes were full of tears. "Never mind Arko's sake, then! For my sake! For mine!"

"Because I love you? Because you've won your way into my heart? You would use it so?" A sound came from his throat like a choked moan. "Kallijas, you are only one man. As am I; what my people will, even if that's sacking Arko, I must do. We're talking the fate of thousands of thousands, here. The forces of history move, solitary people get ground between them."

"No!" he said. "You're evading. You're people will do what you will. You *are* a force of history; I'm speaking to one."

"You think I never got ground between?"

"But you can choose *now*! I'd give anything, Sheng, anything in the world, my life, my honor; would you spit on that?"

"Your love for me, and my love for you too." He nodded, tears raining. "You'd sell me up the river to save Arko, of course you would, except it's got difficult because you're attached to me; you're seeing now you should have killed me when I lay at your feet, and would have, however much it grieved you, had you understood then. Or else you wish the poison had worked. I know, Kall, believe me; you're doing what the demarch or Arko, if there were such a thing, would do. Why do you think I said you'd make a better Imperator than Kurkas?"

He tried to lay his head on my feet, too distraught for words, now; but I sprang up and away, wanting to be standing, my mind made up. "We've been living in the clouds, Kall. However alike we might be, you are Arkan and I am Yeoli, by birth. Maybe someday there will be peace between us; but now, all we stand for is in opposition. Or so you claim; yet you didn't kill me, being torn in yourself. There's no one in the world as good for helping settle things like that as the masters of the School of the Sword whom I'm sending you to. The way of getting there is tricky, so listen hard, or you'll end up lost on the mountain. Most of the day is left, Kall, plenty of travelling time."

From his knees he stared up at me, eyes desolate. "Sheng.
The man I spared, I thought, was a good man. Was I wrong?
Was I fooled?"

On my arm, Mana's ring burned. I thought of Alchaen's
words: "An oath sworn in madness is not binding." To sack
Arko, my people would indeed want; yet should the fate of
Arko, which was not theirs, lie in their hands more than
mine? Or should I follow my own course? I knew, as I had
known all along at heart, and no doubt he had too, why I
was so angry; because he was right.

"Go, Kall," I said. "Sishana will escort you to the edge
of camp." I gave him clothes of my own, a hooded robe,
scrawled and sealed his safe conduct. "Avoid using that
unless you have to; stay disguised instead. Don't wear
gloves, whatever you do, or someone will kill you before
you have a chance to show it. Good luck, go with my
blessing, I love you. I won't sack Arko. No—*Don't* thank
me. Farewell."

I finished the business of the day, including setting Abatzas free, for no ransom. I told him it was in mercy, for what
I'd made him suffer, which he believed; truth was, I feared
if someone higher was brought into it, they'd notice what
was happening, tell me to keep him and appoint someone
smarter. I kept his Raikas pendant, though, to wear as a
joke. When evening came, I went to the campfire of the
Elite, where they congratulated me until I told them to shut
up, and then, looking at me closer, handed me a skin of
wine. I got more drunk than a First General First and a
demarch ever should; they had to carry me to bed.

Two days later, Sishana woke me up at midnight. "There's
a sentry says some people have come in, allies. It's a woman,
her name is . . . Guard, what was it again? Ni-something?
Ni-ku?"

My body leapt up almost of its own accord. "Niku Wahunai? Niku aht Tanra nar sept Taekun?"

"Yes, sir, that's it," the sentry said from outside. "She said
you'd know her . . ."

I went all the way flat out, almost leaving behind the
sentry, who was leading me, while Sishana trailed after me
saying, "Cheng, shouldn't you put on something more than

a half-poncho? Sword and wristlets, maybe?" Before I got
to the torch-hooks I slowed down, had the lights around me
doused and went silently. They were just lighting torches to
show themselves, about seventy-five dark people, with
swords and double-axes.

"*Omores*?" I ran, flung myself into her arms; we kissed
as if the other were the first water in four days, clung to
hurt our ribs, babbled weeping, "I missed you I thought
you were dead I love you we're both out we're both free."

She had brought the child, and sent for her now. She had
never written what Vriah looked like; I saw now it had been
to surprise me, because I had not thought such looks possible. The child was dark-skinned, though paler than her
mother, but her hair was as bright blond as my father's. Her
eyes were mine in small. Though she was barely older than
half a year, she clung and grinned as if she knew me, and
said after Niku, "Aba!" Niah for Daddy.

So I gushed and burbled, while all around me Yeoli jaws
gaped wider and wider. I'd had no thoughts of keeping our
love secret, a good thing; it would be all over camp before
reveille. That was the last of my sleep that night; we had
to tell our stories.

All the way home, after escaping, she'd dreaded arriving;
knowing that I would be truth-drugged, she felt she had no
choice but to confess to her people what she had done. So
she did, before their Assembly, and was almost killed right
there except that her mother, who was one of the elders,
shouted that she should be heard out first. Even so most
argued that she should be put to death, and painfully; many
more argued that assassins should be sent to Arko to kill
me, especially since I was a leader, bound to use the secret
even if I hadn't given it up.

But then the Speaker-to-Sea, the priestess of Sea Mother,
had stood. "It is clear to me by the Betrayer's account," she
said, for so they called Niku, "since Lord Friend sent her
a vision, her own gift which we have all witnessed so bound
itself to this man, and she claims he was one gifted by Sea
Mother himself, that this is a matter of the gods' will. We
must ask them."

Before the grotto of the oracle, six figures were carved,
of sacred camphor-wood: the single-wing, the A-niah, Yeola-

e, the Empire of Arko, Niku, and myself. At ebb tide, to
incantations of voice and flute, they were placed standing
together on the wet puddled sand on the cave's bottom, in
a pattern that reflected life: Arko and Yeola-e locked in war,
me with Yeola-e but close to Niku too, the wing with the
A-niah. As the tide rose, the cave filled, the waves sending
their echoing voices through the sprout at its apex. At ebb
tide again, the Speaker and the people entered the dripping
cave, to make the divination by how the figures were placed
now.

Arko's land-eagle was gone, swept away; the sea-eagle of
the A-niah was more or less where it had been left. Niku,
the wing and the circle of Yeola-e were near one wall,
heaped together. I remember how she told it to me: "At
first my heart fell, for your image was nowhere to be seen;
that means that person will be nothing, or matter none, and
for you, that would mean you were dead. Then as the
Speaker was stepping here and there to see it from every
place, someone else cried out, 'There!' You were on a ledge,
higher than our heads, and standing."

To clarify, they invoked the oracle again at the next tide.
Since Arko was gone and the A-niah had landed in the same
place, which is taken to mean neither a gain nor a loss, just
the remaining four were used. When the water had receded,
they found me standing on a ledge again, Niku near, the
wing and Yeola-e half out the opening to the sea, touched
by sunlight.

The Speaker made her reading of it. "By what Niku aht
Tanra has done, Arko will come to worse grief than we, for
the Sun-clasping Eagle that has shadowed so large in the
sky has come to nothing, while the Sea-eagle flies as before.
He to whom our secret has been revealed will rise to great
heights, but not at our cost. The single-wing touches his
country, and sits bare in the light; the time has come, it
seems, to share it with the world, as we would have sooner,
had the world been kinder. Niku's vision was true; she did
right." On the strength of that, she was absolved.

Memory came, like a thunderclap; while I rifled through
my papers I cursed the rent in my recall. I'd left a copy of
Jinai's prophecy here, and Artira had kept it for me; now
finding it I read. "An animal with metal and wood bits that's

alive, it's moving all over and making noises and I'm thinking, I mean you're thinking, it's a blessing to all the world.
And the wing thing, that too." That had come right after
I'd asked whether I should go to Arko. I'd had to, to learn
of it. I read his first prophecy again, that he'd made when
I was sixteen. "I see a dark-skinned woman. Not Lakan:
short hair. . . . A child with bright blond hair, like Tennunga's, and eyes the spitting image of yours. Terrible trouble
you will have, I can't see what, but you . . . now you have
come through it . . . So many weird things. What does a
green ribbon around your wrist mean? Or a huge orange
jewel? I'm seeing your dreams: the ground wheeling far
below as if you were a bird flying . . ." Niku's jaw dropped.
"This prophet, he's working for *you*?" We both laughed in
glee. "So wise he must be . . ."

Absolved, she had fought against the Arkans, who were
threatening the archipelago more strongly still, until the
child grew too heavy in her. One island is customarily given
to the old and infirm; the A-niah's Haian had been there,
too. The Arkans, angered by their evasive and nimble way
of fighting, killed everyone on it, including the Haian—I
wondered whether this was the other Arkan offense Dinerer
had mentioned—and burned it to earth. Niku's father had
been killed in that battle, something I knew how to comfort
her for. But it was worse for her in that she had been
commanding; she felt his blood was on her hands.

Then had come the news I was dead. Thinking of what
she knew of me, the account of it and the oracle, she disbe-
lieved it; but everyone around her put that down to a lover's
vain hopes, and she could not know for certain. The child
came shortly thereafter.

She showed her people my first letter to prove I was
alive, and my second, addressed to them, to argue for our
plan. It had been a long debate; I'd made strong points, but
they could not help but remember I was an accredited lunatic; in the letter I'd freely admitted I was in no position to
make binding arrangements, and for turning a losing war
into a winning one I had only plans now, no proof. In the
end they had decided to wait and see how I fared.

"I stood back smiling then," Niku said, kissing my nose.
"I knew how you'd fare. Such joy it was to tell them, when

you defeated the Arkans on Haiu Menshir, 'I told you so.' When Laka tore up its peace treaty with Kurkas, 'I told you so.' When the Enchians joined you, 'I told you so.' When you started winning, 'Why do you think he was up on that ledge? I told you so.' So they sent us . . . maybe just to get my told-you-so's out of their ears."

The seventy-five with her were picked from the best in all Niah-lur-ana. In whispers quiet enough to be heard only within an embrace, we set out between us how I would employ them. At all times, four scouts would be in the air above us, looking like circling birds of prey, while others went on journeys of reconnaissance; they had ways of signalling from air to ground with mirrors, bird-calls, and patterns of flying. As well they were good at night-raiding and breaking sieges. I mulled over it all, to settle it deep in my mind where the path unconceived could find it.

Shaina and Etana were still in Kefara with the rest of the family, waiting for the Hearthstone to be rebuilt, so I couldn't speak with them of Niku; still, our agreement regarding a fourth spouse had always been that they would welcome whom I chose. But as well, since I was now demarch, I must make my marriage request formally to Assembly, once she'd proposed and I'd accepted in principle. "You mean I have to ask you?" she said; I answered yes. "Well, will you then?" I answered yes to that too, and decided to write the request tomorrow. Then we settled down to sleep, my head on her shoulder, and fear shot trembling all through my limbs. Never in the time we'd been lovers, close together or far apart, had I told her what I must tell anyone I loved and sought to marry.

I think it was understandable in the Mezem, that unworldly world. Like everyone else, I hadn't been concerned about not living past thirty, only not living past next fight-day. Marriage had been an herb-dream; we'd even forgotten we could procreate.

Her gift was intermittent; sometimes she felt one's emotions, sometimes not; she was feeling mine now, for she looked up alarmed, and said, "What is it, love?" Then the baby, in the clothes chest that served for now as a crib, started to bawl. In Niku's arms e quieted, but only a little. *"Omores, pehali,* tell me."

It's up on the mountain with just the two of us I always do this, I wanted to say, not at night with other people bedded all around, talking over the crying of our child. Still, I owed her no more delay; though it rubbed everything in me the wrong way, I leaned close, and between Vriah's squalls, told her.

She stared, stone-still but for her brown breasts rising and falling as she breathed, until the baby redoubling her wailing brought her out of it. "Hush, Vriah-os, hush, birdling," she whispered, rocking, "all is well, don't be afraid, hush ... then what time we have we must cherish and enjoy all we can, *mi pensi* ... What are you afraid of?" When I told her, she said amazed, "I'd take you for five years over anyone else for a hundred. I loved you when we both thought we might die every eight-day! Two others left you? How *could* they? The young fools! Their loss!" Then it was my turn to cry, with joy, and the baby's to go quiet.

We rarely spoke of it, thereafter. We do not to this day. We make our plans accordingly, quietly. I guess that was what I always wished. But our saying to each other, which had been "Always and forever," was from then on "Always and forever, as long as we have." So it was, I found the love who would make a life with me, knowing.

Next morning, Esora-e came to me, saying he had something urgent. "Tell me what I heard happened last night, that you flung yourself into the arms of that woman, isn't true."

I answered him honestly. His jaw dropped; then his eyes narrowed. "You welcome her into your bed, you claim fatherhood of her child—next you'll want to marry her!" he cried. I signed chalk. "A foreigner? A woman brown as an animal? A savage who doesn't even speak Yeoli or read any language, probably, raising children to be in the succession to the demarchy of Yeola-e? Fourth Chevenga, have you gone entirely out of your mind?" Once started, he never wanted to stop. "Great All-spirit, what did we raise? First it's a slave-woman in Laka, then a Lakan princess, then Kalicha Ityirian, yes, some of us noticed you doing the Arkan thing with him for rather a long time—not to mention that idiot general Abatzas! And now a ... Nyah? Anyah? Whatever, who cares! You've bounded all over the Miyatara, got worldly, your own aren't good enough for you any more! What have we come to, with a demarch who'd marry any foreigner over any Yeoli?"

"That's enough," I said, quietly and evenly. "You were concerned, I've heard you. I will make my request properly to Assembly, and it will be they who choose." I put what I felt into my look; he turned and was gone.

I took up a blank page, and began writing the letter of request. But his words rang through my mind, and fear grew acrid on my tongue. How many of the Servants would feel as he did? Nothing breeds intolerance as well as occupation. What if they refused? It would not forbid my asking again; but I thought of Niku, who'd asked me several times whether all Yeolis were as open-hearted to foreigners as I was, since if she married me she must live here. Told by my people she was below me, would she stay?

As I dealt in my usual way with the stream of people that came with this and that trouble I must see to, as always, I raged my old rage within myself. *Because I was born where and when I was born, I cannot love who I love.*

A-Niah came running. "*Hakan!*" That was their title for me; I found out later it meant one who saves his people. A good forty of the seventy-five spoke Enchian; they'd been picked for that too. "An army of Tor Ench comes, from the east. Some five thousand. At their rate they will be here today." I just said, "Good"; it was Reknarja's younger brother Jakanarja with reinforcements. I hadn't told the A-niah, wanting to see how fast they'd report. Then Krero came. I knew that stern, bearing-matters-of-import look.

He asked me inside; I couldn't be rude to him. "Fourth Chevenga," he said formally, when we were alone. "I'm given to understand you mean to request to marry this foreign woman. Isn't it clear to you, why you must not?" I confessed it was not. "You surely know that many Yeolis and many Servants of Assembly, perhaps a majority, would oppose it?" I signed chalk. "You admit you have a name for stubbornness?" I signed chalk; no point denying it. "You understand the perception of your importance, among the Servants? That you must remain demarch for Yeola-e to regain its freedom? That any threat to your position is a threat to Yeola-e?" I began to see what he was getting at, and made no answer, gripping a tent-pole; I saw my fingers go white. "So they cannot help but feel compelled to consent to your request, whatever their true feelings—and therefore, knowing such a compulsion is in effect, you absolutely must not make it?"

I felt sick to my stomach; he was right. Full of sympathy, he patted my shoulder, but couldn't stifle his grin. "You didn't see," he said. "Well, no one can see everything, even you; it's a good thing Esora-e told me. What are friends for, but to grab your arm before you fall in the pit?"

I could not avoid telling her. Her lips thinned white, though she said nothing. Who could blame her, being spat on for the color she was born? But we told each other, "No matter, we'll just wait for the end of the war; in the meantime we're married in spirit." My people couldn't tell me who I could have in my tent.

As we were drawing up a battle-plan for Michere, Bitha Szten came with worry all over her face, not usual for her, and went down on one knee before me, as I never thought a Schvait would do. "I must beg you, *Stoltzer*," she said, using her word for commander, "else breach of contract." I drew her inside, poured her tea. "Of no information you have asked me, so I am not spying, Abatzas has kidnapped and hidden the *Johtajen* and seconds of his Schvait, being refusing to pay full pay as contracted. They fear orders to fight all they face, even other Schvait. You are our *Stoltzer*, I can only beg you, to not face us against them."

They'd lost again; Abatzas's Schvait had asked more than he was willing to spend. Perhaps the ransom I asked for his command council broke the bank. I had hired Bitha's six hundred to hold off fifteen hundred, a way now closed; but I also saw twenty-one hundred furious Schvait in my camp, if I played things right.

"I won't face you against them," I said. "But in the meantime Abatzas can do anything to them, while he holds the commanders. Something must be done." I asked her all she knew; seeing hope of my aid, she told me. The Arkan Schvait were forbidden to leave their quarter of camp, or send messages, on pain of harm to the hostages. No one knew their whereabouts. If they'd mounted any plans, Bitha didn't know; as they were not the sneaking sort, I doubted it. Yet Schvait betrayed, she assured me, prefer to fight their way out than give in.

With her agreement, I set my spies on it; the prisoners must be found, most likely split apart in several places. In the meantime my promise meant Abatzas could command his Schvait to chase mine at will in battle, so for now I kept them at the rear. If that went on too long, of course, my other warriors would wonder what they were being paid so well for; so we had to act soon.

The battle of Michere was not one of my best days. Any of a good three military histories I know of, probably more that I don't, give detailed accounts. Suffice to say when my first plan didn't play out as it should, I didn't think on my feet as well as I could have. We won, but not overwhelmingly, and taking losses; at this rate we could free Yeola-e in ten years at the cost of every warrior who came of age in that time, not be in the plains by winter. One looks back, struggling for reasons: the Schvait matter distracted me, Reknarja distracted me, I didn't get enough sleep, I was too confident. I wasn't confident enough; they slip through the fingers like water, one tells oneself it doesn't matter, but even that argument gets dragged into the endless circle. One's comrades nudge one and say "Snap out of it, you'll do better next time," then "Shit, Cheng, it's not as if we *lost*." All one can say, in the end, is that one had a bad day, as everyone does.

But they took heavy losses too; the center of the ground afterward was a tangle of dead and wounded, among whom our healers and theirs worked in truce. As always, Kaninjer was among them. My disbelief in my exhaustion was distant and vague; around me people exclaimed, "That Haian . . . where's he going? . . . do you think it's possible for a human being to be that stupid? . . . well there, I guess so. Ah . . . Cheng . . . that's *your* Haian, isn't it?" I watched him walk, leaning close over a litter, utterly engrossed in saving a life, into the Arkan infirmary.

One could hope that he would just as casually walk back out; but he didn't. As twilight came, I knew they were holding him. They would truth-drug him, learn he was my healer, learn all manner of things about me that he knew, demand ransom—sickening thoughts came. I remembered Kurkas wanting those who healed me.

I didn't speak to the command, knowing they'd spend all night, while precious time passed, trying to talk me out of it. I just called together twenty of the Elite. Of course they tried to talk me out of it, offering to do it without me; but I asked them, "Do you want to be led by someone with weapon-sense, or not?" It was not the same as the Schvait captives: there was only one of him and only one place he'd be, being needed there; the guard on him would make finding him easy.

So it was I crept through the Arkan camp by starlight as I had the Lakan camp long ago, though this time with company. It went more or less as planned. But though we shot down both his guards someone sounded the alarm, and Kaninjer was no runner; if some Arkans hadn't come to fear me enough to freeze at the sight of my face, we would never have got away. I stole a horse from the cavalry pen, to find Kan was no rider, either; I ended up galloping out with my poor Haian thrown across in front of me like a sack, yelling all the way. None of us died, though two got small wounds.

They hadn't got around to truth-drugging him yet, to my joy; but he had told them quite loudly, as part of his argument that they should let him go, that he was my healer and quite close to me, so I'd be very worried for him. "Perhaps you understand better now how it is in war," I said. He did indeed, he said, and wept; I swallowed the scolding I'd planned for him, and gave him my shoulder instead. Abatzas had been a better teacher; one of the things he'd said was, "You can heal, Haian, without feet."

The Schvait raid was the next night. Ikal had taken barely two days to find the prisoners, by looking in the end of camp furthest from the Schvait quarters; they were chained and heavily drugged, but all in one place. Perhaps Abatzas didn't expect two night raids in a row. I didn't go myself, this time, fearing to strain my luck. It made even more trouble for the Arkans than I'd hoped, for as the fifteen hundred deserted, full-armed and armored, they happened to take a route right through the sleeping Arkan camp, killing all in their way. Break a Schvait contract and you are their mortal enemy, indeed. I welcomed them, got them

shelter, since they'd had to leave their tents, and saw Kaninjer check the six and the smith strike off their chains
myself. The next day when their minds were clear the three
Johtajen remembered me. They all signed on, for the same
rate I was paying Bitha's.

It has been said, in fact was said even then, that I allowed,
or engendered, far too much reverence for myself in the
Arkan war. I won't deny there is some truth to this. But
none of it was out of conceit; all the deeds for which I was
lauded I did because it seemed to me I must do them; I
played for admiration to bind my army into one, for how
else could I do it? Think of a warrior, fighting for a country
not his own, and forbidden to take spoils (I'd said anyone
who looted anything other than Arkan corpses would be put
to death, and kept my word, beheading a Lakan for stealing
a skin of wine, so that no one would touch even dust now).
To serve his faraway king who sent him in return for aid
somewhere else, or a future favor, or to prevent trouble ten
years later, he won't put himself out. To please a leader
who inspires his love, he will. As for the Yeolis, they were
the worst from the start, having put all their hopes in me.
The foreigners first called me Invincible; it was Yeolis who
first called me Beloved.

VI

Once Reknarja had found out I would be civil and friendly to him, the chill over my teaching him had thawed somewhat. Now, for reasons I could not discern, he'd slowly gone cold on me again, turned as stark and dour as before, the plans he showed me getting stiffer, more strictly conventional, clumsier. He seemed to be holding back anger, but also to be miserable. I thought it might be the presence of his younger brother Jakanarja, who was everything Reknarja was not: handsome, popular, flashy, personable. I'd gathered that all through their childhood Kranaj had been the father no son could please, and the two were rivals. But more and more, Reknarja seemed braced for some inevitable disaster here, and that I could not understand. We have to find out what it is, I thought, before he brings it on himself by believing so hard in it.

Finally, the day after the Schvait raid, I asked him. He gave me a look as if to say, "As if you don't know!", and went into a bitter silence, thinking I was playing ignorant to mock him. I pressed him, mentioning our first meeting, when he'd been fourteen and I twelve. "It would have been better," he muttered under his breath, "if they'd let us roll in the dirt, then." I sprang up, snapping. "You're right!" I took him up onto the mountain alone.

I could barely believe what I had to say to provoke him.

103

As he'd told me in hints here and there, I'd been the stick of his upbringing, the one Kranaj wanted him to aspire to be like, though I was two years younger; it was always. "That Yeoli boy killed five Lakans at thirteen, what's wrong with you?" or "If you had half the wits of that Yeoli boy." My every accomplishment used to lash him, this apprenticeship the continuation of that. Now, hoping it wouldn't be too much to take back later, I said, "Your father's right. I'm better than you at everything." He held still and silent, looking about to burst into flame, for a good tenth-bead of baiting. Finally I shoved him, and that did it.

Against such fearless anger, with nothing stronger in my spirit than calculation, a certain doubt that I was doing right and the knowledge that he wouldn't kill me, I didn't have much hope. I suspected even if I made a decent account of myself, he'd still overpower me; as it was I barely had time for even that, so no one can say I let him win. In a moment I was on the ground under him, his hand with a good half his weight on it grinding my face in the dirt, and his voice roaring, "Take it back, you stinking Yeoli whoreson, take it back!" I fought with all my might, but he was heavier, and however his father might have put down his learning, he knew the tricks of keeping one pinned. I went on, shouting "Never!" and such dramatic things, until my strength and his anger were spent; then I yielded and recanted and said everything he demanded I say, and he let me up.

We stood apart for a time, he to calm himself, I to recover; my brow and cheek were bleeding. Then, looking more broken than I felt, he turned, and threw his bracelet, the sign of the Enchian King's heir, at my feet. When I swore Second Fire come I didn't know why, it finally came out. Kranaj had told me that if at any time I found Reknarja objectionable, I should send him home. Then he'd told Reknarja that if I did, he was no longer heir. This apprenticeship was his kingship trial, and no one had told me.

Kranaj, I wanted to shout, are you *trying* to make us enemies? Are you *trying* to make him fail? How could you imagine he would not think I knew, he would not think it was a conspiracy between you and I, to strike him the final humiliation? You're usually sensible; how could you so play us, and our warriors and countries, since we stand for them in each other's eyes, against each other?

I said this all out in the same words I've written; no reason for Reknarja not to hear. The explanations fell together like dressed stones in a wall: no wonder he'd thought I was so cruel pretending not to know; no wonder he'd been so slow to rush me, thinking he was kissing off the throne of Tor Ench. He still did; several times I had to say, "I'm not sending you home, not now, not ever, even if you make a complete idiot of yourself. It's not for me to choose the king of Tor Ench!" He needed time, to believe, having been preparing for the other so much longer.

Before, he'd cursed me jokingly for being, on top of everything else, one he had to like. But it was only after this, just like the two boys permitted to scrap, that we became friends. A good thing it turned out to be, that very same day.

It was Chinisa who showed the petition to me, that evening: resolved that I be required not to associate with foreigners, particularly the leader of the A-niah—the writer didn't have the nerve to name names, only positions—the heir to the Enchian throne, a certain Haian healer, and leaders of dark-skinned allies.

It was lunacy to be expected, and certain to be ignored, I thought; I didn't know why Chinisa had bothered, until I read the first two signatures. The influence of such a thing depends, almost more than on what it proposes, on who signs it and how close they are to the one addressed, that being a measure of how likely it is to be listened to. This was signed by Krero, my guard captain, and Esora-e, my shadow-father.

I think the paint would have peeled from the walls, had I summoned them into a building; Esora-e even forgot to ask me who'd left his mark on my face. How, I asked them, did they imagine I meant to lead an army of many nations without associating with foreigners? Hadn't they thought what this might do, once it fell into the rumor mill? It was far more, and I didn't let them get a word in edgewise; finally I ended with, "Who do you think will be served best by this? The child-raping *Arkans*, that's who!" One always gets angriest, when it's too late.

The petitioners were busy all that night at the campfires; next day, it hit the rumor trail proper, and jumped the fences of language. Niku understood, being close to me, and explained to her people; it was the curse of their secret that their true worth to our cause—I planned never to have them fight on the ground, no matter what was said—could not be known. Kaninjer said, "I won't stop healing you." Reknarja, bless him, told every Enchian who would listen, including Misiali, that it was the work of madmen.

Jakanarja, on the other hand, puffed out his chest with the family pride, whipped up anger in his warriors, too newly joined to know us better, and sent off a furious letter to Kranaj. That I only found out because Reknarja badgered it out of him a day later, giving his pigeon a good head start on mine. Arzaktaj sent me a note saying that although I saw his men as fit to die alongside mine, he would respect my wishes not to be with him and we could correspond by note from now on. I saw my precious army, barely a month together but having won every battle, falling to pieces.

A demarch cannot start a petition nor command anyone else to; he can, however, happen to mention, in the presence of a few sensible people, that the best thing would be a few sensible people starting a counter-petition and sweating blood to see it got five or ten times as many names in a day or less. The top signatures were the Yeoli command and my mother. Then I called council, with just the allies; other Yeolis present would seem my bodyguards.

Anger eased when I showed them the petition, and spoke my opinion of its worth. But Arzaktaj asked me how I could say it was the work of a small clutch of fanatics when my guard captain and my shadow-father had signed it. I could hardly say, "Because my guard captain and my shadow-father are sheep-diddling idiots"; instead I remonstrated about prejudices and jealousies and how this war had been hard on my people. They demanded I demote Krero and disown Esora-e; I answered that despite their quirks both were competent and good people at heart, so I'd rather flog them both to falling if that was satisfactory, which they grudgingly accepted.

Misiali said he understood, though, that Yeoli kings must act on the will of the Yeoli mob on such things, so what would I do? I bit back what I wanted to say: "A rock-slide on the Yeoli mob, I'll associate with whoever I damn well please," and answered that I doubted this petition would be signed by ten percent of the Yeolis in the army, let alone in all free Yeola-e, which was needed to bring it to vote, which must then be decided by majority. I was sure Yeolis in the army would soon make clear my people's true thought. So I said, and hoped to Saint Mother they would.

All this fence-mending, while I should be planning, never mind doing demarchic work, of which I had a steadily growing stack; and Kaninjer nagged me to ease up, saying, "Remember how much strain you've been under and how much you've been hurt in the last two years," as if I were forty-five, not twenty-two.

Niku had devilish ideas for unnerving the enemy using the wing; asking my spies whether any tales of my coming back from the dead were believed among these Arkans, I heard yes, and remembered she too was supposedly dead. Near Asangal, I called parley, and with Niku smiling beside me, promised Abatzas that if he didn't surrender all his army's weapons to me and begin force-marching them out of Yeola-e today, Hayel would visit them that night.

He laughed at me, as I'd expected he would; so I had Hayel visit them. The A-niah had wings shaped like great bats, a frightening thing to see cross the moon at night, especially if you believe in flying demons; they also had a way of making inhuman screeches with three voices at once, and we equipped them with steel weapons made to leave marks like claws. Visiting now and then all night while my army slept, they dropped fire and blood and clawed parts of Arkan corpses; despite the orders and arguments of the officers, that Arko's gods were mightier and would protect them, the men stayed awake. At dawn, as my demons were settling down to sleep, I attacked with my warriors.

We chased them to Asangal, and kept pressing. I got a cut that festered badly enough to give me fever, but couldn't stay in bed or the wounded wagon, while debate over the petition still raged. Krero renounced his stand and struck his name off, so I let him off the flogging; Esora-e, no surprise, jutted his chin and said, "Go ahead, boy, flog me." I dropped it to twenty strokes, and as always with contentious punishments, did it myself, so it was much lighter than usual; still people called me Notyere, because I'd punished a free Yeoli for petitioning.

To my joy the counter-petition did get five times larger, calming the foreigners; Yeolis waving arms and railing at each other is nothing, I assured them, we do it all the time. Still, Niku started saying, "Perhaps, it's best we live apart, for now." I would answer, "And let fear and bigotry defeat us?"

It was about the same time, while we set camp in Tyicha, when one of the Guard came to me with a half-starved, hollow-eyed man, who looked as if he'd been chased days by a nightmare. The man threw himself to his knees before me, clutched and pressed his brow into my legs. "Demarch!" he wept. "Beloved! You are your people, you can stand for Shakora! Forgive me! Forgive me for living, Shakora! Forgive me!" I took him inside under my arm, fed him a swallow of Saekrberk, and let him cling to me while he told the story.

The worst atrocities of war will happen when an occupied land begins to win back; the conquered get restless, the conquerers, anxious. All through the lines of the underground, I'd sent my advice: stay cautious, don't let hope make you take foolish risks, for the Arkans, Mahid or not, will be harsher, in their fear, if you are caught. Not that Shakora, a city of thirty thousand people, did not listen; there had always been much resistance there, its people being the proud kind. Someone in the Arkan command, I don't know who to this day nor whether he is alive, ordered that Shakora should be made an example of.

They had put to the sword every woman and child, and all the men but ten thousand; in fact they killed everything else living they could find, horses, house-ants, windowflowers, trees. (It was as he told me that, I remembered a part of Jinai's prophecy that my heart had thrust away. "Shakora! I see someone saying the whole city is dead.") The ten thousand they forced to tear down the city at arrowpoint until not one stone was left standing on another, all the corpses flung into cellars and covered with rubble, and the ground sown with salt so nothing would ever grow. Then they killed all the last but one hundred, whom they freed to spread the news across Yeola-e. "Demarch," he said, "when I learned they would leave alive some men to wreck, I prayed I would not be one of them. When I learned they would leave alive some men to free, I prayed I would not be one of them. I've brought the news to you now, the only use left for my life. May I die now?"

I opened my mouth, and no words came out; nor would they even after a decent pause. My life these days was hearing trouble people brought to me, and giving them something to do about it; always I'd had an answer, if not instantly than soon. Now I couldn't think of anything to tell anyone to do; there was nothing.

Nothing but to feel, to stand helpless while pain wrapped all around me like a flock of flies settling on a corpse, and the sword of powerless anger, sheathed in my heart, twisted again; so familiar. *I was here, not there.* I thought, again, and the air around me seemed to be filled with the smells of the city of Arko. *I could do nothing, I can do nothing.*

"*No.*" I seized his hands; he looked up, startled. "Don't die. If the last hundred die, Shakora dies with them. Who else will remember what your home was, who you were, your tales, your ways, your worth?" His eyes had started to glaze again; I shook him, and heard the singing wind. "Strength. You are not alone; we are with you in your grief; and your anger is not helpless. We will free Yeola-e, we will win it all back. But that's a long fight. Anger can sustain us, drive us. Stay with my army, fight for us, spur us forward. You are not war-trained,"—I could see by his build—"but your tongue is deadlier to Arko than a hundred swords, and they forgot to cut it out. Tell us of Shakora, remind us, fire our hearts with why we must win." His eyes sharpened, flashed, seeing a path where before they had seen only an end.

He stood, and his hands in mine now had firmness; he agreed. But his gaze lingered with a thought, and words suddenly poured out. "If there were ever a time we should go out of our borders and ruin some other country, demarch, this is it. *They* should feel, what they have done to us!" He leaned close, gripping my elbows; his fingers happened on Mana's arm-ring. "You could, Chevenga, you understand, you know their ways. You won't fail us. All Yeola-e knows what they did to you."

I said what I must. "I won't fail you. But whether we go out of our borders is a matter of a vote."

"And only the living vote," he said. "May the dead, this time? I can tell you what all of Shakora would vote, if they were alive, the adults, the babies, the dogs, the birds, if they could. Chalk, to cross the border! Chalk, that Arko the city should suffer what Shakora has!" With tears streaming down his cheeks again, he looked in my face for my answer.

I said what I must: "I hear. When the time comes to count, I will remember." After he was gone his face lingered in my inward eyes, tear-stained; but so did Kallijas's, also tear-stained. More distant in memory, ragged with the rents of madness, I saw Mana's face, contorted in agony, on the table of his death. What, I thought, is the expression of my own?

We harried the Arkans by day, sent the demons by night, and every evening now, Kaninjer said, "You are working too much, sleeping not enough." How can I rest, I kept thinking, and saying, while these things can still be done to my people? We were in the plains proper, we'd done it before winter; but best we gain back Tinga-e, to stay there in the worst of the snow; I set my aim for that. With no cliffs near, The A-niah launched using a huge strap of that springy black material from the south, like a giant bow-string, with the flier in her wing the arrow. It took forty people to pull it back enough. In truth I wanted to try it, but Niku said only the very skilled could without danger.

The Lakan cavalry came, to my delight, seven hundred. So did an angry letter from Kranaj, that he must have sent after he got Jakanarja's and before he got mine; he wondered with cold civility if our agreement at an end, or should be. I wrote him again to be sure, explaining and apologizing for all.

There were Arkan reinforcements at Lisere, ten thousand. Bad news came from our spies: Abatzas had finally been dismissed, replaced by one Perisalas Kem, who'd led mostly futile forays against Renaina Chaer in the southern mountains. By the river we fought, and made them retreat to Chinisinal; but it was a long battle, half a day. "You must rest the army," the command council said to me, then privately, "and yourself, Cheng; you know you're pale?" I told them not to be ridiculous, but designated the army's day of rest, and my own, for the next day.

Seizing the chance I dug into the demarchic paperwork, got through a mountain of it, then went campfire-hopping. I'd made it my policy to think no campfire below me not only in the Yeoli quarter, but in all the foreigners' as well; to avoid poisoned food, though, I never let it be known where I would appear. In fact I extended to foreigners the other war camp custom of ours as well, that a demarch should refuse no sexual offers, though of course fewer asked. (It had taken some doing to persuade Niku to accept that practice. Extending it to foreigners made Krero, as Arkans say, shit glass. But the one person who did try to assassinate me that way—and maybe would have succeeded, had I not touched his hand without warning to see if he'd jump—was disguised as a Yeoli.)

I was happily drinking and discoursing on tactics when Handa dashed up breathless. "Cheng! Cheng! They're fighting! Niku and Esora-e are fighting!"

I don't remember the run; apparently Handa couldn't keep up with me, though she was a good sprinter going flat out. I remember the flash and arc of a sword and a double-axe in my weapon-sense, and voice shouting, "All-spirit help us, stop, for his sake, for the war's sake, are you mad, can't you see what a disaster this would be either way?" The story is that I flung myself in between them without regard for my own life, just as two cuts were coming in that between them should have killed me, had some force not stopped them. The truth is I flung myself between them yelling to wake the dead.

Niku backed off, axe shouldered; Esora-e, sword in his good hand, advanced into me, and sheathed it only when I threatened him with outcasting. Then everyone started bellowing their account at once. Each of the two, of course, said the other had been the first intending to kill; what seemed agreed upon was that it had started as a sparring-match, Esora-e challenging Niku, but had got out of hand. I also gathered everyone was fairly well into their cups. Still, that excuses nothing; the dead are no less dead for the killer having been drunk.

I could see the shape of it. Esora-e had wanted to humiliate Niku, perhaps prove Yeoli ways better; Niku, sensing ill intent, had got angry in her way; thick-skulls in the crowd had egged them on and emotion had burned reason away. The calculated malice was no doubt on his part, the mindless rage on hers. I grabbed his wrist in one hand, hers in the other, and held them for the whole tongue-lashing, starting icily with how exactly the alliance would have broken asunder one way, then the other way, so they'd both have the demise of Yeola-e on their conscience, going on to the cry of my own heart, "I love you both! You both know full well I love the other! How could you do this? How could you say you love me and do this to me?" I couldn't help my tears; I was fairly well into my cups, too.

But the difference came clear. Niku saw sense, her anger snuffing out fast as it does, and regretted it almost before I began speaking; Esora-e argued back, that perhaps her death would be best for Yeola-e, what good her seventy-odd darkies were doing us no one had ever seen anyway, and he'd always told me I should take care who I loved.

So I let her off with the scolding, and cast him out of the Demarchic Guard, striking him the blow of humiliation and tearing off his insignia, right then and there. When he could get up, he did not look at me, but staggered away into the dark alone. "All-spirit, it's come to this," I heard him sob, his voice from beyond the trees, clear in dead silence. "Tennunga, heart's brother! Why did you have to die?"

The next three days, I remember, like my madness, in shards. Reknarja asked me out of nowhere if I was well, which I answered yes and he'd damn well better know it. We fought in the valley of Chinisinal, a victory with more losses than it was worth; I can't even remember the plan, or how I amended it on the field, though I do remember Hural asking me sharply afterwards why, when I'd always had so much more in my hand than a hammer, from fifteen years old, every problem now looked to me like a nail. Then he asked me if I was all right, which I answered, "Has everyone turned Haian today? *Yes, I am all right.*"

I'd been sleeping badly, as usual; even Kaninjer, who

believed like all Haians that the least drug is the best, wanted to give me something for it, which I refused, thinking to keep my mind sharp. That night Niku made love to me until I thought more would kill me, and I slept like a baby. No one, I thought as I was fading, remembering what she'd chosen when she'd heard my foreknowledge, not Saint Mother nor Shininao, will keep us apart.

I did not wake of my own accord at dawn as usual, nor did I hear the gong of reveille; it was Krero who woke me, stamping in with a rousing, "Cheng? Cheng! What are you doing in bed? Shit, the sun's half up and some sheep-brain hasn't got around to banging the gong yet, I thought you'd notice by now!" I sent him to see to it; why Niku should send him such a poisonous look I couldn't understand, but it slipped my mind to ask.

That day Azaila ambushed me, but to my amazement, once he had me down, was much more gentle than usual, "Lad," he said, "when was the last time you saw your healer?" To anyone who might be listening I barked, "Next one to say that gets latrine duty for the rest of the war!" I suppose he knew I wouldn't do that to him, for he said, "Lad, see your healer. And listen to him. That's the most important advice I've given you in years."

That gave me pause, as his words always did; but before I got to it, an old friend of Esora-e's, Mirainga Senteni, accosted me. "Fourth Chevenga, he told me to tell you he's sworn never to talk to you again."

"Except through friends, I see. Go ahead, then, say to me what he won't say to me."

Her brows drew down, and her finger stabbed sharp into my chest. "*You*, young man, should learn how to listen. No wonder he has trouble with you—and you our demarch! Imagine, your own shadow-father, who was your father's heart's brother, who raised you, who taught you, who fought in all the wars, who was distinguished before you were out of diapers, who lost his thumb—and the moment you are stronger than he, you have him flogged for signing a petition, and stripped of his honor for objecting to a bad match!"

"*Objecting*?" My voice broke mid-word; it's all the shouting, I thought. "He tried to *kill* her! And I'll have you know

I flogged him to keep this child-raping army together!" So it went, the two of us toe to toe in plain sight before the command post, railing at each other like two brats in a field. It got dirty, with words for dark-skinned people I won't repeat in writing, insults to competence, obscenities, until she stamped away to my shouts that I'd let nothing get between Niku and I. Then I found some three or four people lined up waiting in meek silence, with matters that truly deserved my attention.

Krero came, all full of concern, to ask what I had meant, saying nothing would get between us—not even my people's will? "I agreed to put off the request," I said with a voice of ice and slivers. "I could change my mind. I could send it off today."

He backed off throwing his arms out, as if I'd attacked him. "Cheng, easy! All-spirit—I've noticed, everywhere you are these last few days, there's shouting. No wonder! Cheng, you know you seem madder than on Haiu Menshir? You know what that could do to us? Maybe you should talk to your healer . . ."

I don't have a quick temper; I've seen the blood-red across my eyes very few times in my life. Now was one; had he said one more word I might have gone for his throat. He saw it though, and stepped back. "I've heard you, Krero," I hissed through clenched teeth. "Thank you. Dismiss." But with my anger always comes the urge to calculated action, as well. In my papers I found the letter of request for marriage I had drafted; I signed and sealed it, and sent it off with the courier to Vae Arahi.

Kaninjer had by then increased my squires to four by taking two more of my teenage siblings, Makaina and Ilachesa, as apprentices, and assigning them to me; then he told them all my health was more delicate than I knew, so I should not be allowed to disdain comforts. Now they always fussed like four parents, hardly waiting to get the battle-blood off me before they bundled me in wool, and if I wanted the touch of cold water to keep me hard, I had to find a stream. That night after I'd shooed them and Kaninjer all away, I told Niku what I had done.

Without warning the baby let out a wail as if she were being tortured; but instead of comforting her herself, Niku hailed her friend Beshan, called Baska, and gave the child to her. Now we were alone. She cried, "You did *what*?"

As well to expect thunder from a cloudless sky; I'd thought she'd be pleased. Why, I thought, is everyone around me these days being a senseless imbecile flying off into a rage?

"We agreed we would marry!" I said. "You asked me! I answered yes!" She shouted back, "We chose together to hold off asking! Shouldn't we have chosen together to change our minds?" I don't want to write the rest, I don't remember most of the rest; like all these other times, I said things I knew I shouldn't say even as they came out of my mouth. It ended with us agreeing that perhaps we were erring to think of marriage at all, and her moving out with all her things.

I lay awake, my heart like a stew-pot on the boil. Kaninjer came. "One bit of advice," I said, "and you're out." I didn't make it clear whether I meant out of my tent, or dismissed. He said, "Let me massage you." He had hands of gold and steel, hearth-warm, finding without seeming to search the strings and knots of ache in a body, unhooking the pains, drawing them out and away. It took him two beads to get me into a sleep deep as the dead's. Then at midnight, the Arkans attacked us.

Putting on my armor felt like a floating dream; my feet seemed to bounce on pillows of air as I ran. In the starry darkness I found myself fighting, and commanding, heavily, with mindless anger; *child-rapers*, I kept hearing myself think, *your broke my sleep*. We held, but gained nothing at great cost; and my warriors fought on, keeping faith with me.

The sun rose, its cold white eye revealing all, everyone soaked in drying blood, hair matted, limbs and armor coated as with scabs; there was no firm ground to walk on, only corpses tangled together three and four deep, shifting and slipping, moaning, sometimes screaming underfoot, while above it was strike, parry, strike, parry, arms rising and falling by habit more than intent, mindless, as the running of the Press. It seemed only vaguely real to me that I could stop it all with a word.

Finally they began a fighting retreat, and I called the

same; they would be drawing us to land favoring them. We
picked our way back through the carnage; all around me
faces were bowed and grim; now and then they would find
corpses they knew. But no one said, "Chevenga, how could
you fail us so?"; as ever, they called me Beloved; I need
but speak, and they would charge back into it without a
pause, we all knew. I wondered whether I had lost my touch
for good; then in mid-thought, the sun got too bright, up
and down faded away, and some huge flat thing slammed
against me, making my armor clash. I blinked, and saw
blades of grass growing sideways across my sight.

Voices rose in alarm. "Cheng! Is he bleeding? Get the
healer!" Above me; I was on the ground. Fingers felt my
neck, my brow, my wrists, rolled me onto my back. "*No.*"
It came out of me a whisper. "I'm all right. I tripped; give
me a moment. Don't get the healer, he'll be busy enough."
When I lifted my head, faintness came over me again in a
sickening dark wave. They reached to help me, called for a
litter; I brushed it off. My people were watching; I had to
get up on my own strength.

It took a tenth-bead, and even at that rate was all I could
do. The second time my legs gave out the warriors caught
my arms, and made a chair of their hands to carry me:
"Hide me," I commanded. I remember someone pouring a
bucket of cold water over me, then saying, as I started shiv-
ering, "Oh, shit. I shouldn't have done that." The memories
get more patchy. I ordered Kaninjer back to where he was
needed, he ordered me into bed; he cried, "Finger-wrestle
me!", his slender brown hands raised just like a Yeoli's. But
it was Sachara, a man I could usually beat, who I ended up
finger-wrestling; I remember his whisper in my ear, full of
pain as he held my wrists cocked fully back, "I don't want
to take you down, Cheng"; then Emao-e's face filling my
vision, her voice definite even as it faded in and out, "Fourth
Chevenga, you're incapacitated. I'm in command."

Next I remember waking and sensing it was evening. The
whole day past, and I'd done nothing; I tried to rise. Kaninjer was sitting over me; with one gentle hand he held me
down. "You couldn't make it to the tent-flap."

So long I fought it, as if it were an enemy, an Arkan with
a sword near my throat; I felt it was. I bet Kaninjer I could,

the stakes being that if I succeeded I could do what I willed, if I failed, I had to abide by whatever he prescribed. A bet founded on logic, like my *mrik* game with Astalaz; though at first he said, "It's no gaming matter," he saw this, the curving brows on the copper-brown face straightening for a moment. "Abide by what I prescribe for how long?" We mainlanders were teaching him something.

"For good," I said. He agreed. The black weakness came roaring back the moment I lifted my head, like rock on my shoulders, vitriol in my stomach, a nightmare. With nothing but will I wrung two steps out of myself, then felt my knees unstring; he half-caught me, eased me to sitting. It was like an Arkan weakening drug, that cuts the muscles off from the will. I tried to raise myself out of his hands, the tent-pole still fixed in my eyes and mind; for a moment he held his pose, then, deciding, released his grip, and let me fall with my face in the canvas. "Get up!" he said, his voice quivering. "You say you can, you say you are stronger than any human being can be, go on, then, get up!" I couldn't even find the strength to turn my head; and that was the end of my denying.

VII

Kaninjer prescribed a month's rest, most of it in bed: having lost our bet, I was bound to it. "The war can hold for a moon without you," Emao-e said. Tears came easily in my weakness, with my thought: *I've been here barely two moons, and already lost it. Invincible, they call me.* "We held for a year before," she said, "and that was without allies. We won't let the army fly asunder, either; I'll tell them to settle disputes for the sake of Chevenga." She told me the story she was putting out, that I'd got very bad dysentery, plausible enough.

"I don't even know what I have got," I whispered, that being the best I could do. "No one will tell me, as if it weren't my business."

"Exhaustion," Kaninjer said. "Nothing worse than that. Nothing with any difficult cure. Yes, you are young and have a strong constitution, else you'd be dead. Think of life-strength as a cistern of water, Chivinga. With every injury, to body or soul, you draw some off, to heal it. Of course it replenishes; but only as fast as nature provides. Even after your stay on Haiu Menshir, your cistern was still low, too low to do and bear all you have here. You have run dry. I should say also . . ." He laid his hand on my shoulder, and got that faint look of steeling himself that he did when putting a syringe in me, something I find harder to bear since being in Arko, or giving me some other necessary pain. "Sometimes it never replenishes to what it once was, as a limb cut off heals but will not grow back. Chivinga, you will probably never have the strength you did two years ago."

The first day of the month, I lay in the back chamber of my tent, Kaninjer staying with me constantly but allowing no one else; he wanted not only my body rested but my mind. With incense, his medicine-sprigs hanging and the teas he gave me, he could bring a touch of the spirit of Haiu Menshir here. But in a tent, in a camp, the news seeps through the walls, with the bustle and worry; and people knew I was here. So he arranged to have me taken elsewhere. I had lost our bet; I must bear it. "This, for being away from bloodshed for a month," he said, when I wept. "I could never in ten lifetimes understand mainlanders."

Somewhere north of Chinisinal is a forested hollow, too remote to be touched by the war, where lives a hunting couple kind enough to take in an exhausted demarch and his Haian. My bed was of bound tree branches, my mattress a bearskin; they gave me the best pillow, stuffed with the clippings of their own hair, saved for decades, with a cachet of hops to make me sleep. I remember the great trees in their autumn turning, their leaves gold and orange and red as flames against the burning blue of the sky, almost too brilliant to look at long; I remember the linden tree in the garden, for Kaninjer would carry me out to lie under it in fair weather. To the dancing of sunlight through wind-tossed branches I dozed for days.

My body rejoiced, but at first my spirit festered. If Yeola-e came to some grief my presence would have saved, it would be entirely my fault; and I could not even hear the news from the army, Kaninjer having forbidden it. I had never felt so low in my life; not even torture made me so hate myself, for it had not been my own doing. I felt like an exile cast out for weakness and incompetence; like a baby, so feeble everything down to lifting my head had to be done for me; like a prisoner in my own skin, with a Haian for a jail-guard, but knowing the bed I lay in I'd made myself. I was sick the first half of the month with clinging fevers and fluxes and colds, as well. One pays dearly, for fighting with all one's might against what cannot be fought.

But being in such subjection, my spirit eventually gave over and let it all be. I understood only later why Kaninjer was so strict with me at first, letting me make no move unaided, choosing for me in everything, sometimes even forbidding me, albeit in his gentle way, to speak; he wanted to rest me entirely from responsibility, and those days I would only relinquish that if forced to. As I grew stronger he allowed me freedoms step by step, like a parent broadening a child's bounds as he grows. Not that he wasn't kind; he comforted me with limitless patience when I grieved, brought things to fascinate me, read to me, asked me what in the Haian diet I liked and made it for me again, massaged me for a good bead every day.

I had not known that Haians have such a store of literature from before the Fire: among his favorite possessions, that he engrossed himself in at times, to shut out the madness of war, were Enchian translations of works that had been ancient when the Fire had fallen. I had one of the tiny gemlike verses of the poet Kyam committed to memory on first hearing; it means, essentially, the stroke of the past is in the past, but reads far sweeter than any sword-school proverb: of how neither prayers nor schemes nor all one's tears will wash out what the finger of fate, or God, if you like, has written. He also wrote much and beautifully of death; for instance, how having drunk deeply of life, one must not shrink from the last cup offered one. Many say before the Fire was an innocent time, without trouble. I think times without trouble come only in our dreams.

Stretching out under the great sky with a blade of grass in my mouth like a boy, I suddenly felt the agelessness of all around me, the great trees with their arm-span-wide trunks, Kyam still living through his words, the circling in the sky, lazy as a hawk's, of the Niah scout guarding me, that skill handed down through millennia of generations in Niah-lur-ana, the sky and the earth themselves. These things that obsess me, I thought, my war, my army, my life, they are all just the crawling of ants on a mountain. With feverish work, they build their cities, prosper, languish, fight, win, lose, flee to other hills, hatch, grow and die fast as sparks; but a spring rain would wash them all away, and the mountain never changes, nor even notices.

an out I was to get out of
an attack.

n truth, all the rest of my
nking. Whatever my soul is,
s more frail than tough now.
t through the grinder. I like
re like an ancient sword of
balance and keenness, cutting
never failing on the field—as
eat skill and gentleness, off the
certain cause for being careless
warns me direly, "You'll never
rself out like this!" I find myself

t to find it all set up as I liked;
back. Whether she had not been
injer had forbidden, or she was still
knowing. Emao-e was waiting by my
chamber, to tell me things only she
had told her the secret of the wing,
to be useful with me gone, something
even thought of. Now Steel-eyes was
herself, and telling everyone, "Yes, on
iah really are as precious as Chevenga
cannot tell you why!"
me from Astalaz, half a moon ago, with
ave done much to heal me, had Kaninjer
had released my privateer fleet, having all
the Diradic Tongue. Twenty-two ships,
Selina if they were clever and fought hard,
ae-Aiyen, one who knew how to do that; so
rdered her to attempt it. We'd thought this
wait till later. I made my addendum to the
ne on the ship that could justly be claimed to
est would be rewarded in gold, enough that I
rite it. For the navy, after the first bitter defeat,
d been all grinding skirmishes, then serving
much sweat and blood for little gain. Such
ne cheer and brightness into a warrior's soul,
sh reason to fight well besides his old dull
y and fear.

stop it when I woke up. Until it n...
bed for nothing less than an Ark...
I have lived by this regimen,
life, except for the matter of dri...
I've had to accept that my body
You only get one, and mine we...
the way Alaecha put it: "You...
the highest quality: perfect in...
through steel as through air...
long as it's cared for, with g...
field." Of course I have a...
with it. Whenever Kaninje...
live past forty, wearing you...
unmoved.

I came back to my te...
but Niku had not come...
sent to me because Kan...
angry, I had no way of...
file chest in the front...
knew: for one, Niku...
not knowing how else...
I in my state had no...
learning how to fly...
my crystal, the A-n...
says! And yes, I to...

A letter had co...
news that might h...
allowed it: Laka...
but taken back...
enough to seize...
led by Krena S...
Emao-e had o...
would have to...
orders: every...
have done b...
should not w...
this war h...
under I...
prize...
gi...

a...
sa...
days...
sugge...
making...
calculate...
reveille n...
keep me s...
to tell Kre...
me.

I came into...
dered into, the...
with wine, as if...
they still thought...
truth. I had to refu...
prevent the same hap...
change how I lived: he...
and vegetables with a h...
and required me to take s...
time, every night no matte...
is a little more than five An...
from eight *aer*, more than I e...
had a large sand-timer made...
he put it on my night table, and...
it running when they saw by my b...

She'd called assembly for tomorrow morning already, foreseeing my wish; everything else was in order. "Your letter of request," she said in her brisk way, "Niku tried to intercept, by sending one of her people after the courier. Don't worry: right or wrong, the correspondence of a demarch is the correspondence of a demarch. I reprimanded the curl out of her hair, and she gave over. But I sent a letter to them saying something of your state, and to hold off considering until the next word they got from you once you were well. Did I do right?"

"Yes," I said, "thank you." There was nothing else to say. I would have to write the letter recanting. Then, almost as an aside, Emao-e said, "Did anyone tell you, your shadow-mother's left your shadow-father?"

These days, few things could make my jaw drop. That did. Parents' bonds seem eternal to their children, especially when they've seen no sign of trouble. Yet my shadow-mother had been very quiet of late, more so than before: too quiet. If anyone I loved began saying so little to me, I'd be on my knees begging to know what was wrong; those who've lost faith in words will inevitably, sooner or later, turn to deeds.

I spoke to my womb-mother, who would know. Denaina had left the four, instead of arguing for Esora-e's expulsion, to avoid forcing the choice on the other couple. "She tired of his stiff-mindedness, his unreason," my mother said. "It's been getting worse, these past years. Whether she's trying to teach him a lesson, or is truly through with him, I don't know; I'm not sure she's decided herself; I suspect it depends on him. His fight with Niku was the ripple that burst the dam, I think." Why am I not surprised, I thought, that I enter into it? Sure as the sun rises, he'll blame me.

I went to the A-niah quarter. The guards were more formal than before, chilling to my heart, calling me Hakan, like a commander, where before they had called me by name, like kin. I asked for Niku. More obedient than willing, they showed me to her tiny one-person Niah tent. I sat by the flap, and spoke her name.

There was a rustle of cloth within; then after a pause, that sweet firm voice with its tuneful accent that I'd missed so much. "Chevenga. How are you?" I told her, and for a time we made small talk, about the war and affairs of the army, like two duelists who've just agreed to sheath their weapons, but still eye the other for sudden moves, while the baby smacked her lips sleepily, and make a faint cooing. Finally I said, "Do you still love me? I love you." She said yes, I crawled into the pocket of canvas with her, and we covered each other with kisses. "Aaa . . . *ba!*" crowed Vriah. Soon everything was back in my tent.

In my parents' tent where Karani, on my asking, had left Esora-e alone, he sat honing a spear; I heard the rasp. "You," he said, when he knew my voice. His sounded broken, weak and with edges like splintered wood. "Well. Come in." His head stayed down, deep in his work, his still-thick forelock of black and grey hiding his eyes; even in candle light, his face seemed five years older.

All he said at first, when I spoke of Denaina, was, "These things happen." He was courting her again, it seemed, but so far she would not even speak to him. It suddenly seemed that in defeat, he was finally seeing his part in his fate. "Thank you, lad," he said, for my concern, then, for the first time in my life, "I suppose I should stop calling you lad; you're a man, you have been for a while."

I said, "I don't know whether Shadow-Mama loves you any more, but I do." At that, he let himself cry on my shoulder. "You still want to marry that woman," he said after a time; when I told him the truth, he signed chalk, meaning his acceptance, though he added, "Don't expect me to like her." Beneath everything, after all, was his love. That burned out the last of my anger. I gathered he'd become something of a recluse, for being out of favor with me; I'd have to reconcile with him publicly.

While Kaninjer sat impatiently fingering the sand-timer, and Niku the insides of my thighs, I lay in bed scheming. I asked her when was the last time we'd visited Hayel on them; she said they'd held off for my return, Emao-e fearing overdoing it. I got up, seized a proclamation-sized parchment, and penned on it lightly in Arkan, *I'm back.* They'd guess who. "Hayel, tonight," I said to Nolos, Niku's *kaiyinas,* brother in spirit, who was on duty. "Seize a few sentries this time, and drop their corpses. Do this over in blood, and drop it with a corpse in front of Perisalas's tent." No six *aer* for *them* tonight; I suppose no one knows better than I, the bad effects of sleeplessness. I didn't hear Kaninjer start my sand-timer running.

In the assembly, I saw clear as day my army expected my return to bring the return of running victories. At first, I did not want to promise that, fearing to put myself under strain; then I thought, I was under more strain before, and managed it; now I can only do better. They believed me, I knew by the roar. In command council, someone cautiously raised the thought of my generalling from the hill-top; I quashed it in a moment. "Everyone's been telling me in all their different ways how much more hale I look, and I know how much more hale I feel. No hilltops; I'd get bored." Before a command council and the news-scribes, I reinstated Esora-e to the Demarchic Guard.

They were itching to fight, it seemed, so I let them. It felt just that way; like letting one's sword hand fly after it's been pinned down too long. Though with new reinforcements from the towns to the south, the Arkans had got the numbers near even, we were fired up, they tired and afraid. They ended up fleeing, in effect, with us harrying them, for five days, all the way to Tinga-e. To the cheers of my people I touched the water of the great Ereala, and kissed my hand.

The high Tinga-eni walls were built before Yeolis settled the New Mountains to make a barrier to the south; strange to see them now, topped with scarlet-helmed heads. The Arkans had added good solid harbor-gates, crowned with the sun-clasping eagle, closed tight now. Since the harvest was all in, the Arkans in the city had enough food stored for a year, even with Perisalas's force swelling their numbers. I hardly needed the underground inside to tell me their intent: the *solas* sentries shouted it from the walls, jeering, "Freeze your balls off, Shefen-kas!"

I should say, though I would have died before admitting it at the time, that our war-chest was down to its last two thousand gold *ankaryel*. It was take Tinga-e and the food stored there, or disband my army within a month, see all our work undone, and fail my people, my allies and my creditors. (Though I might add, had I found three thousand

less in Brahvniki, we'd have been done; for this I took the
chance killing Edremmas, and do not regret.)

I gave the order to entrench, and begin massive building
of siege-engines. Soon the still crisp late-fall air around the
city was filled with the clamor of sawing and hammering.
These days I had Reknarja attending command councils;
now he stood up right at the start, good to see in one who
was usually too shy, and said, "First General First, I learned
the principle very early, to never besiege if possible; you
yourself say it even more strongly, never besiege at all. I
understand that this is the largest city in Yeola-e, and cru-
cially important, but surely with their larder and water so
good and a Yeoli winter coming on, this is not wisdom . . ."
His voice faltered, as he looked around him; I think he'd
been expecting more agreement, and instead they listened,
biding their time. (I should credit my command council, if
I have not already; some of our best plans were less mine
and more Misiali's, Hurai's, or crafty old Arzaktaj's, his
touch with the Lakan cavalry peerless.) Seeing this took me
back to another command council, also graced with Hurai's
voice, on a hot day on the plains near Kantila, when I'd
been sixteen. "Go on," I said.

"This is not wisdom," he said more gracefully than he
could have two moons before, "unless *you* have some snake
in your pouch, Chevenga, and you *always* have some snake
in your pouch. Never mind me." He sat down.

I wished I could tell him what it was; I just had to say I
would when the war was over, or perhaps even later than
that. That night in the very late death-hours, while the
Arkans slept easy, knowing by all the work going on there'd
be no assault on the walls for at least a few more days, I
had the twenty sneakiest of the A-niah fly in and open the
gate. We were almost all in before they even sounded the
alarm.

Tinga-e has three concentric rings of wall, built in different centuries as it grew; though the Arkans tried to hold
each one, the inner ones have never been well-maintained
since they were the outer, sections torn down for roads to
pass, houses built into or through them, and the citizens led
us to the breaches. Still, it could have been cleaner; here
and there Arkans seized hostages or found good positions

in strong buildings, and several fires sprang up, lit by accident or spite.

I made the harbor gates a priority, in case someone high tried to flee on a ship; there were seven Arkan river-galleys there, half-crewed. Four we took; the other three managed to heave off and anchor together in mid-basin where we couldn't reach them. It was Hurai commanding that, who had the sense to know them for prisoners, not waste people in heroics, and wait.

The hardest part was winning into the town hall, which in their usual way they had changed into the governor's palace, and walled. As I'd expected, their elite were guarding it. We ended up simply scaling the walls on ladders, and taking it finger-width by blood-soaked finger-width, until Evechera Ano managed to get his Ten, only seven by then, behind the gate to open it.

Perisalas was old-school Arkan; he stripped and wrote a letter submitting himself, but did not stay to feel it, taking a poisoned needle instead; his heart had been still for too long before I got Kaninjer to him. The Mahid, ten of them, all fought to the death or used their poison teeth. The city governor tried to flee, disguised as a servant, but a clutch of Tinga-enil in the street suspected his face, untied his hair to see how long it was, and brought him back to me. The High Governor of the Yeoli Province, as they called it, Kelkulas Immen, had sailed to Thara-e with nine-tenths of their treasury, a day before.

The night turned to wine and ecstasy, as all Tinga-e came out onto the streets. Nowhere is common joy felt more strongly than in a great city, where thousands rub elbows, and no festival is more joyous than liberation. No trouble that the fight was not entirely over, as long as we kept enough warriors sober to finish it; celebration would dishearten the holdouts.

Knowing the governor was under duress, the last resisters would not obey his command to surrender. As usual we were set to ransom the officers, thumb the *solas*, and send the rest out unhurt; now I raised on a dais in the square his bead-clock (one of those classic things in the grand old Arkan style, with brass wheels and arms and golden beads), had ten of the prisoners, chosen at random, beheaded, and

started the clock running. "Send them the message," I told
him, "that I will be merciful if they surrender; but next
bead I will kill another twenty here, the bead after that
forty, the bead after that eighty, and so on, until they do.
Tell them to add up how many that will be, how soon." The
prisoners did, and raised a chant begging them to surrender,
which eventually swayed them. It was ruthless, yes, but
more ruthless with the heart than with blood, I think I
may say. It gave the holdouts a bitter choice, between their
countrymen's lives and their own thumbs, and one could
hear marines on the ships arguing all the way from the
shore; but three hundred and ten prisoners died, far fewer
than in most battles, less in fact than the people of Tinga-e
had beaten to death before we'd got prisoners and citizens
apart.

We sent them upriver by the road, and settled in for
winter, billeted in warm houses with grateful hosts and
plenty of food. More sweet news came: Selina was ours,
with easy losses, and the capture of four quinqueremes. I
saw we were down to a thousand gold, as I wrote the scrip
for the prizes. All was well enough; but now came choices.

The head and heart of Yeola-e were ours once again, and
the feet, the seaport of the great river; some Arkan ship-
captains and garrison commanders on the lower Ereala must
be sweating in their gloves now, hemmed in at both ends.
But aside from all to the west, they still held Asinanai and
had garrisons in all the larger towns up the coast. From
Nakalai they'd been breaking the backs of Yeoli slaves to
build one of those fine Arkan roads to Hirina; they were
probably breaking twice as many now.

A general truly has the reconnaissance of his dreams,
commanding A-niah. For them it was nothing, to find out
how many Arkan warships were trapped on the lower river,
and where: eleven, some heading to Hirina, some to Akara.
In three days I knew how far along the road was: It would
be finished in three-quarters of a moon. We needed to take
Hirina, fast.

Leaving Emao-e in Tinga-e I took twenty thousand, to be
sure, including all the mercenaries; it is a mercenary's fate,
I suppose, that his employers always want to get his money's
worth out of him. At fast march we were there in two days;

the rumor of our coming was enough to set the Arkan garrison at Kolunai to flight. Likewise the road overseers; we took in and healed the crew. Inside the walls of Hirina, the Arkans took all manner of precautions against infiltration, bricking up posterns, truth-drugging anyone who'd come in within the last two days, shift-sleeping so at least half were awake all the time, a hidden triple-guard on the gate at night. To find that out only needed me to creep into within weapon-sense range; I sent fifty A-niah instead of twenty.

Still, they were better prepared and more spirited here than in Tinga-e; they had barricades ready, houses kindled to set aflame, and would not surrender. What I'd hoped to do in a day took three, and when it was done we were a quarter fewer, and two thirds of Hirina was ashes. It is hard to fight in smoke, half-blinded, one's eyes and lungs seeming full of tiny branding-irons, and just when one's knees feel near to buckling and one's sword falling out of one's hand, for lack of breath, enemies closing in out of nowhere.

When they drew back inside the walls around the town hall, and loosed a good arrow-rain, my people hesitated with the ladders, nerve faltering, everyone looking to see if someone else would go first. So I did, climbing at a scamper and carving out a position on the parapet, something one can do alone for only so long, no matter how great. The best Arkan fighters were coming at a run; if mine wanted to keep me they'd damn well better join me. I didn't look back; the people wills. As it was, their war-cries doubled and they came up close at my back. "You know we'd all rather die five times than fail you," a woman said to me in the celebration after, wine making her maudlin. "How can we not, when you trust us so?"

They'd asked no quarter, so we gave none. We captured five Arkan riverships. Their general, whose name I knew from the war-cries was Larianas, we managed to take alive by striking unconscious. An Arkan leader whose men sincerely shout his name to inspire themselves is rare, and more precious than they will pay for in gold; besides I needed it less, his war chest being good for another three thousand. I made up my mind to put him to death, though not without meeting him.

"Well," he said, once he was fully awake, "we took a good

many of you with us, didn't we?" I answered the truth. "Though I was very much hoping to take you, Shefen-kas. It wasn't meant to be; my Steel-armed God wills. Are you going to kill me?" I answered the truth again. "May I beg one mercy? At no cost to you? Will you tell me how you got behind my *fikken* gate?"

I laughed, sensing he was strong enough to bear it, then said yes, if he agreed to have the cut made in his tongue that renders a person mute; it having been such a hard fight, I meant to execute him by giving him to my warriors, as they had asked, and a gag might get torn off. To my surprise he consented without even considering; a general to the bone, he had to know. I used the knife myself; he was brave, making no sound and holding still. Then I told him.

Never have I seen Arkan-blue eyes so wide; he waved the fingers of his bound hands desperately for pen and paper. It was not something I could refuse him. I still have them, Larianas's last words scrawled, not that I would have forgotten them. "By the blessed gods, is it you, not us, who will return to the stars?" I said, "Whether you or us, I hope it's someone, at any rate." On that we could agree. I'd fed him a long draught of Saekrberk before making the cut; now I gave him a syringe-full of painkiller, leaving time for it to take effect, before I led him out to his death, which I will not recount.

That was as much as we could do, down the river; as if in warning, a finger of snow fell the first day of the march, enough to wet boots and get everyone complaining, except for the Schvait who never do. None too soon we were back in Tinga-e.

A pigeon came from Denaina Kotelai, the next day.

Though Kaninjer could not know, it still seemed suddenly unreal that he should still be puttering about in his office next to mine, humming some Haian tune while his remedies bubbled, when this had happened. Arko's face having got dung on it, losing in Haiu Menshir, they'd had to make good. This time they'd sent five quinqueremes.

The scene that I could see so clearly, those slow-moving gentle brown people gathering in thousands around the harbor, and Dinerer walking out under her canopy, had been set again; but this time the play ended differently. They had done no more violence than was necessary: seized the poppy of state and, right there in front of everyone, struck Dinerer's head off.

I could torment myself, if I wished, wondering what would have gone differently had she accepted my offer of aid, or I'd left before provoking the first attack, or I'd died and never arrived there. I did, somewhat. But there was nothing to remember in the end, but that firm ancient voice, when I'd offered anything in my power, saying: "Heal."

Denaina and her staff were in hiding, waiting for their chance to slip onto a friendly ship. That was all she'd had room to write on a pigeon-paper. Or could it be, I thought, she still thinks me delicate, and doesn't want to write more? I remembered Kurkas's orders to seize my healers.

I could not know; these were thoughts to put out of mind. Now, I must do what must be done. There were a good twenty Haians attached to my army now, the number so high, I do not doubt, because they had been called out of Arko, and knew the reasons. Kaninjer represented them to me; as well it might be worst for him, if Kurkas's revenge reached to the families of my healers. I called him in, and told him.

I won't write much, except that he took his Haian poppy on his hand, and crushed it, before I could stop him and say, "Haiu Menshir lives in the heart of every Haian, wherever he is!" I did all I could do, offer him and his people my comfort, and anything I could give; he said only thank you, and it was best I did not join them when they gathered to grieve. A private thing, like a family; yet perhaps some of them blamed me, as well.

I thought of sending the privateers to retake Haiu Menshir, now Dinerer was not alive to protest. But that would be yet another violation of the Haian way even if I set them free afterwards, or so I knew she would see it; it would be spitting on her pyre. Besides I could hardly do it and then leave the island unguarded again; it would be in essence Yeola-e's, afterwards. The other way, of course, depended on a vote of my people, to invade.

The square where the Haians gathered was near enough

to my room to hear their dirge, which I knew from Haiuroru harbor, and the occasional voice rising into keening, the song not bringing release enough. That long night I lay awake; Handa tip-toed in now and then to start the sand-timer, and I kept having to say, "Not yet, love." The thoughts that I was best not thinking came; too tired, I could not stop their thread. Alchaen, Kaninden, Merchoser, perhaps others, in the cellars of the Marble Palace; what would Kurkas do to them? Again from afar, I felt his hand, closing cold on my heart, the weight of Imperium.

We settled in Tinga-e. The Hyerne went home for the winter, and though we'd shipped in skis, I released the Schvait until snow-melt, not seeing to need them till then. Most of the rest of my mercenaries were content to stay for room and board, and pay if I sent them on raids, expecting little action in winter anyway. The river froze, closing off ship traffic; snow grew deep on the rolling fields; covering the ashes, smoothing the harsh corners of ruins to innocent white curves. As often as not the first exercise of the drill in the square each day was the Yeoli shovel-push, as foreigners came to call it.

I began getting promises of alliance from all manner of people, should we cross the border; news had evidently reached the north that we might. From one tribe from near the great northern sea I got a gift of a scarf-snake, a creature I'd thought mythical. It is unmistakably a snake, winding and flicking its forked tongue like one, but it is covered all over with fine short fur like on a rabbit's paw instead of scales, and warm against the skin. It will spend all day coiled warmly around one's neck, in fact gets quite upset, releasing heart-rending birdlike peeps, if prevented.

Winter ground on. The solstice is a festival for every race here, I found out, and in fact everyone's rituals seemed to call for light, whether torches or candles or great bonfires or the evergreens the Enchians burn in sacrifice. All peoples, I suppose, are subject to the length of the night.

A longer letter came from Denaina, who with her staff had escaped to Selina. The orders had indeed been to seize those Haians who had healed me here; interpreted broadly that could mean every assistant in the theater of surgery (a good ten), the strong-arms of the House who'd saved me from myself and every apprentice who ever checked my pulse or sat a night with me. They had interpreted it sparingly, All-spirit be thanked, taking only Kaninden and Alchaen. Again I remembered his face, imagined him on a Mahid table, and had nightmares I cannot speak.

Reknarja and I got closer. One night, sodden drunk, we laid bets on who had suffered worse in his life, the stake a kick in the rear for the other. In my tale, I'd barely got to Arko when he conceded; but since I refused to kick him until I'd heard his, he told me. He was a virgin. "Agh!" I said, facing away from him, "kick me! Kick me, hard!" When I could sit down again, I thought to myself, some injustices in the world one must work without surcease until righted. Virginity can be remedied.

Most things I set out to do, I do; but often they are no slight task. He refused to let me arrange it in advance, insisting that it must be his own charms and nothing else that won the woman; also, I had to twist his arm almost to breaking to make him wear any color other than black; also, every move I tried to teach him he'd say would only work for me, or a Yeoli, or someone handsome, and so forth. Still, incentive will out. He was tired of pretending to have done it, and the whispers at home that he lusted for men, which is great scandal in Tor Ench. I won't write on which night or with which woman the deed was done. He wore a glow for a time, and was happier ever after.

Niku and I revelled in loving in a place where we did not have to slap a hand over our mouths whenever we wanted to cry out in ecstasy, or do anything more than whisper. I will not say it was entirely peaceful. I have a way of always knowing best, she has her temper and we are both rock-stubborn, so before we'd learned to know well where our misunderstandings would come, we often fought tooth and nail. It didn't necessarily help that she felt my feelings. Once Krero came in, watched us for a while and said, "No wonder Arko wanted you two for fighters."

Vriah grew, and learned more words. She would scream death and eternal cursing if we fought near her, one way to make us stop. Yet one day it struck me, she'd as often as not yell before we did, even at the first black stare. Like plums released by a rent in the basket they came to me, ten or fifteen times I could remember her crying or fussing when someone near felt strongly. I tested it, by carrying her towards the infirmary. She began writhing as we came near the door, tiny tears forming in her dark eyes, so I had to carry her away running. She had her mother's gift.

Niku was at once thrilled, and afraid. She herself had not had it at all until thirteen, old enough to understand causes and cures; what can a baby do, but cry? And here; we'd chosen a fine place to raise an empath, in a fighting army.

I thought of sending her back to Vae Arahi to Shaina and Etana; but how to explain to her why she could no longer be with her Ama? In the end we just resolved to be careful, and then set about learning how. It was not so simple, as keeping her away from people who felt badly; for one thing, in the command-post, one never knew when they'd come running. It helped that she was quick with words. Most children cut their teeth on "up" and "down" and names for things; our Vriah did on "angry" and "afraid" and "happy."

Denaina was not moved by Esora-e's courting, in fact she told him to leave off. I remember coming to visit my mother, and hearing voices: his, anguished, "But I can *do* nothing!" and hers, calm, "Doing nothing is something. It's what she wants. She won't forget you, love."

Just after the solstice I got a cold as one does in winter, except it put me into a raving fever for a day, for no reason Kaninjer could discern. It could hardly be overwork, now. A half-moon later I got another, a cold, nothing more, with the signs everyone knows, the raw throat and stuffed nose. The fever was worse, lasting two days. It is the hardest thing for a Haian, to have to say to one who trusts him with his life, "I don't know what it is, or what to do." He couldn't even send a sample of my blood to Haiu Menshir now; the Arkan garrison watched the University like hawks, he knew, having managed one exchange of letters with his mother. It was only the officers who were at all cruel, she wrote; one sensed among the common soldiers a certain unease at being here at all, armed. The spirit of the unwritten compact lived, if not the letter.

From then on I was very careful not to get chills, bundling myself up well with Little Hugs, as I called the scarf-snake, inside, staying away from those with colds. But I was demarch; I couldn't wall myself away. The third one came about a half-moon shy of the equinox, and almost killed me. I can't even remember being laid in the ice-bath, or having the snow packed around my head and neck; they must save not only my life, but my mind, already scarred.

After that, I began at least in part to think of the war as something to finish before I died. The time of action was soon; the Schvait had returned, everyone else was itching. News came from the coast; all the Arkan garrisons had been stripped to skeleton guards. I almost feel sorry for those Arkans ordered to stay; they must have known what would come. The towns of Miniya, Nakalai and Forekanai had already overthrown theirs, giving every man a slow death. That left Asinanai, and Akara on the river.

Yet still, within the heart of victory curled the snake of trouble. These places are far-flung. Even replenishing our funds, we didn't have enough numbers to split to take them, at a good risk. No more aid would be coming from Astalaz, nor could I ask Kranaj for more, until we invaded. I could order Krena to take Asinanai, since its support from land was cut off; but she was near broke too, having to pirate, which kept her busy. Thus I found myself in the same place as many in history; pulled toward attack for the sake of defense.

Through the talks and arguments, one thing came clearer: we must take Thara-e, and the Arkan treasury. If we did that, we'd be both flush and close enough to the border that I could reasonably write to Assembly suggesting the vote be initiated, so as not to keep us waiting at the border and give the Arkans long warning.

I recall someone, though I don't recall who, saying, "What if we lose?" I answered the bare truth. "We lose, we're done. Dead, slaves, failed, a nation living only in history, die cast gates fast and all go home. Just like every other battle we've fought. So we will *win*."

I called in Jinai Oru, and asked what our fate would be if we marched now. Facing me to the empty wall, he cried out as if wounded, tore his hands off me. "You were dying," he said, when he caught his breath. "I saw the river, all blue, speckled with white ice. You said, 'Throw me in,' because you wanted cool before you died."

"Right, we're not marching now," I said. I had learned to listen to him, even when I didn't see the cause. "I've decided; what do you see now?" This was less frightening: an Arkan in chains, long-haired and well-dressed, being led to me.

Two days later, Kaninjer came to me with Bitha, and a Schvait I didn't know. Had we set off before that, I suspect, this meeting would not have happened until too late, and it was that Jinai foresaw, nothing more. A roll of the die none could see but him; it is with such things augurers truly come into their own. "With all due respect, *Stoltzer*," the black-shirt, whose name was Hilai, said, "may I examine your snake?" At first I didn't know what he meant; I'd got so used to Little Hugs coiling around my neck by then she almost seemed part of me. "*Gotrung*, there!" He showed me, the weeping from her tiny bead eyes and the sweet musky smell about her, that I had not known for a sign. Coming from the north country, he did.

There is a sickness that scarf-snakes get that also infects people, but only shows its deadly side when one catches something else. In time it kills. The cure was simple; remove her from me, and my blood would cleanse itself. "But she was always that way," I began to say; then saw the meaning.

The letter sent with her, bearing the name Ucust of Tiri-tsa, had assured me no reply was necessary until spring. I sent one, by Schvait ski-courier. "It is my pleasure to reply," I wrote, "in gratitude for your gracious gift of the scarf-snake, and your offer of three hundred warriors of your nation." I got his answer in three-quarters of a moon; the seal was the same, but the writing different, the style rougher. Some mistake had been made, he vowed, Second Fire come, or someone was playing false; he'd sent me no scarf-snake, nor offer of warriors, having been waiting to see how we did in spring. Some Mahid posted north, I thought, deserves credit, for deviousness.

In the meantime, from the small box where we impris-oned Little Hugs while Kaninjer tried to cure her came a constant anguished peeping; she scraped her nose bloody rubbing the lattice. Her disease was incurable, another

northerner told him, and commonly dealt with by a quick
twist of the neck. He gave her a syringe of sedative—enough
to put a man to sleep should kill such a small creature—
and I let her wrap herself one last time around my throat.
I wept more to feel those soft coils loosen than the last time
I'd seen a hundred people hacked to death before my eyes.
War makes for such strangeness, Haians say. Or perhaps it
was her utter innocence that undid me; those hundred all
die sword in hand, while she'd never meant to give anything
but warmth. Or perhaps it was that even as she died, by
my order, she never ceased loving me.

High Governor Kelkulas had taught us his policy, in
Tinga-e; if the city he was in were threatened, he would get
out well in advance with the treasure, to keep himself and
it safe. With the river iced now, he couldn't sail, but must
take the road, which had been paved with poured stone,
Arkan style, from the border to Thara-e. I sent a force of
five hundred with Renaina Chaer upriver secretly on skis,
to lie in wait for him; then at the first thaw that bared the
ground, ten days later, we marched.

As usual with Renaina, the ambush went well. Kelkulas
came out with the treasure-wagon and a guard of two hundred, apparently, almost as our boots first tasted the mud
of the road; his spy must have sent his fastest bird. Renaina
just split her warriors, half taking the road in front, half
behind; the Arkans, all ordered to fight forward, got cut
down from behind. Kelkulas tried to get around by driving
the wagon off the road, but it mired in the mud; then he
seized the satchel of most precious papers and ran. He was
slender and quick for an *Aitzas*; since I'd not asked for him
alive, as long as we got the treasure, they brought him down
with an arrow. He lived only long enough for the first question of Renaina's truth-drug scraping, the secret he'd least
like known a personal one, no one's business.

They came away with some twenty thousand gold *ankaryel* in chains and coin, as well as documents. He'd had a
limitless line of credit from the Marble Palace—I knew that
gold writing, and that eagle seal—and plans for all manner
of work all over Yeola-e, roads, bridges, canals, sewers,
which in truth would have been useful; the designs I kept.

But now I kicked myself for not having him brought alive.
How much I could have drawn on Kurkas had I forced a
signature out of Kelkulas, and sent someone impersonating
his representative to the bank in Roskat before the news of
his capture could get there, I'll never know.

The next night I had his corpse laid near the gate of
Thara-e, to be found in the morning. Then I called parley,
standing where all those on the wall could see me, wearing
his collar of office, which was all gold coins in two wings
balanced over the shoulders, to show who had the treasure.

I'd hold off attacking for an eight-day, I said. Any desert-
ers I would allow safe conduct home; the first ten and every
tenth after that up to five thousand who came equipped, I'd
give five gold chains (about five months pay, for common
rank), and let them keep their gear. Five hundred and fifty
chains well spent, if it got rid of five thousand of them. If
the army surrendered, we'd neither thumb nor ransom anyone, but set them free with enough provision to get to the
border; if we had to defeat them, we'd have mercy on none.

They were not locals defending their beloved land, who
would come away from many defeats with their resolve
made harder in desperation, but far from home, missing it,
wondering whether they would ever see it again; they'd be
shamed for deserting, but still able to bear a sword, as was
their craft, if they kept their thumbs. They were people
capable of believing their Steel-armed God, whose gaze on
this war had first blessed, but now soured, meant to reward
their vanity with defeat; in case they hadn't thought of it
themselves, I played on it in my speech. They were twenty-
four thousand with gear for thirteen thousand, who had just
borne a second bitter Yeoli winter and seen Kelkulas's
death; they knew, some from witnessing it, our way with
sieges; some had been driven all the way from Ossotyeya.

The first two hundred came the first night, looking to be
the first ten, tip-toeing with bent shoulders, hiding faces in
scarves as if we knew their names and would shout them.
We took a shoulder-flash from each, to keep them from
sneaking back into the city or coming to us twice. One
fellow in the insignia of a centurion came with his whole
unit, twelve worn scarred men; I think they split the five
chains. By the eve of the eighth day, almost thirty-five hun-

dred had come through, to steal back across the border in twos or threes or alone.

The city governor, Hamadas Forin, called parley. "It's a base nature that plays on the basest natures of others with bribes," he said when we were alone, superior-to-inferior of course. He had his Imperator's liberality to thank for that, I answered. Next thing I knew, he was quietly saying, "You were willing to expend five hundred fifty chains for five thousand desertions. Are you willing to spend two thousand for surrender, letting us go without arms but with animals?"

This plan obviously did not have his Imperator's approval, else he'd say it aloud. I bit back my question about base natures, and haggled him down to twelve hundred. A sweet little egg-basket for an *Aitzas* second son, as he must be to work here, not idling on his father's estate; he could buy a house. I would have let them retreat with arms at a lower price, but he didn't ask, wanting to make good. I feel for those of his warriors whose swords were heirlooms. I suppose he was doing them a favor, but he never asked their wish. It was part of our deal, of course, that I keep the payment secret. "As long as I live," I swore. This book being sealed until my death, I have kept that.

So we won back Thara-e without bloodshed. I sent the letter by pigeon to Vae Arahi, and ten thousand gold chains to Krena in Selina, with orders to take Asinanai if she thought she could on that. Then, while I itched to move, I had to wait, except for negotiating: I offered Kranaj the Arkan-settled part of Nellas in return for help if we invaded, to which he agreed.

Assembly voted to convene in Tinga-e, that being close to the war, and central, for ease of vote-gathering; they were understanding of the bounds of time. So it was I put down the sword and picked up the Crystal, and reminded myself as I did, "This is what I truly live for; not that."

The exact issue was whether the law forbidding the invasion of foreign land should be struck down temporarily. Involving all Yeola-e but having to go through quick, it required a ten percent petition from ten percent of counties (already done), an Assembly debate, then the vote.

Some called the idea the preposterous spawn of a young, vengeful and headstrong warrior-demarch tempted by greedy foreigners, (as if I'd had time to push petitions); some took my early request for dangerous enthusiasm. Others wondered how we could threaten Arko less than a year after being nine-tenths conquered by it. I was asked how far I thought we could get, and answered as I must, truthfully. "With alliances, and the ground's been laid for invading alliances," I said, "we could take it all." I gave the evidence: my estimate of Arko's true strength, reckoned from its claimed strength, less how much its claimed strength had tended to exceed its true strength in history, less its losses in wars. Besides us, at that time, there were Tebrias, Hyerne, Ibresi and Nellas, all of which had dealt Arko losses, and Kurkania, of which little was heard, good sign of trouble there too. Of alliances I said what I could, they were good; even as we debated a letter came from Mirko of Roskat, promising an army of eight thousand if I'd grant Roskat independence. I spoke as I saw: "The world wants to fell the Empire, knows it must unify itself, and sees its chance in us."

I had answered as I must with no thought in my mind but to tell the truth; and yet even as I read them back on this page, the words sound eager.

Hands signed for the Crystal; Alatha Tirini, Servant of county Halthelai, stood. "Demarch, in modesty, you obfuscate. You counted into your figuring your own service as First General First, did you not?" I signed chalk, my teeth on edge for what he might next ask: how I thought we'd fare without that, in case I died. Instead, he took it for granted, saying, "It does not see its chance in us, Fourth Chevenga: it sees its chance in *you*.

"So the question must be asked, all made clear, your heart laid open so the people may make their decision fully informed. In the world of ideals, a demarch does what his people commands with all his heart; in the world of truth, his inclinations cannot help but touch his actions; and you've always shown a clear tendency to follow your inclinations quite knowingly." I felt my nails claw my knees under the table. "I put the question to you, then: Is it your *wish* to invade Arko?"

I replied, "I must answer only questions that are relevant; a demarch's *wish* is not. I will do what my people require.

For me to say my wish, either way, might be seen as an attempt to influence the vote."

"But that's exactly it," he returned. "Your wish will and indeed *should* influence the vote, for the reasons I gave. The people must know whether it takes such a risk with a commander who is whole-hearted about it or half, because that will decide the odds—"

I cut in, though I did not have the Crystal. "The people wills. If they send me, I will go to it whole-hearted. If you doubt that, impeach me. It's against the spirit of the law and the principle of my office for me to answer this; so I refuse."

Once I'd been censured for speaking out of turn, others leapt into it, voices echoing loud in the high ceiling of Tinga-e's Hall. I set my teeth. This was not a command council, where I could leap up and shout back, or have the field-gong brought in and banged until everyone shut up.

Those favoring invasion guessed I did too, and wanted weight on their side; the pacifists wanted either the same, or good grounds to brand me a war-monger. Those leaning toward accepting my refusal mostly cited principle; Sharaina Anina of county Aratai argued furiously that letting me speak my wish would engender the corruption of power in me, one of the few times in my life we agreed. Finally they proposed voting on it.

I tried to stop that, citing points of order, until I was thrown down from presiding, for debating. The vote went strongly chalk. I threw up every barricade I could think of, insufficient mandate, demarchic bounds, demarchic privilege; they got more stubborn as I did, and hungrier, like wolves sensing the prey at bay; in the end I sprang up and strode out.

This is something not done, a symbolic abdication; the jaws of the hangers-on outside dropped when they saw me. But to me it seemed I had seen the soul of my people fought over, between faith and cynicism, goodness and baseness; the low had won out and now wanted me to serve it; I should resist to the end. No one had asked me what I thought the consequences would be, how invading Arko would touch Yeola-e's soul, whether it was wise; no one seemed even to think of it. At the same time I remembered the dark water of a foreign harbor, and a wise elderly voice, "The more your people know you, the more they'll command you to do what you choose"; then a young desperate one, "You *are* a force of history." To them, the Assembly, my people, the world, I wanted to cry, "You're saying I am what Notyere dreamed of being! No! I'm not! I can't be!"

Two keepers of the peace trotted after me, seizing my arms with utter gentleness as if they were sacred objects, their faces pleading, don't make us drag you back, Beloved. I let them stop me, begged time to master myself. One kindly put his arm around my shoulders, easy, since he was a half-head taller than me. When I felt the flush mostly gone from my face, I went back in. "The demarch must answer the question posed," the Keeper of the Arch-Sigil intoned, "on pain of impeachment."

I took a long deep breath, and ran my hand through my hair, like a child playing for time. What did I wish? I didn't even know. When I told them that, the Keeper spoke out of turn as ancient people in sacred posts may with impunity. "Young man," she said like a great aunt, dashing me down to a child again, "you will stand and we will wait, until you have an answer."

What is in my heart, I thought, laid open? I remembered Haiu Menshir, and felt only a distant abyss, howling with black wind; I thought of the Mezem, the Palace, the City, of what I'd yearned to do then, when it had been hard to imagine having a say in the fate of a dust-speck. What do I wish now?

I clasped my crystal, and said what came. "To do it."

Krena took Asinanai a moon later, as the grass sprang high and the branches of the leaves were just bursting out green. The national vote was counted a half moon after that.

The sum of all votes was some two-thirds of what it had been last time, and this a referendum no breathing Yeoli would abstain from. So that is how much, I thought, we are diminished. One could not wonder that it went as it did: seven in ten chalk.

VIII

No need to wait for Astalaz and Kranaj's reinforcements before moving, I thought; in truth we were better off moving now. The news of the vote would get to Arko as well. I can't even remember learning the principle that one does not wait for four enemies to join together, but takes them one at a time, apart. The entire campaign would have to be that way, lightning-fast.

The Arkans had already called in fresh troops from Moghiur and Roskat, bringing their strength to near twenty thousand, to our twenty-eight, Hamadas entrenching at the border. Then a message from the wing-scouts came to me, as I was considering battle-plans for the next day: the garrison barracks in the city of Roskat were in flames. Mirko, I thought, and stood on rank in command council to hold off attacking. The day after, sure enough, the scouts saw trees in the forest moving, as a host came towards us. Roskati: Arkans would use the road.

I'd never used a Niah for a messenger before; it would be tricky, but this message must not fall into Arkan hands. I wrote what day we would attack, at dawn, and suggested that as soon as the Arkans were positioned against us, the Roskati start a bonfire party in their camp, to lure them back. Mirko answered back agreeing, and added, so I would know for certain it was him, "Since it's on pain of death, I won't call you lad."

Now the Arkans were fighting, if not for the town of their birth, for the borders of their Empire; I could feel the difference the moment I eyed them across the field with its dung-sticks and pits. But the smoke and flames suddenly rising from their tents, and then the arrow-rain coming from behind as well as both sides, distracted them; one could hear the commanders furiously shouting *"Stand fast!"* As I stood ready to give the gong-squire the sign, the people near me kept saying, "Shouldn't it be now?", but I waited, hoping for more to turn.

What Mirko did then took great trust in me, considering we had not planned it; I could have let him carry all the losses to preserve my own strength, if I wanted. He formed up and ordered a full charge at the Arkan rear. That made them turn.

So just as he struck his gong, I struck mine, and we cut them between us, the north half fleeing into the woods with Roskati hard after them, the south hemmed in against the river. Best not to fight those cornered; we pulled back, rained arrows on them from all ways for a time then demanded surrender. As I disarmed and put on the ivy wreath to meet Hamadas, the light of the path unconceived flashed in my mind. "We will not thumb nor do any other harm to any of you," I told him, "not now, nor again in this war." He was considering another bribe, selling off a bit of his Empire this time; but I was in a position to threaten this time, so I did. To save their lives he gave in.

Why I had chosen to be merciful came clearer to me, as I watched the footmen stack their arms, grudging slow, and unfasten their red-lacquered armor, looking wretched as Arkans always do when they strip. I spelled it out to the officers around me, who'd all looked at me as if I were mad when I'd ordered no thumbing-crews formed. "We're not in Yeola-e any more. This is an entirely different shape of war. We are no longer defending, we're attacking; all the rules are changed. For one thing we can imprison; for another, we are not trying to make them never return, but, in a sense, win them over. If we do this, what will they be? Not our foreign enemy, driven off, but our *citizens.*"

It came to me that night: so far I'd fought and led this war more with my heart than with my head. From now on, conquering, I must be gentle except where harshness was necessary and could be made good later; what we'd done in Yeola-e I could always say was out of anger—the truth, I saw now—but no more.

I ordered a compound built for the prisoners, assigned them decent rations and what freedoms they could safely be granted, and forbade anyone to harm them unless they tried to escape. I had them guarded by local people, commanded by Yeolis who bore no grudges. Their first task was to watch the prisoners for the fifty quickest and loudest spreading news, and set them free. As well, I had the Pages writer called out of hiding on my oath, wined him and told him my change of practice with all its reasons. I wanted all Arko to know.

As I was seeing things put in order after the battle, I heard a Roskati-accented voice I knew. "There you are, much happier than last time I saw you!" I grinned and took Mirko's bear hug. "And older," he said more seriously, looking into my face. He looked, and acted, just the same. To my delight, Vaneesh was with him, and gave me a smile full of affection; or perhaps with a touch of the Lover in it.

We ate together, and afterwards spoke plans. With the lifting of the Arkan yoke all but accomplished, disputes were heating over who should rule Roskat in its freedom. Suddenly I found politics here was my business; I was the power, now and to come, if I chose to be.

There were only two true contenders for the throne, the other a man named Fuun who claimed descent from the old royal family, and wore and sealed his letters with an ancient monarchic signet. Mirko wanted to be a demarch, though, Yeoli-style; in fact he wished to be regent demarch, pending the coming of age of a child trained to it from birth. "I take it," I cut in before he went any further, "you are looking for my backing."

In a flicker of his brows, I saw the thought, *This certainly isn't the grief-fuddled youth I dealt with before.* Smooth enough for an aspiring king, though, he answered, "I merely wish to inform you how things stand, since it is your concern."

"Since Roskat has lent me warriors," I said, "once my army has passed through, Roskat is to my mind independent, free to settle its own matters, as agreed." There were those who would say I was allowing too easy an interpretation of the agreement, that I should keep them beholden to me until the war was over, since they were on our border. Krero's words: "One would think a Roskati never led you into quicksand." But I wanted to show I trusted those who had trusted me. "I wouldn't like to see bloodshed," I went on, "but it won't be for me or mine to sit in judgment over rivals. To my mind there is only one fair way to choose: put it to a vote of your people."

"I don't know," he said, with a trace of old grudge, "that Fuun can be convinced of that."

"Is he here?" I asked, though he must be; Mirko would hardly have left a rival at home to garner support while he fought. He stepped out to send for him; I whispered to Vaneesh, "You, I trust to be even-handed. What's really going on here?"

After she laughed, she said, "Mirko tells no lies, though he is a little harsh on Fuun; I think he'd be surprised at what Fuun can be convinced of. I prefer neither man over the other, but Mirko's course, I think, is the better one for my people. Of course you didn't stop to hear all of it." I began to say it was none of my business, when Mirko came back in. The second Roskati, with a heavy seal-ring on his finger, followed soon.

I spoke the same again. When I was done, Fuun, also a big man but slenderer and greyer-haired, fifty or so, stood up and began pacing, his hands clasped behind his back. With a sudden turn, and half-gesturing in the Roskati way, he said, "Do you mean to require this vote, Fourth Chevenga? You certainly have the power to, now."

Yes, I wanted to say, so watch your tongue. I've got too used to being able to make threats, I thought, veiled or open. But requiring a vote is like trying to force free speaking at sword-point; the count might be questioned, the people would remember not all had submitted willingly, resentments would linger. "No," I said. "Be assured, Roskat hasn't exchanged Arkan masters for Yeoli, if that's what you are thinking. I just believe it is the fairest way, and the least likely to lead to bloodshed. Tell me, both of you, how did you propose to settle it before I suggested this?"

They eyed each other like duelists. "I suppose each of you was looking for the other to back down, out of concern that there be no bloodshed, thus leaving the greedier and more careless of his people's lives in office?" I saw what each was bursting to say—"That's why *I* didn't back down!"—and wished I could be the ancient king who judged the two mothers, awarding the baby to the one who would give it up to the other to keep it from being cut in half. "What are each of you in this for, anyway? The greater good of Roskat, no? Is that not more important than your personal gain? If so, you are not rivals in that, but share it."

Fuun looked angry, in truth, at my impertinence; to him, until three years ago, I'd been a stripling Ascendant. He kept it in, though. Mirko said, "I am willing to submit to a vote. It is the way I stand for, after all, the way of demarchy; it cannot be brought in by force, only by choice, and only by a vote will the people of Roskat have that choice. Win or lose, I will abide by Roskat's will." One could see the old royalism, the feeling the people should serve the king, not he them, stir in Fuun. But he had integrity in him enough to answer Mirko's courage with his own. He agreed too, and I got them both to sign on it—Fuun using his signet—before they could change their minds. As I signed as witness, I said casually, "You know, if the loser has good ideas or ability, it need not be lost; the winner can always give him some high position. You do both have the greater good of Roskat in mind." They eyed each other again, with a different light. Obvious; but rivals don't think of it.

I brought out Saekrberk for four then, to celebrate. "Now I know he's no longer trying to persuade me," I said to Vaneesh, "what is the rest of Mirko's plan, that I didn't stop to hear?"

She laughed her wise-woman's laugh again. "And you said it was none of your business! Well. He wants to be regent demarch, until the child comes of age. Because I am priestess, and impartial, we thought it best the demarchic line start with me. All dependent, of course, on the people choosing Mirko's course."

She said this aloud; none of it was secret from Fuun,

then. "The father, I guess, must be neutral too," I said. "Who's he?"

The rivals traded a glance, both stifling smirks; I wondered when the last time had been for that, even as I wondered why. Vaneesh just let her beautiful smile broaden, picked up my sword hand in her tender narrow fingers, and touched the signet. "One who is neutral, fertile, and can give the child proven demarchic blood." In respect of my freedom of consent, she let go my hand, as my jaw fell. "If he will."

It's a rare man who would say no to that request, especially with a woman such as her. Underneath the pain of that night three years ago was the pleasure, like embers under ashes; as I remembered, Mirko laughed and said, "Look, the Invincible's blushing." Then he was somehow suddenly reminded of urgent business he had elsewhere, and Fuun similarly suddenly reminded, and making their regards they left.

It's a rare man, and I am not him. As I looked on her with Saekrberk blowing a warm breeze through my heart, I wondered whether she might like to begin that child right now. But it lay with the vote of her people; I knew she wouldn't try before permission had been given, since justice must be seen to be done. As well, I could hardly pass this off to Niku as a roll in the bushes for demarchic duty; a child would come of it, something that always changed everything, for her. "The people wills," I said, and kissed her hand. "If they choose it, and my wife-to-be permits, I will do it." Then for a while we flattered each other as would be unseemly to set on paper.

We marched to Roskat City, led by Roskati. It struck me then that the further into the Empire we got, the harder it would be to get local guides. I am the first Yeoli commander, I thought, going deep into land where I and my warriors will be hated, our dead, if we leave them, spat on, not cared for. But I, like all the others, was taught the details of defense only. Everything I didn't know about invading suddenly came into my head, too fast to keep if I did not write it down; right there in the saddle I took out a waxboard.

I borrowed books from and spoke at length with Misiali and Arzaktaj (who both joked that Lakans and Enchians were old hands at invading), and gleaned from works I found in the spoils. One thing I saw I should do immediately, and did: say again that spoils would be split justly, so looting was forbidden on pain of death, regardless of race, unless I said otherwise. I didn't say out loud, that means Yeolis; to my mind it was clear enough.

I must also count into the bookkeeping that food for this ever-growing host—we'd soon be seventy thousand—would cost double or triple, unless we seized it; people would hide, not give of their stores. It was spring; I forbade my warriors to disturb any planting, wherever we were, steal seeds or trample crops unless commanded to. One would think it didn't need saying; but warriors are careless in lands other than their own, worse in a hated enemy's.

In Roskat, people poured out of doors to greet us, with kisses and tears. There was a greater depth to their joy than in Yeoli towns, the sorrows preceding it layered on far thicker; they'd been slaves of Arko seventy years, not one. There we camped to stay, for a little. There are two Arkan roads into Mogh-iur, one going through Roskat, one passing north; I wanted to see which one the Arkan reinforcements from there would take, and at the same time wait for mine. The Lakans had to get through the New Mountains, and the Enchians all the way across Yeola-e, while we sat on a road smooth as paper and wide as a village square, built for moving armies. If we kept on they'd never catch us until we met a fight, where we'd need them.

My wing-scouts reported: Arkan reinforcements were on the northern route, having heard Roskat was fallen and thinking to head us off at Osijitz. I split off a flying column to take that city's stores first, in and out and back, fast.

That is Arkan territory proper, having been so for better than four centuries, the blood a mix of Arkan and whoever was there first, their language and customs long lost; it is Arkan practice to efface those things as soon as it can be done, as they would have done to us had they won. Many Osijitzans fled, having heard tales of a barbarian horde burning and killing everything; the governor tried to get out with the treasury and his art collection, but I sent cavalry to catch him. I'm just a Yeoli bumpkin in the end, I guess; I never imagined wealth such as in the City Itself could exist, until I saw it; then I thought it was only there, and never imagined it could be all over the Empire.

When we got back to Roskat, the vote was finished. Mirko, to show his people his convictions, had done the Kiss of the Lake where the river touches the town square, and dared Fuun, who had refused. It went some sixty-forty for the former.

So, once I had cleared it with Niku, Vaneesh came along with us, staying with the Roskatis, to enact the plan. As brood-slaves do (we'd both learned the tricks) we made love every other night for three nights in her fertile time, both holding off from others. Niku put up with it because it was a state matter, and Vaneesh her people's priestess, as opposed to an old flame. One cannot hide them from her.

The people I've loved, I've found, come in two kinds: those I love because they shape their lives by ideals, and those I love because they do not. Vaneesh and Kallijas shine like gems; I feel the God-in-Myself reflected, and hope for some light to rub off on me. With Niku or Skorsas I can cast off the pristine mantle, spit, kick walls, shout, "incompetent lazy glacier-slow shitbrains!" or "Why *me*? Why do *I* have to deal with all this crap?" without fear they will think any less of me, or give advice. To my mind, one needs both.

The Lakans and Enchians arrived, fresh and eager to conquer, as did a contingent of Mogh-iur under Truszan Steln Betkov, the King of Mogh-iur's son by the same name, and not particularly steady-minded; he was here in part to live down a javelin-wound he'd got in the back, on a slaving raid up the Brezhan. We got all manner of others, too. From the next cry of "*Ai-yae-ohhh!*" we never traced our own trail back again.

All through that war, almost to the end, the same tale played itself over.

We never faced an army as big as our own, out of all the Empire, but once. The reason comes clear if one plays it all out in one's head. We cast ourselves in a straight course like a spear's for the City Itself, instead of chasing armies, knowing they'd come to us; we laid no more sieges because deep in the Empire the towns are not walled. Arko's armies were far-flung, and most had their hands full. For a force to be called away from its post to face us, the news that we had won the latest battle and not been contained had to get out (past the wingers stationed in ambush, for one thing), travel to the force's commander, and be believed; he then had to send for permission to the City Itself, which may or may not send permission back, depending how crucial *his* campaign was seen to be. If it was granted it had to get to him, then his force had to get to us. Usually by then we were well-past where he expected us.

Add to that the single-wing, which was like having eyes where everyone else was blind; more than one Arkan commander, as he sat bound waiting to be ransomed, asked how in Hayel did I always know where everyone was and how the land lay everywhere. In the tales, we travelled fast as fire; the truth is we did most of the journey at a slow march and rested a day at least before and after every battle; I would not do to my warriors what I had done to myself. (Now and then camp would be broken before I'd got my six *aer*, making me the only First General First, I'm sure, who ever led the march on a horse-litter, fast asleep.)

I will not detail the battles; I have enough. Within the infinite number of forms the tactician sees and uses, it is always the same substance, of the same nature. The weapons flash out, the two sides close; war-cries turn to death-cries; into the smells of metal and sweat rise the reeks of blood and innards laid open. People move, with courage and skill or without, following orders or forgetting; they yell curses or the names of gods or leaders, in fear, in hate, in pain; they kill, and laugh that they did not die that time; they die, and fall still, this time finally, with tears in their eyes. The generals lay out their plans, form up their ranks in the cold light of the day; as the battle swirls they see the weaknesses and snap out the field-orders; they curse what they've missed or how they've been had, and try to make up for it. They see it all work, and secretly thank the gods or the die while they receive the hails and give the prizes, or they see it all fail, and damn themselves as they kneel bound to serve the victor.

And they all learn—what do they learn? How do they

change? Haians say it is all mainland madness; but even Kaninjer came to admit it was not so simple. The madness had to have a form, a cause, a key, in human nature or circumstance; but he could never find it. I went to an infirmary—we had several, now—after every engagement, and walking from patient to patient, seeing who would heal whole, who crippled, and who was dying, finding friends or bushes-mates, I would wonder what the cause was as well, so I might help to root it out somehow, someday, when I did not have to dance to its tune. While I held a bloodless hand, and listened to a fading whisper of home and bothersome sibs, the youth not believing his or her whisper was fading, I would think, "Kurkas in his gilt palace sent his *rejins* to make his Empire bigger; so my people sent me and ours to destroy it, and others joined in. That's the cause, Kaninjer. That's all of it. If that explains too little, if there is no answer to this thousand-fold agony in that fifty-year-old face that carries no mark of power—well, as Alchaen once said, to some questions there is no answer."

The chest and the larder we kept full by foraging; once we'd passed the border, mercenaries, seeing which way the wind blew, would join us just for board and spoils (though those with us from before I paid the same as before, their reward for joining us at the start, when our odds were longer). It is said in the tales if not in the books, every sell-sword, vagabond and beggar with a grudge against Arko tagged along; true enough. If they would work and abide by our orders we would not turn them away. I appointed a clerk, with full mandate to appoint more clerks, just to keep count.

We got everything from urchins in rags to Megan Whitlock, a tiny woman from F'talezon, at the source of the Brezhan, so far north the sun barely sets in summer or rises in winter, who had a snow-white streak in her coal-black hair, more weapons than one could count on her person (including fingernails she'd somehow had turned to steel) and powers commonly called magical, as one hears her people do. She could make herself appear to be a monster, by what process, whether in her mind or the watcher's or both, I don't know, or cast a glow on a weapon that looked as weapon-sense feels; she even claimed to have killed a man once with powers of mind. Not all the demons haunting Arkan camps after that were A-niah. Working together—I went on a night raid or two with her, before a mishap convinced me it was too risky—we became friends. Like many others, we found what we shared, both bearing the marks of use by Arkans; she was seeking her long-lost son, sold into slavery in the City Itself.

Her wife and lover, whose name I know only to render as Shkai-ra, was a cavalier from across the great ocean of the west, who put on an extravagant show of archery and riding. (Truszan had to snatch a kerchief from the grass with his teeth at a full gallop too, just to show he could. They shared one thing: a story that they'd worked as slavers while in exile.) This was on a creature of the east steppe, half-horse and half-wolverine; its favorite food was human flesh, and it would eat whomever she pointed it at. I grilled her at length on Fehinna, the empire across the ocean, which had sold us weapons unheard of on this side, then, as soon as we'd started winning, began selling the same to Arko. Otherwise, their colony of Nubuah, on the coast outside the western gates of the Miyatara, keeps its head low; gathering strength, one must assume. She was a good cavalry commander, too; I thought I'd have her commanding the whole mercenary cavalry, but she went missing in Aijia, dead, we presumed.

More than a hundred Haian healers in all joined and tended us, gratis, a marvellous number even for this host. They all spoke Arkan, and at first kept their hands hidden, by habit from living in the Empire. We got northerners with faces painted blue and scarf-snakes around every neck, southerners of every shade between snow-white with pink eyes to blue-black, people who counted me as being allied with old greater Gods the Arkans were trying to slay, (hence my demons), people who worshipped me as a god, or God's chosen, as Skorsas had. Of course they all had ways that turned each other's stomachs; one sees it particularly with burial customs. Bereaved A-niah, for instance, eat the heart, something I wasn't about to tell Esora-e.

It made my work of being the mortar between the stones harder. Many contingents brought gifts, often of timepieces, the word having gone around that I collected them, news that made itself true. Not so pleasant was the gift a tribe made to me of six hundred fifty blond heads from an Arkan border-post they'd passed through, neatly stacked in a pyramid in front of my tent in the morning, while they stood beside it, bashfully smiling, waiting for my approbation. It was obvious that the border was several days back, and I had drunk quite a lot the night before. But I smiled and said what they wished to hear, smoothed it over after Kaninjer, who came out before I could warn him, threw up right there and fled in tears, and had it all cleared away for burying before the Pages man, who'd make hay of it and perhaps find a face he knew, came for our daily chat. Let anyone say, I could not do what must be done to hold my army one.

To lie bare-chested by the fire in the tender night air of summer, listening to Truszan strum his long-necked string-box and croon his lewd lyrics, and see which women's eyes lingered on me, was sweet. To be told by Kaninjer what illness I'd caught was sour. At the start of the war I'd sworn an oath that I would keep no secret from my warriors I was not willing to say publicly; besides, certain of them should be warned. So I announced it in Assembly. I was not thinking to improve my name for honesty, only to do what was necessary. Kaninjer managed to cure it in a short time, though, with his miraculous bread-mold extract.

There's a tale that I made love with everyone in my army. Though how anyone could imagine one man could possibly bed one hundred thousand people, I don't know, I suppose I should lay it to rest. I was in the bushes with three Yeolis; we all got tired, I'd given more than I'd received, and they felt miserly. "If I were a King, I'd have gold to give to my people," I said. "But I'm only a demarch; I have only myself to give. Take that one extra, give it to the next person you're in the bushes with, say it comes with love from Chevenga, and tell them to pass it on." That would have been enough, but I added, "That way, I can say in a sense I've made love to all my army." I suppose I was asking for it. Rumor loves such words.

A short way out of Roskat, one of the A-niah broke a wire flying, and fell near the Arkan camp.

Usually when they find themselves in trouble that cannot be saved, they aim themselves for some place impossible to get to or hidden, and go at a dive, so the *moyawa* ends up too broken and the person too dead to reveal anything. This man was on a night-raid, low and close to the sentries. He'd been killed, certainly; but the remains of his wing, the Arkans had seized.

So the A-niah took the decision then to reveal the secret more broadly: to build more wings and train Yeolis to use them. Arko couldn't hope to have seventy people as skilled as my flyers for years even after they managed to craft wings that worked; but best we get a good start keeping up our margin of numbers.

So Niku set her people to work building wings, and training first the Elite, then warriors of the general Demarchic Guard; they were picked by how they'd answer when someone casually asked them whether they'd ever dreamed of flying. They trained by night, or in a hidden valley near camp; when I wasn't too busy I got my own practice in, on a wing I had sewn blue and green with the mountains, like a Yeoli banner.

As the saying goes, three people can keep a secret if two are dead; the rumor got out that we were trying some kind of flying device, and the archivists and Pages people started pestering me to know. "All will be revealed when the time is ripe," I would answer mysteriously. Niku sighed. "I suppose I sealed this," she said, "when I told you." But I looked ahead to when the war was over, and saw wing-couriers, wing-healers, wing-travellers the world over.

Our daughter grew, and learned whatever an empath learns in a war camp. I got into the habit of taking her on my shoulder to parleys. The Arkan would protestingly ask me why I must bring this noisome brat to such a meeting; invariably I would answer, "I have to take care of her, her mother got wounded last time we trounced you." The truth was, Vriah from a year and a moon old could read people better than I or anyone, and knew when they were playing me false. She would fuss, or, when she learned the word, would say, *"Bad. Lie."* Some have said I used her as no child should be used; but Niku told me, "If you keep her

near you, she will be well. Your love is a fortress strong
enough."

Once I said something about bullshit, and to my horror
it became her favorite word. Niku asked me from whom
she might have heard such language; "It's hardly avoidable,"
I answered, "in a war camp."—"Bull-*yit-t*! Bull-*yit-t*!" our
daughter cried, pointing at me. I had to own up.

We sacked no cities, left the golden sun-discs on the temples, touched no farms or farmers, paid them for what we
wanted at the higher prices an army carries around it like
skirts. The citizens would come creeping back; eventually
the poor stopped leaving at all, the whisper being, "Shefen-
kas wants the City Itself alone." Those with property fled
with what they could carry, to keep it. In each city I
appointed a regent-governor, choosing the ungrudging and
fair-minded. We killed or harmed no prisoners who surrendered, but imprisoned them as in Roskat, to be freed when
the war was over.

Now and then I beheaded one of my warriors for looting
without leave. All through I prayed, let this be finished
before a Yeoli tests my word. It was not granted.

I don't recall his name. Someone in Ikal caught him stealing firewood from behind a house. As they led him to me,
all through camp he said loudly, "Oh, come off it! He won't
kill *me*. Not for two sticks!" Else, with an oath of silence, I
might have let him off. Justice must be seen to be done.

There was plenty of argument, as people gathered around
the block, Yeolis asking whether I was sure I should do this,
foreigners wanting to see whether I'd stick to my word with
my own as I had with them. As I signed him to lay his head
down, he threw himself at my feet, and wept, "Beloved!
Beloved, my demarch! It was only two sticks, I'll give them
back, I'll never do it again, Second Fire come! Should they
cost my life? Demarch, hand of your people, should they
cost a Yeoli's life?"

"Should they cost a Lakan's life?" I asked, pitching my
voice for all to hear as well as they had his. "Or an Enchian's? They *have*. I am demarch, yes, but I command an
army of a thousand colors, whose blood all runs the same
color and we shed as one. You relinquished your will to me.
Twice I've said what would come of looters. If you think I

lied, that was your error." While some friends or kin of his
railed about how all Yeola-e would agree this was wrong
and they'd see me impeached, I had him held across the
block, and did it fast before a fight could start, or my own
tears blur my sight.

They turned their backs on me when I asked forgiveness
for doing what I must; understandable in their grief, I guess.
Then one of the Yeoli officers who'd argued most vocifer-
ously to spare him, said just loud enough for my ears to
catch, "Well, Beloved, you're an old hand at killing Yeolis,
now."

Through my tears I looked to see who would say such. It
was a millennion I barely knew, recently promoted, a tall
portly man of thirty-five or forty, with thin red-brown hair
in curls small as a Srian's, named Inatalla Shae-Krisa. He
stared at me with what seemed to be utter hate; the eyes
of those around him were grim; it was only those further
away who stared at him, not me.

Now I know what I should have said; "Start a move to
impeach me, then, Inatalla, if you think I am wrong and
you are right, and we'll see how it goes," or, "Does Inatalla
seek to make a bigger little warlord of himself by cutting
me down today?" He was that kind, and people knew it; I
should have known he did not truly hate me, but had some
other aim, for we barely knew each other. But I was too
upset to see sense fast enough; instead I charged him—I
remember how his loyal comrades faded back—threw him
down by the collar and ground his face in the dirt. I don't
know all I said, but one part that was remembered was, "I
hope I catch *you* looting, you child-raper!" Afterwards, most
would forgive me, for an understandable rage, in which I
could not be held accountable for my words; but others
would say I hurt a Yeoli, again, for speaking his opinion,
and what I said only proved how I had it in for my own.

At Setzetra, at Kirliana, at Minkemmenik, at Fispur, we
fought *solas* pulled from southern wars, their faces brown-
tanned, *solas* tired from being force-marched over the
mountains north of the great peninsula of Arko from northern border-posts, marines so recently off ships they'd barely
found their land-legs, youths, oldsters, untrained *okas*, slaves

and serfs levied at sword-point out of villages and manor-fields and made to stand unarmored in pike-hedges with spears at their backs while we rained arrows on them. We fought, and won, and marched on.

Ahead of us, the scouts would see them, in caravans threading the great highways, their carts full of paintings and marbles, silk gowns and gold-trimmed furniture, the gentry of the countryside, streaming onto the *lefaeti* and down into the great pit of Arko, day and night. The Pages announced a levy of every man sixteen to sixty, regardless of caste, without admitting the Empire was in deep trouble; next eight-day it listed bread prices five times higher than when I'd been in the Mezem; the eight-day after that the price was doubled again and only *fessas* and higher were allowed to buy meat. All through, where in his place I would have spoken inspiration every day, Kurkas was silent.

One day, as we neared the City, it came to me so strongly I went dizzy: *I walk with a hundred thousand people at my back who would go wherever I led, do whatever I asked, kill or torture whomever I pointed to, die at my word. It's been a long time coming, but this I'm suited for. What couldn't I do?*

The answer sprang to mind, making me laugh out loud, so those beside me glanced. *Arm-wrestle someone with a stronger arm than mine.* It's a fool who doesn't learn from others' folly.

Yet that night, just as Makaina peeked in to see whether he could start the sand-timer yet, I again found myself in my little stone chamber with its wall-scrawlings in the Mezem, on a night as dark as this. Gold glowed again on my wrists and fingers, then covered my body, and the thought came, like an invocation read from stone by a historian, *I am Imperium. I am perfect.*

I sprang up in a cold sweat, making Maka start back against the tent-wall. "What do you need, Cheng, sir?" he said, before I could even apologize. "Food? Wine? The maps? Someone? I'll get them on the double." All-spirit help us, I thought, my little brother is my lackey. "Was it a nightmare, Beloved? Shall I get Kaninjer?"

"It's nothing and I need nothing, love," I said. "Thank you. When this war is over, you and I are going to have a tickle-fight. Or maybe before." *My hand rules all*, that old voice ran through my head. *I am God*. You fool, I shouted at myself, when he was gone. You laughable moron, thinking it was only being the other, that night, not knowing fore-knowledge when it hit you in the nose.

IX

Beside the cliffs of Arko on the eastern side lie the plains of Finpollendias. It was there, they fielded an army as large as my own. Hearing news faster than they received orders, many Arkan commanders had chosen to play it safe and bring their units to Arko; as well there were the children and ancients and untrained of the levy. The city being crowded, they encamped on Finpollendias. We encamped by the mountainside to the east of that, to rest for a day, a place from which the prevailing wind was right, for what we planned.

That night Megan Whitlock, my tiny F'talezonian illusionist, came to my fire, and we happened to speak of revenge. She'd lost her mercantile house to an underling who'd drugged her, sold her off and announced her dead; fighting free and finding allies she'd set to winning it all back, her vengeance made all the worse by his having been almost a lover.

"It almost ate me alive," she said. "If I'd caged and killed him, I'd have tied myself to his memory." She paused, scratching at one steel nail, that flashed in the firelight. "I'd have driven everyone else away and been alone with my hate by now, more than a little bug-crazy."

"Are you worried," I asked her, "that I might lock myself

in the cage forever with Kurkas as you almost did with Habiku?"

She smiled a slanted smile. I should perhaps say here, she was not grieving for her lover Shkai-ra, still holding out hope she would come back. "That thought might have crossed my mind."

Peyepallo, Segiddis's rival who she'd sent as leader of the Hyerne, was here too. In her way, she snorted, and said, "I'd have just killed him and that's the end of it, and I think so should you, Invincible. Death ends all disputes."

People were listening. "One thing to get out of the way first, Megan," I said. "You spared your tormentor—he got killed, yes, but you let him go, without care whether he died. I can't do that; mine must die, as a matter of political necessity." That was a lesson my teachers in conquest had repeated, worried that I might be too merciful: one does not leave the old powers alive, to work trouble underground, to keep hope of a return to old ways alive. Peyepallo hummed knowingly, making me think of Segiddis.

"Have you decided how you're going to kill him?" said Esora-e, as if it were my sacred duty.

In truth, I hadn't; I'd been too busy. Now the question was put in my mind, though, I tried to imagine. I could not see myself even touching him; each time I raised the image in my inward eye of him, and me close, it slid away sideways or wisped off like smoke. "In truth, no."

That led to a rain of suggestions unfit to write. "Then it seems vengeance doesn't obsess you," said Salao, "so you needn't worry." Kunarda said, "Still, anyone who harms you should come to an end, as the Mahid like to say, ten times worse." He had never been as close to me as Mana or Krero, yet in the Lakan war he'd called me Cheng and we'd come to know each other well. Now he called me Beloved or even Invincible, leapt at my orders, would guard me like a watch-dog even off-duty, trying to see what I wished before I asked it. When I drew him aside and bared my heart about it, he did not understand; never, to his mind, had we been closer, and he happier. I could only watch, as I lost him.

"With all due respect, *Shaikakdan*," said Arzaktaj, "I've heard the tales, as we all have. It is not natural for a man, even kind-spirited, who's had done to him what you have, and who has a good prospect of getting the one who did it into his hands, to have no thought at all of what he means to do to him."

The wine-skin was going round; I reached for it and took a long draught. Like a child evading, I wondered what business was it of theirs, as if they were not urging me to face it for my own sake. Is it madness, Alchaen? I asked inwardly; then turned away the thought of where he was; that sight came too easily.

"Chevenga, I hope you'll forgive me for saying this." It was Alaecha, who'd seen me on Haiu Menshir. "But Kurkas . . . he had you, you can't deny, he put you in fear, he mastered you. If you don't do it, if you give it to someone else, will you be able to say to yourself afterwards that you truly did overcome him in the end, or will you feel at his mercy forever?"

I'd never thought of this either. One's friends will be one's psyche-healers now and then, if they are decent friends. Two argued over how I would or should answer, until others said, "Let him!"; then around the fire there was silence, but for the crackling of the flames and the sizzle of the meat.

"Listen," I said. "However it goes, *I* will not come away feeling the victim. Believe me." Laughter broke the silence. Decent friends will let up on a hint, as well, even if not sated. This was not the House of Integrity. I saw several elbows nudge several ribs, and then we went on to other matters.

Day broke bright and clear, an Arkan day like those I remembered, though cooler up here in the hills. In the morning I had Jinai aim me to the blank tent-wall, and asked him, "If we do as planned today, will we win? Tell me nothing else." He said, "Yes." Later, Niku asked me if I would like to go for a fly. We were free about the secret now, so I did it often before battles, to get a better feel for the ground.

We would attack late afternoon, when the air was settling down to sleep, as the A-niah put it, teaching us their thousand words for wind; my army had orders an army rarely gets, stay in bed as long as you like. Now, though, the breeze was brisk and good to ride. As always she strapped Vriah to her back. Mainland parents toss their babies over their heads or twirl them to thrill them to laughter; A-niah take theirs into the sky.

So it was we launched ourselves off the cliff, and glided out over the city of Arko.

So this, I thought, is the sight I saw in my flying escape dreams, in reality. It was not so different—I'd imagined well, perhaps aided by prescience—with the buildings shrunk and foreshortened by our height. But those dreams were rooted there; and everything was too familiar. There was the Mezem: to see it was to remember. I felt more than thought, with the rhythm burned into my body and soul, *two days hence: fight-day*. There was the Marble Palace, with its roof of gold blinding in the sun, the stronghold of Imperium, the house of destruction, the place of my unravelling; even as I wheeled in the palm of the wind, my mouth went dry and my arms weak, sweat broke out all over my skin, and everything inside it seemed empty. Here I was with my host one hundred thousand strong, our sword poised over all this for the death-stroke, and I felt helpless, and alone, enough to falter so that my wing showed it, and Niku cried out to me. Such is the power, by which we may fly or be bound, of mind.

Be bound, or fly. I turned my wing, banking, and looked down on Arko again, this time remembering all that was, now. In the streets, I saw the people walking antlike, the dots of their heads all blond; I could hear, if I listened, the bustle as they went about their business, thinking as they must that the city could not fall. *Arko,* I thought, and wanted to cry. *Did you think I would never return? Or that I would stay your slave and your victim forever?* It struck me then: it was near high noon. The bells would ring, and the girl-children's chiming scream; then all would stand silent to listen for a voice from the sky.

So when it came, I dove low. "*Arko!*" The words came, and I let them pour out as they would, into the silence below. "*Arko!*" Their own tongue, superior-to-inferior, to all. "Arko! Do you know whose voice this is? You should have listened better, then, when I was here before! I said

I would come back, and do what I will do; did you think I lied? Did you think I, and the world, would wear your chains and suffer your whip forever? All is different now, isn't it, Arko, city of masters! To whom do you pray, now, with your last breath? Did you think your gods would listen to you, or ever will, speaking through one who holds none, who reveres them only as helpmates in ruling you? Pray to the one who matters, Arko, pray to the one who will listen, and hear—pray to *me!* For it's in *my* hands, your fate! It's *my* will, that you will dance to! It is *I*, who will hold the chain! Pray and say amen, Arko, to *me!* Amen, Arko, ah-*mehhhnnnn!"*

X

May every army a Yeoli ever leads go into a battle of even numbers so high-spirited. As the sun sank towards the west, they were jesting and laughing everywhere one cared to listen. Too much so, in fact. In my speech to them, I showed myself alarmed and sobered, and spoke a lie of war: "Wipe off that cursed grin and listen! I asked my augurer to prophecy for this battle. He went death-pale, and told me I didn't want to know. 'I see the Arkans with their backs to their homes, now, set to fight to the death, like never before,' he told me. 'And us—we think we're going to win, like always! In our heads we're already lounging in Arkan houses, sipping Arkan wine, forgetting that for once there's as many of them as us, not seeing the look on their faces, thinking the prize is in the bag, and we don't have to do anything for it! But, All-spirit help us, Chevenga—in truth, we're doomed! Arko will find its strength in the nick of time, and we'll be lost on the brink of victory! I see the corpses in heaps; I see you in chains again, flung down before Kurkas; I see him laughing, and all Arko heaving a sigh of relief. I see it written in the history books: "they failed in the end, because they thought victory was certain!"'"

"So he told me, my people." I let that sink in for a bit, watching horror fix on the near faces; then I said, "Such is the future, that only foreknowledge can change. But we've

165

had foreknowledge; we've been warned; if we listen, there's hope. It's not as if we've never had our backs against the wall before; we know how to fight against all odds ..." I went on, in my usual vein for a hard battle on which everything hinged, until I'd got them fired up again, properly this time. Afterwards Jinai came running, crying, "I never said that!" Right in front of everyone: I had to say, "Yes, you did, you just forgot."

It was time. The lines were drawn; from the mountain they looked formed of figures on a map, too distant to know as people, spread out before me across the plain, too still, waiting for the signal. Time: the sun was near to touching the hills: "To wings!" I cried. "Lamp-lighters!" They dashed down the line, setting the one torch each had fixed to his bar, and the two I had, alight. "*Ai-yae-oh!*" I ran, and flung myself into the air.

"Look up! Look up, you straw-haired child-rapers!" The air all around me sang as we flew, "*Ai-yae-oh! Ai-yae-oh!* Here we are, shit-eaters! Look back! It's too late! Look back and see Arko burn! Say farewell to the sun, whoresons, for when it rises again, it will see you in everlasting darkness! *Ai-yae-oh! Che-ven-ga! Che-ven-ga! Che-ven-ga!*"

Arko could not know, for we'd kept it secret, how many wings we had now, and wingers, trained enough for a downward glide in still air, to a clear target: fifteen hundred, a flock to fill the sky. As we were over them, the faces upturned, mouths open, the bows loosing arrows to fall far short, I struck free my second torch to fall, the signal. Niku started the A-niah making their awful screech. All down our lines, the great gongs crashed, and the roar of war cries rose.

Rose, to fade behind us in the rush of silk through wind, and our call. The five hundred who would take the Gate from within split off; the rest of us set our course for the roof of the Marble Palace. Across the city we dropped our fire, to land where it would land. In the streets, screams began.

The Palace roof is flat, with only two towers, for show. Guards poured up, too late to catch us in the air; they formed strong positions around the stairwell doors, but they were not their nation's best, and we were; expecting Mahid,

I'd brought the Elite. Soon enough we were in the marble halls with their gold braid; "I don't *believe* this!" my warriors kept saying as they looked around them, too astonished even to be greedy, yet. I sent off detachments to secure the gates, and called the rest to me: the Palace guard had set the cry, "To the Imperator!" Then, what I'd thought would be a hard but not-too-costly fight turned into Hayel.

I had my spy-filched maps of the Palace; but they knew it with their feet, had narrow places to hold, and I could not know where Kurkas was. All that I'd expected: but there was also what I had not known. There is not one Marble Palace, but two: within the shining one hides the shadowed, a warren of secret passages no fewer or less complex, nor less well-known by the Mahid.

We'd think we had a wing sealed off, then find them inside or creeping up behind us; we'd charge an empty corridor, only to see an onyxine shape ghost in through the wall shooting poison darts or flinging caltrops tipped with venom among our feet, happy to die as long as he took as many of us as he could with him, hungriest for me. Twenty times over I would have been killed, if not for weapon-sense telling me where he waited, so I could put steel through him before he put poison in me. I fought in dread, for Niku and Krero and the others I'd sent away to take other corridors.

Evechera went down beside me, then Salao; we all learned soon that if the wound was not apparent, it was mortal, being from a dart. Once as we were playing stepping-stones over the stream through a patch of caltrops, for our lives instead of dry feet, Sethara on my sword-side yelled to Kunarda on my shield-side, "Shit, I can't stand this! Grab his other leg!"; together they carried me across. Halfway I felt Setha flinch, and growl, "Child-raping shit!"; she'd stepped on one, half my weight added to hers making sure it drove deep through her boot sole. No matter how great the skill, how long the training, how invincible one may be in a clean fight, poison works the same in all of us. She lived just long enough to put me down on clear floor.

We were in the Imperial chambers now, the marvelous decor hauntingly familiar, the servants who fled by us wearing satin. A Mahid waited around a corner, tube at his lips;

I showed my head just long enough to fake him into shooting, rushed him to cut his lungs in half before he could reload, and knew his face. "My old friend Meras." He was groping for some weapon in his kit even as blood bubbled through his lips, those pale eyes fixed on me with the same reptile expression as always, from the floor, like those of a dead snake that still writhes. I chopped off his fingers. "I'm not one to keep count of how many I kill with my own hand," I said. "But for *you* baby-rapers I make an exception. That's eighteen Mahid, smothering in Hayel by my doing—nineteen, with you." A dribble came from his lips, and by his eyes I knew it was the best he could do for spitting at me.

I knew the door beyond him; it led to the first anteroom before Kurkas's parlor, the chamber of strip-searching. From here in, there'd be spring-darts. "Shield-wall head to foot!" I ordered. We heard the thorns hiss out of the walls, thump into wood and ping off metal beside our ears, skitter through our feet. The people who trigger them sit in a booth behind glass that is clear from their side, reflecting from yours; my people were surprised, when I smashed and leapt through a mirror, striking. They were regulars, easy work. "Through the passages from here," I ordered five Tens, "they likely lead to the trap-booths of the rooms ahead; if not, come back."

Beyond the next door, in the purification chamber, three Mahid waited. "Archers!" I flung open the door, keeping behind it, letting through a volley of our arrows; then we rushed. A dart hissed by my cheek; then I let Chirel whistle through bone and the air was filled with spattering blood. They were all three down; beyond the next door, in the chamber of prostration instruction, waited five Mahid—light on numbers, I thought, it's probably no more than fifty, who are so hashing us—and a solid crowd of Palace guard regulars.

By weapon-sense, though, I knew there was blood spilling in that room's trap-booth; that fight had got ahead of this, having easier opposition. I commanded halt. A wristletted fist smashed away the mirror-window from within, and a grinning bloodied face leaned through. "Cheng? Do you know how to work these things?" I scrambled through the darkened passage. There was the console, with its polished brass levers, there through the window, the Arkans all waiting in stance in the chamber, weapons aimed or levelled; their gaze was fixed on the door, teeth set against the knowledge of death, with no idea I, and it, were here, not there.

I studied the ivory plate by each switch saying where it was aimed, said, "Like this, I think," and with my forearms, banged down both banks of switches all at once. A good half of the Arkans fell, stunned or dead; I called *"Charge!"*, heard it relayed back, saw my people burst through the doorway, and vaulted over the console and through the window to join the fight.

The Arkan guard opened the last door, with the Lukitzas beside it, to make a fighting retreat and hold us there; with so many of ours crowding in behind us we just had to push our way through bodily, the first rank on both sides corpses. I touched the little bronze's bald head as I passed, as one should. The fight boiled out into the room; I let its edge get ahead of me, and jumped up on a chair arm that looked solid. No spring-darts were flying. I looked all around.

They'd converged here, falling back, we'd followed them; I heard hails from the split-off units from across the room. A knot of Arkans in the middle had formed a ring-wall of shields; inside it I saw the bright satin sleeve of a robe. Then came something that seemed out of a dream; from the forest of red-greaved legs squirmed a naked boy who might have been my twin brother, if one could have a twin twelve years younger. His hair was black and curly and cut just the same as mine; he even had a scar down his cheek in the precise same shape as mine. For a moment his eyes, mine in small, froze on me, not frightened, just still, with wonder; then he scuttled under an embroidered silk couch. Kurkas, I knew, was inside that shield-ring.

"Stay arms!" I shouted with all my might, three times, in both languages. Most did, as if in unspoken agreement. There were no Mahid left standing.

I spoke to them, not him. He would think nothing of sending them all to their deaths, if it meant a few more last chances at me; it was only their lives, after all. I had no breath for anything grand, just, "Give up, lay down your arms, and I'll spare you all. It's been a cursed shitty dirty child-raper of a war, but it's over." In the heartbeat of silence, I and they waited for him to order them to stand fast. They would have, had he spoken. They were the loyal ones; they'd fought this long. But no order came. The ranking officer showed himself, said in a voice full of tears and exhaustion, "All right, Shefen-kas, I'm yours." He tossed down his sword, and it truly was over.

I sat down on one of the great cushioned chairs, and felt my own fatigue wash over me in a wave. A score of orders needed giving: to finish the securing of the Palace, aid the wounded, imprison the prisoners, ring the tower bells, our victory signal, to find out what was happening on Finpollendias. It seemed almost more trouble to worry later about what would come if I left it all undone. Someone in the Demarchic Guard put his hand on my shoulder and handed me a wine-skin, and someone in the Elite said, "Cursed shit, how many of us *did* get pecked?" Like a marionette worked by another hand, I spoke the commands, hearing my voice break from overuse.

We'd been a thousand; now, as far as I could tell, we were some four or five hundred. The A-niah were mostly all right, having stayed back as I'd commanded; Niku, they told me, had got badly but not mortally wounded. I got a precise count for the Elite. Fifty, they are, the fifty best in all Yeola-e, with all the training and talent, rare as diamonds, that requires. Putting them in the vanguard all the way in, of which those left would probably rather die than complain, I'd lost thirty-nine.

Sethara, Alaecha, Evechera, Salao, the roll went in my head; all I could think at first, in some stupid part of myself, was, "The national Unsword tournament will never be the same." From somewhere I heard a steady gasping for air; four people were carrying another, whose face was blistered red where it was not bloodied, and streaked with tears. It was Krero; he'd had poison gas flung in his face, so no one could know whether he was dying or not. I had them get his armor off and lay him half-sitting with his head back, to wait for the Haians. "Cheng," he whispered between straining breaths, when I clenched his hand. "At least you're alive." It came to me then, there was more cause for his tears than the gas. Sachara should be here. I looked up to the others, and made the sign of Sach's long red ringlets. They just signed charcoal. I thought of Tera, his wife of just more than a year.

"Beloved." It was one of the people I'd sent to the roof, breathless and grinning helplessly. "We've won on the plain. The gate's ours, and so are most of those rafts hanging on ropes." All around me victory whoops rang out. I just said, "Good," and stood up, and turned.

He was sitting just as he had been when I'd first set foot in this room, in the chair by the pure glass table. The Arkans had all backed away from him, none in the end wishing to share his fate; mine stood back as well, waiting with smiles, to leave him for me. The chessboard, with its king-pieces crowned with real jewels, was set up for a game. He looked up from it, to me.

I know how I would look, in his place: bloodshot, un-kempt, haggard as if I had not slept for a month, mad with shame and despair. He looked no different than before, the smoothness of his face as unassailable as the cliffs. Is this the God-in-Him, I remember wondering, that keeps its calmness even in the ultimate extremity, like a sage; or is it plain madness? Then I looked into his eyes, of that purebred porcelain blue.

Their gaze was a lover's, bright with joy and yearning. He spoke in barely more than a whisper, but I heard it over all the din of celebration around me, like an inward voice that silences all else. "Shefen-kas. You went from me; but I always knew you would come back. In your heart you know where you belong." With his soft hand, naked but for the flashing gold of one Imperial seal, he beckoned me to him.

As set in heart and mind as the stonework of sanity, are the vines of madness, curling unseen where one thinks one has routed them out.

My people, shouting and laughing and raising skins, were suddenly ghosts; Chirel fell out of my hand; my body moved of *his* will, as it always had, it seemed, and always would; those few little things that had happened since were a vain dream. I knew nothing but his eyes, creasing in the begin-nings of a smile, then his lips curling in it; no scent existed in the world but heliotrope, wrapping me all around. The pit in my soul screamed its laughing invitation; the fires began to burn, and the glass shatter.

"Shefen-kas," he said. "I missed you." There had been a psyche-healer's name to cry, but I'd forgotten it; besides he too was here, broken in this hand. "Kurkas and Shefen-kas." The black lightning bolt that does not move cracked across my soul; and my body, knowing only one answer for that, knelt before him. I felt his hand twine in my sweat and blood-sodden hair, and my face press against his warm naked knees.

His laugh rose in the deepening silence, his fingers scratching the back of my neck like a dog's. "Shefen-kas, who knows true power. Shefen-kas, who would teach me! Here you are, the greatest warrior in the world, the most brilliant commander, the one whom all the world's warriors would follow to its end, the conqueror of the Empire of Arko, master of all, lord of lords, king of kings! But still, you move to my hand, as I taught you; still I need only speak, and I am your master. Hah! *That* is power." He was wearing a loose robe and nothing under; now he opened it.

A hundred voices and hands held me, shook me, flung cold stinging liquid in my face. *Cheng! Beloved! What the shit? Fourth Chevenga, where in fik are you? Get a healer, the child-raper had something in his hand. . . . No. It's what they did to him. Cheng . . . make him stand. Bring his sword.* Arms hard and strong lifted me; I felt the grip of Chirel in my hand. "Chevenga, we're with you. We're here, Beloved, we're yours, we've won, what *you* say goes now. *Chen,* Chevenga, come back."

I opened my eyes. It was wine on my face; I licked it from my lips, then took a long pull from the skin they handed me. Someone said, "I think he's himself," making everyone laugh. Kurkas was on the ground, pinned by Kunarda, who held a knife to his throat, and looked at me for the word.

"No," I said. I took a long deep breath, and turned myself steely hard within. "Take the seals from his hands." He fought, clenching his fists, so they had to strike the tendons of his wrists to palsy his fingers loose. I slid on the rings of the seals, clasped the bracelets around my wrists, and raised my hands for all to see. The room filled with whoops. "Strip him, bind him," I said. When it was done I had them make him kneel before me, and cut off his long hair with Chirel, almost to the skin, remembering Alchaen's words. I need not stand alone; my people were with me, would save me. "No," I said to him, spreading my arms, to mean them, and pulling the two nearest, a Yeoli and a Niah, in beside me. "*This* is power."

He kept his countenance through all my taunts, about his sanctum and the glass city and so forth; when I decided to show him what an Arkan slaver first does to a captured slave, he yelled but not excessively, to my mind, for what he was suffering. Perhaps he had matured; or perhaps he thought it was all a story he was in. But when he understood where we were taking him after that, he almost bolted out of our hands, and screamed without shame like a baby. We had to drag him, thrashing and scrabbling at the inlaid floor, then the tiles, all the way.

Alchaen, I thought, as I looked down at my hands with the seals on them, trembling so the chains joining ring and bracelet on each seal danced even as I kept my mind calm, you were right, that I am not entirely healed. I will find you, wherever you are, whatever state you are in. But you are not here now.

I had my people get blood, "I don't care how," I said. To muddy red; let him have not even the clarity of water. By the way my stomach clenched when we came in, I guessed I'd been in the Imperial bath more than the once I remembered. Had he had me flung in to see if, soul-broken, I'd sink?

The work was done well; with half the torches doused, as I'd also ordered, one could imagine it was pure blood on which the flames and gold fixtures reflected, shimmering. I took off all but my jewelry, and dived in. Pure blood would feel hot like this, I thought. I stood in the center where it was about the right depth for the Kiss of the Lake, and called. "Kurkas and *Shefen-kas* forever, you say! Then come to me, true lover, come to me!"

What a person who holds to no gods, not even one in him, sees when he faces death, I do not know. He might have been braver facing a death other than this one, his most terrible fear. Or, I wondered, were you prescient too, and feared this because of today? Truly that would have been self-fulfilling foreknowledge. He begged, and screamed, and vomited, and voided, while I saw how many times I could drown him to senselessness—with my hand over his mouth and nose at the end, like the Ritual Monk—and revive him, before his heart gave out.

It was longer than I expected; under that fat was some strength, after all. All the better, for his mind gave out first, as mine had. The begging turned to babbling, the fighting to random convulsions; his eyes began to wander. In time, I got what I wanted; he learned to duck his own head, mindless, like a puppet, on my command, to move to my hand, mewling, to serve me willingly.

When the struggles of his spirit were long over, his body began to weaken too. When I knew he was nearly done, I unbound his wrists and ankles, and drew him close to me. "Kurkas and Chevenga forever, you wanted," I whispered to him, lifting his hands to my throat. "I will give you your chance, to take me with you." A light came into his half-dead eyes; he understood. His fingers clenched, harder than I'd thought they could; I tumbled over backwards, his weight bearing me down, and we sank, clasped together.

Sealed in black water I saw and heard nothing, only felt. He had me pinned, the tile hard under my back, his fingers feeling my neck for my life, finding the arteries, pressing until they screamed in rhythm; the wings of Shininao, and the silence between, filled my ears like quicksand. In his death-throes the grip turned into a death-grip; my senses began fading in and out.

But one of my first tastes of the world was the stream; later I went to it again, of my own will. I think in the end he knew, felt my steadiness while he thrashed, heard my soul laughing as his began to detach, and his fingers went limp.

I flung myself upward and gulped air; my people raised a savage cheer. His pale shape bobbed up, buoyant with fat, still twitching; so I trod him down again, pinning his head

ys that to you!" Kunarda made to chase him;
m by the collar saying, down, boy. The party
, close, to the room across the corridor, whose
window faced the city. I threw back the curtains,
iding pane, so the wind could blow in, hot and
d and full of screams and whoops and mad high

feet, Arko burned. Beneath running legs the paving
reets was black, but reflected the flames as Kurkas's
lected the wall-torches, though it was not raining.
s lay like boats aground, each contributing its tribu-
the river, made blood-sibs in death regardless of
or age.

t my people pull me back from the window, and slide
sed, at which they felt safer, and let me go. Candles
behind me, night dark outside, I saw my reflection,
blood-streaked, hands flashing with gold. What I see
ng into your eyes, Kallijas had said.... "Drink,
ng," Emao-e said. I toasted the other Chevenga, made
glass—at which they all laughed, thinking I was toasting
dying city—and threw it straight upwards again. Across
face of blood ate flames, in a shower of glass, crystal
attered, water-drops. *I am Imperium,* I thought, seeing
e seals on my hands. *I am Arko. The people wills.* I flew
t myself who flew back at me, while an anguished cry rose
from thirty voices as one.

In a story, crafted elegantly by some master author, I
would have died neat and clean then, my skull smashed on
the flagstones three floors below. As it was, when I was
through the window and the flow of time slowed, I found
myself, and the hovering swarm of glass chips frozen as in
ice around me, crashing through leaves and branches; a
wooden crack against my shield arm took my breath away.
I'd looked out, not down, and not seen the tree. Startlement
made my body do what it willed, not I: curl to roll out of
the fall, then, since my head was still going to hit first, get
my arms under it. I remember the crescendo of shards hit-
ting stone below, a rush of tinklings like a waterfall; then
came another snap and white flash of agony, and just as
suddenly I was lying still, in quiet, looking back up at the
window where a thicket of heads leaned out shrieking my

to the bottom by a foot on his neck, until I knew for certain
the blood-water had eaten his mind, and cut the cord of his
soul.

If Megan was right to worry, I thought, *It's done.*
Somewhere in this great rat's nest, I said to my people,
there are two Haians, a psyche-healer and a surgeon. Find
them. Free them.

"Victory!" I learned the word for it in all the languages I
hadn't known already. "Peace! We can sleep tomorrow! No
more child-raping marching!" Someone reported to me,
from Finpollendias. The Arkan line had broken easily, half
its spirit looking over its shoulder to its homes, lying under
winged torches, or to the Marble Palace.

"Get pissing drunk, lad," Emao-e said. "You deserve it.
I'll take care of things. Wine, here, now!" In the knot of
friends who kept close to me, I kept looking for Sach, hearing his voice. Then Mana, even as his ring clasped my arm.
We found the hundred-year-old stuff, worth several gold
chains a flask, and flung streams of it at each other; we
threw jade lamps through the windows, danced on the tables
till they broke, yelling each time, "We'll buy another!" The
last time I'd so embraced the pleasure of destroying, so
sweet for the things being precious, came back to me: Kurkas's sanctum.

I heard Chinisa's voice. "Demarch, where shall we set up
office?" I answered the truth, I haven't a clue; let's look
upstairs, on the Aestine Floor. Here, that's the third, I
explained, and the second is the Arkine; you have to be
careful, for in some wings the Aestine is the second floor,
not the third, and the Arkine the first, it all depends on
where you are. I smelled smoke, but someone assured me
the Palace wasn't burning, there were clear orders about
that.

I was sprawled over a couch when someone came running. "I was looting a very nice office when I found this,
Beloved." It was a letter, addressed to me, in the golden
ink.

"Well!" I said, breaking the seal, and staggering to my
feet for a proper rendering. "Let us see what deathless
words he left me!" But in the candlelight the gold swam on

the page, doubling, blurring; I was too drunk. It was in Enchian; I passed it to Chinisa, to read.

It was not deathless, more mildly insulting to bland; he went on and on with this and that tangent, around in circles. Then she read, "My revenge is complete, for if you have read this far ..." Her delicate old voice cut off, and the paper fell from her fingers. I reached down for it, suddenly sobered. She snatched it away, bellowing "*No!*"; I had not thought she could move so fast, or shout so loud. "For if you have read this far," she went on, her voice quivering, "you are dead; this letter was impermeated with a poison that works through the lungs." With movements almost formal, she took up a candle, went to the broken-open window, and holding both outside, burned the letter in such a way that no one would breathe the smoke from it.

I jumped up, barked, *Get Kaninjer!* People scrambled every way. Chinisa, precious, I said, sit here, near the window, half-lying, head back. I loosened her collar and cuffs, covered her in the spreads they brought, and took her hand in mine. Again I smelled smoke. Her hand went cold and she broke out in a sweat. "Burning, in my lungs ..." I watched each breath become harder than the last, and spoke to her as if I had no doubt Kaninjer would save her, we'd be at work tomorrow bright and early as usual. Still, no Kaninjer. I took her in my arms. A smothering death, I thought, just what he'd have wanted to give me. "Demarch." She shaped gasps into words. "Chevenga. Better me than you. I can be replaced. I'm old, lion cub, I've had a good life. Grieve for those who die young."

Yes, I thought, cradling her bony aged body, and feeling life ebb out of it sinew by sinew while Kaninjer did not come, I will grieve, for all who have died or suffered for being near me. First Naiga and Senala-e and my escort, next Mana, then Alchaen and Kaninden, today Sachara, the Elite, Sethara who stepped on a caltrop so I would not, maybe Krero—and now you, not even a warrior, choosing the risks clear-eyed, but my scrivener, just because I was too drunk to read, and take the death meant for me. My life is a blade, that cuts whoever comes up against it, or even close.

"Cheng," someone said gently. "We'll take care of her.

The people wills. Drink[...] gone, like a ghost. "Swee[...] "this is Saekrberk! I've fille[...] Saekrberk! Heh heh; Cheng[...] hand. "Hee hee! You know [...] back. I dare you!" "You'll kill m[...] alcohol poisoning!" "*Korukai*, C[...] ing. "Bottoms up, that's glass, we l[...] *Korukai!*" The Invincible turns do[...] ishes I did it, croaking *Korukai!*, and[...] upwards against the ceiling, to make[...] shards.

"*Chivinga!*" The room was inverted; I[...] on the couch, for a different view of the w[...] ing by feet stuck somehow to the floor, stoo[...] hands bloodied to the elbows extended befo[...] right, I said, you're too child-raping late, she[...] worry.

"Child-raping!" he cried. I'd never heard his [...] and choking; he was trembling from head to f[...] eyes looked as if they'd known only horror in[...] should speak of child-raping! I should have brou[...] should have brought the baby that fell at my fee[...] insides torn out! Chivinga! How can you let this g[...]

I swung my head up, making the room spin e[...] end. Emao-e had him by the shoulders, saying,[...] Haian, later. *Leave him alone.*" "No," I said. "From[...] on all speech shall be free in the Empire of Arko, so dec[...] the Imperator." It wasn't fear shaking him, I saw, but ang[...] I clasped his hands, though he shrank away a little, the[...] kissed them, drew my face through them so my cheeks and[...] brow were wet with blood, and leaned back laughing. All[...] the mainland laughs with me, I thought, though everyone[...] in the room stared at me as if I'd gone strange. Hypocrites, I thought.

He stood like stone for a moment; then spoke more certainly than I'd ever heard him. Good to see: my heart applauded. "You rabid beast. You barbarian. You fooled me, all through. I resign. I cannot work for one I despise." As eyes popped all around, he turned on his heel, and was gone.

name and my use-names, an idiot part of me wondering, "How did I get all the way down here?"

I should at least have faded unconscious while the messy threads of plot about me were neatly knit clean. Instead I stayed awake, unbelieving, cursing, weeping, yelling "Kill me!", as they came running, laid hands on my brow, argued over whether to move me, pinched my feet to see if my spine was broken. Some Haian I didn't know dosed me groggy with pain killer, set and casted my arms, and reassured them I would live.

XI

One knows the settings of one's recurring nightmares like real places, the scene of the death, or the bad back room in the house. One of my worst is a chamber, one wall black and sheer with the Aan family sunburst on it, the other three made of hanging golden chains, fine as jewelry or Arkan money, but with sword-sharp blades like cat's claws woven into the links, glistening in the candlelight like golden stars. The ceiling is a distant vague sparkle; the floor moves under me like something alive, or a skin full of liquid. I always thought it was my sleeping mind's symbol of Arko itself.

I never expected to wake in it. Now the shining chains wouldn't go away no matter how many times I blinked or shook my head; under me, through the bedclothes, the strange motion stirred, like a faint earth-tremor turning ground to mud. The only odd thing was a Haian, Akinaer, as he introduced himself, somehow drawn into my nightmare, poor soul.

My mother sat near; I was not on a floor, I saw, but in a bed. Kunarda stood grim-faced, just inside the chains; Emao-e wandered in, making an opening in them by pushing them aside with her dagger. "You're awake," she said, hands on hips. "Better shake out the spiders, lad, form up your head and start telling us what in shit to do. You're Imperator, remember?"

I saw the Imperial seals lying on the pillow beside my head, fastened to my crystal-thong. The Haian was holding the stem of his Haian-bottle, full of water, to my lips, guessing I was thirsty, which I was, desperately. I thanked him and turned away.

"Niku's wound's in the great blood vessel of the leg, so she can't be moved or excited, which is why she isn't here," Emao-e said, more gently. "Your spun-gold-and-mahogany child is with Niku's friend. The rest of your family here's all right. Krero pulled through. What's bothering you, lad? You keep looking around as if you expect a ghost to knock." I asked her where we were. "The Imperial bedchamber." I understood my nightmares; it seemed I'd been here before. "I can't believe this place, how fancy it is . . . shit, I'll say it, it's beautiful. All ours now, Cheng." She went on for a time about the fires being out, the rich quarter having got razed, the state of the treasury and so forth, then trailed off, seeing the Haian shake his head. "I'll make the full report when you're up to it. Don't worry about a thing, precious."

I said, "Thanks. I won't." An awkward silence fell; Akinaer leaned close with the bottle, and I turned away again. The silence deepened; they'd seen, this time. Emao-e drew herself up. "Let's get clear what everyone is afraid to say. At least then we'll all know where we stand, even if it's in shit up to our noses. Your sword-side ear's still got a standing invitation to Shininao, doesn't it, Fourth Chevenga?"

The past is an illusion of memory; in the history books, which friends who will praise me are left alive to write and enemies who would damn me are not, this chapter will get left out. Yet much as I'd like to, I cannot deny it.

I hadn't even thought of dying, just not wanting water: now I saw it was and should be so. I'd allowed the sack of Arko, and the world knew it. Now the war was over, and time for peace and reconciliation had come, I who had wielded the firebrand could hardly say, "Let's all forgive everything and join hands." The best thing I could do for peace was die, letting Arko purge its hate with me, and go

on with someone else. Put as a state matter: I was Imperator, and had killed my own people wantonly. Put as a military matter: my own looting decree, which I'd always
enforced with death, I had broken. It was the same answer,
every way.

They all started yelling at once. *"What?* What are you
talking about? You can't die now—we just *won!"* Shock
wore off after a time, turned to reasoning. "You mean to
leave us alone with this mess? Chevenga, none of the rest
of us even speak the cursed language; you're the only one
who has a clue about this place! Who else in the Garden
Orbicular can run it?" "This shit-pit deserved all it got and
worse. They didn't leave anything breathing or standing,
after all, in Shakora." *"We're* your people, *not* those straw-
haired child-rapers! Did we give you leave to leave us? What
about rebuilding Yeola-e, *your* country?" Intimations came,
mostly from Esora-e, of selfishness and cowardice. All
through Akinaer, a soft-voiced Haian, tried to say, "No, let
him be, this is the last thing he needs, let him rest, let him
sleep, and it will pass."

That reminded me. "Has Alchaen been found?" Emao-e
answered; they'd searched the Palace from top to bottom,
and found neither him or Kaninden. "No one saw him?"

"Yes, yesterday." She changed the subject, too fast. I
asked what state he'd been in. She knew better than to lie.
"Cheng . . . don't ask. If he's in the City, we'll find him;
only then will we really know. Until then there's no point
worrying. I'm sure he can be healed, at home. You were."
Answer enough.

My mother had said nothing. Now she brushed back my
hair from my face, and whispered, "My poor child. Such
strength you have, steel and water; but so many arrows have
come your way that would pierce even the strongest armor.
There's pain in you I cannot touch. Perhaps no one can,
and this time is your time. Either way, you'll have rest."
Her tenderness undid me; I wept like a child. But I didn't
change my mind as they'd hoped, seeing no reason in my
tears. "Karani," Esora-e said then, "be too accepting of his
intent, and you'll help kill him." She froze, stunned; I called
him what I thought, for that. They pulled him out of the

room, before it could go further. That night as I slept they tried to wet my lips, but apparently I turned away, even in the deepest sleep.

The pain of my arms was less the next day, the thirst worse. "Whatever these others have said," I told Akinaer, "you are free to go where you'd be more use, which is almost anywhere in this city. They can't force you to heal one who is not consenting." I felt sorry for him. He admitted he was no psyche-healer, and left shortly after. Emao-e was furious, but there wasn't much she could say. Fearing I'd find some way to harm myself, they bound me to the bed with linen, loose enough that I could shift only a little. The bed, which was indeed a skin of some sort full of water, was bigger than the floor of most rooms; I felt like an island in a sea, sinking, and out of place, black and Yeoli, tanned and sweaty, in cream quilted satin threaded silver and gold.

They tried reason some more, yelling and waving their hands reasonably, until I rasped "Chinisa—or whoever my scrivener is now, dictation. Write out my whole cursed argument and when these idiots start again as if they've never heard it, nail it to their faces!" And I turned away and would not speak or listen to anyone.

They spoke of force-feeding me, of linking my veins to water, as any well-equipped Haian could do, of drugging me. "I will drink, and eat, and let my arms heal," I would say, "then run a sword through my heart. Do you plan to keep me drugged or bound all my life? Have you ever seen me not do something I set out to do?" I had no care, what I saw in their faces.

Esora-e made it a point to sit by my side with a huge glass mug of water and either swill it gulping, or sip it with savoring noises, or spill some, ice-cold and wet as I could feel down to my bones, on my face, apologizing profusely of course. Others argued that this sort of thing would only drive the blade of my trouble, whatever it was, in deeper, that only gentleness would heal me.

Mid-afternoon I dozed. After a time in which I knew I must have been asleep, for I'd been lying in the stream on Hetharin drinking for beads without my thirst quenching, I felt a hand I knew on my brow.

He looked as if he hadn't slept since the night before the sack, as no doubt he hadn't, haggard-faced, red-eyed, his long black hair in lank tendrils. "Kan," I said. "How are you? Tired, I know, from working. You should rest."

With his deft brown hands he folded back the covers to check me; I took the breaths he always asked as he listened to my chest, by sheer habit. My arms being in casts, he had to take the several pulses Haians feel for, indicating this and that organ, on my ankles. "More hale than you," he said. It's a good change in him, I thought; he was never blunt enough before.

"What are you doing here?" I said. "You can't work for one you despise." I felt his fingers clench. I'd meant no reproach, only a plain question, but he did not look up at first, his eyes hidden behind his hanging hair.

"I did wrong," he said, quietly. By weapon-sense I could tell several people outside were poised to listen, hoping he'd influence me. Beyond the gold chains are thick velvet curtains: I got him to draw them.

"I cannot know what you have lived," he said, "so I have no right to judge you. So I was wrong to leave you, I am sorry, I beg forgiveness. I will be your healer again, if you'll take me." Words long rehearsed, I could tell. In his honest way he looked at me to say them, but afterwards hid his face again; I saw the ends of his hair quiver, so that I yearned to clasp his hands between mine, as usual, and say "Don't be afraid."

"Kan," I said. "There's nothing to forgive. But I forgive you, if you need that, of course." He looked up, and I saw the spark, of the candle flame, reflecting from a tear.

I asked him how he'd come to this. "In the city," he said, "there is a great building someone said was being used for an infirmary, so I went there. When all the injured who came in had been dealt with, this morning before dawn, I slept for a little; then I spoke with the man who was running things, an Arkan healer. He asked after you as if he knew you, and was one of those who one finds oneself opening one's heart to; so I ended up telling him I had been your healer, and why I was no longer. He introduced me to a young Arkan man, the boy you sometimes cry out for at night. He looked angry when he heard what I'd done, and showed me . . . I hadn't even looked at the place, too busy with patients. I didn't know it was the . . . bloodsport palace."

"Skorsas Trinisas?" I said. "And the man, was his name Iska? Iskanzas Muras?" He signed chalk.

The Mezem had been spared, I think, by chance; Arkans had brought their injured to it for shelter, perhaps seeking a familiar place. "Skorsas had messages for you," Kaninjer said. "He still loves you, he says. He has all your things. And the fortune's safe. He said you'd know what that meant." I thanked him and said, "If you see him again, tell him I still love him too, and it's all his." He just nodded, and went on.

Skorsas had taken him on the grand tour, it seemed, with full accounts of what had happened to me in each place. Now Kaninjer listed them off, his voice dropping to a whisper, and asked me if all were true. I answered yes.

"Why did you never tell me these things?" he said, after a silence. "I was your healer." His whisper broke. "You never let me truly understand you. How could I, not knowing this? How could I properly heal you?"

"It was in the past," I said. "It wasn't important any more. You would have wanted to speak at length; when was there time?" No more time, I thought, than to clasp hands over the gulf between Haiu Menshir and the mainland, you and I. He just shook his head, then wrapped my head in his arms.

After a time he asked me again if I would take him back. "I have no need," I said. He laid his hand on my brow again. "I will stay with you anyway, until you die, if you don't change your mind." To that I agreed. Though I would not let anyone touch me with anything wet, he thought of other things, I found out, such as the braziers with steam-pots to moisten the air. My tongue swelled, and he got a smooth marble stone (with a chain, in case I tried to choke on it) for me to keep in my mouth, which eased the thirst; every now and then he would cool it for me, keeping the ice-water out of my sight. Of course he got a scolding from Esora-e for making my death too comfortable.

o   o   o

When next I remember, I'd been moved to another room, with an ordinary bed. As things were being set up, I saw a tall shadow at the door, moving slowly. Wearing an Arkan silken robe with brilliant embroidered flowers and flames, his Vae Arahini half-poncho over it and a breath-mask attached to a flask under his arm, Krero came in, leaning on the arm of one of his squires.

"You shouldn't be up," I said; it was plain from his face. *"What!"* he hissed, with just a scrape of gravelly voice. "You're telling me I shouldn't be up, and you're cursed killing yourself? Eat shit, Fourth Chevenga!" He started wheezing; his squire made him lean back, lifted the mask slightly and misted some soothing spray into his nostrils. "All-spirit, look at us," he whispered, when he could, the ravaging of his voice giving it a sound of desperation. "When I think of ten years ago, when the rest of us all wanted wristlets to match yours . . . I thought we'd all be married with two or three brats each by now, hanging around the School of the Sword and Assembly Palace influencing you all day and drinking you under the table all night . . . Mana, Sach, soon you, and my lungs half burned-out, what a child-raping boneyard." He wouldn't get on the litter, but let them take him on a chair. "Farewell, Fourth Chevenga, suicide. I never want to see you again if you don't change your mind. I love you. May your soul rot." He didn't look back.

Alchaen's face leaned over me, alive, moving, with heart and mind still behind it. I thought I was dreaming, but he was truly there; it was him who'd had me moved, knowing my nightmares. Now he told me his story.

Kurkas had ordered exactly what I had feared: that my healers be administered what they had healed me of. By the same person, First Amitzas Mahid; but he could not bring himself to do it, to Haians. He'd faked giving Kaninden the *grium* with some other substance, but not told her; Alchaen, though, had had to be in on the deception, which at first he'd thought a ploy, to torture him with hope. Luckily Kurkas had taken almost no interest in it himself; the one time he'd inspected, at month-end, Amitzas drugged Alchaen for the proper effect.

That had been months ago; thrown into the dungeon after, Alchaen had had to keep up his act as catatonic, with all that entailed. Now and then Amitzas would come down and speak to him alone, bringing books; they'd become friends. Alchaen being Alchaen, the Pharmacist had eventually let out his heart, torn for having broken his Mahid trust, in being merciful for a moment with me—neither of us had forgotten, then—and now with the Haians.

On the night of the sack, he'd come to the dungeon to free them, in case the Palace burned, before going to die with the rest of his kin. They had dragged him out with them to hide in the woods, and persuaded him to submit himself to the judgment of the new Imperator instead.

That, I recalled, was me. No wonder Alchaen proposed it, I thought, and no wonder Amitzas agreed; he'd expect the worst. "I'll put it in writing," I said. "Chin—scrivener." I absolved Amitzas for all he had done against Kurkas's will, then for all he had done by Kurkas's will, rewarded him for saving Alchaen and Kaninden with rights to a chamber in the Marble Palace, double-guarded. Signing took as long as dictating; my covers had to be turned back, my hand positioned, the pen put into it, then when that was done five seal-marks made: bracelet and ring of each Imperial seal and demarchic signet. I fell asleep before it was finished. I'd lost track of time. This room had no windows, only flamelight; my dreams, of parched lakes, of fire in my mouth, of being fried on a skillet the size of a sea, never let me know how long I'd slept.

I woke from a dream in which I saw a slug melted to water with salt, and wanted to drink it, to find Vriah sitting by my head.

Her tiny brown face was creased with concern as no child's that young ever should be; whoever brought her, I thought, I'll have skinned alive. But she said she'd come, " 'Self!" She was two or three moons shy of two then; how she'd got all the way from the audience chamber downstairs, our infirmary, where Niku was, past all the guards I presumed were in the halls, I could not fathom; she had, though.

"Make the wall, Vriah-riah," I said, our words for whatever an empath throws up against others' feelings; Niku was teaching her to use it at will. I wanted her to have none of what I felt, now; nor ever again. She stuck her tiny fist in the crystal ewer of water on the night table, and tried to stick it in my mouth. "Aba *thirsty!*" I turned my head away, said I was all right, I needed nothing. "*Bad!*" she snapped, frowning. "*Bull'yit-t!*" She wrapped her tiny arms around my neck, hard. "Aba, don' die!"

A blade of purer pain running through my heart, I have never felt in my life. I could not tell myself she was just imitating the word; she'd been reared in a war camp. I wept like a child, and so did she, who could be excused, being one. I could not make the wall.

Kaninjer came in, having heard, and snatched her up from me, which made her scream as if he were torturing her. He put her back on my shoulder, at which she pressed her face into my neck and quieted. Hurai was acting guard captain now; he rushed in, and managed to get out of her that she'd got in through a cat door.

That, his duty, done, he straightened, folding his big arms, and fixed his eyes on mine. I knew what he was asking; I whispered, "Charcoal." Even rethinking it all, I still saw the same. His eyes flicked to the child, who was half-asleep now. "I never would have believed," he said, "that you had such evil in you. Chevenga ..." His eyes suddenly filled with tears, as I had never seen before. "All-spirit, what can I say? If *this* doesn't move you, what can *I* possibly say that will?"

I was crossing a desert, though I'd never been in one. I swam through sand that moved like water, golden waves, dunes with smaller ripples all over, heaving past me silently under a burning white sun, while wind blew sprays of scalding grains into my eyes. I chewed and swallowed sand, crunching between my teeth, digging like thorns between my sucking-stone and my tongue, its dryness eating. The island ahead, where there was a well, receded, or turned out to exist only in my dying-visions.

I woke, and knew they were covering this all up. Why else would the command be taking shifts here? I heard whispers. "Three days ... The steel in him ... far gone ...

accept he won't ..." I said as best I could, "Call in the command, the foreigners too, and my family."

Eager, hoping I'd changed my mind, they propped me to sitting on pillows and put my half-poncho on me as I asked, and crowded in around, as they must to fit all. "The war's over," I said. "It occurs to me, I've never spoken my pride, or my gratitude." As the First General First should, I went all around the room, person by person, remembering the best deeds each had done, giving the praises due. Soon enough I got them laughing, which they all looked in need of, with remembrances, and at the same time, in tears, for the dead.

When that was done I left a pause, and said, "War is over. With one time ends another. You love me, and I love you, but it is war's love, as I am war's creature. Peace, I leave to you. I called you in to say farewell."

The room froze; some took in a sharp hissing breath, as if feeling a blade go in. The foreigners stared, puzzled; sure enough, they'd known nothing; there were quick whispers, and their puzzlement deepened.

Then a scream like a death-scream split the air. Kunarda; he flung himself backwards, flat, tearing out two long dark strands of his hair; others had to catch him. He'd accepted that I would die. Someone gestured, and he was pulled outside; I heard his keening fade.

"Farewell," I said. On tear-streaked faces, I saw the word, pressing to come out, hiding again, wavering.

Esora-e's voice cut the air, like a sword. "Let me say why I will never say farewell to this one, not this way. If I did, I would have had a hand in killing him." He turned to stride out.

"And you wished me," I cried, "to call you father!"

How he got back so fast, I don't know; everyone melted out of his way, I think, seeing his eyes. He yanked me up by the sidelocks. "Is *this* the son he made? Is *this* the son he gave Yeola-e? Who would do this to all of us who loved him and raised him and died for him like so much flea-shit? I don't believe it! *You* are more than an ingrate, *you* are a stranger, an aberration, I don't know what you are—but *he* would have cast you out!"

"Or killed me, Esora-e?" I said. "So, it took a little more

time." He wrenched an arm free from those trying to pull
him away, and struck me the blow of shame, with his wristlet. When the stars cleared, I found blood on my lip, spat
it away. "So you'll do it, Esora-e." His shrieking sobs flung
me back seventeen years, to my father's death; I hadn't
heard him cry that way, since then. There was more confusion; I remember Alchaen with his hands on my shoulders
saying, "Calm," though I hadn't thought I was excited; and
Krero rasping, "What do we do? Mana was the best to talk
to him, Sachara second best, and they're both dead!"

Then someone ran in yelling, "Cheng! That straight-
haired shitbrain got all the Palace servants mourning, and
now it's all over the army that you're dead!"

"It will be true, soon enough," I said; but Emao-e and
Renaina cursed as one, and started yelling orders. "Everyone who has legs go out and announce he's alive! Sound
the gong, 'stay arms'!—no, sound it for Assembly, sound it
for *both*, announce Assembly, in the Palace square! Find
that idiot Kunarda, bring him to me! Litter, here!" Her
steely eyes fixed on me. "You're always out of it when this
happens, and no one tells you after. You don't know what
your army does when it thinks you're dead."

I learned then. As they carried me through the corridors
I smelled smoke long before we got to the balcony over the
square, from which Imperators make their speeches. Through
windows as I passed I saw the blue sky stained black, heard
cries that seemed strange in daylight, since I knew them as
things of the night. The gong-beat, the announcements, the
orders, were all too little too late. As they held me standing
against the rail, to show those who happened to look up
from what they were doing that I still lived, I saw Arko
sacked again.

"Drink, damn you!" It was Hurai, holding a skin in my
face. "They'll stop now; would you have them do it the *third*
time?" But all I saw, written even thicker and clearer on
the skyline of the city now, was my death sentence. This
only compounded my wrong, compounded it ten times,
thrust Shininao's beak deeper into my head. I turned my
face away. "Speak to them at least! Tell them they have no
cause!" I answered, "I would not lie." So when the army
was finally assembled, as the sun was sinking, I heard her

say I was deranged with fever, and so could not speak, but would hear, if they hailed. She had me dragged forward again, and I heard the chant of my name rise deafening, from their ten thousands of throats.

"Chevenga, just say *gihit*. Say the word *gihit*." Arkan, for "rise"; I blinked my eyes open. Something pricked my ankle. "There's an Arkan here; he flung himself flat on the ground and swears he won't get up until you and you alone say that."

I did, and saw Skorsas's bright head come up over the edge of the bed, and his face, lit with joy. He was taller now; when I grinned back, he ran to me, and flung his arms, now thicker than a youth's, let alone a boy's, around my neck. His hair was unlawfully long, made *Aitzas*-length with false extensions, and he was dressed sumptuously; it seemed things had got too dangerous for Karas Raikas's boy, so he'd left town and come back disguised as a young lordling, no surprise. "I know," he whispered, bringing his lips to my ear as he covered my face with kisses. "After-fight grief, I know, jewel of the world. You must have a very bad case of it. It's all right, we'll get you through."

I didn't have the strength to spit out the stone, so I could not speak, to ask him what he had lost, in the sack. I looked to my feet. The pain was a water-needle; Kaninjer was just hanging up the bottle on the pole. "We decided against it, except as a last measure," he said gently over my railings, easy since I was good as gagged, and no one helped me. "The time for last measures has come." Though Skorsas tried to soothe me, I fought so hard Kaninjer gave me a sedative too, by the same tube.

"*Ai*. Cheng. Wake up, come on out of that desert." A hand shook me. Not believing I'd heard that voice or felt that touch, I opened my eyes. He was there: Mana.

"You can't be," I said. "Unless I'm dreaming."

"I'm half-here, and you're half-dreaming, which is why we can touch." He nudged my shoulder with his fist, and grinned, that grin that was Hayel to remember, Celestialis to see. He was wearing the arm-ring, as in life. "One of the good sides of being dead is knowing what will come. I know you don't like foreknowledge, heart's brother, but you'd better listen anyway."

I asked, "Did I do the right thing by you? To swear my oath, and keep it?"

He made the brush-off sign. "Stroke of the past. Shut up for once in your life and listen.

"You're dead. Who takes over?" I answered, my sister Artira. "Yes. As demarch, which she can do well enough—*and* Imperator. Tell me, what does she know about Arko?" I answered the truth; it might as well be nothing. "And this isn't Arko as it was, but conquered Arko, Arko in a shambles. Hungry armies on the borders, underground kings wanting independence, maybe some *Aitzas* general in Kurkania or Marsae or somewhere deciding to declare himself Imperator, slaves rebelling, whatever. You think she has any kind of a feel for all that?"

I was stuck for an answer; he went on. "Now. Remember the saying, about what happens to a Yeoli coming into money? What do you think the kind full of hidden greed is at right now, while no one's giving them anything better to do?" I stared, knowing even before he said it. "There's lots more to grab up, than just gold goblets and paintings. *Who kills becomes*, remember? He chops up an Arkan lord, and the butler presents him with the papers for the house, the estate in Kassabria, the slaves, the ships, the Arkanherb business. . . . Imagine Inatalla Shae-Krisa or Rao Irae getting their hands on all that." My stomach turned. "Never mind that they *could*, Cheng—they already *have*.

"So. Will they do what every sensible Yeoli wants to, go home? And give it all up? Shit, no! They'll stay—and set themselves up as the new Arkan lords, the Yeoli *Aitzas* caste, higher than the Arkan *Aitzas*. You're dead, cockerel, so Ardi comes into this all wet behind the ears. Who does she trust, with you gone? Yeolis, that's who. The ones who are here to talk to her! No Arkans are going to make a peep, not to an Imperator, Yeoli or Arkan, who doesn't urge them to; and only you would. And what do you think Inatalla and friends will tell her, Cheng? To be a good people-loving demarch, the Hand of Arko instead of Yeola-e, hear them always, teach them to vote? You think so? Or will they say Arkans can only understand and respect an Imperator who's an *Imperator,* by the Ten Gods, that they must prostrate themselves to as usual? Or answer me this one: do you really think Ardi's not going to run into trouble here, that will play into their hands—because of what Arkans think of women?"

I lay silent, blinking. He patted my shoulder, and said, "I'll leave you with just that, Cheng. Enough to think about for now." Then he wrapped his arms around my neck, kissed my cheeks, and faded away.

"Tell me," Alchaen said, "why you are doing this." He cut me off as I started my argument. "No, no, not that. Tell me what was in your mind when you leapt out the window. Trace it back, follow the threads."

In truth, this conversation I had with Alchaen didn't come all at one time, but in fits and starts. So he tells me and I must believe; perhaps the logic of it makes me remember it as one.

"You thought, *I am Imperium,* saw your own reflection and the burning city as one, the seals, glass, mirrors, water . . . The sense you made of it was to kill yourself. How did that fit? What was the thread you picked up?"

Every answer, I found, had a counter-answer. It had not been to escape punishment, for it was punishment; it had not been what I argued now, for that hadn't come into my head yet; if it was remorse, why had I permitted the sack in the first place? Instinct, I said. "But you always hear wind, and the song of the harmonic singer, when you do that," he said. "Did you then?" I had to say no. In the end all I could say was, "I don't know, Alchaen." Yet it was the true answer, for it had the ring of truth I knew from doing this before on Haiu Menshir.

"I don't know," I added, but there are reasons, there must be. I still feel them. Do *you* have any idea what they are?"

"Oh, yes," he said, "a very good idea. We'll get to it. Tell me, what passed through your mind when you decided to sack the city?"

I tried to remember. That meant putting my finger on when I had decided, and it kept slipping out from under. He kindly extricated me, as he often did. "We should remember how it went. You had a general forbiddance on sacking, but you must have known it would not hold in Arko. You took no measure to prevent the sack. Yet you took no measure to order or encourage it, either. Tell me, did you ever make the decision at all?"

A clanging started up in my head, like a signal-gong. "No. All-spirit help me, Alchaen, I never did." Like secret doors opening on great caverns, memories came echoing, their echoes rising to a thunder: being unable to see myself close enough to Kurkas to kill him, Arzaktaj's words, "It is not natural, to have no thought at all of what you mean to do to him," the feeling of bonds, while I flew free over Arko with my army below.

I slowed my breathing, seized myself. "I didn't, but I did. Even in not choosing, is choosing. I can hardly say, 'The First General First sat on the fence, so none of it's his fault.' I'm absolved of nothing."

"I never said you were. Or meant you should be. We've never spoken of what passed with Kurkas. Will you tell me that?" I did, and felt more fall into place. I'd never faced him in my mind, never looked straight and clear at what was in myself. "I think we have something here, don't we, Chivinga?" he said, smiling in his way.

"Yes," I wept. "I understand. I did all through. I'm still mad, I fought the whole war mad, Saint Mother cast me out!"

His hand pressed my brow. "Remember the rules. No curses on yourself. Enough come from elsewhere. To say you're still mad is too simple. You aren't; ninety-nine times of one hundred you know what you are doing, and why: better than most. That one was the weak point, the thing you hadn't finished settling within: remember how you said back to me, when I asked you on the gangplank whether you meant to sack Arko, 'To some questions there is no answer?' But to all other questions, you have them. Tell me, what do the mad fear most, in their sane side?"

"Their madness," I answered, as I had learned.

"Especially those who have great concern about the effects of their actions, as you do. But do they ever say, 'I am afraid of my madness,' right after? Not usually, for it seems something much greater than that. They say . . . what do they say?"

I gritted, " 'I am afraid of *myself.*' "

"And they seek to leave responsibility to the sane. I told you, I had good ideas why you are trying to kill yourself. You think you've proven yourself unfit forever; you want to purge the curse of Fourth Chivinga from the Earthsphere. Yes?" My eyes burning as if full of hot sand, I nodded. "But see it clear. The trouble isn't *you*; it's only the remnants of your madness, that Kurkas gave you. Do you think it can't heal?"

In his arms, I felt small as a child, like a thousand times on Haiu Menshir; I could almost smell the sea. When I was spent with crying, he smoothed the covers in around me, and said, "Think on all this, sleep on it. You have more time now, vein-linked to water. I will stay with you. Sleep."

What I knew in my mind and what I felt in my heart stood on top of and through each other, quivering, vying for my attention, like a reflection of sky shimmering over the stream's pebbled bottom. Then I am only mad, I thought, not evil, not lost; then: but a mad Imperator should be a dead one. If Kurkas didn't prove that to me, I proved it to myself. Not once but twice, has Arko been sacked by my doing. Not two but one, should anyone, especially a demarch, be.

His words came back. "Forgive yourself, for what Kurkas put in you." But he doesn't understand one thing, I thought; I'm a demarch. It is not for me to forgive myself; only my people. How can he think Arko would?

A hand seized my hair, and jerked my head around to face another face, with blue eyes flashing. I saw his anger, a spark and crackle of purple-white lightning through golden hair, all around his head. Agent of Shininao, I thought. He tore the stone out of my mouth.

Always, he was one who acted; words came hard. "I thought so much of you. Your honor, your word."

I grinned into his narrowed eyes. "Kallijas." No one else was in the room, I knew, by weapon-sense. They were desperate for anyone who might persuade me at this point, so he'd been able to demand to see me alone. "I still have the tenderest affection for you," I said. "As I do for all those I can play so easily for fools." His face and his hand on me tightened, and a scraping sound came from his throat. "Kall, love. What did you expect from me, a simpering apology? Begging for forgiveness? You knew when we last parted, you should have killed me."

"You said . . . !" The words hissed between his teeth, twisted and awful; I saw a vein grow in his temple. "I believed you!"

"I lied," I said. "Don't get me wrong, though; I love you, I always will. I change my mind; I want you to serve me; I know how good you'd be."

His hands flew at my throat, froze. "You heathen whoreson." He shook away tears. "I'd kill you right now, and not care what your stinking minions did to me afterwards, except I swore an oath—I signed up for your guard! My honor's on it! You know you can always get me that way, you bastard!"

"I absolve you of it." For a moment he crouched pricking all over, disbelieving; then his tear-filled eyes brightened, full of my death, and his hands locked crushing around my throat. I closed my eyes and lay still, while my heart rose to hammer-banging and the veins in my head gave their dying whimpers, in rhythm. My lungs started their struggle, so familiar.

But I erred, doing what I was inclined. If I had struggled in his hands, begged, tried to call guards as if I valued my life, he'd have done what I wished, what I'd tried to play him into doing. Instead he saw. Breath and light came shrieking back, my skull seeming to split with blood rushing in. "What are you? Which are you? How can anyone understand you?" Kallijas's face came clear, sparkling as if his skin and hair were lake-ripples in sun, no longer with anger but with the brightness of his soul. In his expression was only confusion. "Are you playing me for a fool again? Answer me: if you are such a monster, why do you want so badly to die?"

My tongue would not move, and I felt the moment for the answer that would convince him pass, and fade into distance like a falling stone, lost forever. I could only look into his eyes, and feel the hardness of malice I'd called up strip away; watch him unclasp the breastplate and find the bleeding underneath.

"*Sheng.*" He leaned close, took my head in his arms, pressed his lips to my brow, while I wept, with my failure. "Celestialis, Sheng."

"Who and what did you lose?" I whispered between sobs. "I would say I am sorry, but that doesn't begin to be enough. I should know: tell me."

"My parents and the house are well. My brother got wounded on Finpollendias, but he'll live. My betrothed and her parents our Steel-Armed God saw fit to take, Celestialis receive them." Keeping one arm around me, he lifted the crystal ewer, poured a cup. "My love, who forgives Arko so much he would punish himself with death, for doing what conquering Imperators have always done—after all we did to you, and your country. I love you, Shefen-kas, my Imperator. I forgive you." He took a long draught from the cup—I heard him swallow—then caught my head in his arms so I could not wrench loose, and kissed me. His mouth was still half-full of cool water, which, like a mother bird, he let trickle onto my tongue. I have tasted wines only an Imperator can afford, fare from the most lavish kitchen in the world; but nothing in my life ever tasted so good as this. With steel-strong hands he held my head still, until I swallowed.

Thus, I was cured. I could do nothing but weep, in relief, in exhaustion, in horror at what I'd done these past four days—it had been four days—and I could say nothing but, "More, All-spirit, please, more!" Holding the cup to my lips, he didn't want to leave me, so he called, making my guards run in with spears levelled, ready to kill him; then they were leaping and dancing, kissing his gloved hands, which made him flinch, and throwing him their shirts. He got enough to fill a wardrobe.

There it is, then, the hidden chapter, the worst thing I ever did in my life that was little known, coming so soon on the heels of the worst thing all the world knows. Perhaps I'm a fool to reveal it, expose my name to the mud, make people wonder what I truly was. But I'm writing under the Oath of the Scrivener. Excuse my squirming, and judge me as you will.

XII

The next day, they hung the Imperial robe over my shoulders, hiding my casts, and carried me to the balcony in a chair, ten husky Arkan servants appearing so fast out of nowhere that Krero almost sounded the alarm. The Palace staff, knowing the hiding places, had suffered few casualties; now they came creeping out in hundreds to serve us, seeing no hope of pay from anyone else.

I didn't have the strength to make my voice carry, so we used three heralds, Yeoli, Arkan and Enchian. The rail was draped; I leaned my hips into it, while crouching hidden, Krero braced my left leg with his shoulder and Kunarda my right, to keep me standing. Thus I first spoke, to Arko.

I had thought it out last night; a few more things came to mind as I spoke. My and Yeola-e's vengeance on Arko was finished, I said, and the world's as far as I could prevent; I was Arko's Imperator, and so considered it my duty to do best for all people of the Empire; Arko would rise again from the ashes less grand a nation perhaps, but more just. In the meantime, all Arkan laws were still in effect, those regarding life, limb and property to be strictly enforced.

The Arkans gave me fearful applause, the army, exuberant. Then my people carried me back to bed. I had them pile the pillows so I could sit, and began work.

I was the son who kills the father to inherit the house; victorious, he walks into the front door to find the furniture smashed, the well poisoned, the food eaten and the roof on fire. On top of that he's killed the carpenter, well-digger, farmer, water-carrier and everyone else who can tell him how to do anything.

What Emao-e had done in my absence concerned itself mostly with my army, not anyone else, except for the corpse-burying; for instance, she'd found those Arkans who had anything left and taken it for our wounded, who'd missed out on the looting.

Every *Aitzas* or official of any sort found had been clapped in the dungeon, to be given the choice, swear allegiance to me or be beheaded. A good hundred, many very highly placed, had died already. I put a stop to that, and spoke to those who had sworn and those who had yet to choose, together. The latter could help me rebuild the city, I said, or not; either way, I'd free them, unless they meant to foment trouble. I gave them a day to think on it, to wonder where else their learning would be useful, except where they honed it. Many more swore after that, lining up before me kneeling, to kiss me where Arkan men do to swear fealty to a superior. Why one of the Arkan signs of office is a robe with no belt, one can see. Once in camp near Vae Arahi Kallijas had told me the gesture of the oath had changed; in ancient times it had been pressing the face into the superior's hand, meaning "My breath, my life, is yours." I decided to change it back. But my arms were in casts; it couldn't be now. As well as those Arkan officials, I sent to Vae Arahi for high bureaucrats, pulling half the Assembly Palace staff.

Water was no trouble, coming from the river, but the conduits and sewers were damaged in many places; that would be first, in the rebuilding. Food was short, of course, few sellers willing to come into the city; ships that usually bring grain through Fispur were standing off for fear of being plundered. No one had much to buy food with anyway, except my army, traipsing about in satin and gold, and no one in the command had thought to stop feeding it out of our war chest. I did, and some, believe it or not, complained. My inclination was to spend the Arkan treasury bare feeding the city; but what was truly needed was the work and pay, the give and take, that makes for prosperity begun again. That needed order, and rebuilding.

Nothing could be done about the pall of sick-smelling smoke, which the wind held hanging in the pit. Everyone from poorest beggar to Imperator breathed it, swallowed it, wore it, washed hair and clothes a thousand times in vain, got sick with it, as one. In port taverns all over, it was said, you could tell someone had been in the City Itself the moment you got downwind.

I wrote proclamations: one for garrisons, ordering stand pat, except for those on Tuzgolu, Ro and Haiu Menshir, which I ordered to move everything to Fispur, and one for citizens, saying more or less the same as my speech. My heart almost stopped, with a thought. "The Press," I asked Emao-e, "was it damaged?"

"Damaged?" she spat. "Smashed to dust . . . well, it *should've* been, anyway, after the Pages that came out of it the other day. But we can't find the child-raping thing."

"The Pages came out?" I gasped. "*After* the sack?" She signed chalk; it had appeared the second night after. I sent someone at a run, not for the Enchian edition, but the Arkan. As I'd expected, while the former spoke tragically of the sack, the latter the writers had considered their last word, to be given like heroes. It recounted every atrocity imaginable, including a few false ones at my own hands, cursed me for a Hayel-demon whose claims of having been tortured were lies, and called all Arko to arms to overthrow us. Three days head start it had, on my proclamations.

"You must know where the thing is," said Emao-e, grinning. "Can we smash it now?" Instead, I had an invitation to tea sent to Intharas Terren, who was still high editor. They'd barricaded the doors; my messenger had to shout up to a high window.

Intharas came putting a brave face on, but I could see his hands shake from across the room. Like all Arkans, he did the prostration, flat on his face with his arms outstretched. I hadn't known the Imperator must say *"gihit"* before they'll even think of rising, until Skorsas taught me; the first time Kallijas, ever formal-minded, did it, I almost kicked him, having no way to haul him up.

I gave Intharas a good cup of Saekrberk. When blood came to his cheeks, I asked him what he wanted for Arko; it took another few swigs to get an opinion out of him, since Arkans aren't inclined to admit they even have opinions to Imperators. More war he didn't want to see, he said finally, so I asked him why the latest Pages read as it read. A misunderstanding, we ended up agreeing. He had not known, he could not know, that I did not mean either to leave Arko once I'd destroyed it, or destroy it even more thoroughly.

On matters of Pages policy, I first had to make it clear I meant not to smash the Press to bits. Then he began angling for my rules of censorship. I said, "Write the truth."

"But each person has his own truth, Imperator, Whose Wit is the Wisdom of the World," he said, as I should have known he would. "What is *Yours*?" (Of course he spoke to me in inferior-to-superior twice removed with all the flourishes due to an Imperator, so that I had some trouble understanding at first.)

"You've been in the Pages since you were an apprentice," I said. "You must know like the back of your hand what truth you couldn't write because it was not Kurkas's or his father's truth, but was still searingly true. Should I call it accuracy? Should I say, leave out nothing of concern to the people of Arko?"

Of course he wouldn't believe me. "If you write something I don't like, I'll warn you, not punish you," I said, and swore my oath on it. That wasn't enough. "Ask me a question," I said, finally. "Any question, except military secrets, and I'll answer true." He took another long draught. I'm writing this conversation shorter than it truly was; he'd drunk a lot by now, but, a true news-scribe at heart, he could hold it well, having lost neither clear speech nor his nose for the secret heart of matters. "How," he said, "did You break Your arms?"

To go back on my word would ruin everything. So I told him, how, and why. He was so stunned he didn't take a scratch of a note, and kept asking, "How can you tell me this?" Time ran short, so we turned back to policy; I'd give a half-bead every day to writers, I said, and have my ministers do the same. I thought it a little short, but he thanked

me as if it were a fortune in gold. Kurkas hadn't spoken to
writers at all for more than fifteen years, it seemed, and
then only when he felt like it; it took spy-work to even know
who his ministers were.

So the Press was unbarricaded, and my proclamations
made up and sent out. The military ones I sent by Arkan
messengers; they were less likely to be shot. It was for this
I cursed myself the most, for my wasted four days: an army
can do much in that time. Learning Arko's strength was
no sweet task either; Kurkas hadn't had one high military
commander, considering the position dangerous, since several Imperators had been overthrown in coups led by one
who held it. Instead there was a council of land, sea and
espionage commanders, all rivals. Only Adasanatetzas Itzan
of the army and Meras Timmen of the navy were still here,
and they admitted no one had ever trusted anyone else's
numbers. I didn't trust theirs; for one thing, Meras still
believed Milforas Tatthen's reports of having conquered
Hyerne.

Having no fear Hurai would overthrow me, I made him
First General First and handed him this mess. We released
the Enchian, Lakan and Hyerne armies, their obligation
done. Most of the mercenaries who'd joined too late for
regular pay had gone their way already; those we were paying wanted either release or more work. Most of the Yeolis
were clamoring to go home; the war was over. One secret
I kept strictly was how few my army now was.

I paid off my Brahvnikian loans, wrote to Astalaz, Kranaj,
Segiddis and the others to finish our agreements, giving over
the islands I'd promised. Had I been Kranaj, taking over
the disputed land in Nellas, I would have parleyed for peace
with the Nellans, who fight fiercely, and made a long treaty
to keep Anska with its ship base. But as a king whose nation
was once an empire will, he saw the amount of land the
Arkans had taken and did not want to relinquish it, guaran-
teeing himself a long and bitter enmity. "You fox," Misiali
would say when he embraced me farewell, "you knew he'd
do that." Perhaps.

It was a hard farewell with Reknarja, such good friends
we had become; I think he would have wept if he were not
an Enchian, for I almost did myself. "You pass, with hon-

ors," I said. "I wrote your father that. Don't make too many women mothers, stallion." He said, "I'll miss you, you slip of a boy."

I stayed up late, though Kaninjer kept saying, "Six *aer*, Chivinga," and finally snatched the papers off my lap. Outside in the main chamber I heard Irilai say, "We shouldn't bother him with this. No, not just now—ever." I called her in; it was my duty to be bothered with everything. She came with Krero, and the boy who looked like my twin. Though he was Yeoli—he could be nothing else—he began the prostration. "No lad, you're free now," Krero said. "That's not an Imperator, that's a demarch."

They told me what he had told them. His name was Kaminika Shae-Liren. Arkans had picked him out from the gathered prisoners of his village, near Tinga-e, and he'd been brought here, cut on his face to make the scar, and given six months training in serving the Imperator (so he phrased it), all the while forbidden to speak his own tongue, or know himself by any name but Shefen-kas. Irilai, seeing my face, cast Krero a glance as if to say, "I told you we shouldn't bother him with this."

Worse, he was only one of two; Karas and Raikas, the servants had nicknamed them. They'd worked in shifts. "The other one the late Imperator-rest-he-exalted-in-Celestialis gave to his Son-whose-whim-is-the-world's-command, and they went," Kaminika said, near tears; torn from their families, the two had become brothers in spirit. I had wondered why no one had seen sign of Minis, and some of the Mahid were unaccounted for.

I will find them, I thought, for no other reason than to free that child. Right then and there, with Kaminika as witness, I set Ikal on it. Then while I had his family searched for—praying they were alive—I introduced him to Alchaen. Worn and ailing from the dungeon, my psyche-healer wished and needed to go home, but was waiting until Haiu Menshir was free of Arkan marines. Practicing his craft was a balm; so he did, on Kaminika and me, two scarred former pleasure-boys of Kurkas, who could look at each other, and better understand our own fates.

Alchaen spoke of returning from Haiu Menshir after a time, to finish healing me. "Whatever you do," I said, "don't come back to the mainland just for my sake." He said, "You are Imperator. It's not only your sake, but the world's."

Niku was here now, healed enough to be carried; we had time only to snuggle together in the bed, I using my legs, she her arms, and say laughing how comely a pair of cripples we were, before sleep took me like a hammer-blow in the temple. So ended my first day as Imperator.

My term lasted two and a half years. A thousand times more I would think, "It's winning the war I get acclaim for . . . but that was *easy*."

The traditional Imperator's life beggars belief. Skorsas, who always does as he plans, had indeed quit the Mezem and apprenticed himself to a Haian, making him probably the richest apprentice healer in all Arko if not the world; now he slavered after the post of Most High Chamberlain, so I gave it to him. I hadn't thought he'd have to study out of several great tomes to learn the protocols surrounding the Imperator; good thing I taught him how to read. For instance, the ritual of getting me out of bed, to my foot-itching frustration, required forty servants, each bearing a title such as Scenter of the Footbath or Purveyor of the Lingerie Imperious, and taking a sacrosanct pride in having no other worldly function. The closer to touching the Imperator's person, the more exalted the post; Palace servants wanting to alleviate the boredom have been known to knife each other in the back to raise their standing.

My inclination was to dismiss ninety-five out of a hundred. "You can't do that!" Skorsas said, shocked. "It's blasphemy—besides, they'd starve." So, at an expense I didn't like to think about, I waited to be rid of them by attrition. They didn't like him, a mere *fessas* calling himself *Aitzas*, so he felt he must keep heavily reminding them whose words had kept them off the street. "Don't worry," he'd toss over my shoulder to them as I stamped out of some delicate rite a tenth done: "we'll fashion an Imperator out of this raw silk yet." No wonder Kurkas did no work, I thought; he didn't have time.

Once at dinner I happened to mention absently that the oyster, the round bit of flesh between the thigh and the spine of a chicken, was my favorite part. Next day at dinner

I got a whole plate of chicken-oysters, in a sauce delicious beyond description. I was raised in the Hearthstone and went on to the army; all my life I have eaten what was put in front of me without thought of anything else, having been taught complaining was for children, who know nothing of going hungry. Now I almost couldn't enjoy this, for wondering who those many people were, who must be eating oysterless chicken tonight. As well there was twice as much as I could possibly down, so I ended up desperately passing them off to anyone who would take them to keep them from going to waste. "How could you embarrass yourself like that, with those peasant affectations?" Skorsas said afterwards, with the horrified expression that was threatening to grave itself permanently onto his flawless face these days. "Born a king, and still I have to teach you how to be rich!"

He and I were in the bath together once—the small bath, I stayed away from the great—when he said ingenuously, "You know what they're selling? Your bathwater. I caught the servants tapping the drain, bottling it and selling it. Touched the person of the Imperator, you know . . . Of course I couldn't let them go on doing that." After a pause: "Not without taking a cut."

I laughed so hard that anyone who had come in would have thought my sanity had finally broken entirely. I elbowed a splash over the rim; "Whoops! There goes a copper chain's worth! All-spirit . . . how much would they pay for my crap?" He put on his calculating look, and I gave him a faceful of water. "We don't bottle it *all*, just *enough*," he yelled, through the sheets of water now flying. "We wouldn't want to flood the market." Yet it was the laughter of denial; I'd lie sleepless that night.

I must always be carried when I was on the ground floor of the Palace, or outside, for the Imperator's feet never touch the ground (though I know Kurkas cheated in this one). I wondered where I would train, until I thought of the flat roof. Yet I could walk naked out onto the street, if I wanted, and they'd prostrate themselves as usual, for nothing about the Imperator is less than sacred; if I took a mind to piss on every head, they would take it as Celestialis raining blessings on them. And not because I'd sacked the city, either: Minis had done such things.

You might wonder why I abided by these trappings of tyranny; certainly the words "conceit" and "power-mad" and "second Notyere" were bandied about, in Yeoli. Skorsas said Arkans would have no respect for me as Imperator if I didn't; but the true reason in my own mind was to give them what was familiar. In the chaos stability was needed; I wasn't so much worried Arkans would not respect me— they dreaded me—but that they would not recognize me, and know they had an Imperator at all. Bad enough that I was Yeoli, and dark-haired; best everything else show them what they knew. Once things were settled, I'd start changes.

So I began the traditional way, never seeing an Arkan bearing himself in any way but submissively, speaking in any tone but deferential. Skorsas was less formal, but had considered himself my servant from when we'd met; Kallijas still carried the subservience of defeat, albeit proudly. My parents and sibs went home; my friends were all still in posts to take orders from me, and, though they were contemptuous of Arkan nose-scraping, as they called it, they had their own ways of it. The likes of Inatalla, who made as my equals to make others bow to them, I did not let close. Soon I had none near who'd kick me if I slipped except Niku and Hurai.

Treat a person like a slave or god long enough, the saying goes, and in time he'll come to think he deserves it. I was doubly vulnerable, I saw, by my very training in being what my people willed; my teachers never knew I would end up in a place where my people would will me divine, and see my every act as the work of the Gods extant. On nights after days in which I'd felt my power working on my heart, I'd lie awake in fear, or wrestling it back and forth in my mind. Once I had a dream: fat and lazy Yeolis were being borne in carrying chairs by groaning Arkans, under a bronze statue tall as a tall building and fearsome with sword raised like the lightning bolt of a punishing god, of me. I woke sweating, and clung to Niku. Neither Kallijas nor Skorsas could understand why it frightened me.

I took measures, which I have left to become Imperial tradition if my successors see fit, if they are wise. I appointed Hurai to watch me, or keep his ear cocked for it; if I went beyond the pale, he would finger-jab me on the shoulder when next we were in private. Then I would go to another, whose name I keep secret on his asking, to undergo at his hands humility-training. Always I came out dashed down from an Imperator into a demarch, exhausted and refreshed both at once, with my spirit singing. I fulfill the Scrivener's Oath well enough, I think, to leave it at that.

This, all on top of my debility, which in truth was probably good for me. If memoirs are only justified when the author has lived as no one else has, as I've heard, I think I qualify: who else who can say he has been the most powerful person in the known world, and unable to eat, dress, bathe or use the midden unaided, both at the same time? Good advice for Imperators, demarchs, and all others who must perform such tasks of life: if you must break both your arms, do it one at a time.

Everyone took it as going without saying that the fights were abolished. Everyone with a mind, that is. The name on the audience list I didn't know, but the face in my office I did: the Director. He fawned and flattered and mewled, "Who can understand better than You, O Living Greatest Turned Greatest Patron, the excitement, the drama, the grandeur of the Mezem?" Who indeed. I refused his request. All but a handful of gladiators had left the moment they'd finished their part in the sack; those citizens who had chips would only come to seek refunds by night, fearing my minions would spy them.

I wrested free a half-bead, to go down, with Niku and Skorsas. It was by carrying-chair this time, with the necessary honor guard. But when I got up and walked, through the colonnade, it was as if the past two years and all their battles were all a dream, the Imperial seals only here by my playing Kurkas, and I would presently wake up on my tiny satin-sheeted pallet, between stone walls covered with tallies and prize ribbons, and hear Skorsas chirp, "What suit today, diamond of the Mezem? Breakfast is coming." In the Ring I went dizzy, and wanted to throw up, in a way I never had before, with the emotion that comes when the suffering is over and the heart can unshield itself. It was the same for

Niku. Skorsas just stood silent; this place had once been his path out of squalor. I could raze it, I reminded myself, tear stone from stone just as I wanted to then. For a while we sat in the Imperial box; that cured my trouble.

I didn't raze the Mezem; I had the lion trenches filled in, the gates torn down, and the Ring made into a stage. Now one goes there to see *Ilesias Imperator* or *The Deliverance of the Tinga-enil,* an athletic contest or a circus; the quarters are now dressing rooms for players, the scratching on the walls looked upon solemnly as reminder of a more barbaric age. The Mezem retains its decadent gaiety, its look of circus wrought in real gems; but the horror is gone out of it.

First things must be set in order; then we could think of changes. So I planned. It soon came clear, though, that setting things in order would take months, at least.

I had always thought the Arkan ethic of who kills becomes a curse; now, in dealing with what was left of Arko's *rejins,* it proved a blessing. Taking Arko by force made me rightful Imperator, by the reckoning of most.

Not all, though: during the four days I'd been idle, word had gone out on the sea that the general in Kurkania, Malaradas Kazien, had declared himself Imperator and was calling all loyal Arkan warriors to him in Marsae. The word was that Malaradas himself was a figurehead, past the age, and it was his young high aide, one Toras Meneken, *solas,* who truly ruled, and meant to do so in the Marble Palace as well.

We had a fleet in Anoseth, that Hurai had called in, but by all reports we could count on Malaradas's to be bigger; once there, he could march to Arko in four days. We had a fleet in Fispur, but they would have to sail all the way around the peninsula. We still had some twenty thousand mercenaries and another twenty thousand Yeolis in the city, but that would make the numbers about even, with half of ours war weary and wanting to go home; and what we needed was not a long drawn-out fight but a quick and complete victory, to discourage others.

Many of those surviving from the Arkan standing army had sworn allegiance to me and signed up again, seeing, like the servants, no other hope of following their profession. They were nineteen thousand, fully equipped, plenty to make good odds against Malaradas. But I'd made a promise at least to myself not to make Arkans fight Arkans.

That evening as we were making ready for bed I happened to mention it. By that time, I should explain, Niku and Skorsas both claimed bed-rights as my lovers, and Kallijas slept in one of the small adjoining rooms. Niku was not jealous, and had always known of Skorsas; Skorsas had known of Niku, and my preference for women; Kallijas had always known other claims came before his. The worst trouble came at first between the two Arkans, since I paid no less attention to Kallijas than to Skorsas; as well, each thought the other an upstart. Kall was quicker to defer, but never enough for Skorsas, who wished him gone entirely. When they spoke, each used the superior-to-inferior inflection, no matter how often I told them they were equals in my sight and heart. I suspect all that kept Skorsas from having Kallijas poisoned—an easy thing for the chamberlain—was my saying, when I first thought of it, how my heart would break, should he die.

Yet, considerate to me, who wept inwardly every time they fought, the three made their compromises. Niku slept on one side of me and Skorsas on the other, in the great Imperial bed, the place of my nightmares, being the only one large enough.

So it was, all three were there when I spoke of the trouble in Marsae. "Why not send Arkans?" said Skorsas. "An oath of allegiance is an oath of allegiance. You're thinking too much like a Yeoli, Celestialis's delight. We've had civil wars." Kallijas kissed my shoulder, and said, "I'd fight my own brother for you."

I saw the hint of the light of the path unconceived. "Why?" I said. "I'm a barbarian, I sacked Arko, I'm the enemy. There must be some compelling reason, Kall, such as can be explained, and shared."

He saw what I was getting at. "To them I am a traitor, Sheng. They wouldn't listen."

"Not to words," I said. "To deeds, perhaps. This Toras Meneken, is he much in a fight?" He shook his head; he'd heard nothing extraordinary. "Then you could take him,

Kall. Here's what we do: you go with the army. Before any fight, Renaina, the general we're going to send, calls parley; and loud, so all can hear, you give challenge. Not to Malaradas, in respect of his age, of course, but to Toras, the next highest young enough, who is *solas*. Then they've taken a deep wound, for if he accepts, he's dead—forgive me for pricing the unborn calf, Kall, but I know how you are in a duel—and if he refuses, he's shamed for a coward. Whatever you have done in the war, they all still know your name as a warrior, they cannot help but wonder why one so strict in honor would turn; and you will have the chance to say it, while the strength of his argument is weakened by his failure, either way."

He looked bewildered that I should have such faith in him, for some reason, but agreed to do it. Perhaps I should say here, he had reconciled with his family; they knew he'd stayed in Yeola-e and was now with me, that was all, and it was not spoken of in the house. I called in Hurai and Renaina. On hearing my scheme, they eyed Kallijas, and I knew their thought. As the saying goes, turned once will turn again; even truth-drug might not predict the leaning of his heart when Malaradas's army called him over, when old friends in it cried, "What is your honor? What is your loyalty? Prove it now!"

Near that office is a balcony, two floors above a courtyard; saying something about good air I brought them all there. I let them take the chairs, and sat myself on the rail, nearest Kall. Rocking back, I teetered too far, and overbalanced backwards, letting out a yell; my arms in casts, I could not save myself. One could barely see him move, it was so fast. When he'd seized my legs and knew I was safe, he went pale, and clasped me to him; then when he saw I'd done it purposely, the pallor turned to flush, and he said under his breath, "You whoreson." Hurai's alarm changed into laughter; Renaina remarked on my sanity. But my point was made.

His scarlet and gold scalloped armor had been put on display in the new-built School of the Sword; though we'd ordered it shipped here it would come too late. So he went wearing standard issue. On the Palace stairs before the assembled army, I bade him farewell, with my blessing for all the strength that could give him, and let him cut a curl from my hair to carry with him, though it caused a hundred gasps from the Demarchic Guard. "Your love is strength," he said. "Gods bless you, heal, listen to Kaninjer, don't over-work," he said. "I'll be back soon."

It was something I had never done before, see someone so close go off to war without me. That night I woke up shaking, imagining Toras had got in a lucky stroke and killed him. "Shh, world's treasure," Skorsas whispered, trying to draw my head onto his shoulder. But it made me pull sharply away and turn my back on him, so that I'd have to apologize later, to know what he must truly wish for Kallijas.

I'd given it into their hands; I must let them take it, and turn mine to what was here. There was plenty: trouble on the north border, whose garrisons had been half-stripped to aid against us, Mogh-iur declaring independence and raiding along the Arkan border, the Srians, having retaken Tebrias, swarming across the strait to the peninsula to wreak vengeance. The story that had gone out was not that the Empire had changed hands, but fallen. At least I had my Vae Arahi bureaucrats, now, so the administration could run again fully in hands I trusted, and a scrivener almost up to Chinisa's ability, Binchera Shae-Lindel.

In Yeola-e, where there was much to be done as well, I asked my sister to be my proxy, again. You can be sure I took arrows for that. A thousand times I heard, "Did we send you to conquer Arko to serve them, and forget us?" One would think from the whispers, I never went home in the time I was Imperator, when in truth I twice toured Yeola-e from one end to the other. But I can't deny they were only visits; I spent far more than half my time in Arko. I had good reason, which many of my own people were too plain up-country to see: the fall of this empire, as with every other through history, would touch off wars all over the Midworld, a good century of bloodshed, unless it were pre-vented. I saw no one else who could or would do it, and it could only be done from here. Some Yeolis couldn't care less if foreigners killed each other all off; I am not one.

To the northern border I wrote a proclamation for my warriors—strange to think of Arkans as my warriors—to show the enemy: the might of Arko will descend like flaming talons on all who dare to doubt it is not still great, or something overblown like that. All bluster, of course, while we fought Malaradas; but fear of Arko was well-enough ingrained up there for it to work for long enough.

Mogh-iur, in truth, was a matter of protocol; I should have liked the courtesy of having been informed. "You guessed right," I wrote to Truszan the Elder, "that I would not begrudge your people's independence. Did you fear it would show weakness, to inform me, as if you were asking the master's permission? Have I ever put on airs, or been less than a friend to you? You sent your son and your warriors; I led them to victory with few losses. How could you think I would do anything, had you written me, but congratulate you? Call off your raiders, and we may speak of embassies, and trade."

He sent an envoy with a letter saying the raiders were being reprimanded, and his son most of all; apparently the lad (which I suppose I shouldn't call him, since he is three years my elder) had been charged with dealing with me about this, and forgotten. I wasn't sure I should trust this, since it seemed so unlikely, but it didn't matter; the raids ceased, and we began diplomatic arrangements.

The Srians were not so easy, sacking their way happily along Sikil, while the retreating Arkan army begged me for help. I thought for beads what to write to the Srian rulers, who were as per custom a married couple, until the reason I could think of nothing good came to me: I was writing from the weaker position. They needed to be thrashed once before they'd listen. But my strength was in Anoseth.

It took a shorter time to think what to do than what I'd wasted on the letter I would not write. Srians are a desert people; what navy they'd had had been smashed by Arko. I ordered in thirty ships from all the near bases, Kreyen in particular, since I'd called them off Hyerne (Milforas I'd tried and beheaded by then). This was three eight-days or so after the sack, and aside from my arms I was strong; so, over Kaninjer's objections, I went myself. I properly announced my intent in advance, to come for peace negotiations, adding that as a wartime precaution I would bring a light sea-borne guard. I sailed into Tebrias on one ship, leaving the other twenty-nine at anchor outside.

I was met with all due pageantry, grass-fringed shields, lion-skin capes (everyone who is anyone in Sria wears one), leopards on chains, gold baubles shining on oiled blue-black skin. I had seen Srian warriors before, but never the nobles, who are even taller; I felt like a child, barely coming up to their shoulders. The city was still mostly ruins, mud-brick houses crumbled by fire; no one could say war had not hurt them.

The reigning pair are known as Mefweo ra Binte and Mefweo ra Masil, meaning High Sister and Brother. He wore the skin of a maned male lion, she the unmaned skin of a female. Claw-scars shone pale against the dark skin of her face and neck; her lion skin she'd got honestly. They looked in their mid-thirties or so, and gazed at me with a certain coldness.

When the formalities, the meal and musicians and dancers, were finished, we withdrew. So I was in their hands, with only a few guards and my arms in casts; but their city was in mine. Masil spoke only Srian, so I dealt mostly with Binte.

At the very start she cited the Yeoli custom of seizing land to compensate for war losses, and said they'd invaded Sikil for that, so retreat was out of the question. That doesn't explain the sacking, I answered, the burning of so many valuable things; when she said it was only land they wished, I asked why they were taking slaves. That led to one agreement; I would see all the Srian slaves in the Empire freed within five years in return for all the Arkan slaves in Sria; the first they wanted were those knowledgeable in irrigating desert land, for whom she gave me a list of names. Sria's only way of growing southward was to win land from the desert, a fight as tiring, if not as dangerous, as war, and using one weapon alone: water.

"But what we've taken of Sikil we fought and died for," Binte said, "and it is a matter of the Mefweo's personal honor. A Srian is in the bitterest disgrace who must retreat or order retreat." "If you would prefer for your honor's sake to fight it out, I will of course oblige you," I answered. "I've come prepared." They didn't look game for that. I reminded them why their opposition had dwindled enough to make invading Sikil possible in the first place; until I had struck into Arkan land they'd been fighting in the streets of Tebrias. That she could not deny. By their looks, and the Srian words they spoke together, I guessed trouble would come to them personally out of this. But that was not my affair.

Knowing she was defeated, Binte hinted that she and Masil would lose no face among her people if they agreed to retreat as the loser's payment in some personal wager or contest, like my game of *mrik* with Astalaz; she even hinted broadly she would not try as hard as she might on other days to win, though I doubted I should trust that. With my arms casted I had less rashness in me than usual, for this sort of thing; there was nothing to gain in it for me anyway, only for them, to whom I owed no favors.

They spoke with a certain resignation, from then on, having agreed in spirit. While we were making the terms of the peace treaty they said I should renew it with their successors to make sure. I saw what fate they faced. Not fatal, since Srians, like Yeolis, can impeach the Mefweo, and choose new by vote: but still, a great sacrifice, which they would make for peace.

I forced them, I cannot deny it. By duty I had no choice. Yet one could not even find in it a clear mistake of theirs, that they were paying for; only their people's imbecile pride and narrowness, that would ensure Sria was ruled by those most rigid and unreasonable. They had guessed that I, being Yeoli, would not notice or care what they did in Sikil, a reasonable guess; quite a few Yeolis had shared it. "I can't understand," Krero asked me later, "why you'd get so worked up over a war between black and straight-haired foreigners." I answered, "Call me an idiot. I care for the world."

So I'd won, but with a sour taste. Binte and Masil were indeed deposed, a year later, and went into exile in the desert under their born names, Ogi and Ada. By Srian custom they must do that or divorce, so as not to linger as a threat to the incumbents, and they loved each other. I sent them a gift, of what I will not say, since to Srians gifts are secret things, and have corresponded with them ever since.

Last I heard they had a child. The new Binte and Masil—
the name goes with the position—were as I had expected,
older and stiffer-necked, speaking contemptuously of their
predecessors as lacking in honor, weak, spoiled and so forth.
Of course it was not for me to speak my opinion, of either
pair.

In the Arkan garrison in Haiu Menshir it had been whispered that the sack was God's wrath for what they had done,
so they were happy to leave. Blood was shed over whether
to go to me or to Malaradas, though, the compromise in
the end being to split ships. At least the wounded had healers; Haians will begrudge no one.

Haiu Menshir is free, I sent my envoy to say, the province
or base of no other nation. I requested permission for the
Yeoli embassy to re-open, but not the Arkan. It was for
them to say, if they wanted such on their soil. The recon-
vened Council of Elders rescinded the call on Haians not
to practice in the Empire, the words I had been hoping for
the most, but spoke nothing of embassy. They were grateful,
but cautious of me. So I did all I needed to, an easy thing:
left them alone.

It was a year later before I could visit, while taking the
long tour of the Empire, visiting cities, inspecting garrisons.
I dreaded to find Haiu Menshir changed by the occupation,
but it was just the same; Haians, if anyone, know how to
heal. They welcomed me well, but with hearts torn two
ways, so that I got some people kissing my hands with tears
in their eyes, and some giving me cold looks as if they
wanted me far away. Everywhere I went, children with huge
dark eyes dogged me, touching the seals, asking me, "Why
do you mainlanders have wars?" and "Is it really true
you've—excuse me—*killed* a hundred thousand people?"

On the last day the new Speaking Elder, Mitaer, took me
into his office in the Hall, a room and desk I remembered
all too well, and said, "Fourth Chivinga, we were once
uncertain of your intentions. Now, seeing we may trust you,
we wish to show our gratitude as we should have already."

I began to say no matter, they owed me no gratitude,
when he held to me a bracelet in a jewel box, clearly
ancient, made of two joining leathern straps fastened to a
stone set in metal. I thought stone, at any rate; looking

closer I saw it was at least partly glass, with four characters in some unknown script. Then I saw the motion, a double mark appearing and vanishing. That made me understand how old it was. "Mitaer, I can't take this," I said. "It's a treasure of Haiu Menshir; it should stay here."

"It's a timepiece," he said. "How precisely the characters are read will probably be a mystery forever, but they change regularly, and follow the same pattern every day. It has sat idle here for centuries, a thing that should be with the moving, the active. Studying it we have found it only works when someone carries or wears it; not even the nearness or touch of life-force activates it, only movement. Your care for such things is known, Fourth Chivinga. Accept it, please, with our blessing."

For at least part of the day, every day, I wear the Haian timepiece. I cannot think of it as mine; it is the world's. In that distant epoch we all look back on, when wonders greater even than we have it in us to imagine were real, it was probably the most ordinary thing. Someone wore it on his wrist, and glanced at it when he wondered how late it was. Now I do, having learned the pattern, so that in some way he clasps my wrist, and I his.

I set about to sign treaties with all my old allies, and had success, everyone agreeing we needed to lick our wounds. No one, though, would sign a treaty longer than twenty years, or fifty for the Srians, though I asked a century or two. They all gaped at that. "So, you're planning to attack us twenty-one years from now," I kept saying. "How are we to know what will happen then?" they kept asking. "Why not *plan* what will happen then?" I kept asking back.

In time it came to me: in countries where they take no census but for tax rolls, and have no laws on childbearing, they cannot know how much land they will want, in twenty years. It was then the idea came to me, of forming a federation of nations.

It sprang full-blown into my head, as artists sometimes say their paintings do, or story-tellers their tales. Instead of warring the member lands would settle differences in council; in war against outsiders they would ally; in trade they would favor each other. Best that joining have several attractions, so that anyone claiming not to need military allies, for instance, could still join without loss of face, citing another reason. By no means should it have a hint of empire, since that would keep everyone away sure as a reek; the Executor, as I came to title the head of it, should serve in the way of a demarch, obedient to the vote of council, and hold no other title. To join a nation would be required to begin censuses, to see the future clear so peace could be planned.

It burned in me, throwing my mind off imperial business for a day; I wanted to write the letters and draft the constitution and run to people like a child saying, "Look what I thought up!" But it would get its best start from Arko, and Arko was not settled, nor my position here strong enough. The curse of my life: I had no time. Bitterly, I did what I must: put it aside.

Serving two countries who have just fought a war so vicious, there is no pleasing both. I gave money to rebuild both. "The plundering victors are being aided?" muttered Arko. "Here we are devastated, cut to two-thirds our numbers, and *our* demarch helps those who did it!" thundered Yeola-e. I kept giving money to both.

The war was over: I could ask approval to marry Niku. Some argued I was still too important not to be forcing my will on Yeola-e; I would be till the end of my life, no doubt. Assembly saw my way. (In one Servant's words: "This man saved the nation. What does he have to do before we let him marry who he loves?")

We went to Yeola-e, and did both the Yeoli and the Niah ceremony, with just family and friends; one should not flaunt the contentious. I wanted to move the family to Arko—there were positions for Shaina and Etana, and all were willing—but objections were raised to Fifth being exposed to foreign corruption at such a tender age. Assembly voted against that, though narrowly, so I had to split my family, Niku and Vriah coming back to Arko with me, Shaina and Etana staying at home with Fifth and Kima. Fairly soon after the sack Niku and I conceived again. I had not known there were twins in her family; nine months later, we had two boys. It settled the argument over whether to name our first son after my father or hers, for they both survived the stream, to become Rojhai and Tennunga.

Vaneesh of Roskat and I had failed to conceive during the war, so she started making the journey, every month, to Arko. Niku was tiring of doing without me for those five nights, since she no longer had me to herself, and it went hard indeed with Skorsas. It was great relief, when on the fifth moon a letter came saying Vanaesh was with child. They named the girl Shadavie, which means Shared Grief, for the time Vaneesh had first made love to me, in condolence, and proclaimed her Ascendant of Roskat. Whenever I passed through Roskat from then on, I visited, and so saw her grow. Her face was mostly Vaneesh's, though there was a touch of me around the nose, but her hands, if you looked closely, were entirely mine.

When we took Arko, the masters, journeymen and apprentices of the Mahid fourteen and older all died defending Kurkas. But they'd killed the younger apprentices first, and the women had slit the remaining children's throats, then their own, or taken a knife-thrust from Meras's wife, their Senior, if they hesitated. The Mahid did nothing in half-measures, nothing whatsoever. So was the tale: in truth, Amitzas was still alive, as was Ilesias.

He'd been on a table suffering correction during the sack; three of the Demarchic Guard found him, saw his scar and remembered the order I'd given, about taking a young Mahid with a scar like mine alive. In the dungeon, though by Mahid dictate he should refuse and die, he swore to me.

So I called him in, and gave him back the crystal as I had promised. He was seventeen now, and because I was Imperator, moved like a stone doll with seized joints and would not even look at me until I commanded him to. Since there was no Senior to tell him, he wanted to know what it was my will he should be, and do, and say, and think. "What you wish and think right," I said. "That is my will." It would have to be that; there was nothing else for him. With the clan dead, he was chained to freedom.

I assigned him to the Palace Guard, under Krero, set to guard Amitzas's door. The Yeolis spat on him at first, remembering the fight through the Palace. But Krero forbade him to wear onyxine, memories faded, and having sworn, he was flawless, in his Mahid way, going so far as to learn fluent Yeoli in four moons. "I wish all the rest had half that boy's dedication," Krero would say wistfully, then quickly add, "*Not* that I like him or don't still wish I'd never got him, don't get me wrong, Cheng." There were incidents—someone gruesomely killed a kitten I gave him in his room, and someone tried to poison him—but he won friends. In fact he eventually married a Yeoli woman. I'm getting ahead of myself, though.

I picked up my friendship again with Norii Mazeil, who had come into trouble writing in support of my claims I'd been tortured. The Pages people were gaining nerve, in their freedom; it was about that time one of them asked me whether I'd answer the same under truth-drug. Yes, I answered; very well, he said, and drew a vial and a syringe from his satchel. I made sure I didn't blink, saying "You'll have to use one of the veins in my ankle—no, wait. We must do this right, or it will be said I had it faked."

I called in the full Ultimate Court, all nine judges, the *Fenjitzas,* or high priest, and his aides, and other witnesses, mixed three vials of drug from three reputable pharmacists, tested a dose on my food-taster and another on one of the judges, and called both a Haian and an Arkan healer to examine me once I was under the influence to swear to its authenticity. That lessened the number of doubters.

The first report of what happened at Anoseth, came by pigeon from Renaina; then the accounts clamored in, by scores.

She'd encamped at the land and sea crossroads, so Malar-adas could not go around her by ship. An eight-day later, the rebels arrived, having taken their time to gather strength.

She called parley, and made the challenge for all to hear. When Kallijas stepped out, there were flapping lips and taunts all down the rebel line; they challenged his honor, as I'd expected. But he kept his countenance and said, "If I have done wrong by the gods, Toras, why fear that they will not favor you, when you face me? When I did wrong before, they struck me weak."

"The gods!" Toras called back. "It was *you* who failed Arko, traitor. Why do you think you can succeed for your snake-haired dog-master?" Kall just smiled, and said, "It seems you are accepting my challenge."

My watchers gathered then that Toras's true importance was, as we had hoped, little known among his army, for as he hesitated they began exhorting him, calling on him with cheery fierceness. If his conviction was faltering, theirs was not.

He asked time to consider, and the armies shouted their chants, each trying loudly to call the other over. Finally he announced he would send a champion to fight in his stead, if that was acceptable. From behind, Renaina quickly whispered, "Kall, say yes only on the condition that if you win, Toras has to forfeit *his* life, since it's him your quarrel's with." Kall did that; Toras refused, of course; Kall lambasted him for a coward and a doubter of his own cause's divine favor, and offered to ease the stakes, letting Toras have a fair chance in a second duel against him. "I'll be tired, maybe even wounded! Or are you scared of me even so? Ask your priests for a good long blessing, since your cause is so holy!" Toras could hardly refuse that.

He chose his champion, Idiesas Firnean, whom Kallijas knew from war-school tournaments, and sparring in war camp. No surprise, since he loved great swordcraft and all who could do it, they'd been friendly, making Idiesas's barbs sting.

It was a hard fight, with perfect conviction on both sides; I know I was happier not watching. Kall fought in his way, diamond-pure; Idiesas did likewise. "I kept wanting to say," Kall told me later, "Idiesas, understand! By your touch I know you could, if you would!" After several close misses and minor wounds both ways, Kall got a stroke through onto Idiesas's head, with the flat but hard enough to knock him senseless. I knew that stroke. On waking, Idiesas conceded, and Kall helped him up and gave him to Malaradas's healers, though by Arkan standards the insults he'd spoken warranted death. "Whichever way this goes," Kall told him, "Arko will need you."

So it was Toras's turn. It was a long time coming, for he gathered a clutch of gold-robed priests with a sun-disc standard to do some ritual over him; the better for Kallijas, giving him time to catch his breath, and take painkiller. Watching the rite, he thought of praying for strength himself, but decided against in the end. The Gods have already made up their minds, he thought, to let me do this or not; what difference will a word or two more of wheedling make? Do I not trust them? With naked sword he went out into the field again, his only prayer, "My thanks for your justice, Steel-Armed One, though I cannot yet know what form it will take."

Toras advanced boldly enough, but as they came close he went death-pale. In the way of those who aspire to hidden power, he knew everything, including that it would take a miracle for him to beat Kallijas Itrean; he'd been hoping time and the rite and the yelling of his army would cow Kall's spirit. Now in Kall's face he saw that would not be, and perhaps did not trust the gods to preserve him after all. As it happened, they didn't. To Kall's mind, Arko did not need this man, so he made a clean kill.

My side gave its victory roar; Malaradas's with its coterie of priests stood stunned and silent. It looked to its leader; but of course it had none, Malaradas wondering "What next?" as much as everyone else. Then Kall, who had not moved, called them to attention, which for want of other orders they obeyed.

He'd never had training in oration, but he heard the flute of his god, and that can make up for it. As was best, he did not think of it as a speech, but only what he must say, heart to heart, to those who, like him, were Arkan and warriors.

"Every *solas* knows, whether he speaks of it or not, what the plague of the Empire was; for none suffered more often by it than we," he said. "There are a thousand words that mean corruption, from apathy to cruelty, from laziness to choosing favorites, lying, murder, torture. One might say the Gods intervened to punish Arko, or that it was by our own failure; what matter? We gave ourselves to masters who treated our lives as dirt to be thrown away; we followed blindly as the corrupt in power, corrupted by power, led us over the precipice."

I balk at writing what he said of me. "But now a man has come who is worthy to be our master, for he made himself so by strength and by spirit, while we let our spirit wither away into lassitude and decadence. If the new Cur-lion, the fresh wind blowing across the face of the world, is a foreigner, not an Arkan, it is that the gods punish our pride, to remind us that we are not the only people, that no nation can be the Eternal Victor, that greatness can come in a thousand forms, not only ours, and we must embrace it in whatever shape it comes.

"We thought he came to destroy," he said, "but he came to correct, and inspire, a father and teacher, not barbarian, not demon." He spoke of the rebuilding of Arko; they'd been fed with lies that we'd razed the City as they had Shakora. "Nor did Shefen-kas desecrate the robe and seals, and say only his signet has meaning now; he took them up, follows the Imperial protocols, and has changed no law." There'd been disinformation on that too, tales it was now legal for wives to knife and eat their husbands, and so forth.

"You are leaderless now," Kallijas said, "for Toras was your leader, as you will find soon enough if you don't believe me. Why has Malaradas not stood up, and spoken, and seized the reins?" He left a moment's pause, for them to see that. "Such is the deception of the old way. And now when the war should be over you bring Arkans to shed Arkan blood, you seek to tear the Empire asunder with more war. How long, how badly, must Shefen-kas punish us for our foolishness?

"The Gods' will is written, upon the page of the world." He tossed away his shield then, drove his sword into the ground beside the corpse, and walked away unarmed. "Those who see it, come across to us; by Shefen-kas's own order, nothing will be held against you. Those who doubt the truth of what I say," he said, "let any one strike or shoot me down." And he knelt facing them.

Some surged forward, to cross or charge, it was hard to tell, but were held back by others; some turned to fighting among themselves; all argued. Then one commander of archers ordered his unit to shoot Kallijas.

He stayed still kneeling, looking a hundred paces into a thicket of arrowheads, each bearing his death, without his eyelids creasing. Some of the archers unstrung their bows then, crying, "I can't do this!" or "This is a parley!" while the officer threatened them with death for insubordination; others, Kall could tell, meant to aim wide. Of the volley, most whistled past, two glanced, and one caught him, through his breastplate into his chest, a little to the right, mid-height.

Its force jolted him, the witnesses say, but otherwise he did not move or make a sound, nor lose his countenance; the only sign was his cheeks going ghost-white. Then a warrior strode out from Malaradas's ranks, some of his unit following, took Kallijas's hand and stood beside him. It was Idiesas. "You gave me my life," he said, "and would give your own to make us believe you; so I will. Keep still, Kall, the healers are coming."

Four thousand or so came over to us, right then. More would come in at night, not wishing to be seen; others never would, but faded into the woods, so that Renaina could not bring the army home, but must skirmish all the way to Marsae to secure the city and the border. Malaradas's sea-forces, finding no other leader, turned to privateering, as goes on to this day.

So it would be; but Kall could not know it. He stayed kneeling, Idiesas holding his hand; when the healers did come with a litter, they had to lift him, for he could not unlock his own limbs. When they did, he gave a writhing thrash all through his body, spat a gout of blood and passed out.

Kaninjer was not there, but other good Haians were. He was three beads in surgery. The arrow had gone through the sixth rib, shearing part of it off, through the lower lung and into the rib behind; he was lucky it wasn't on the left, else it would have struck his heart and killed him instantly. They linked his veins with others' to replenish his blood, and aided his breathing with the Haian bellows and tubes; even so, his heart stopped twice while they worked. An Arkan would say it was by the gods' will he lived.

When he was strong enough to be moved, Renaina sent back half the army, including all who'd turned; when the column marched into the city, it was said, every other Arkan in it looked surprised to see anything standing. It is not for such an army to parade, but I went out in the robe to meet Kall in his litter on the steps. I'd found out the highest

award for valor an Imperator can give to a *solas* is to elevate
him to *Aitzas*, which must be done by elevating his father,
if he is still alive. So right there, on the steps, with his
parents and his brother Joras who, I saw now, had lost a
forearm on Finpollendias, I did the ceremony. As Dammas
Itrean took on the silver satin robe with its border of the
family's sigil—I'd had it made to his conception—all but
Joras wept. "It was you who were my strength, Sheng," Kall
kept saying. "I thought of you all through." But no one can
borrow spirit, who doesn't have it himself.

(Of course elevating Kallijas required elevating Skorsas,
if I didn't want him to pine to death with jealousy. "In
spirit," I told him, "I elevated you in the Mezem, the night
before my false execution." His eyes and lips softened and
went tender, remembering, and he whispered, "True." All
we needed to do was the paperwork.)

We nursed Kallijas in one of the higher rooms with plenty
of windows and air, away from the bustle; he was still there
when Kaninjer freed my arms from the casts, so I could
show him by sneaking up while he faced the other way and
hugging him. We'd feared he'd lose his wind; but the way
the arrow had gone in and the lung healed, he was lucky.
Three moons later he beat me five of nine times in sparring,
which says enough, I think.

XIII

Things settled, and so I set my mind to rewriting the laws of Arko. It was like walking on a knife-edge: best to go slow, but all the longer my feet hurt. I gradually got a feel for how to use such power, and for Arkans, who spoke more and more freely, learning to judge how long it took them to swallow one change so I could go on to the next, how to shock them with an extreme proposal, then ease it to the more moderate one I'd been planning all along, like a rug merchant haggling, how to distract them with something striking here so I could slip through something more important there. Teaching the vote was my dearest wish; but all Arkan society leans against that, so that other things must be dealt with first. How could slaves vote, for instance, if they were not free? How could women vote, so much under the subjection of men? The high castes felt only they should have the right, of course, or at least the count should be weighted in their favor, the choice of a *solas* counted as ten to the one of an *okas*, and so forth.

I walked the knife, raising indignation here, crushing hopes there, letting the Pages write what it would all the way through, sometimes teetering, getting cut frequently. I remember the editorial writer who was harshest against me, Nil Kinnian, who either hated me or wanted to test what he could get away with, I think, writing such things as,

"Shefen-kas is taking further vengeance on Arko with this woman's literacy law, turning all womanhood against all manhood, wife against husband, sister against brother, daughter against father." Not that it mattered what I felt; I feared only that he would be believed, and Arko lose what trust it had in me.

My worst opposition, believe it or not, was not from Arkans, but Yeolis. Just as Mana had predicted in my dying-dream, my own prescience wearing his face, a hundred or so had thought beyond shiny things when they grabbed in the sack. They had huge tracts of land, country palaces, merchant fleets, whole towns of slaves, all duly acquired under Arkan law which, they took relish in pointing out, had not changed. They did set themselves up, with astounding speed—things should have gone much better if they'd spent half as much effort helping me as helping themselves—as the true *Aitzas* caste. They came to be known about the City as *iolias naakasi*: the Yeoli hawks.

No matter to me if they grew their hair long, or wore their crystals on thick gold chains; it is, as the saying goes, what crawls inside the shell. Inatalla Shae-Krisa, Rao Irae, Faraika Terero, Alai Shae-Chano and the like did all they could to rule Arko through me, pretending concern for the poor conquered Arkan with one breath then claiming reward for conquering him the next, endlessly demanding reward for their selfless effort in the war, as if they hadn't got enough, or I hadn't had some small part in it myself. Out of fear or greed, which they played on with little scruple, Arkans would toady for them, as they always had for such, which gave them more power.

It was not enough that all Arko opposed reforms to the laws that oppressed them, not seeing the gain to be made, but the hawks did as well, taking up the most retrograde Arkan causes with Yeoli fervor, becoming the spokespeople often as not. As the saying goes, politics makes strange bedfellows. "They *want* to be oppressed!" they'd say. "The people wills!" After yet another audience with Inatalla contending that no people without a long tradition of demarchy could be expected to make reasonable and responsible choices by vote, I lost my patience. "Of course you don't want them to—they'd confiscate all property acquired by the hacking up of its former owner, and all you sheep-turds would be out your fortunes, wouldn't you!" He stamped out snorting, "See how long you last, displeasing everyone," and other such things. Since his first words to me, after I'd executed the Yeoli looter, though, I'd never mistaken him for a friend.

I feel bitterness in my own words as I read them back; but whatever the style reveals, the content is nothing but the truth. I don't think there was true hate in their actions, actually, only calculation, as with Inatalla's first words. At the most there was envy; they'd have liked nothing better than to make one of themselves Imperator, and then everything would have been as they wanted it. Nothing hurt worse than when they accused me of breaking the principle of the people wills, which they did often, seeing the effect. So many times I looked in the mirror, asking myself, "Is it true?", renewing my answer the same way every time, yet afraid to stop asking lest I get jaded, fooled by the false alarms into missing the true. But there was nothing to be done about the hawks, now. So much I wish those four lost days back, to have cut their feet out from under them before they found their balance.

Then there was the high priesthood of Arko, with whom the Imperator has no choice but to deal. They keep a hierarchy as strict as an army's, the *Fenjitzas* being First General First, the lowly citizen who marches faithfully every eight-day to his or her local temple, the wretched footsoldier. Yet, since the church is entwined tight as a vine on a cord with the state, one stands highest: the Son of the Sun, the Gods' Agent on Earth, the Imperator.

When I met with the *Fenjitzas* and his two high aides the first time—after we'd settled the dispute about the audience list, which they seemed to think they could jump at will—they were determined to see that I changed only those matters of law, religious or secular, they approved of my changing, that is to say, none whatsoever. Their first tactic was trying to convert me, out of pure concern for the fate of my soul after death, of course (he said the word right out and with great weight, thinking to scare me). "I shall do what I always have," I answered him, "my utmost to act rightly, and let the gods judge me then; but I should warn you, that might not mean doing what you say." He undertook then to educate me, the ignorant barbarian, on things spiritual; but he was as easy to tie into knots as certain philosophy students I recalled, if not easier, his mind having had more time to wear in ruts than theirs. Soon enough I got them doing what is traditionally an Imperator's due: supplicating.

One mark I will leave indelibly in the Arkan history books, at least wherever the date is mentioned. Everyone knows the Arkan calendar counts backwards; what is less commonly known is why. I had learned that as a gladiator: when Arko fell from the sky, the story goes, the Gods gave them a century to find their way back to it, (the First Age) the years to be counted down. Then the Gods kindly gave them another hundred, (the Second Age), then, very kindly, another five hundred (the Third Age), a second five hundred (the Fourth Age) and the last five hundred (the Present Age). I'd become a gladiator in 58, and it was now 55; the deadline was impending, and if Arko was any closer to returning to the stars it was by borrowing the A-niah's device.

By what mechanism the Gods granted extensions, I had no idea, and despaired of living to find out. As it was, though, the *Fenjitzas* and his two high aides came to audience, one day, looking so miserably humble my heart went out to them. In an achingly long exposition full of liturgy I couldn't make out, they inquired whether the Great God had spoken to me yet, as it must to the rightful-by-the-express-will-of-Celestialis Imperator, on whether in view of Arko's eternally shameful failure to attain the sky, it should be granted heavenly mercy again, or consigned to everlasting Hayel. At first I didn't understand, though by their faces full of solemn terror I knew I had better. Then it came: they were asking *me* for an extension.

My inclination was to look thunderstruck and say, "Ah! The vision comes . . . oh oh. Looks liked everlasting Hayel. Sorry, I did my best . . ." *You make fun of what they hold sacred*, the singing wind said, in my mind. I got up and went to the window, looked up into the sky. Since *you're* here, I asked it, what do I do? *Few more stupid questions were ever asked*, it said.

"Arko has another five centuries," I told the priests. "So

the god has told me." Looking at those three old faces, eyes flat and unreadable as blue glass, I wondered who among them if any believed me, and who bitterly thought a heathen barbarian was playing a game on them and all Arko. How amazed the latter would be, I thought, to find the former are right.

The first thing they supplicated for, after this, (and my assurance that they should continue to receive the plentiful tithes whose burden, they assured me with straight faces, kept the faithful citizen to a properly spiritual asceticism) was that I preserve the purification.

Of course my heart cried out to abolish it; at noon when the birdlike screams came carried in on the hot breeze, I wanted to make it punishable by death. But, as the priests argued, how could I consign all the female sex of Arko to the eternal smothering of Hayel? For I most certainly would, in their own minds at least; belief, no matter how perverse, is belief. On the other hand, as most Yeolis argued, after a generation they'd get used to it, having found out no vile fate awaited them, but a more pleasant one in fact, and in time would thank me. Then there was the matter of the people's will, that I'd sworn to live by at home and here. I knew what Arko would vote for.

For all my loves urged me and I wanted to unburden my heart, I wish I had never breathed a word of it in the bedchamber. Skorsas and Kallijas, of course, were dead against any change. Niku cried, "What? You are even thinking of not forbidding it? Fakhad shkavi! I won't sleep with that!" and stamped out in her deadly graceful way. "That's all right," Skorsas said brightly, "I will." All well, and I laid my head on his shoulder; but when he muttered, "There'd be much more peace around here if she were purified," I drew away from him sharply, to moans of "What did I say? What did I say?" and he and I ended up sleeping on opposite edges of the great bed.

So my loves were scattered to the winds, and no solution in sight. I have to say that this was one conundrum I never finished solving—the purification, I should say; my loves did, to my heart's relief, return. I set a number of scholars on it, searching through old versions of the Arkan gospel for anything that might call the custom into question. They discovered the Imperator who had instituted it, some 400 years ago, bearing the opinion of women in general that they were innately evil, conniving, lustful (hard to believe a man saying that of women), and hence correctible only by the glass knife. I asked them whether the man ever had a mother; it turned out she had been terribly cruel. Still, the priests argued that his vision had been true.

I made this all public. To put outright abolition to a vote, it struck me, would be too unsettling; I could see killings; the chances of chalk were nothing anyway, with no prospect of changing quickly if at all. So I proposed that the age of purification would be changed to third threshold, twenty-one, to be done only with the sworn consent of the woman. They could hardly say that violated their beliefs; if she believed, she'd choose it. It was in the back of my mind that this meant effectively there'd be no cutting for some fourteen years; they might get unused to the idea by then. It will go to a vote, I announced; since Arko is unfamiliar with the process, I won't require a majority of charcoal even, just a fifth of the population—including women and slaves—unless there are more chalk. If they wanted to see nothing changed they'd better mark it so.

The *Fenjitzas*, of course, supplicated; surely the Great God, he argued, could not have willed such a thing. No, I said; the vision he sent me was that he would speak his will to me through the people of Arko; if the priesthood thought that was charcoal, they'd better go forth and preach to the flock what to do that crucial day. Three times I told them this; each time, they left bewildered. I should have guessed I'd put them in the impossible crossroads, and they'd do nothing.

We all carry the blindnesses of our upbringing with us as well as the clarities; here I found mine. I hadn't thought it possible that anyone, even Arkans, could go without debating something of such import to them. Maybe they're putting it off, I thought after the first four moons, and it'll warm up as the day gets closer; maybe they're doing it in secret, I thought, with a moon to go. It came clear afterwards, as always; those who were against the proposal kept silent, fearing to go against the Imperator's will, while those few who supported it (mostly women of secret education, who in effect whispered it in my ear) kept silent fearing those against it, or assumed it would go through and therefore felt no need to speak.

All through the Empire I sent heralds, since so many people are illiterate, to teach the procedure in every village; the chips were fashioned, the boxes set up, the scriveners hired to count. All through the Empire, barely a thirtieth of the people came out, and the result was an almost even split. By my own declaration, not enough; so I put the law through.

The night after word came out in the Pages, all Arko grieved. From my window I heard keening, and shouted pleas, "Have mercy on my daughter, great God!" Not a protesting cry, at having their will crossed, but a lament such as people make after a flood or an earthquake, a vagary of fate over which they have no control. So they have always thought the will of the Imperator. The worst of it was, several fathers killed girls younger than first threshold—sometimes tearing them out of mothers' arms to do it—to make sure they got into Celestialis. They were tried by Arkan judges, who, of course, understood.

"You see?" the hawks all told me. "We told you so. Learn something more than those naive ideals, Fourth Chevenga; Arkans aren't Yeolis. They can't understand voting, they never will." History might have been different, I think, had Kallijas not been near me, to say, while I sat despairing, "Sheng, you're not starting to take those buzzards' opinion of us seriously, are you?", kicking me back into sense. He'd voted: charcoal, he confided in me. I kept that secret from Niku. The path is there, I thought; I just haven't conceived it yet.

The bitterest thing to my heart came about a year after the sack, when I was turning twenty-five. The town of Temono, on the east coast of the peninsula where it starts to round the heel, was taken over by rebelling slaves.

Before the conquest, the whisper along slave grapevines had been *Shefen-kas will set us free*. True enough, in time; but because the Empire ran on the shoulders of slaves, I could do it only gradually without bringing famine. My plan was to change the laws slowly, so that in time it became more of a hardship for a master to hold slaves than to grant them shares, or at least wages; I'd already made existing laws on the treatment of slaves much stricter. Then I'd make it illegal. But it all would take time. In Temono they had not been willing to wait. Those who had argued that any lightening of the slave-yoke would unleash rebellion now crowed triumph.

It was no dilemma to me, since I'd thought out before what I'd do if this happened; only anguish. I must put it down; I had no choice. If I looked the other way, slaves from Kurkania to the Roskati border would take it as permission to revolt, and the Empire would be awash in blood. I put out proclamations saying any further uprisings would be harshly dealt with, called up an army twenty thousand strong of Arkans, only my personal guard Yeolis, and marched to the town.

The mayor had got birds out to the near seaports before he died, so enough marines were here already to have made the slaves seal and stay inside the walls. The tales from those Arkans who had escaped—gentle masters who'd been spared, or the fleet of foot—were as terrible as one would expect, of whole families killed, overseers chained and whipped to death, babies impaled on pikes. Several thousand Arkans, they said, had died. The revolt had been started by slaves of the great iron-works.

I ordered the army to surround the city, and called parley. The leader came out: a Srian, tall even for one of them, a good head and a half taller than I. His name was Lasatro, and though his eyes were wary, they seemed honest; I cursed inwardly, having wanted him to be one I could hate, for I liked him on sight. On his great black shoulders, bare in the hot southern sun, the whip-scars were furrows.

He would speak alone with me only carrying weapons, he said, that, I remembered, being a matter of honor for a Srian; we agreed on his sword alone, no daggers, and I kept Chirel. He addressed me inferior-to-superior, but only once removed, as an Arkan Imperator would take as inconceivable insolence. Nor did he make the prostration; I could feel the ripple all down the lines of Arkan warriors, when he came near me without doing it. In the cool shade under a cluster of trees, away from the lines, I sent for iced juice and fruit, and we spoke.

I got the whole story from his side. How bitter life was in the iron-works, he said, he could not describe; but he spoke of things that went far beyond the new law. It seemed, I found when I asked him, no news of any changes had ever come to the slaves; the last they'd heard was my proclamation I'd change no laws for now, news half a year old. Nor had they heard that of the agreement I'd made with the Mefweo, to start freeing Srian slaves, of which many here besides Lasatro were; he didn't even know I'd been to his homeland. Now the word was, Yeoli or not, I was an Imperator like any other, and planned never to abolish slavery. The few literate slaves here had been forbidden to see the Pages lately.

It came clear: the master of the iron-works, seeing losses in the changes he must make to obey the new laws, had decided not to, or at least to delay, and had persuaded, bought or pressed every other slave-owner in the town to go along with the lies this required. Fearing unrest they'd hardened on the slaves, with floggings and executions; then one slave had turned on an overseer and struck him dead with an ingot. Rebellion spread; Lasatro had directed it in such a way that it could win.

So, I had a mess caused by false news, and the people I must punish, not truly to blame. I had wanted to say to Lasatro, "Why couldn't you wait? Did you not trust me?" But what else could they believe, but what they'd been told? He and I had no argument; I was at a loss for words. I ended up saying, "Tell me, Lasatro; imagine you are in my place. What would you do?"

He was no fool. That I was Imperator and must keep order in the Empire, that if they did not surrender it was my duty to fight them, and mete out some punishment even if they did, all this he understood; it had been an eight-day or so since the revolt, the frenzy had worn off, the limbs stiffened, the eyes cleared. The iron-works and its ways would be changed as the law demanded, that we agreed on; since everyone in its owner's family was dead, by Arkan law ownership reverted to the Marble Palace, a grand way of saying me. That I should not be merciful if they refused to surrender and lost, we agreed on, too. I'd have known he was not a second generation slave even without his accent, at that. Srians accept such things. "But if we surrender," he said, "I would say you should be gentle with us, given our circumstances, at least with those who did not lead it, and set us free in stages in the years following."

My heart went out to him, seeing him willing to take punishment himself to spare the others; but I had to say, "Then you'll have done exactly what I cannot let you do, if this is not to happen again all over the Empire: gained, by violence. You don't want to suffer; none of us do; all those Arkans you killed didn't either, parents or children, and nor do the ten- or hundred-fold more who will if all slaves see their best course is killing."

"But isn't it?" he said suddenly, standing up to pace, so that beside him I felt the size of a child. "How can it not seem so, to us? How long must we wait, before you do what you say you will?"

"You had reason to distrust me before," I said, "being permitted to know only falsehoods. You have no reason now."

"You say the rumor was a lie," he snapped, "that you know how it is for us because you were a slave yourself; but in truth you sound like any other Imperator, saying you have to think of the Empire, Arkans and nothing but Arkans, coming here to keep us in chains, and you a Yeoli. This is a lie, that's a lie, how do I know it isn't all lies, to get us out from the walls?"

Though I knew it was only past falsehoods keeping the chasm open between us, a flash of anger came. "I'll bet I have more marks on my body, put there by Arkans, than you have," I said. Skorsas had chosen a gold satin jacket embroidered with birds and orchids for me for today; I threw it off. "Look!"

His deep voice turned quiet, but lost no hardness. "*You* killed your owners for it. And quite a few innocents, too."

I sat still, half-naked, stuck for words. He was right. In his place I would do, had done, exactly the same; the only difference was I had had a bigger army, so I could win. It was laughable, to call justice into it. Exactly the same, I thought, seeing him cast a nervous glance at my eyes; he was trying to read me, to see if I was one whom words that struck home would turn harder, fearing it would cost his people, as I would have. Don't regret, Lasatro, I thought; you judged me right.

"I would not lie to you," I said. "Second Fire come." He sat again and sipped, his great callused fingers black against the gold of the juice in the glass cup.

The trouble had come through others' fault; the way around it was there too. Where slaves had been driven to violence by abuses, there was grounds for lenience; to see them let off lightly would make other slave-owners move faster to obey the new law. "Consider this," I said to Lasatro. "You surrender, and stand trial. Two trials it would have to be, one of the leaders, one for the followers as one; no doubt it came down to chance who killed whom and how many, anyway." I knew how such things went. I explained to him, how the law was to some extent on their side, how they should make their case with accounts in writing of every abuse. There was no law on the books now, of course, allowing slaves the right to trial at all; while they were gathering evidence, I would slip back to Arko and write it.

"To be tried by an Arkan judge?" he said. "Or the Ultimate Court, all Arkans? I know what they will say!" One thing I had done early, I was coming to regret: set down that Arkans in Arko should be tried before Arkan judges, and Yeolis before Yeolis. It had been to save Yeolis from coming under Arkan power; it failed when a Yeoli wronged an Arkan, or vice versa, or in the case of slaves.

I said, "*I'll* judge it." The Imperator has such rights. "Taking recommendations from the Ultimate Court, but only recommendations." I'm dealing, I thought, as if he had any hold on me, but my conscience. A chain as strong as his: and he knows it.

For a long time he looked down at me, pupils and eyelids the same brown-black, whites the color of ivory but still bright against the dark, searching into my soul. Someone less slavish, I thought, I've never met. Finally he said, "I must ask the others." Without an obeisance he took his leave.

They debated it long, while my Arkan officers, seeing them withdraw from the parapets to gather, said eagerly,

"Shall we now, Shefen-kas, shall we?"; it is Arkan custom that an oath made to a slave is not binding, if the Arkan feels like breaking it. I went among the Yeolis, who would understand, to pace and swear.

Lasatro came out, by the same way, still bearing his sword; but there was a difference about him, as if he had shrunk, like one aged. I felt sickness grow in me, understanding. When he said, "I give you our answer, Imperator," he looked straight at me, with the free spirit still in his eyes; but when he knelt and bowed, laying the sword along the nape of his neck and the backs of his hands to yield it to me, his gaze went dull and did not rise above my feet again. Where I could hardly have imagined him a slave before, now I could see him as nothing else.

In my eyes I felt the burning of tears, as I took it, my only comfort in thinking, as now I must keep to myself, *Some day, Lasatro, I will give it back*. I drew him up, by the hand.

Having made myself their judge, I wanted to see the place of their suffering, so had him guide me through the iron-works. Despite the revolt, they'd kept it going, not knowing what else to do, I suppose, or perhaps considering it, as slaves secretly will, their own.

I had not thought such a place possible. These masters had truly thought their slaves tools, to have as much use pressed out of them as possible until they broke, then to be discarded, and replaced. One would think they hadn't heard of windows, and this was a hot land already; in nothing but a loincloth and jewelry I still sweated rivers, while he didn't even seem to notice, and when I mentioned it said, "You should be here in summer." Once, seeing him lean on a stack of ingots to speak, I put my hand down too, and whipped it away by reflex, lest I burn; they all had hands and feet callused like horn. Over the foundries, there was not so much as a railing; about once a month someone falls in, Lasatro told me; the masters say it gives the metal quality. The cells used to punish slaves were high under the roof, where it was hottest, and only waist-high, so one must crouch; one felt baked in an oven. "No one lasts longer than three days here, without water," he told me. "Or they go mad after two, and hit their heads against the wall until they die. Sometimes for nothing, just for an example . . ." His throat closed suddenly, and he turned away; I wondered who he'd lost that way. He was not one, I'd seen, who was easily upset.

I sailed home, writing the law in my mind. They made their case well, a hundred tales to turn the stomach, that all stood up under truth-drug; the advocate prosecuting could say nothing that everyone didn't know already, that nine hundred odd Arkans—that was the true count—had been slain.

The majority of the Ultimate Court, of course, recommended death for both the leaders and followers, by torture for the former; it was only three of the four judges I'd appointed myself who favored what to their mind was lenience: that the followers be flogged and forced to watch the executions of the leaders. As they spoke I saw Lasatro, in his prisoner's chains, serene of face, resigned to death, a shining of his pride returned.

In announcing my decision, I made all my points in full. We look away from the hardship of slaves, I said. We ignore their agonies, though in their place we would feel no less. These ones were driven: I spoke at length of the unlawfulness of their circumstances, how they'd been deceived, that some might say the dead had deserved no less. Those who had only followed would be flogged to falling, I said, those who had led would suffer the same, but as well, live all their lives, imprisoned in the dungeons of the Marble Palace, toiling as slaves to their dying day, though all other slaves in Arko be set free.

Lasatro's eyes caught mine. They stared, gone strange, his face holding smooth, but full of a terrible twisting just under the skin. Death he had been ready for; not this.

You became a pawn in a game of state, I thought that night, when I could get away from my desk, and went down to the dungeon in a robe; it is the fate of such pawns, as I know myself, to be flung up and down, from life to death to heartbreak to ecstasy, feeling they have as much of a hand in their destiny as a leaf does in a fire-wind. He sat in the corner, his huge length curled. "Lasatro," I said. "Come close, so no one else hears."

"No," he said. "I don't think I could keep my arms from

trying to strangle you, and I shouldn't blame you, for you think you are doing me kindness. You are a good Imperator, a boon to the Empire, as snakish clever as the best of them: it must be your Yeoli subtleties."

"It was either this or death," I said, dropping my voice low. "From death I can't quietly spring you, and the others, in a year or two when the furor has died down."

He laughed, a dry barking. "The iron overseers, they used that too, the most useful whip: hope." In the next cell, a steady thudding started; I guessed soon what it was. No words, no moans, just thudding, even and resolute. "Why don't you tell *him* that?" Lasatro said. "He might believe you, so you'll be able to draw it out longer."

My oath, even Second Fire come, would mean nothing to him, since he thought me forsworn already. Only the proof would prove itself, and that I could not give him, now. I could only hope he didn't go mad first. He was a blacksmith, whose owner had rented him to the works; I had his things, his anvil and hammers and half-finished pieces brought, and set him up a forge in the dungeon, hoping practicing his craft would help him keep his mind. I did likewise for the two others who survived. Sometimes I had him secretly brought up to one of the courtyards, to see daylight; though it did not shake his distrust, it seemed to bring some balm. In my bitterest moods I would visit him, beg him to believe me, let him see my tears, let him be my master and laugh his deep razor-laugh, hoping that too would help him stay sane.

Spring turned to summer. One night, at the time when one sleeps deepest, Kaninjer shook me awake shouting, "Drink this, Chivinga, no questions." He lifted my head on his arm; the cup shook in his hand, chattering on my teeth, as I drank. "Your food-taster took ill," he said. "Tell me the moment you feel anything amiss. No, stay lying down."

There was already some panic in the room; I remember thinking he could have done it more quietly. I ordered everyone to keep this silent, and move the children away. By the time I'd sent for Emao-e, I was in a cold sweat, sick to my stomach and light-headed in too definite a way to be fear. I could hardly get out the words, that she was in command, for vomiting.

After that I don't remember much except pain and confusion, and fighting. It was a poison that attacks the muscles that work without thought, the heart and lungs and gut. I remember feeling as if my ribs were two walls of stone, immovable, so I couldn't get air, while all around me people yelled, "Breathe! Breathe!" I remember Skorsas exhorting me, as he had from the Ring gate, "Fight, jewel of the world, treasure of Arko, you can beat it, you are stronger, fight!" The candles got too bright, so Kaninjer blindfolded me; I remember the feeling, in shreds, of hands gently pinning me, a long needle going into my heart, and then fire just like in the heat of battle pouring through my veins, making me want to leap and thrash and tear up mountains. It was all I could do to walk leaning on two arms, though; I remember begging them to let me rest, and Esora-e's stabbing voice: "You lazy good-for-nothing brat—if your father could see this!" which took me back to the training ground, where I'd learned how to go beyond fatigue that felt utter. Apparently, all through, I kept asking after the taster, whose name was Barabbas Kallon; Kaninjer was running back and forth, between him and me.

I fought it all night, all but died three times, and woke up the evening after, feeling as if I'd fought a *rejin* of *rejins* all alone. The news-scribes were waiting, though, so over Kaninjer's protests, I let them in; it wasn't my fault I was in bed, death-pale, getting dinner through a glass tube running into my arm, so I didn't care who saw.

I'd had raw oysters whole; that's what Kaninjer guessed had carried the poison. When they asked me whether the culprit had been found, I was at a loss; Emao-e, it turned out, had been waiting for my word before she did anything. It came to me how we could find him without subjecting every scullion in the kitchen to truth-drug; I asked Niku, and Vriah, and both were amenable. I had Krero quietly surround the kitchen; then Amitzas walked in, robed and with his box, a terror every Arkan knew, followed by Niku with Vriah on her shoulder. She need only finger the one who suddenly became afraid. It worked; he ran straight into the arms of Kunarda and Herenna, caught before my interview was over. Ikal had the other two involved, one of them the son of a noble who'd died in the sack, in the dungeons that same night. A simple motive: revenge, for the father, and Arko.

The writers asked me another question I didn't know the answer to; how my food-taster was. I looked at Kaninjer, whose face tightened. He had given both of us blood-fire, as the last resort; but I was young, and my body and soul used to such strain. Barabbas had died while I was still in the worst of it. Of course they couldn't tell me that, then.

For his good life, he had paid in full, saving mine, for which I am forever grateful. I give his name so he may be remembered. His son Amas is to be commended for his courage too, for he volunteered to take his father's place that same day.

I wasn't good for any work the next two days, and for another two worked in bed, because Kaninjer wouldn't let me up. Krero wanted to fire every Arkan in the kitchen and have the assassins publicly tortured to death; I agreed to having my and my taster's food go through Yeoli hands only, but reminded him that law ruled in Arko and would decide on a sentence, not I.

That turned out to be wrong. Being Arkans they were subject to Arkan law, and at that time there was no separate provision for assassination—Imperators had always dealt with it themselves—so it was a plain murder and attempted murder case, sentence to be decided on by the victim's next-of-kin and almost-victim as per Arkan law. I had never felt for myself how fast Arkan justice worked, either; Kaninjer testified, the truth-drug transcripts of the accused were read, and that was it. Their fate was tossed back into my lap before I was strong enough to walk.

Those favoring lenience reminded me of how the attempt had not succeeded; those favoring hardness felt lenience would be as good as declaring open season on me. In the end I gave the scullion, who had done it, and the noble's son, who had paid for it, death by the same poison, for no other reason than that was what Amas wished. The third man we let off with a flogging, since he had been only an accessory. The executions I had one writer witness, public enough. They went to it with decent courage, the *Aitzas* youth in particular, it had been a good home he'd lost, and he'd done this in love and rashness. I couldn't bear to watch it through to the end, my own memory of the poison too close.

On assassination attempts, I write only those I know of; probably there were many more that fell far short, or that Krero didn't want to trouble me with. Aside from vengeance, I suspect assassins feel towards an Imperator much the same as mountain-climbers do towards an unconquered peak, daring it for no other reason than that it is there, a challenge to their craft. I expect to die by assassination; it seems likeliest. I've had so many near-misses, and such luck can't last forever.

One morning in the shower I tasted oysters at the back of my tongue, and felt a touch of burning; thinking the water must be a touch bad I ordered it changed, and thought no more. A few days later the oyster taste came again, much stronger, and my skin turned to fire. Amitzas knew after one look: the poison is called Hayel-rain, and was popular for murdering the Imperial family some two hundred years ago, until everyone put a guard on their cisterns. We, of course, had done away with the guard, not knowing the reason. That assassin must have put in a small amount the first day, and more the next when he'd seen how fast I got in and out. We never caught him. To heal me Kaninjer had to shave off all my hair, even my eyebrows.

Ikal had had no luck finding Minis and his Mahid; they are good, of course, at covering their tracks. But I was waiting for their assassination attempt. In the winter after I turned twenty-five, just after Jitzmitthra, I had a bitter fight with Niku, one of those that shakes a marriage deep, calling up fears like ghosts out of the crematory ground. One thing I said: "No great matter if I'm a curse—you're not stuck with me for much longer." There was no sleeping together that night. That saved my life.

With the aid of Ilesias and Amitzas, Krero had mapped out the grid of secret passages in the Marble Palace, and now had guards at the heart-points. But even Amitzas did not know them all. It was twelve beads, two past midnight, and Skorsas was sitting on the edge of the bed, brooding, when his shadow appeared on the chains where it should not, thrown by a light behind him; turning, he saw a Mahid with a blow-tube creep out of the obsidian column, looking for my head on the pillows.

Skorsas flung himself down beside the bed, yelling help; that saved his life. Niku woke up and, seeing the assassin right beside her, and two others spreading to cast about for me, set on him close so they could not shoot. The guard in the trap-booth then forearmed the switches, ending the action.

I, if you should wonder, was on the floor outside the chains, where I thought, since I was so vile a husband, I deserved to sleep. And so I did, through all this; even when the guard came to rouse those who should be roused and chain those who should be chained, Krero could barely wake me. I remember it all vaguely, bustle and bother and candlelight and a tiny fountain of water spraying from where a dart had pierced the bed; I thought it was a nightmare and told it all to go away, irritated. I was full of a sleeping-drug strong enough to deaden weapon-sense. Amas was the same—the food-taster's attendant checks only his vital signs as he sleeps, not his mental state—so it had been in dinner; an all-round well-laid plan, that for dumb luck would have got me. The door in the column was so cunningly made that we had never even noticed the cracks, the rock so thick it sounded solid when one struck it, beneath, a spiral staircase inside a pilaster.

Happenings went on below, longer than we knew. As usual one Mahid had hung back, to report; the guard who stood in his way as he fled was Ilesias. Both froze dead, each seeing his brother.

I heard it this way from Ilesias. Itasas said, "By the Mahid oath, brother, you should have been with us or died long ago. Stand aside, by the will of the true Imperator, or all Celestialis will know you as a traitor twice over." Ilesias did not answer, but did stand aside, his heart torn two ways. Not between his oaths to Kurkas and to me, but because his brother had not raised a hand against him as a traitor, his proper duty. But as Itasas's back receded into the darkness, Ilesias knew he would be forsworn to me, to let him go. So he raised his blow-tube. Some falling Mahid will use their poison teeth when stun-darted, and some in the end will not. Itasas did.

The next day, when my head was clear, I went to find Ilesias. He was in the Mahid chapel, now a supply store, urns and crates stacked on the pews, dust-motes catching in the sun-shafts from the high narrow windows. He prayed, naked-handed. On the altar lay the corpse, straightened, the onyxine smoothed, the hair unbound and combed. Four new names were carven into the cenotaph. He'd been here all night.

When he paused, lowering his hands, I tapped on the doorpost, to let him know to put on his gloves. He leapt up, then down again in the prostration. As he rose to kneeling I saw his eyes, more Mahid-flat even than usual, but red-rimmed all around.

"We all strive to follow the truth we know," I said, "whether that be Mahid catechism, or more. He did that; and so, though it was the hardest thing you could have done, did you. No Imperator had a Mahid more loyal." I kissed his gloved hand, and then drew him onto my shoulder. He did not weep, but clung.

Only one of the assassins had failed to use his poison tooth, not the one, unfortunately, who knew where Minis was, or who had put the drug in my food. We did learn in his truth-drugging though that Second Amitzas led Minis's guard, and considered himself the true Imperator; the old law is that if the Imperator dies with his heir underage and no regent chosen, the highest Mahid succeeds him. I suspected it was Kurkas who had told him of the column passage, or perhaps Meras. Krero didn't want to bother trying the one survivor, just do away with him in private; but laziness is no good reason to overstep justice. The trial went fast anyway; even without truth-drug the Mahid denied nothing, regretting only that he had failed. Death by dart-poison would have been a surprise and painful, but only for an instant; so I had him blindfolded, and a pin-dagger thrust through his heart.

For all being Imperator was a curse, I count myself lucky. How many callings are there, in which one can fashion dreams with the stroke of a pen?

For me, abolishing slavery was one. By the end of my second year, it had been more or less accepted that I meant to, and was doing it gradually only out of necessity. Slave prices had been steadily dropping; that summer, several large land-owners sold off their whole staffs, thinking to get something for them while they could. That started a run of panic selling, prices fell like a stone, and next thing I knew a delegation of slavers was in my office, begging on their knees for me to close the markets until it blew over, set a price by law, lend them money, anything. Every slaver in Arko, they warned direly, was in danger of going out of business; one man even spoke of "our ancient and honored profession." All through I fingered my manacle-scars conspicuously; when they didn't notice that I mentioned the heat of the day, and took off my shirt. Crude, to Arkans; but they seemed blind. "Hard it is, I know, to change one's work," I said finally, scratching my whip-scars. "But you'd be amazed what suffering people can come through, perfectly able to do so."

I set the date of abolition for three years hence, though I was not sure I'd live to see it. Those who owned slaves set about making do. Sometimes they came up with arrangements less shackling only on paper, such as manumitting their slaves in return for a life-long oath of serfdom, or giving them loans to be worked off, then arranging prices so that a hundred years of work would not repay the debt. A great game of cat and mouse we played, between slave-owners and law-writers.

As the saying goes, the Marble Palace can't have its eye on every field. As always it was ignorance, or more to the point, illiteracy, that caused the downtrodden to let themselves be rooked and abused. They knew it, too; it was an oath every slave just manumitted seemed to swear, to make his children read, somehow. A law forbade teaching except by accredited tutors in approved schools, charging fees that only *fessas* and up could afford; another law forbade any but those who worked in the Press, who are all sworn under truth-drug, to learn the workings of the machines. I struck them both from the books.

Building another Great Press is something only a nation or great city can undertake, and none have yet as I write, though there is talk in Brahvniki. But in the Press compound are smaller machines, including one about the size of a desk that one person and one drafthouse or ox on a treadmill can work happily. The same day, the Press people could barely run it, for the crowd of smiths leaning and poking. Not only in Arko were duplicates of it crafted—spawn-presses, they came to be called—my own too-literate people seized them up as a cat does milk, despite our alphabet with its ten times as many letters. Within two years there was a chronicle full of opinions in every square or cenotaph in Yeola-e.

The single-wing would have caught on of itself; I merely speeded things, spreading the news, setting up a proper wing-courier service. Sometimes the wind forbids; sometimes a fast carriage on a smooth road or a good pigeon is quicker. But roads and pigeons don't go everywhere, and the wing does. Most of the couriers were A-niah, of course; but a crop of Yeoli and then Arkan youngsters came up, in love with flying enough to want to do nothing else. It is dangerous; they often die falling or go missing; but it is the same with sailing or riding, or anything that brings such reward. So I played out Jinai's prophecy.

XIV

Some say I lost the stomach for Imperatorship, when Vriah was nearly assassinated. Someone somehow had got poison into the cough medicine in Kaninjer's supply, and it was her who happened to catch the first cough. He managed to save her; but fearing for all their lives, I persuaded Niku to take her and the twins back to Vae Arahi to live there. It was safer.

I didn't lose my spirit; but life was bitterer without her or any of the children, the Imperial bedchamber seeming cold and dead and too big, like a catacomb, even though Kallijas and Skorsas did all they could to cheer me. I feared for their lives as well. The old feeling worried at my heart for a while, that my life was a curse to other life near it.

I had more trouble with the hawks. As time went by they saw the futility of influencing me, and turned to undermining me. Callous, naive, cruel, ruled by feelings, tight-fisted, narrow-minded, bloody-minded, stubborn, weak-willed, stupid, ignorant, corrupted, competent only on the battlefield, a second Notyere, still insane; they said all these things of me, at one time or another. My favorite of all was "too Yeoli." Inatalla gets credit for that.

One of their tactics was working on Krero. I'd said from the start that in Yeola-e I served Yeolis first, and in Arko, Arkans; he, like they, felt that I should serve Yeolis first wherever I was. Among other things they gave him a house in the new *Aitzas* quarter. It seemed to them, they said, that the fruits of his labors, considering he'd been in the fight through the Marble Palace, got gassed and lost his best friend, seemed a little stingy; *they* had no qualms about sharing fairly. "Are you such a fool you can't see why they're doing this?" I said. "As if they care a whit about what you suffered!"

His eyes narrowed. "I thought you might call me a fool, Fourth Chevenga. So did they, actually. What sort of friend are you, to think I'd feel beholden to them enough to influence you? Or influence you for any reason—*me!*" There was no reasoning with him, on that; they'd found his weakness, and played it to the hilt.

They also set out to discredit me in Yeola-e. One of the first spawn-presses in Tinga-e was bought with money gleaned in Arko, though that was concealed; Yeola's Children, the nationalist party in whose hands it turned up, couldn't have afforded it any other way. Foreign corruption was rife in Yeola-e, that chronicle argued, (in the perfect script of an Arkan machine); its instrument was me, the absentee demarch, the only Yeoli who'd ever killed other Yeolis and not been outcast, the vainglorious swordsman who'd been too willful from a child, spent too long in Laka as a youth and too long in Arko as a man, and found, leading an alliance, that he liked ordering around submissive foreigners more, and so made himself Imperator.

Everything noteworthy I'd ever done they claimed I'd trumped up to carry my own legend; every word or act of mine more meaningful than a scratch of my behind they called conceit or grandstanding; the war was all my fault anyway, they said, for undertaking that naive peace mission. It got someone angry enough to smash the Children's press one night, probably a warrior who'd loved me, but the act played into their hands: never until my time, they said, would such violence against a device of free opinion have been committed in Yeola-e.

You might wonder, after all I had done, who would listen to this. Yet some anger I could understand; my people certainly hadn't sent me against Arko to lose me, I concede that. And there are those, like my old friend Elera Shae-

Tyeba, whose souls suffer for anyone else's victories, who can't bear another doing well, and so must find some way to shrink it, prove it false, find some comforting flaw. They drank such words up like water.

The worst charge the hawks had against me was that I believed myself, and accepted homage as, divine.

The worst of this was that it is true. I believe myself divine, as I do you and all that lives, but myself no more than anyone else. The homage started in the war; or, in fact, in the Mezem, with the fight-fanatics who curled their hair and dyed it black. Skorsas will call me Celestialin, Savior, till I breathe my last. You might recall, our last night in the Mezem I'd said that my death would prove I was not; that I'd lived he took as damning, or should I say blessing, evidence. To his mind I *had* saved Arko: "sometimes the cure," he said, "needs the cauterizing rod." Kunarda, who in our youth had been a friend, worshipped me too, as everyone knew, taking away from me his friendship.

Its roots were in those things, then, and my position as Imperator; from the start of my term it blossomed. Alchaen, who understands such things, explained it thus: they desperately preferred to think a god conquered their Empire rather than a mere man, and a barbarian at that, and so took no half-measures thinking it. Being Arkans they were organized and hierarchical about it; the most numerous group called itself the Temple of the Enlightened Followers of the Deity on Earth Shefen-kas (my penhand squirms just at writing it). They wore crystals, spoke their liturgies in *Aitzas*-accented Yeoli, and raised portraits and statues of me in their temples; learning their rituals involved choirs trying to replicate the sound of my own singing wind, something which to me is as personal as the beating of my heart, I shrank from knowing more of their practices. At least they stayed away from me, except to bring breathtakingly expensive offerings. These I'd turn around immediately to good works, and eventually got them handing them straight to the orphanages, hospitals and so forth, in my name.

Krero took delight in playing with this, as everything else; "You could get them to do *anything!*" he would say, with a pernicious light in his eyes. "It takes Arkans," he sneered; then the Disciples Chevengani sprang up, in Yeola-e, and he had to eat his words. They at least didn't hold I was divine, just wise, and contented themselves to study quotes of mine, though I couldn't recall having said anything profound. They will have a heyday with this book.

To keep a fair balance I should write, as I reminded myself then, that for every worshipper I had a detractor. A business prospered in Arko, in chamber-pots with a face in the bottom, the same one that graced the halls of the Enlightened Followers. I think—I like to think—pots outnumbered altars.

I could not abolish worship of me, for I'd allowed all people in Arko freedom to practice their own creed. I couldn't laugh it off, for they grew so many—an even million Enlightened Followers, last I heard, and thousands more under other names—that by my own creed of the people wills, I must listen to them. I realized the worst when after hearing one report, I leapt up saying, "This is madness; I've got to stop it. I'm going to deny the whole thing—newsscribe!" Kall caught me by the shoulder. "Sheng, what are you doing? Everything's so upside-down already ..." I saw, with heart turning sick: I was Imperator, God's Agent on Earth, Son of the Sun, *officially* divine. By what Alchaen had said too: if I didn't want to foment despondence at the best, bloodshed at the worst, I couldn't deny it.

And so, in Yeola-e, the hay was made. "He claims visions from gods," the spawn-press tracts read. No less than the truth, of how I spoke to the *Fenjitzas*; and I could hardly wink and say, "Look, it's really the God-in-Me; I'm lying to them," in the hope that no Arkan news-scribes who happened to speak Yeoli were near. Far easier for my people, with their remembrance of Notyere, their knowledge that I'd worn the green ribbon, and their fear brought by four years of turmoil, to think power had gone to my head.

Another arrow came, to dent the shield over my heart. Benaiat Ivahn's cough had never improved, since I'd come to Brahvniki asking loans; now a letter came from Stevahn saying he'd taken a sudden turn for the worse, and was not expected to live long. My schedule was drawn up too tightly to allow even a half-day visit, for therr months; I set aside time for it after then, hoping silently it wouldn't be too late.

It was; he died in a month, leaving Stevahn to succeed him, having seen nothing more of me but my letters and gifts.

A half-moon after that, Kall took me aside, and said, "Your grief seems a shade inordinate, for a death so long expected." His teeth were set; it turned out there had been long discussion on who would say this to me, everyone dreading my answer. But I'd known without knowing myself. I looked into my heart, and told Kall what I saw: "I feel somehow I failed him." Seeing it clearly I could reason with myself.

On my twenty-sixth birthday, I looked in the mirror; so much I looked like that black-haired man now. I feel, I thought, like a rider whose horse has turned into a dragon, fire-breath burning the reins away in his hands. I rule Arko, but I no longer rule my own name; I have done everything I could, and that is much, my power absolute, but I have less control over my fate than when I was demarch. I must have done something wrong; what was it? When was it?

I let out my heart to Kallijas. "You did nothing wrong," he said, gripping my shoulders. "That's the problem. In your goodness, you call out to the rest of us, who are imperfect."

I tore out of his hands. "Kall, if *you* turn, if *you* become one of them, who among Arkans will I have left?" He seized me again. "No, Sheng. Let's spar, and I'll show you whether you're God ... I'm seeing it clear, I'm certain. You're not perfect, but you're very good, and it's that they see. Good enough to think of something, when you stop worrying, to find your path unconceived. You always do. I believe in you."

Then came the matter of Haiksilias Lizan, the great painter, who'd done my portrait as a gladiator.

He'd come to me after the sack, begging a commission for a mural, to my joy; I'd feared he'd died, or lost his art, as artists sometimes do (which I suppose would be as bad). In one of the great old parlors, that I'd opened again to the public, was a suitable wall; I had the paintings hanging there moved, and gave it to him. Only one condition, he asked; that until he was finished, some two years, no one be permitted to see the work. Knowing artists are fickle in such things—the greater the artist, the greater the fickleness, some say—I agreed, and he began.

Now I had all but forgotten. It was two years; he came, made his obeisance, and said it was finished, with a look on his face like a child's, barely able to wait to show one a scribble he has done. Since I had no appointments right now, only paperwork, I put my pen down and went with him. We met Krero in the corridor. I wonder how different things might be, had I not thought he looked as if he needed cheering, and invited him to join us.

The curtains were drawn, so that one could see only darkness at first; on the wall, my eyes caught only the sense of motion, and of flame. When we were in the best place, Haiksilias pulled the cord that threw all the curtains open.

Words are weak, in describing an average work of art, fail entirely describing a great one. Suffice to say, it was painted so real it seemed alive, the figures moving, the fire hot; being on a wall large enough that I could see little else, it threw me back two years; I could all but smell the smoke, thick with its stench of wrongness, hear the whoops and the screams, feel a gutter-stream of blood splashing my feet. I had not seen the sack up close, but from the Marble Palace. Now I did.

Seized in feeling I barely had time to think, to understand what this meant, to admire, as well as his mastery, his courage, the strength of his conviction—he must have expected to die for this—to think what it would move in Arkans, when they saw it. A sound came, that did not fit: his chuckle, to see me so shaken. Two years, I thought, he's been looking forward to this. Then a sound and a movement came that did fit; Krero's snarling cry of anger, and his sword, which being guard captain he always wore, springing out of its scabbard and drawing back over his shoulder.

I saw a moment's flash, of him holding Haiksilias by the throat, the hands that had such brilliance in them thrown up to ward off the blow; then I was between them, barely knowing I had moved, since that was my hands' skill, catching Krero's wrist. "*You child-raping, Saint-Mother-spurned moron!*" Krero blinked, astonishment cutting through his rage. "I'm in the same room. In full sight. *Who'd get blamed, Krero? Who'd get blamed?*"

"Well!" he cried, straightening, and not sheathing his sword. Haiksilias had got knocked over; now he scrambled, quick for an older man, away and up, eyeing the door. Over my shoulder Krero barked to the guards to shut and bolt it, which they did. "Look at this, Cheng! Look at this monstrosity! Why do you think the child-raper did this? What do you think will happen when people see it, and have all the old wounds that have healed ripped open again? This is subversion, this is rebellion in the guise of art! If someone did as much in the street, we'd whip off his head without a thought!"

My mind was coursing ahead. Haiksilias had been threatened, and abused; it wasn't only assault, but attempted murder, the sort of thing we sentenced people to ten years in the dungeon for. A warrior's instincts don't serve, in peacetime. Haiksilias might not bring charges, counting himself lucky; but it had been in my presence, and I was law, in Arko. I told Krero that. He stared at me, frozen and silent, as if I'd stabbed him. "You wouldn't," he said, after a long time. Then, catching up his mask again, "Cheng! Cheng . . . where are you going, Beloved? Does it matter nothing to you, who loves you, who are your friends, who got you here?"

I looked at my hands, saw them shaking like leaves, the gold chains of the seals dancing. I heard Haiksilias chuckle again. "How many times have I told you, Krero, in Arko I serve Arko first? How many times have I said, even I am not above the law?"

Now he saw fit to show a face of anger. "You and your child-raping laws! Isn't there one against stirring up trouble and bloodshed by telling lies, in writing or with paint?" The mural followed the first Pages' tale of the sack more than the second, and had me standing triumphant; yet nothing was overblown, it had the subtlety that a master knows how to invoke, that makes for a harder and deeper ring of truth. "Isn't there one against fomenting hate against other residents of the City, putting them in danger? Don't you see, Cheng? This stinking cowardly Arkan did this *counting* on you to be soft on him! It's a stroke against all of us, you too, why do you think I got angry? And if you put up with this, what will be next? We can paint it over but *he* will go on . . ."

"Paint it over?" I said. That was inconceivable. Whatever feeling it evoked, it was a great work; a thousand years from now it would be counted so. I'd destroyed enough Arkan art treasures. "Are you mad?" we asked each other, in one voice. "Cheng! What on the Earthsphere are you thinking? We're going to let Arkans through here to *see* this? Why don't you give them the charge order against us, while you're at it!"

"That's enough," I said, quietly, which froze him. "Go to my office and wait for me, if you want to say more." While he yelled, I couldn't think. He started to protest, wanting me to make no decision without his voice in my ear, until I threatened.

I stood alone, in silence, with Haiksilias, and the sack. I don't know what to do, I thought numbly; I have no idea. *Think,* I commanded myself. *Choose.* He knew to say nothing, somehow; with a long breath I seized calm. What would you say, I asked, God-in-Myself?

It answered. Could we hide from Arko the work of its own, out of fear? Were we pretending the sack hadn't happened, and no one felt anything about it? I would tell all Arko through the Pages of Haiksilias's duplicity about it, which one should take into consideration while wondering whether everything he'd painted was true; then let them look. What am I, I thought, if I fear truth?

I opened the door. "You've been duly paid," I said to Haiksilias. He stared at me amazed. "I suppose you thought I'd punish you for this." I gestured to his rendering of me, strutting over the flaming ruin, with a cruel gold-toothed grin. "Because *he* would. But I was never that. You are a great artist, Haiksilias, but not an honest one, and you know it; you're too great not to. That takes away from your greatness." His eyes seemed to flinch; great artists feel truth deeply. I beckoned to the door, and he went without a word.

"So what are we going to do about this?" said Krero, in my office. "Let's think this out sensibly, Cheng."

"I've already thought it out, chosen and done," I said. "Except the last. Someone who shows such bad judgment even once, I can't keep on. You're out of the Demarchic Guard."

I remember it word for word, but won't bother to write it. Suffice to say he called me a traitor, and said the hawks were right in everything about me. I told him time was up, I had work to do. "A demarch who won't listen to the people's will is no demarch!" he cried, finally. "I'll see you impeached!"

The flash I saw was bright as lightning, a wide bolt that for a moment binds the sky; the voice of the harmonic singer rang clear, with the wind. "Go right ahead," I said. He stared, startled; for a moment, I thought he'd guess. So I made it into a sneer, as of defiance, *"Go right ahead."* He sprang up and stamped out, snapping, "I *will*!"

I stayed up that night, and by the morning it was on the books, an impeachment law as close to Yeola-e's as it could be. There was no Assembly, to vote the ten percent once a petition was in; as well most people in Arko don't know how to sign their names. So I set out that a mark would suffice, and ten percent in any city or district, including the City itself. Just as in Yeola-e, everyone sixteen or older would be allowed to vote, man, woman, slave, any caste; owners and husbands must allow their slaves and wives to go to the chip-boxes. When Krero came asking about it that same morning, I showed him the page, with the ink barely dry.

His eyes had been flat; now glaring put some life into them. He'd always been against Arkans being given the vote. "Weren't you going to start this here?" I said. "You need some voters. You think I'm going to let a small clutch of Yeolis, not one of ten thousand in this nation, throw me out? Is that the people's will? Or did you plan to start this at home as well? If you want to *really* get rid of me, you'll have to: Yeola-e might accept Arko tossing me as Imperator, but not demarch, unless *they* vote on it."

He looked as if he'd swallowed a peach pit; I suspect he might have backed down then, except that he'd already spoken to the hawks. "You have some cursed trick," he said. "You always do. On me or them ... What is it, you turd? You think all Arko is going to fall over in gratitude for the sweet things you've done for them, is that it? You want to prove that? Or that all Arko will become Enlightened Followers?"

"If you can't see what I'm doing," I said, with a smile and a wink, "just trust me. I know what's best for the people." He strode away, trembling with rage.

I spoke my thoughts on Haiksilias's painting in the Pages, and threw open the doors. How Krero had thought it would evoke only anger, I don't know. Not that there was none; the guards, to whom I'd given orders not to move unless threatened with harm, got spat on and called names by people in tears more than once. But it didn't start a revolt; sanctioned, indeed paid for, by the oppressors, how could it be a rallying-cry? Only Haiksilias made a call to arms, and got called an immoderate artist by the Pages for it, while they praised my courage and honesty, and wrote another reminder of what I'd really done during the sack. I'd made friends there, by freeing them.

I gave the writers the news of the impeachment law, and when they'd hit themselves on the head enough times to believe it, they wrote it. Shortly after that the petitioning got properly underway. Inatalla came in for an audience, praising me now for my integrity in upholding our sacred principles. But it struck him, he said, that Arkans and Yeolis being two different peoples with two different philosophies, that two separate votes should be held, one in Arko over my position as Imperator, one in Yeola-e over my position as demarch. "I understand your concern," I answered, "that were it held as one vote, more people in Yeola-e might vote charcoal than Arkans vote chalk, since Arkans aren't used to voting, and then you'd still be stuck with me. For shame, that you'd abandon your own people to the mercies of such an incompetent, mad, corrupted second Notyere, as long as Arko was rid of me . . . well, no matter. I'm afraid you'll just have to go out and campaign, and get those Arkans voting. One vote it will be, with Artira succeeding me should chalk win."

"You can't just choose that," he said.

"Choose *otherwise* is what I can't do, Inatalla." I told him. "We conquered this land, as you're so constantly reminding me; it's part of Yeola-e. Anything so major as independence would require a full vote of the Yeoli people, and if you think you can convince them to do that, two years after the war ..." He strode out with resolve in his eyes. Shortly after that, it was chalk, chalk, chalk, a speaker waving papers on every street in Arko, Chalk Societies, tracts and lessons on voting going out to every corner of the Empire ("once you have your chip in hand, take up the white chalk ..."). The hawks had money enough to hire an army of speakers.

Because I didn't do the same, having no money of my own, my friends began to run scared. "Would you let Arko fall to those vultures?" Kallijas and Skorsas kept saying. "You're the only Yeoli who cares for us at all!" I spoke, in Assembly and the Pages. That was as much as I could do, in decency, to my mind.

Inatalla liked to stay off the podium, I noticed; it was Faraiko Terero who did most of their talking in the city. They mostly stuck to the sack, uncovering a number of atrocities I'd done they'd been forced to keep quiet but could hold in no longer, their consciences bleeding. I submitted to truth-drug again, but of course they cried fake. They were quiet on the rough handling of Haiksilias Lizan, though; it might come out that their first signatory had done it.

Krero's voice, I noticed from early, was strangely missing. Then he struck his name from their petition. A change of heart, was all he told the Pages.

He stayed in the house they'd given him, now, and never came near the Palace; our paths could not cross by accident. Then his name was on the audience list. He came in, cold as ice. "I'm only here for one purpose, demarch and Imperator: to tell you what you should know.

"They're out for your blood. I've never seen such a hunting party, sharpening arrows, going around the circle dreaming up the most plausible atrocities, revelling in lies ... they hid it from me before, saying they were concerned for you as well. But once they smelled meat ..." He seemed to become himself, as if by habit, as he spoke. "One would think you'd spat on their mothers' ashes, not shed your blood and got them all where they are!" News to him, perhaps.

"Cheng," he said at the end, "—don't tell me what you

feel towards me ... please? Just let me say what I must. You were right; they played me for a fool. I ... I'm sorry."

I began to say what I felt, thinking despite his asking it was for the best. "Krero, it's all right, if you hadn't, someone else—" He cut me off, tears springing to his eyes. "No! No! Don't! I know what you'll say! You forgive me! And you still love me! And you'll embrace me! I couldn't stand that! I couldn't stand that! I'd rather die!" He ran out before I could say more.

"It comes as no surprise," Inatalla said in the Pages. "He called Chevenga his best friend, after all. Once turned will turn again." And *then* he opened the matter of Haiksilias. Why hadn't he pressed charges? Had I, who was the law in Arko, not told him he could, by the new law? Or had I said something else, to prevent it?

I had, in truth, been leaving it to Haiksilias, who hadn't dared. Now, seized up like a standard by the hawks, he did. When the Guard went to arrest Krero, they found his house ransacked, and empty. He'd done it himself, his servants said, then fled; I had to send Ikal after him. Because truth-drugging will show ill of him and well of me, I thought, he thinks I mean to abandon him, or toss him up as a sacrifice to save myself; if only I could say, *Ikal, don't find him.* As it was, they didn't, before the vote.

The debate in Yeola-e was furious, and full of feeling. The hawks used their spawn-press there too, but at home there were many more loyal to me to be angered. All manner of insults which I won't repeat were flung, from both sides. When I went home, a number of people came to me, asking as Inatalla had that the vote be divided in two: no Arkan choice, they contended, should ever be permitted to tear a Yeoli demarch away from the Yeoli people. This was the price, I answered, of spreading our ways by conquest. Of course many answered that Arko didn't deserve our way; then I should not be their Imperator, I answered, for I know no other. A number of others pulled me aside quietly and said, "Are you suicidal, or just idiotic?" I would just smile and say what usually shut people up when I said it: "I have a plan."

The date was set, two moons before my twenty-seventh birthday. Of course the debate heated up almost to madness in the days before. In Arko there were fights, and even some killings; gangs threatened to examine every voter's hands after he came out to see what color dust was on them, so we had to arrange a heavy guard for every box, and a bowl of water for washing.

I finished up some affairs that must be finished if I lost. One of them was freeing Lasatro, and his command. Of the four, one had died, of beating his head on the wall.

I don't think he believed me, even when I turned the key, opened the door, helped him load his shop-things onto a cart, which taxed his muscles, and strained mine. When I gave him back the sword he'd surrendered to me, he believed. He apologized for everything he'd said then, and gave me a sword: a short sword he'd made here, that fit my hand like an *Aitzas's* glove. He'd measured my grip, he said, when I'd raised him by his hand after he'd knelt to surrender. "It has a name," he said. "*Hope.*"

We embraced; in those huge arms I felt like a boy, and cried like one. I'd never much hidden my heart from him. Whatever the rest of the world might think me, I was redeemed in his eyes; right now, that was enough.

If I could somehow have been in both places, for the opening of the result, I should have been; as it was I went home. That much I owed my people, my first people, who bore and raised me. I was asked, was I frightened; no, I answered, for it will be good either way, whether you see it or not. My poor sister was more frightened than I, understandably.

All the world knows how it went. In Yeola-e, sixty-nine in a hundred charcoal, in Arko, seventy-five in a hundred chalk. But, All-spirit be praised, even if too few of them were women and slaves, some half of the population of the Empire voted. That, of course, is far more than twice the population of Yeola-e.

So the demarchic signet was taken from my hand, and then in Arko, the seals; I ceased being Fourth Chevenga Shae-Arano-e, and became Chevenga Aicheresa, taking the surname of my mother. How humiliating the ceremony is, I had not known, never expecting to suffer it. Several times, one must say, "My people, I have failed you." It was worse than usual for me, too, having to do it twice, and the second time to such jeers.

I stayed in Arko, to do the transition. The night it was done, the Guard gathered to console me, privately, no scribes. I ended up consoling them, my eyes, I think, the only ones to stay dry. Kunarda was the worst by far, carrying on like a teenager who'd lost his mother. Near the end of the night, one of the younger ones, Sithena, came up to me. "Beloved," she said. "We can still call you that. . . . Whatever you say about the people's will, everyone knows: you could have stopped this. You didn't have to do it. Why did you?" I called for silence, owing them all an answer.

"You know what I always wanted," I said, "and how it kept falling short. Remember when I tried to get them to vote over purification, how well that worked? I saw; they needed something that made it clear. How, really, could they know the law is truly subject to a vote, and the Imperator to the law, unless they saw the Imperator is subject to a vote?

"The hawks decided to impeach me, and I saw the chance to teach Arko the vote, to get even my enemies sweating to teach Arko the vote. You think because you love me that the best I could have given to Arko was more of myself; you're wrong. I am finite; one day I will die." In three years or less, in truth, making my choice all the easier. "What I have given them will last forever. They've ruled an Imperator: they've seen him cast down, because they wanted it, and they will never forget. It can never be taken from them, whatever the hawks think or plan. I've shown them their own power, and how to use it. That is far greater a gift, than myself."

I awoke past midnight. The Arkan air lay like a huge sweaty hand on my skin, full of tendrils of heat. A lamp was burning; I heard voices. I was alone in bed—not the great bed, since that was no longer mine, but another. Skorsas was speaking quietly with Kallijas.

"He seems all right. . . . That means nothing, you know how he is. Alchaen says he won't be able to help it. . . . It was his life . . ."

"Alchaen's going back to Haiu Menshir, isn't he? Or ... can we afford ..."

"He's going to talk to him in the morning. If anyone can head it off, it's him. ... thinks we should visit Haiu Menshir."

"Stop worrying, love."

A little while later they had to pull Alchaen out of bed, and bring him. His hand pressed cool on my brow, ruffling my forelock, but I didn't truly feel it. For the work for which I lived was done, and I understood that; no reason remained for my heart to beat nor my blood to flow, my muscles to flex nor a single more thought to pass through my mind, and so, like a wheel rusted in an instant, it all seized up.

XV

I lay on a bed that must be on land, not ship, for it was not tossing. I heard movement before and behind me, though I paid no heed. "Chivinga." Alchaen shook me by the shoulder, fairly hard. "*Look*." Before me on the night table stood a cup. "At me, now." In his hand was the green ribbon.

"This is the fork of the road," he said. "Before you is death; I mixed it myself; no tricks, it will work. Behind you am I, and the ribbon. It must be one or the other. Choose."

I lifted myself onto one elbow, facing the cup. I knew him; he didn't lie in this sort of thing. Healing or death was the nature of my choice, as always.

I took up the cup in my hand, gazed down into it. The liquid was clear, and had a bit of a tang for smell; it was some Haian stuff I didn't know. Painless, no doubt; he wouldn't make me suffer. If he feared for me, as I did this, he didn't show it.

I drew it up close to my lips. I thought, what is my life? Nothing, or worse than nothing, a lie: it masquerades as something. I am dead, my flame, burned out; but my heart still beats, my lungs still draw air, in and out, in and out, mindless as obedience drill, pretending some purpose. What's the sense, in refusing an end to this absurdity? I put the cup to my mouth, ready to tip it, and my hand turned to stone.

Trembling took me, all over; the cup jolted, splashing a trickle of the poison on my hand, and tears came to my eyes. My flesh, I thought, why won't you do my will? There's nothing in the world left me but this draught, that will put all things right; my soul is gone, it only remains for my body to join it. Even the God-in-Myself, the singing wind, was of the demarchy. What is it, flesh? Not cowardice, for you must know that here lies nothing but the blasted waste, madness, forever; there, freedom, truth, justice, reason. But you are only flesh, mindless; you don't mind living mindlessly; you know no better. That's what my will is here for; to make your choices. I made to tip the cup, and was defied again.

Patience, I told myself, drawing breath against trembling, and heard my teeth chatter on the rim. Since six, I'd trained my body to be stubborn in clinging to life. Like the nine-tenths dead twisted pines on high talus, barkless from the wind, it clung. I sweated cold, and tears ran down my cheeks; I fought off a child's wail of helplessness, and drew myself up to kneeling to hold the cup to my mouth in both hands, afraid to let it further away in case I could not bring it back, like a patient joined to his medicine flask. I made love to it, lip to lip, remembering Shininao in my Mezem dreams; the wings and the silence that smothers all sound in between filled the air; the acrid liquid with bubbles around its edges was familiar, as if I'd been intimate with it all my life.

I give myself, I thought, closing my eyes, foolishly thinking not seeing it would make a difference. I give myself to an end; but my hands would not lift, my mouth would not drink. Why? I felt my tears splash into it, and my shakes turn to wracking sobs. Long ago, in some dream or myth, I thought, I could do anything asked of me, even give my life in a lake; now the only thing that I should, I can't. I slammed the cup down on the night table, spilling poison all over it, and stabbed my wrist out to Alchaen, crying like a baby now, knowing it was not my body that was the traitor, since flesh cannot will, but my soul; that in this I would always fail, even if it brought the Second Fire; that I was chained forever to the wheel of life, however short a way was left in its path, however much it hurt. I felt him tie the ribbon; I had chosen.

My second stay on Haiu Menshir, Alchaen was with me much less. It was a malady of change, not an injury done me; to his mind I was past the worst, having chosen, and needed only time, and rest. As well he separated me from my loves; I could not truly rest, or keep my mind on myself, as to his mind I must, unless I was alone. It was for their sakes too, I think; being near me then, I know, was nothing but torment. Niku, on Alchaen's urging, visited Ibresi. Skorsas and Kall stayed in Haiuroru, though sometimes, I found out later, they would hide in the rocks by the beach, just to see me.

I recall several times sitting on the sand alone, looking at the ribbon on my wrist and thinking, "Now what? Alchaen's left me with this, all I have, without a clue what to do with it, curse him!" But in the end he was right, as usual. My life had been the demarchy, but life goes on, and like nerves healing around a wound the soul will find new ways.

From the Hall of Elders Alchaen borrowed a silver mirror, and I finally met Chevenga Aicheresa face to face. That next month, since we were stuck together so constantly, I got to know him, and his habits. Once his vitality returned, he was always burning to do things; long training every day barely sated him. He was very good with a sword, could be impetuous if he didn't take care, thought and moved fast, spoke honestly, loved wholly, lusted frequently, slept badly, was obsessed with time since he knew he would die soon, and needed a hot bath every night. In fact, he was remarkably familiar. Whatever of my character was innate and whatever bred into me by the demarchy, I found, it was all still there, as much as my arms or legs.

Yet it was all purposeless. Again Alchaen asked me what I wanted to do. I could think of nothing for three days, so thoroughly broken of the habit I had been.

In time, I found my rage. Alchaen thought from the start it was in me, but I was keeping it secret from myself. Never, I argued at first; it was all justly done, the people wills, I had been behind the whole thing; all in all, really, I didn't

come off too badly for sacking a city. No one had ever hid
from me that of four demarchs impeached in history, two
killed themselves within months. (That brought back like
yesterday our childhood game, and Nyera saying after I'd
been impeached, "Now you have to kill yourself." I remembered not believing I had sadness that great in me for anything. It seemed I'd been right.)

He took me to a farm where there was wheat to thresh,
in a barn out of anyone's hearing, and put the flail in my
hands. As I worked, he ran through it all. "You were slave
to cruel masters, Chivinga, once Fourth. You toiled, you
shed your blood, you worked to collapse for them, and
finally you offered the utmost sacrifice, to set them free.
And in return they cast you down, stripped you of your
name, your craft, your life's meaning, ground your face in
the dust, killed your soul if not your body. Chivinga Aicheresa, once and never again Fourth Chivinga Shae-Arano-e:
they killed him, and what becomes of you they don't care
a dust-speck."

My reason saw the contradictions; but it was to my emotion he spoke, and it listened. I choked on a pain like an
ember in my throat; then flat and tooth-edged and dead as
madness, the anger came roaring up, shot like lightning
through my arms and into the stroke of the flail. Those
wheat-grains died a thousand deaths; nor did I care when
the chaff was beaten off, but went on, howling mindlessly,
making them into flour. As always in such a rage, part of
me stood off impassive, and thought, *he brought me here
so I wouldn't kill anyone. He was wise.*

He kept me going until I was so tired I had to sit down,
and when I wept then, said, "Chivinga, haven't you learned
yet, not to demand perfect justice from your feelings?"
Always he knew without my saying what upset me.

Doing this every day wasn't enough, as it turned out. I
know how a Haian psyche-healer would phrase it: I was a
mainlander, war-trained, having lived a life awash in violence, and hence hardened to its effects. A ruffian, no question. That night, lying awake, I wanted to draw blood. On
Haiu Menshir that is not so easy to arrange, for all I managed it last time; there'd certainly be no Arkan attack for
an excuse; I'd arranged that. Yet, as is my talent, I managed

it. In short, I slipped away from the apprentice watching me, did a quick Mezem warm-up, and started a tavern brawl in Sailortown.

The memories are hazy. I do remember standing by the bar realizing I didn't know how to do this; I'd fought forty-nine death-duels in the Mezem and commanded an army of a hundred thousand to conquer the Empire of Arko, but never started a tavern brawl in my life. I remember deciding the first step was to get drunk, and the serving-woman asking, "Which self-induced poison will you have, sweetheart?"; It was then I realized I had no money. She saw the ribbon, and gave me one on the house, provided I went home to my healer after. The cheapest wine: she could not know I'd tasted an Imperator's. I drank, thanked her and left; a place with such kindness in it did not deserve what I meant to do.

Next I remember a rougher place, and one of its huge brawny peace-keepers laying a heavy hand on my shoulder. "I'll be entirely honest with you," I said, for it seemed the right thing to do, "I carry a great deal of buried anger, which, as my healer tells me, I have need to release; yes, I admit, I came in here to do that. I am telling you this so you will know not to take it personally." I next remember the sight of him sprawling on the dirt floor, and people shouting all around.

It gets much hazier from there. I remember the hot pleasure of my own body's motion, yells and whooping all around, wood cracking, a cup smashing on stone, flames leaping up from an overturned lamp, wild laughter, snatching up half-empty cups from tables and quaffing them in between comers, wondering, as I saw the fighting had spread all over, what anger everyone else had kept buried. I ended up declaiming from a memorial in the harbor, while the crowd hailed me mockingly, raising flagons. Alchaen found me there. Later, when I could stand it, he repeated back to me what of my speech he'd heard.

"I am the *semanakraseye* of destruction, the Imperator of war! Every duel in the world, I am the gladiator, every battle, I am the army; my hands have killed and died a million times! When ten thousand Lakans died in Kantila, I was the poison! When Arko burned, I was the flames! The

Arkans who conquered Haiu Menshir and struck down the compact of peace, I *brought* them here! Wherever people turn mad against each other, I am, wherever blood pumps out into the dust, my heart beats! Hail me, child-rapers, barbarians, cowards; fight me if you call yourselves human, kill me a million times again, if you can!"

So he tells me, and I must believe. Apparently I greeted him cheerily and innocently as a boy, saying I was well, thank you, my only regret that all these people had turned too lily-livered to fight me. He talked me down.

As we went away, I glanced over my shoulder at the stone, and broke out laughing. It was in remembrance of the one battle on Haiu Menshir, the inscription mentioning someone by the name of Fourth Chevenga Shae-Arano-e.

Apparently all Sailortown raged with debate, the next few days, some swearing the rampaging madman was the very same Fourth Chevenga, his face unmistakable, others scoffing that no one so far gone could be him. Let the dispute be put to rest now: no, it was not him. It was one Chevenga Aicheresa.

How long, I wondered, will it be before the evil I do in my life outweighs the good, and the credit of love I have earned runs out? The House of Integrity was sued, of course, and we paid the damages out of Skorsas's fortune, which he considered mine. After bargaining the plaintiffs down, that is: they'd hoped through my weak-mindedness to bilk the House, if you can imagine that, claiming I'd laid waste to two establishments I hadn't been near, and caused two-thirds of all sixty-seven injuries. I did that negotiation myself, actually, hiding the cuffs on my wrists and ankles (a custom of the House, which I accepted as justice) under the table, while the plaintiffs, a tavern owner and an Enchian ship-captain, peppered the conversation with such remarks as, "You should be chained to a post," and "Where I come from they lock people like you in a bricked pit and throw the key in the sea."

The night after, I dreamed of being put in a pit covered with a steel grille and lined with brick, just as the captain had said; now he was sailing into the great ocean of the west which is as deep as the mountains are high, since the judge (Yeoli, since I was Yeoli) had decreed that nowhere in the Miyatara was deep enough to throw my key. But I had a note, signed Amitzas, that showed the pattern of bricks to tap; the secret door, which led to a passage in the Marble Palace, sprang open.

The next day, I looked at myself, and saw, though I'd been stripped of seals and signet, I had things that had always been Chevenga's, not Fourth Chevenga's; not the Ascendant's or the demarch's, but *mine*. My crystal, my father's wisdom-tooth, Mana's arm-ring, the Haian time-piece—they hadn't asked for it back—even my gold teeth, come to think of it, and my scars. These things I would never lose.

From then on I could hold to sense, my anger bled out. After the first thought of what I wanted to do with my life came to me—to take a decent amount of time raising my children—more followed. I wanted to spend more time with Niku and Skorsas and Kallijas, train, teach in the School, practice my flying, write, visit people and places I hadn't been able to before, such as Megan Whitlock in F'talezon and Niku's family in Ibresi (it was about time); since I'd lost my trade, I should keep house for my family. Barely had I begun to see what a marvellous amount of time I would have, when it was filled.

He freed me of the restraints, let Skorsas and Kallijas back in, so I could make all my apologies. Niku came back, and we had our tearful reconciliation. Several days later, Alchaen untied my ribbon.

We both wept this time, bidding each other goodbye, though we swore to write. In my future, I could not foresee anything to force me back here again, and if I should leave my family for any reason it would be to visit a place I had never been. I was twenty-seven. Most likely I would never see him again, and we both knew it.

Niku persuaded me to go home by way of Ibresi, since it was close; we spent a moon there, while Skorsas and Kallijas sailed on ahead. Arkans were never well-liked on Niah-lur-ana, and they had some business to finish, they said, in Vae Arahi.

Her home truly is Celestialis on earth. A sea turquoise in the depths and crystal-clear in the shallows breaks on beaches white as snow, or pale pink with coral sand; under the ripples, fish of colors more brilliant than jewels play among plants as bright, while in the sky above winged children loop and wheel like brilliant birds. Though the islands are not far south of Haiu Menshir they are somehow much more southern, perhaps because the sea is warmer; aside from the palm trees with their fronds swishing in the wind, plants that Haians would think fanciful grow in abundance. It soon comes clear where A-niah find the time to so master the craft of flying; for a fresh meal, one need only ponder what one would prefer, then pick it from a tree or dive to the bottom of a sea warm as a bath. It became hard even to imagine cold. I kissed Niku's hand, and said, "I never understood until now, how much you love me. You left this place."

They welcomed me like a king, with a feast of Ibresian boar and giant cormorant eggs, and the gift of a man's pareo of purple silk. It was strange to hear my secret Niah name, New-Wings-in-Sunlight, spoken so openly by so many, or to be called, still, *Hakan*. To them, I had not changed, nor what I had done. They showed me the cavern of augury, at high tide and low. I learned why A-niah wear so little—anything more is unbearable in such heat—and why the brilliant colors: to match nature. Against the flowers and birds and fish that live there, no human-made dye can look ostentatious.

I met Niku's mother, a white-haired ancient woman with skin like bark from the sun and the cripple's wizened legs, yet in whom one could see strong beauty like Niku's. She was not one for sentimental homage. "Well, here he is," she said, once we'd been introduced, "the lad who ferreted out the secret of the wing and made us cast our fate with the world's, who conquered Arko and lost it. Sit here, boy, and let's see what sort of deal my only daughter is getting for leaving us. . . . Are you over your madness yet?" Niku said something to her in Niah, exasperated; to me she said in Arkan, "She's testing you." I'd gathered that.

She grilled me as thoroughly as if we were doing some deal, except with personal things as well, making me tell my whole life story. I kept honest and civil but gave her back as good in bantering; she'd like me less, for weakness, if I didn't, I knew. She was Niku's mother.

A wheeled chair is little good on an island of sand, so she must be carried everywhere; that month, I was her horse. My tour of the islands I did with her on my back, using my ears like reins to turn my head where she wanted, making mock propositions and announcing me wherever we went with a pat on the head and a loud, "Here is my Chevenga!" It was not such hardship, in truth. She weighed little, and was one to learn from. We were soon fast friends. As Niku had said, she did indeed still fly; she just needed a height and a pair of strong arms to hurl her into the air. Later when I got home, Esora-e would ask me what I'd done in Ibresi; I casually told him, crystal in hand, "I flung my mother-in-law off a cliff." He almost hit me.

Too soon, we had to leave. The night before we sailed into Selina, I could not sleep, the creaking of the ship and the chatter of the ripples on its planks too loud. Of impeached demarchs who had chosen to live on in Yeola-e, there had only ever been one other. Hiding my face would be cowardly; but what would people think, to see it?

I found out, the next day: I would have to hide it, if we meant to get anywhere. Mostly the crowds came to embrace me, tenderly, and give me blessings; it was no secret, where I'd been. "I voted for you!" they'd say, and "Curse those Arkans, they shouldn't have been able to take you away from us! Why did you let them?" Or the warriors: "Is this what we fought them for, Beloved?" I would ask whether they now thought Arko and Yeola-e should be two separate lands; as often as not they'd say, "Now I'd say so, yes!", or "Yes, but they should be under us." Not that it mattered now, what I heard.

I meant to go through Terera on the sly; but Niku took a mind to throw off her hood, and announce to all and sundry, "I'm here, so you know who else is!" Out onto the street and roofs they came, calling my name like a new demarch's, but with a note of concern, as the people of one's home will do. With waving and clasping hands and hugging and saying, "Yes, I'm all right, I'm fine, thank you, I love you too," all the way to the falls, it took me a bead.

Skorsas and Kallijas were waiting at the lip. I'd thought the children might be too, a half-frightening thought; one wonders what madness is still hiding in one, to touch them without one knowing. But Skorsas said, "They're waiting at home, life's heart." We walked together up the path, my loves' faces all shining like children's about to see a secret gift they've made found. Where the road forks, they all went left, to Haranin instead of to the Hearthstone. "Well, we should blindfold him, shouldn't we?" said Skorsas, as I stood confused. "Yes, yes, we should," Niku and Kallijas agreed. They forbade my questions, saying, "Trust us," and tied a silk scarf over my eyes.

All I could tell of where they were leading me was that it was up the mountain on a path my feet didn't know, that went quite high. Ahead I heard a child's giggle, bird-high with excitement, that sounded like one of the twins—how long, since I'd seen them?—then a door creaking open, though I knew of no buildings this high. "Here," said Kallijas, and they stopped me. After turning me in precisely the right direction, they untied the scarf.

Standing before me, so new that the ground around it was still raw and sprinkled with mortar dust, was a stone house, built in a style like the Hearthstone Dependent. Mansion would be a truer word; the center was three stories, the wings two, and sprawling. Everything spoke restrained quality: the windows were all pure-glazed, the roof tile, the door oaken and carved with patterns, but none too elaborate. It was one of those places whose outside did not shout, but whispered, to one who could hear, of subtle wonders within. Though it was too new and unlived in to look homey yet, that would not take long, as long as there were plenty of people.

"All-spirit help us," I said. "Who built this? And why?"

They'd been peering at my face; now they all broke out laughing, as if they'd been waiting a long time for this. Kallijas said, "Read the keystone."

It said, "This house was built in Summer 1554, with the funds of all those thousands who wished to aid in his welfare, and by the planning of his family, with the deepest love and gratitude, for Chevenga Aicheresa."

I dropped my face into my hands, and almost keeled over; Skorsas caught me. The door burst open, and a wave of shrieking children flooded out and washed all around my legs, grabbing my fingers, my belt, my kilt, tugging me towards the door with all their might. There were adults in the ambush too, waiting inside in the sitting room, which was as big as most houses in itself: all my parents, my grandmother, my aunt, my surviving sibs and their families, all my close friends in town. Esora-e knifed open the first jug, while the children dragged me off on the tour. I hardly saw anything for tears.

It doesn't befit me to describe what was given me. I squirmed enough to have got it. Suffice to say the style of the whole place was understated but with a touch of whimsy where one would least expect it, there were more than enough rooms for all of us, they'd thought of everything, and it was indescribably beautiful. The thing most worthy of note was in a chamber of its own, and almost made me fall over again: a fully-functioning and fully-equipped spawn-press. It even had a brass plaque with my name on it.

When I came to my senses, I pulled Skorsas aside. "Tell me in truth, how you did this."

He answered, "What do you mean? Do you think the keystone lies, treasure of the world?" It seemed while I'd been in Haiu Menshir, in no state to know it, people from all over Yeola-e, knowing I had none, had sent me money. He'd put in some of his, too, but not all that much; the use of the land, which was higher up than anyone else used, had been approved by Assembly. I saw now why, when I'd healed faster than expected, they'd sent me to Ibresi, and what business Skorsas and Kallijas had been doing. "As for the press," he added, "it'll pay for itself in a few years. There's enough clients in town to book it solid; half of them even know how to run it. Yes, the Palace people said they'd teach you. You have friends everywhere, heart of the world."

So, it seemed, it had all come by the people's will; I would never have accepted something so huge, in the end, except for that. If anyone objects to their extravagance, I have yet to hear it. Yet, wandering the corridors a few days later, I thought with a pang, all this they've given to me, to have for maybe three years. When I am dead, will Niku be chastised for building it for herself and her own, since she knew? Yet everyone else didn't; it could be argued she had to go along to keep it secret. Then I thought, how small-hearted is the world? Not so, surely.

* * *

So began the private time of my life.

It was, as I had expected, filled. One can start with the letters, which they'd sorted into a stack a hand-span high, from those I knew, and a cabinet full, from those I didn't. I'd barely been back a day when Azaila visited to ask me to teach at the School, someone from Terera University offered me a share teaching state philosophy, someone else offered me a share teaching general-craft, archivists and Pages people wanted me to write about this and that. The Workfast Literary, that had seized on the press and blossomed to ten times its old size in Arko, were after me for a book. There was a letter from Artira, in the golden ink on Imperial stationery; but it was all personal, nothing political, though I had thought she might like my counsel. Still, she sought to be out from my shadow.

I lazed for a time, until the itch to do outweighed the tiredness; then I took up teaching at the School, though not at the University, and found my hands more than full raising our horde of children and trying to keep the house in some slight order. It came to be called the Hearthstone Independent, the play on words winning me no friends among purists, though I didn't invent it. People were always coming and going. Kaninjer, whom of course I could no longer employ at state expense, asked for chambers in which to set up a practice, so his patients were always about; the petty-press drew its clients; the children brought their friends to track mud through the library; and with Skorsas in the house, of course, we could not help but host parties, though he always cursed me for holding down the ostentation. I kept away from news people. Much time I spent in the sky; there, clinging to the air and life by a delicate device of silk and bamboo, hearing no voice but the wind's, one is truly alone.

It didn't seem to matter to Workfast Literary what I wrote the book about, as long as I wrote it, so, slavishly imitating the style of Norii Mazeil as best I could in Yeoli, I wrote whatever came into my head. It seemed to divide itself into four subjects: warcraft and general-craft, politics, ruminations which, if one must dignify them with a category, could be called philosophy, and tales from my past. The first three

I imagine will someday be collated into books; the fourth, which the workfast got most interested in, became this one.

I'd noticed from the moment I'd got home that Fifth, now ten, had a constant look of carrying a boulder, again. Esora-e had started giving him extra training once more, while I had been in no state to protest and Niku away; he'd convinced Shaina and Etana. Abjuring wasn't enough, it seemed; if I wanted my son free of this after I died, I would have to give it in writing to the School.

So I did, then took him up the mountain for a long talk. He was old enough now, the idea of appearances and deceptions well enough worked into him, that he was still afraid of me even after I carried him on my shoulders. When I asked him how he was liking his training, his eyes went glummer than an adult's should, let alone a child's, and he said, "I'm not doing well enough, sir." Sir, of all things. He might as well be standing on the far ridge, my own son. That night when I fought with Esora-e about it, I got so angry I nearly struck him.

"I didn't ask you how you were doing," I said. "I asked how you are liking it, what is in your heart." He stared at me with his pure green eyes wide, full both of terror and wild hope; then he bowed his head, one hand clenching and clawing at the other fist. That was answer enough. "You may quit extra training if you like," I said. He looked up shocked, like an innocent wrongfully charged hearing his reprieve, but not quite sure he deserves it. "But if you go on, it will be with me. What do you say to that?" He considered for a while in his way, the brows furrowing just like my own, but more thoughtful than I at that age, then thrust his hand out, chalk.

"We're training now then," I said. His eyes popped; he didn't have his sword, I didn't have mine, he wasn't in his training clothes, and his Teacher, of all things, started a tickle-fight as the first drill. "Trust me, lad," I said when he asked me what I was about, "I know what you need." That he asked me in itself was an improvement. On the mountain we trained, taking joy in playing games, taking joy in talking philosophy, taking joy in straining our bodies until we were dizzy and sweating rain barrels. He could barely wait for the next day.

I picked up the thread of the news again, and kept abreast of it. Though these things were my work no more, I found myself still fascinated by them, after everything; it's a snake-bite, I suppose. Artira was listening, as Mana had predicted in my dream, too much to the hawks. Laws that favored Arkans at Yeolis' expense got delayed or forgotten; the feel of the Pages got more cautious, easier on the Marble Palace. She did start writing me with questions, after all, on things Arkan; but of course I could not make her act on my answers.

I kept up my urging on this matter of federation, drawing up in detail the proposed treaty, and sending it around. But all I could do was urge, and my arguments had lost some force, it seemed, for my impeachment. More than anyone else, my sister could have acted. But she kept saying Arko kept her too busy, and my impression from what got into the Pages was that she thought of the whole thing as my typical-crack-brained idealism. I hardly need say, some people fobbed it all off as power-mongering, my trying to set myself up as Executor since I was no longer Imperator. My friends on thrones all waited, for I know not what.

Centered in Vae Arahi was a fairly well-organized campaign to reinstate me, of all things. They called themselves the Alliance Chevengani, but were commonly known as the Bring Back Chevenga-ists. They'd kept it alive through Yeoli sentiment, clear-eyed regret—no one claimed I thought myself god now—and anger that a Yeoli majority had not got its way. They were split over whether they should press for the division of Yeola-e and Arko, which they feared, or seek support for me in Arko, which seemed starry-eyed, to put it politely.

There was no law allowing for the reinstatement of an impeached demarch (part of their proposed course was to write one); to my mind that also meant no law required an impeached demarch to accept reinstatement, either. Despite this, they did not approach me to ask how I felt about it. I think the wisdom had gone round that given my delicate state, the time was not yet ripe; or as it might otherwise be put, after all I'd gone through getting over it, they'd have a cursed lot of nerve to come to me about taking it on again. Or perhaps it was the principle, the people wills, the demarch has no say, though I was one of the people now. Still, they made their intentions for my life no secret. Even though I could not see it coming to anything, I'd learned to feel a sense of my life as my own, so I rankled.

I asked after Krero. Haiksilias had dropped the charges after my impeachment, and Krero had come back, to stay in Arko, with Arkans and hawks, whom he despised, and who despised him; his letters to his parents were strictly formal, and infrequent. He felt himself a traitor, not worthy to come home. I wrote him, to say I forgave him, so he should forgive and stop outcasting himself; he did not answer. I took it on myself to write him every moon, telling him my news and my heart, as before, and making my argument in different words each time. No answer ever came; I could only hope it was working on him.

I visited F'talezon. It meant leaving my family; but that might not be all bad. The truce Skorsas and Kallijas held had gained some warmth, and might do more in my absence, good preparation for my longer absence. Niku understood, it was now or never for me these days, with all things.

I went on one of Megan's ships. The journey up the Brezhan is long, and has been described well in other books. What I remember most is my first sight of Shamballah, the star that is said to be a machine, built before the Fire. I watched it set on the same horizon from which the other stars, Nature's, rose. F'talezon itself is a spectacular city, set half on a mountain, half in a gorge, with the royal palace— the Dragon's Nest, it is called—and the rich quarter half dug into the mountainside, underground places being considered superior. I remembered Mikhail's rooms, buried in his mansion in Brahvniki. All the people are tiny, and steer clear of foreigners; I felt like a gawky white Srian who hadn't bathed for a month.

As to state affairs there, one could not imagine worse. The power of the Woyvode, Ranion called Dread Lord, was absolute, and Megan claimed he was worse than Kurkas; I found that hard to believe until she told me some of his atrocities. Kurkas had at least kept his secret, and few, and spared his own people. Ranion, it seemed, spent all day at it. He was openly insane, thinking he was the Dark Lord, the Zak people's devil, and played with people's lives and deaths as a child does with insects. It was his wife Avritha called (behind her back) the Viper, who ran the state, her spies and secret helpers thick as fleas on a sick dog, a sane tyrant keeping a mad one in power. Zak politics is complicated—or simplified, some might say—by the great water gates at the foot of the lake, which if closed would flood the city. Each day, a key must be turned and levers moved in a secret sequence, to keep them from closing of themselves. Only the Woyvode knows the sequence, and wears the key around his neck.

Intrigue is a national pastime, more for sport than any greater purpose, so people couldn't believe such a political soul as I hadn't come for some subtle game. Everywhere I went, my whole stay, I was shadowed by a tiptoeing tableau of never less than fifteen watchers, the number increasing as time went by and I did nothing surreptitious, making them think my game must be of a heretofore unimagined, fiendish subtlety. There'd be fewer beggars here, I kept wanting to say, if half the citizens weren't sneaking around instead of doing something useful.

Better not to deal with the powers that be, Megan told me. But I'd sent a letter to the Nest saying I was coming, strictly on personal business, a courtesy, from one such as me. I had got back a dinner invitation from the Woyvodaana Avritha.

By the Oath of the Scrivener, I must write all, or if I leave out part, I must give good reason. Accordingly, the details of what passed between Avritha and me I omit, because she herself asked me to. Some day, she says, she might tell her own story; I leave it to her.

Suffice to say, despite all I'd heard, we became friends, and shortly thereafter she took the decision to cast off the madness of the Dragon's Nest. That meant plotting to overthrow her husband; despite all that had been said, she did not have it in her, in the end, to leave her people in his hands. I will admit I had some part in convincing her. But again, that is her tale. She and I wrote to each other, and she would tell me her auguries. Like all Zak, she had a gift: hers was to halt mid-sentence, her white face framed in its wonderful fine black hair going blank as a doll's, say some words in archaic speech, and then continue the sentence as if nothing had happened, unaware it had. People around her had long since learned to record the words, for they always played out true.

I have three loves, I thought one day, when I was back home, and I have told only one. Because we fell into it rather than planned, because I was not thinking of marriage . . . Rarely, since we were young yet, but too often, Skorsas or Kallijas would plan or joke of our old age. One can hardly call it loving twice as much, I thought, to live so falsely.

Yet I wondered, now that the time was so soon, whether it would be crueler. I feared more for Skorsas, who leaned so completely on me. I spoke long with Niku, but she couldn't make up her mind; my mother likewise, saying she did not know well enough the mind of Arkans on such things. It's another Arkan I need to ask, I thought, spurring myself to do what I should anyway. Up on the mountain after a long sparring session, I told Kallijas.

He took it like the great warrior he was, one who lives hard and happy though clear-eyed that he or anyone can die any moment: dry-eyed, concerned for me before himself, and saying, of course, how now he understood me so much better.

"Don't worry for me," I said. "It's no shock; I've never really known anything else. It's others, it troubles."

He said in his sincere way what I'd take as the baldest flattery from anyone else, how every fall makes me shine brighter and so forth. Finally he asked, "Is that why you kept it secret?"

"Well . . . it was for my own sake too. I thought people might put bounds on me I didn't want." He nodded, and said, "You were a child, and perhaps that is a child's thinking; perhaps it would have bothered people less than you thought. You're from a family of warriors, after all . . . yet people want a king who'll last, you certainly got trouble for taking risks in the war. Perhaps they wouldn't have approved you; and that would have been worse, for all the world."

Having chosen young and put it behind me, I'd never

thought out with an adult's knowledge how it might have been the other way. Later that night, I would, imagining I had done nothing else differently: and I would come, at least for a moment, to the awful conclusion that it was a child's thinking, and I should have told. My mother would have convinced my shadow-father my foreknowledge was true, and not to try to save me; I would have shown the same promise, and been considered worthy of demarchhood by my people as I had by her; it would have made no difference in the Mezem, or in either war; and I would have lived entirely free of falsehood, taken for what I truly was.

But one cannot regret things done so long ago; and besides, on second playing-out, I saw it more soberly. Probably it would have gone thus: Esora-e and some others I would have got along even less well with, bucking their precautions; I would have got a name for recklessness, and not been approved for the demarchy. Therefore I would not have gone on the peace mission and got captured; in the Arkan War I'd have worked my way up through the ranks to First General First, perhaps, if I'd not got killed in the first Arkan push. Yet we might have lost the war, since I would not have been empowered to forge alliances or ask loans. I would probably have been remembered as the demarch's doomed warrior brother, who'd gone down with my country. Perhaps; or perhaps not. Such knowledge is denied us.

Kallijas looked on me as if I were even more precious than before, while I told him who else knew. I didn't swear him to silence, knowing I need not. Finally I said, "Do you think I should tell Skorsas?" After some thought, he answered, "No, I don't. I think he'd start mourning the instant you told him, and lose all the joy of his last time with you."

This had a sound ring, but wanting to be sure, I wove into a conversation with Skorsas himself the question, "If I happened to have a dream that foresaw my death, would you want me to tell you?" He answered emphatically, "I wouldn't want to know!" My question couldn't be answered more clearly.

In the next few days I found myself wondering, "Had my father foreknown, would I have been thankful for his not telling me—or angry that he would hide such a thing? Angry, I know. Angry that he had not trusted my strength." Fifth was ten, Kima six, Vriah five but old enough in mind to understand. I owed them no less than my lovers.

Niku and I talked long on this. In the end, we decided Fifth would most likely feel as I would have, and when we told him, Vriah would feel the ripples, and come asking, from which as always there would be no hiding. Kima was too young yet; when later in life she found out, she would not blame me for telling Vriah and not her, knowing what Vriah was. So I hoped, at any rate.

So I took my Ascendant up on the mountain after training. Once he guessed its importance he knelt like a warrior. I had a sudden remembrance of him the size at which I'd first seen him, and thought, "So big. Almost a man." As always, I could not look him straight in the face all through, as I told him.

His first words were a blade thrust through my heart. "If you knew, why weren't you with us more?" When I'd caught my breath I made my answer, the truth: necessity. I was lucky he was old enough now that that meant something to him. But he made me swear never to go away without him again, an oath I will keep to the last.

Vriah asked what was bothering me as I readied myself to tell her, and tried to soothe me; then she took it with unearthly calm. Perhaps she had always sensed it, from the shape of my feelings. She asked me her sensible questions, did I know for sure, could I stop it, and so on; then spoke her heart in her water-drop-clear way: "I'll miss you, Aba." People die, their loved ones grieve, then go on; she knew all that, well enough not to imagine it could not happen to her.

There were tears and tantrums; they went through all the phases like everyone else, even while keeping the secret. But children are rubber, resilient, soon accepting all that comes as threads in the cloth of life. I would die, and so it was meant to be, and as with every other circumstance of life, they soon came with questions. "Do you know if you're going to get 'sassinated?" "Who are you going to leave everything to?" "If you're a ghost like Grandpa, will you come back and haunt us?" "Are you scared?" It was both pain and balm to my soul, at once. No adult would ever ask or speak of such things with me so forthrightly; it banished the shadows of secrecy, let me be accepted, for once in my life, in my entirety. In the meantime we all got on, they more hurried now, with the business of life: enjoying each other's company while we had it. Fifth and Vriah even urged the others, without saying why, to be with me. Perhaps they know they will be thanked some day.

This was all in late summer, the moon in which the shepherds begin to bring their flocks down to lower slopes. After the first snow dusting of the Hearthstone Independent, I heard through the grapevine that Krero was home, to visit his parents. I went there, thinking I would drag him out by the ear if I had to. His father let me in, led me straight to where he was sitting by the fire.

He was changed so much I had to look twice to know him. No more Arkan satin flash; he wore rough black, collar to toes, not so much as a jade bracelet, with his hair long and unkempt; he sat with head bowed and shoulders curved, the set habitual, like an old man's; shame had eaten at his face too, hollowing his cheeks and creasing his eyes. At his hand was a cup, though it was still morning; coming close, I smelled wine on him, too much.

He flinched when I put my hand on his shoulder, as if it were a brand, knowing my touch without looking. "I didn't mean you to know I was here. I wish you didn't. No, please don't . . ." I embraced him anyway; he was like stone in my arms.

"A deep crevasse, you've let yourself slip down into," I said. "All-spirit!" I'd seen no crystal, hoped he was wearing it inside, but now feeling for one, found nothing. "Krero. I did that once. You know what I was, then."

"I should not wear it. I am no Yeoli. I cut down my best friend."

"The sword wasn't in your hand, Krero. You didn't cast a thousand thousand chalk votes. Besides, the wound didn't kill me, and doesn't hurt any more. I want you to see my new place."

"I began the stroke. If I hadn't—"

"Someone else would have. One of the hawks, as soon

as he thought of it. Or worse. I'd trust you with my life, Krero."

"You always trusted me too much! You turned your back, and I stabbed, just like . . ." He spoke the name of the Enchian who murdered my father.

"What you are is a man with a good heart who's occasionally a bone-headed idiot, not knowing when to stop pushing, because your heart sometimes fears. Like anyone."

When he spoke bitterly of having played Trust Me Trust You, I thought, that is the answer. "Come up on the mountain with me, Krero." I made it a command, though I had no right: *"Come."*

At the cliff's edge I almost regretted bringing him, by the way he looked over. I kept a grip on him all the time. Again and again, I kept wanting to say, "Where you are I have been, I know your heart, listen!" But from being there I knew he would not.

He climbed over the edge first, to hang from my hands. "I trust you," he said, when I commanded, and let go my wrists. Heavier, he was, than in childhood; but my fingers were stronger. Somehow it was a balm to him, for he threw his head back and closed his eyes, and whispered, "All-spirit." It made me remember why I'd had a childhood affair with him. Then he closed his grip on my wrists again, swinging and shifting to get it tight, and said, "I trust myself. Let go, Chevenga."

His eyes were too still, too set; if there was determination in them, it was the wrong kind. I said, "You always try to choose my way, Krero. First you won't let me forgive you. Now you want to make me your murderer."

He let go again, and bowed his head so his face was hidden; I saw a tear flash in the sun, beginning a long fall. "Why not, Cheng? It's justice!"

"Oh yes! The one friend betrays the other, so the other betrays him back, and such a betrayal, playing Trust Me Trust You! A powerful little tale, Krero! But the villain begs to be excused."

"No one would ever know!" he cried. "You could say I slipped!" The wind was rising; he swung in my hands like a pennant.

"*I* would know. And that is enough. Do I have to drag

you up like a drowned dog or will you help?" He half-helped, which was good; my arms were tired.

He didn't want to do the second part, my turn to hang, afraid that even if he held with all his might he'd somehow drop me. I convinced him by grabbing his wrists and slipping off the edge, like an otter off a rock. He gasped and his clasp went so hard it hurt my wrists. When I said "I trust you," and loosed my fingers, his tears fell like rain on my head, or into the great distance I saw fade away under my feet. "How can you? How can you?" When we were done and I was back up and safe, he made a move for the edge; so I grabbed his hair, clamped my arm around his neck and dragged him back. This hadn't been the answer.

What does he need? Not kindness; it hasn't made a scratch on his breastplate. His madness shown back to him, then, in its full truth. "Are you afraid there is some secret anger in me," I asked him, as we sat together in the meadow, "that I'm too polite, too forgiving, too loyal a friend, to show?" Without raising his head from in his arm, he signed chalk. "Well . . ." I seized him by the collar, flung him back flat, and let my eyes pour fire into his. "You're *right*." He blinked, startled; but the fear in his eyes turned to a sick and ugly hope.

I sat beside him, pinned his shield arm under mine, took his little finger in both my hands, and snapped the bone. He cried out in pain, flinching all over, but didn't protest. "Do you deserve this, Krero?" I whispered. I worked the tiny splintered bone back and forth, feeling him writhe; as I stopped he lay panting. "Do you deserve this?" I went on to his ring finger, and when he said nothing, broke that too.

I had no doubts, would not turn back, would have no regrets. Regret nothing, do nothing you'd regret; I try to live that. I would go on until he protested, until he said "No! I don't deserve *this*!", or until I killed him, one or the other. He had wanted me to kill him anyway; let him feel all that death truly meant, and see if he still wished it.

On the middle finger, his arm jerked, half pulling away, but he made himself relax again, though he was weeping with pain. "*I deserve this*," he rasped on the forefinger, but it was a chant to himself, as people make when their conviction is failing. I drew it out, doing what no word properly describes but torture, until he was shrieking like a child. Then I took hold of his thumb.

"*No!*" He broke loose, with the strength of panic-struggle, his breaths coming in tearing gasps. With the broken hand tucked under the arm and the look of a cornered animal in his eyes, he crouched, in stance. He had been trembling; now it was gone. *"Come any closer and I'll kill you!"*

I came in slowly, low, like a fighter, keeping the vicious light in my gaze. "You don't deserve this, then? For what you did to me, you don't deserve more?" He backed away, panting. *"No! No, you mad son of an Arkan! Get away from me!"*

"Then how," I said straightening, throwing my arms wide, "how can you deserve death?"

We stood staring at each other, still as two wooden figures in a story-carver's tableau of the tale's crucial moment. Then he said quietly, "You shit-eater," sat down, and started laughing.

Soon he was rolling on the ground, gingerly, tears pouring anew. "Shit-eater. Child-raper. Arkan-son. Wart on a donkey's sphincter," he intoned, as I heaved him up, and took him down the mountain and into Kaninjer's clinic, with his good arm over my shoulder. "Illsprite. Toad. Dung-knot. Sheep-diddler. All-spirit, when will I ever learn? There's no matching you. There's no arguing with you."

He stayed in the Hearthstone Independent, with my children being his other hand, bringing him flowers and making him laugh, for a month. His fingers healed clean and straight, though Kaninjer wondered why, if he'd had a fall, they seemed to have been broken one at a time. "I bounced off four rocks, landing on my hand each time," Krero told him. "Chevenga tried to catch me, but kept missing." Living with me, my healer has learned when to stop asking. Krero went back to Arko when the splints came off; but it was only to pack his things, to move back home for good.

XVI

One day in the summer before I turned twenty-eight, the courier from Arko brought me a packet from Inatalla. The loyal Yeoli residents of Arko wanted to raise a statue in my honor, "so that the citizenry of the City Itself may never forget Fourth Chevenga Shae-Arano-e and all he stood for." They had found a suitable sculptor and were negotiating for funding with Artira, who, he wrote, was quite enthused. When I unfolded the plans, my stomach went cold. It was the statue I had seen in my nightmare, surrounded by Yeolis on carrying chairs borne by Arkan slaves.

Looking at the specifications, I found my dream had indeed been prescient. The thing was to be twenty Arkan paces high, which is some ten man-lengths, and pure bronze from head to foot. They planned even to hire Zak metal-sealers, so the seams of the sections wouldn't show. I didn't want to think about how much it would cost, but Inatalla had kindly written the estimates for me. "I anticipate with delight the feeling that must swell in your heart as you read this," he wrote.

I can imagine, you pig-turd, I thought. For an amount that could feed the poor quarter for a year, they would raise my image to loom shadowing over Arko, reminding the people forever of the sack; I could see Inatalla laughing, "Chevenga will help us oppress Arko, whether he wants to or not!" From where did they plan to divert funds: the sewers, the schools, the orphanages? Or did they mean to wring more out of Arko in taxes? So I would be remembered.

I could not stop it; like any citizen, I was helpless before the will of the Imperator, now. Never had I felt it so hard. Kima, who was watering Ibresian plants by the window, calmly said, as someone must have trained her, "Daddy, do you need Kaninjer?"

I could do one thing: write to Artira. My hand soon ached, from emotion. I spared no strength of wording; the gist of it was, "If you love me, my sister, you'll nix this." It was using a personal bond for political influence, yes; but one's likeness is a personal thing too. Certainly it would be for all City Arkans who saw it, which they'd hardly be able to avoid.

It was all being done on the sly, else there should be word of it in the Pages; did Artira fear debate? I thought of sending a copy to them, but held off in wait for her answer. In public she'd be more likely to dig in her heels, especially with me.

I sent the letter by wing-courier. A half-month passed, and no answer; she's angry at me, I thought. A month passed; I sent a pigeon asking whether my letter had been lost. A day later, Esora-e, who was coming to dinner, stamped with grey eyes sparking into the clock room, where I was with Kallijas. "Fourth Chevenga Shae-Ara—*Chevenga Aicheresa!* You preening little gamecock, even now you have too many cursed flatterers, turning your fool half-addled head. How in sheepbrains did you talk Artira into *this*?" He slapped down the latest Pages, just in to Vae Arahi, on the table.

They started in on each other, a distant yammering while I read. Artira had announced the statue. It would stand at the head of the Avenue of Statuary; they planned to tear down two University buildings to make space. No mention of cost. No mention of protest, either; was it too early? The speculation was I would be delighted at the compliment.

Deep voices rose; Esora-e and Kall were glaring, near to blows. "Shadow-father, shut up," I said. "The hawks conceived this, not me. I'd like you to see Inatalla's letter to me, if you will; and a copy of the letter I sent to Artira. If you wonder why I told no one, it was in the hope of heading it off."

It was a sickly quiet dinner, except for the tantrum Rojhai threw, I think, just to distract us all. My food went down cold.

"It's not as if we can't lobby," Skorsas and Kallijas kept saying to cheer me, despite their perplexity on why I was bothered. "We've got money; we've even got a press. If you come out against it publicly, how can they go through with it?" They made plans, to write letters, to print tracts, to make speeches. I only half-heard. I was reading the opinions, even as Esora-e said, "I suppose in a man's own house he can be rude enough to cut everyone else out at the dinner table with a wall of paper." Like the first tendrils of fever, a streak of cold crept slowly up through my heart. The piece on the statue, favoring it, had been written by no writer; only bureaucrats have such a dead style. But it was signed Nil Kinnian.

In Haiu Menshir, I had learned a sense of my own life. It clung with a spider-grip in the end, as Rojhai's rage had clung to him; I guess I threw a tantrum of my own, in my grown-up way. "I'll have to go to Arko to deal with this," I said. "I don't *fikken want* to go to Arko. It's been so good, so beautiful! Why does this have to happen? Why can't I be left in peace, like everyone else!" Skorsas twined his fingers tenderly in my nape-locks, and kissed the top of my head. "The world won't leave you in peace," he said. "You're too bound to it, and it to you."

I closed my mouth. It will be more merciful, I told myself, to tell them what I'm doing after it's done. I offered to walk Esora-e down the mountain, since it was dark, and put on my hooded robe. "I didn't really think you'd want that metal monstrosity, lad, not the way we raised you," he said as we climbed down, his voice small in the night wind. I was glad it was him here and not my mother; she'd have said, "You're too quiet, my child. Tell me what you're planning." I embraced him goodnight at the Hearthstone Gate, then took the falls road down to Terera.

I didn't even know where they kept office; I had to ask someone outside a tavern. "The Bring Back Chevenga-ists?"

he slurred. "Thataway, on Lake Row, has his name, his *real* name, on the doorsign, in gold. They're in the whole building now, you know, and busy as a beehive. . . . More power to them, I say. Beloved, he's my man, no one ever got a straw-haired child-raper licking under his kilt better and quicker than he did, no sir!"

I found the sign, in gold paint, Arkan-style. There were lights inside; I heard voices raised, sounding more eager than angry. Oh, to be a fly on the wall. When the bright-eyed young man who answered the door saw me, his jaw dropped far enough that it snapped when he shut it. He was so obsequious I wanted to kick him; but under that was a glint in his eye like a miser's finding the long-sought fortune close at hand. Working in such a campaign will do that. Between two glass lamps, like an icon, was a painted low-relief of I hardly need say whom. My soul itched.

I knew many of the names and faces, and with them, the reasons. The bureaucrats liked my style better than Artira's; the warriors wanted to see a warrior on the Crystal Throne; the demarchists wanted me to finish making Arko a demarchy. The pacifists trusted me to make Arko and Yeola-e separate, washing our hands of oppression; the nationalists, the same, untangling us from foreign corruption. The enemies of the hawks trusted me to cut them down. Two of the three Arkans present looked for me to grant Arko independence, probably backing for Imperator some *Aitzas* whose name was as yet none of my business. The third was an Enlightened Follower, doing this to pave his way to Celestialis; the Arkan prayer homage he did to me was a dead giveaway. Gazing at me, they all looked like the miser near the treasure.

I didn't know the leader, a heavy young man with ruddy cheeks and a halo of brown curls; he introduced himself as Iyana Vilasena, of the Hall Workfast of Asinanai. "You cannot imagine how pleased we are, dem—" Bureaucratic tongues need a title to roll off, but my proper one, Impeached, he could not bring himself to say. "Just call me Chevenga," I said. Their copy of the Pages lay on the table, front page up, the statue article marked all over with pen. They see opportunity, I thought.

I sipped my tea, and found my hand shaking so badly I

almost spilled it. "Iyana, is there anything stronger, please?"
A cup of nakiti came as fast as if Marble Palace servants
worked here. It went down fire-hot and ice-cold at once.
"So. How's it doing?"

They slid paper at me, eagerly. "As you no doubt understand," Iyana said, "we've had to wait before we start gathering signatures publicly until we know it will not die at the
petition stage. In Yeola-e, we could win tomorrow. In Arko,
as one says, a different wind blows."

"They'd have voted to chop off my head if we'd let them,"
I said. "I did sack their city." I could almost hear tongues
being pinched between teeth; some controversy had brewed
here. "That lightning-flash honesty of yours," said one of
the bureaucrats. "The world misses it." The Enlightened
Follower drank in my every word as if it brimmed with
divine wisdom, his blue eyes unblinking.

"Yet things have changed somewhat," Iyana went on. "We
have suggested to Arkans that they did better with you as
Imperator; recently we find them increasingly agreeing. I
think, as one says, our time is at hand."

"Inatalla and his ilk hold far too much sway in the City,
all to the detriment of every Arkan," said one of the hawks'
enemies, "and every Arkan has noticed."

"One can hardly help it," said one of the independentist
Arkans. "Only an Arkan Imperator can truly have the good
of Arko in mind—aside from You, Whose Arm—Shefen-kas.
You were always extraordinary."

"In a way beyond mortal understanding," said the Enlightened Follower. "We'd be fools to expect such out of a mere
man."

"Let alone a *woman*," said the other independentist. All
the women around the table took deep breaths.

"You aren't in favor of this bronze colossus, are you?"
said one of the demarchists. "Did no one ask you your feelings? Or did you protest, and were ignored?" The Enlightened Follower stared at her as if she'd spoken hubris; he
favored the statue, of course, for pilgrimages, perhaps. It's
a good thing no Lakans are here, I thought; they'd be lobbying for human sacrifice.

"What's the official Bring Back Chevenga-ist position on
this?" I considered asking. It would be as good as throwing

a live asp among them. "I'm very strongly against it," I answered instead, and listed off my reasons. Two or three people said meaningfully they'd thought so. "I protested, though no one asked my feelings. *And* was ignored. But, mind you, there are others who have not asked my feelings on matters touching my life."

I heard the patter in the wall, of a mouse's running feet. It was as if they'd all instantly died.

Iyana cleared his throat, glanced enviously at my nakiti, then poured himself one. "Well," he said. He cleared his throat again. "We have always intended to, dem—Chevenga. It has seemed to us until now the time was not ripe yet, just as with petitioning . . . I pray you will forgive us."

"As no doubt you planned to ask me before you started petitioning," I said. His cheeks grew brighter.

Then he took another draught, and said, "Strange that you happened to come here now; we had just, as one says, grasped the nettle and decided to pose the question."

He was one who sweated easily; it formed beads under his forelocks. Yet I was no drier, my shirt clinging soaked to my back; my heart raced and I had to will my breathing slow. I'd come to this place bravely enough, as the condemned will marching to the block; but what he feels when he sees it, nicked and bloodstained, before him, here and now, is another matter. I thought of kissing the lip of Alchaen's poison cup, the riot in Sailortown, the three days it had taken me to think what I wanted to do with my life. I downed my nakiti in one toss, wishing it would hurry up and numb me. On the Pages my own form, drawn as it would be sculpted, mocked me from its victory pose.

"I am authorized," Iyana said formally. "Chevenga Aicheresa, formerly Fourth Chevenga Shae-Arano-e, do you wish to be reinstated, to the demarchy, and the Imperatorship?"

"Do I *wish*?" I heard my voice crack high, like a youth's just changing, and papers crumple under my hands as they curled. "Do I *wish*? What does *that* matter?"

They all spoke at once. "It matters! Of course it matters! Do you think we don't care for you? Do you think we don't love you? After all you've gone through, it's about time someone cared what you feel; who can it be if not us?"

"Very well," I said. "You've asked me do I wish it, I must answer honestly. No. I don't."

They all died again, Iyana turning to stone with his arm reached out to refill my cup, with the look on their faces that their lives' striving had been for nothing.

"I don't," I said, standing; even at little more than a whisper my words seemed too loud. "I would not lie to you. The world knows I loved being demarch, and, in its way, Imperator. I had a cursed hard time getting over not being demarch and Imperator. But I learned as I never could before what a life of one's own is, how sweet it is. I can be with my family for as long as I want, and they need. I don't have to give every drop of my time and strength to demands. I am free to go where I will without a hundred guards, and say what I will without it fomenting bloodshed. I don't have to worry about everyone and his brother trying to kill me. All the deaths of an Empire's wars aren't on my head any more, I don't have to throw any more slaves in the dungeons, I can tell anyone I don't want to speak to to go copulate with a turkey and if the lands of the Midworld sink to oblivion, it won't be my fault!"

I fell back into my chair; the quivering breaths I heard, I realized, were my own. My hands were trembling too hard not to show; wanting darkness I buried my eyes in one, hiding the other in my lap. Hiding, as a politician does.

The neck of the nakiti flask clicked against the rim, and I heard the trickling. Iyana said, "But *you* came to *us*."

It was all I could do to keep the sound of tears out of my voice. "You know what was bred into me. Do I have to spell it out? You asked me if I wished to. You didn't ask me if I *would*."

On their urging ("Yes, get me to sign something quick before I change my mind," I said laughing) I put my consent in writing, short and without arguments, since that would be unseemly; then as they brought out wine to celebrate, I wrote my letter protesting the statue for the Pages. They kept at least one hand always on my shoulder, and my cup topped up. Being unused to that kind of service these days, I didn't know how much I drank. When we'd finished planning and it was time to go home, I could barely walk, and

Iyana assigned two people to take me. I remember saying, as we got to the door, "Maybe you should come in. My spouses are going to *kill* me," and all three of us almost falling over giggling.

Niku, Kallijas and Skorsas were all up, it being late enough to worry. "Celestialis, something's up," said Kallijas, when he saw my state. "He doesn't do this. Sheng, where were you?"

"In Terera." They froze when I said which building; no delaying after that. "I agreed to it."

For a moment the stillness held. Then Niku brought her fist down on the side table, one of the thick oaken ones, so hard that under the thump I heard a crack. "After all we've suffered! After all we've wept! What do they want out of you? Your heart on a platter, swimming in your life-blood? And you'd give it to them, curse you, you'd give them anything, and they know it! The vultures! The *a-fahkad shkavi*! Why did I ever marry you?" She slammed the door so hard behind her the walls shook.

"What did I tell you?" Skorsas said over my head to Kallijas, his hand stroking my hair one moment absently, then with infinite tenderness, like a healer's. "The world can't do without. Along it lumbers, Arko and Yeola-e and all the Midworld nations pretending they know the way, blundering about in the dark, gaining not even a step. But this one needs only speak one quiet word, and like a flash from the heavens, everything will change again. He'll be Imperator again within a quarter year, Kall, just you watch."

I left for Arko the next day. Skorsas and Kallijas came. Kima and Vriah wept; Fifth's lips and eyes narrowed. "You swore you wouldn't go anywhere without me." I had; so I took him.

We came into the City near evening, gliding down from russet sun into purple shadow between the great cliffs. Both at once, a shiver stirred between my shoulder blades, and it seemed I should step into the chair waiting, take the sweetmeats the kneeling servant offered, and hear Hurai's and Pinchera's reports.

Artira met me, gold-haired on a roof of gold, her tunic gold-threaded too. I saw new cares on her face, no surprise, and a coolness shadowing her eyes as she watched me come; but her embrace was happy as a child's. With unfamiliar smoothness in her command-voice, gained from her new practice here, she saw us all settled.

As I told her all the news of home and she told me all of her family here, I found myself aching for protocol; how does the impeached brother of an Imperator sister raise the sticking point? She didn't speak of Arkan affairs at all until I asked her, and then it was a cool "They're well enough, thank you," and no more. She was right: it was none of my business.

Finally I asked her why she had not answered my letter. She stared at me surprised, her hazel eyes blinking. "What do you mean? You haven't written me in better than three moons."

"You didn't get it? I gave it to the Niah courier, saw it right into his hands, a month and eight days ago. Eight days ago I sent a pigeon asking if it had been misplaced; did you get that?" She signed charcoal, and for a moment we sat staring at each other with hard brows. "Don't tell me Binchera's getting disorganized," I said, "now that he has children."

"I dismissed Binchera," she said, "three moons ago."

"Whatever for? He could make your day run smooth as oil in his sleep."

Her eyes hardened a little; to me it was just gossip, but she saw it as questioning her judgement. "We had a falling out."

"A falling out?"

"If you don't mind me saying," she answered coldly, "I began feeling always with him that he much preferred working for you. That grows tiresome."

I held my tongue. It wasn't for me to answer that, however much I felt it was no reason to dismiss someone excellent. "Then the new scribe perhaps misplaced it."

"He doesn't make a habit of misplacing important correspondence. The courier might just have well."

"A bonded Niah? Without owning up? Besides, what of the pigeon?" She thinks I'm blaming *her*, I thought; this needs settling. "Artira, love, may we have the coop records checked? I made a note of the device on its leg-band."

"Very well," she said, and summoned her new scribe, though I would have preferred someone else; those asked to check their own mistakes often will cover their tracks. As he came in, with a half-bow to her such as I had never seen a Yeoli make, so that it looked like overly-solemn play-pretend, I knew his face, from some function where he'd been presented to me. He was Kosai Ninangen, who I'd known as Inatalla's scribe.

Cold went up my spine, prickled out into my limbs. "Artira," I said, before she could command him. "It's not necessary; don't trouble your staff." Her brows peaked, half-puzzled, half-angry. "Imperator," Kosai said as he went, bowing again, and to me, "Impeached."

The gold she wore, Kosai's half-bow that she'd taken as a matter of course, the quiet way everyone spoke and moved near her, all so ill-matched to her nature—it was someone else's doing, I saw. This room was spring-trapped, my chair the one at which they were aimed. Whose agents, I thought, are behind the glass? How far do they fear my suspicion reaches?

If I get up to whisper in her ear, they might argue they had to follow policy with any threat. What will be said, while I lie unconscious? I remembered the drug which acts precisely like stun-dart serum, but kills a moon later in a way that looks like illness, something I suspected she didn't know, since it wasn't the sort of thing she liked to. Then I thought, have I gone mad? I'm afraid in my sister's court; I'm imagining Yeolis would kill me.

Yet a mind like Inatalla's had plenty of things other than death in it. This all might feel unreal; but if it was a play, I was a character in it, subject to its laws; whatever hit me would be a weapon, not a prop, and no blows pulled. She was staring, about to ask, I think, what child's game I was playing; I clasped my crystal and said, "Ardi, may we speak where no one at all will hear? It's important, I swear." Whatever else was between us, she knew I was no oath-breaker. We set off for the Fountain of Silence, a loud-splashing ring of water in one of the Palace courtyards, built for two people to converse on the island in the middle of it without being heard.

Outside her office an erstwhile young warrior did that

little half-bow and asked her where she was going. "Demarch and Imperator," he said, "the Guard Captain must be consulted on this."

This was too much. "The Imperator must consult the Guard Captain on her sitting in a courtyard of the Marble Palace?" I said. "Don't tell me the courtyards are left unguarded." He turned pink, and said something about policy. "Well, it's up to you," I said to my sister. "If you want, since they're so nervous, I can arm up, and anyone after you will have to get past me." She looked at me smiling, in spite of herself, the grin of the girl I'd played rough-and-tumble with twenty years ago.

The youth stammered something else about policy regarding the presence of people not on staff. Finally I understood: it was me he was worried about. "If you don't have a sister, boy," I said, "imagine it. What would you say to someone who suspected you of meaning to kill her?" He clammed up, and off we went.

As I slung on my weapons I heard a creak in my closet. Someone had gone through my things, I'd noticed, though nothing was missing; no matter, since everything I might have wanted to hide was on my person. But he was still here, not having expected me back so soon. This is like Kurkas's day, I thought, and the sickness I'd been swallowing came on strong. Probably he was made up as a valet; if I called him out in front of Artira, he'd say he'd been tending my clothes. So I pretended to have forgotten something, and went back in alone. No doubt he was watching me through the slats, so I gave him a grin as I jammed the chair up against the latch, wedging it hard as I could. Let him knock and yell, and have to be rescued by the regular servants. Someone would get mud on their face, who deserved it.

Curtained by the rush of the fountain, Artira and I knelt together. "Well," she said, "here we are, my big cloak and dagger brother, no one can hear us. It's you who's been mysterious, not me, you know: you haven't said what this all-important letter was about, or even why you're here. I suppose I'm messing up so badly you need to tell me in person."

I drew in a deep breath. It was like trying to think how

to win a death-duel against someone armorless, without
drawing blood. Knowing eyes were on us, I kept my arms
folded all through, speaking gestureless like an Arkan.

"The letter was about that statue of me you're planning
to raise. I'm against it, Artira. Very much so. All my reasons
were in the letter, but I can argue them again . . .'"

Had I any doubts that she truly had not received it, they
would have died now, for she looked as if I'd struck her.
My sister, I thought, who lived with me most of my life: do
you know me so little? "We all thought you'd feel honored,"
she said. "Fourth—*Chevenga*, why say this *now*? The sculptor's already working on the models, the old buildings are
already torn down; money, that you're so concerned about,
has already gone into it!"

"I tried telling you," I answered, "in a letter that's van-
ished. I wrote the same day I first heard of it. Ardi, think
with me. Inatalla wants this thing—in fact I'll wager it was
his idea." She signed chalk. "He tells me of it in a letter,
whose tone, on my crystal, is gloating, over my not being
able to prevent it. *He* knows how I feel; when I was Imperator he suggested several things of that kind that I vetoed.
Immediately I sent a letter and a pigeon to you, both of
which disappear. Your scribe used to be his; did he recommend him to you?" She signed chalk. "Ardi, demarch,
Imperator, don't you see something here?"

Her eyes widened. "Chevenga. You aren't suggesting . . .
All-spirit!" She suddenly seemed near to tears. Too easily;
your life is not going so smoothly as you say, I thought.
"How can you? I defended you to him! I defended you!" I
asked her what she meant. "He said you'd got more suspicious, towards the end . . . seeing plots everywhere. The
danger of a brilliant strategic mind, in power . . . I said you
didn't have it in you, to think such of Yeolis."

My prickling turned to sweat. Had he known I'd come
back, or was he just providing for the possibility, in his
careful way? Her envy of me, her wanting to see the draw-
backs in my strengths, her hatred of my shadow; he knew
how to play everyone's weaknesses beautifully. Mine no less;
he hadn't cast doubt on my honesty, as I could have dis-
pelled in a moment with an oath or an offer to be truth-
drugged, but on my sanity, after I'd been twice in the House

of Integrity. I knelt tongue-tied. How much of anything, I wondered, does she believe?

"Don't trust me, then, if you think power turned my mind," I said finally. "Check the pigeon coops, personally. Ask the A-niah when my courier came in. Get out the truth-drug and see who turns green. If none do, then you'll have been proven right. In my term, I'd have suspected Kosai enough for a dose, Yeoli or not."

"Oh yes!" she cried. "Everything was perfect in your term, wasn't it!"

From the past I heard an echo, faint in its antiquity. *Everyone loves you and no one loves me and it's always Chevenga this and Chevenga that.* I couldn't ask her to be me; we'd already been in each other's places.

"Not so perfect as it is in yours," I said. She stared, stopped in mid-thought by surprise like the tug-of-war player with nothing to pull against, my intention. Then her eyes said, clear as day, *What are you heaping in my ears?* There was the truth I'd known in some part of me: that she knew in some part of her she was failing. "Or is it?" Her eyes caught anger, then; she bared her teeth, just a slight white crack.

"Ardi," I said, "you know I'm at your mercy, here. You could do any number of things that are perfectly legal: cast me out, try me for slander, declare yourself my guardian and commit me to the House of Integrity, issue a proclamation discrediting me. All these things would free you of my pestering. So, if you get nothing useful from it, what I think of how you are doing is chaff in the wind. Even what the people of Arko think of you would matter nothing, if you didn't wish it to; you and I both know they are too new to the custom of the vote that you couldn't wean them from it again. No one's estimation of you matters, but your own; the rest is nothing. Had you forgotten who rules here?"

Her eyes gave off a hundred emotions at once, most of them pain. My anger went out of me. "No," I said, thinking aloud. "You've just forgotten how alone you are in it." For a few heartbeats longer she gazed, then sprang up and turned away. In the din of the fountain I could hear nothing; but as I stood she thrust her hands into the arcing spray, and splashed her face with water. Droplets hung in the gold of her ringlets and the chains of the Imperial seals.

I got up and laid my hands on her shoulders. "Ardi, you find yourself having to be strong before everyone, don't you? Is there no one here who will comfort you and yet let you rule?" She flinched, as if stung. I thought of her husband; it must not be well between them, if he didn't do that. "Well, I'm your big brother. *I* will." At that she let me comfort her. Right then I remembered the office with the golden sign in Terera, and what I had put my name to, there, and travelled here to tell her.

"So much to do," she said sobbing. "So many little things . . . Did you never get tired, Chevenga? I am Imperator. All paths lead to me, I know everything, I keep track. It's all clear, even when it's complicated; I understand everything I'm doing. Yet sometimes I feel as if I'm in a mist; as if there is a veil over things, that turns out not to be there every time I try to tear it away, then reappears . . . Yet no one can be hiding anything from me, for who would? Am *I* too suspicious?"

I was about to say, "Put faith in your own senses, Artira. I was never too suspicious, that's untrue, and nor are you. If it seems someone is lying, perhaps he is, and you must face that." But over her head I saw a figure coming along the path. How his timing was so good, I couldn't imagine.

He'd put on weight, his belly standing out round, and wore a long robe, exaggeratedly Yeoli, the patterned border done in gold. I remembered what the boy had said about the presence of people not on her staff: it seemed he was. "Imperator!" he called, over the fountain's din. "Something most urgent!" She dashed away tears.

At the gap in the curtain of water, he greeted me with a curt, "Impeached," showing me a flicker of a smile he plainly wished he could make me see longer. Then he saw her reddened eyes. "Imperator! Saint Mother forgive me, for coming when you are troubled. . . . Always good at stirring the waters you were, Chevenga Aicheresa. Are you telling her again what she's doing wrong? Did you come back here to be on the throne again?" That stuck my tongue too long to interrupt. "It means nothing, Artira. It's only your own measure of yourself that matters. At any rate, there's something that needs you alone, and can't wait. Forgive me."

"Who says what's important," I whispered in her ear. "Him, or you?" She asked him what it was, as if he wouldn't say it was something not for my ears. I thought of whispering that if it wasn't in truth important, something would be proven; but it might turn out to be, and make my case look worse. "You are up to it?" Inatalla said, all businesslike concern; then, like a father, "Of course you are." So beautifully, he played.

Artira drew up from me, and shook off her tears. "It's only emotion," she said to me, "I'm all right, Cheng, don't worry. I've got to go, the people wills." The people wills, if it breaks her, I thought; that's one way she's trying to prove herself. Another way they had her, I saw: keeping her running, since she would allow it, with little things so she'd lose sight of the big. There's only one person who both knew what to teach her, I thought, and would do it honestly. But like a fool I went mad instead, and by the time I was healed it was too late.

Some part of me wanted to cling to her presence; so this, I thought, with sudden bitterness, is how fawning sycophants feel. But it would help nothing, to look weak. All-spirit knew what he would pour into her ear; for all I knew, he might somehow have learned why I was here. All I could say was, "What time for dinner, then? Or will you summon me?" She looked back with pinched eyes. Sickness and darkness pressed harder around my heart; I suddenly feared she would not call at all, out of anger, or worse, pretending to have forgotten. I'd be safer in the streets, if that happened.

"I'll call for you." I made the sign of the fist, and gave her the best smile I could. Alone in the ring of the fountain, I watched them go, Inatalla speaking emphatically, but gestureless.

She did call me. But almost before I sat down at the table she said, "Don't start speaking ill of Inatalla again, Chevenga. The past is the past. He's my closest advisor now, appointed by me, and there's no one better; I don't need to hear it." On the statue, when I brought it up: "It's too late to stop it now, when buildings have been torn down and the artist has begun. Don't you care what a fool I'd look?" Every path of conversation I could conceive came to a dead end, and she, I suppose, had nothing to say to me; so we ended up eating in silence. The meal, masterwork of the greatest chefs of Arko, tasted like mud.

When the dishes had been taken away, I said, "You still don't know why I am here, and I've waited far too long to tell you. I feared how you would take it. Forgive me." And I laid one of the copies of my letter of consent before her.

When she looked up, I saw on her face for an instant a flash of relief, that she might have it all off her hands. But it was only an instant; after that it changed into the look of one learning the truth one has always feared, and froze in that shape. "So I've failed entirely," she said, in a voice half-dead.

I wanted to cry no, not at all; but that would be a lie to my own mind. "What I think," I said, "you would know, had you been listening. Call it failure, if you want, though I never did, or would. I think you're doing wrong."

She laid her head on the table, and wept, no silent graceful tears now, but long quaking cries. The day our father had died came back clear as yesterday, and her, so small then, with his bright hair, standing dazed in the courtyard. I reached for her, standing, touched the gold satin of her sleeve. She drew back sharply like a snake recoiling, eyes full of hate. I realized I'd forgotten caution even as I heard the snap and hiss, and felt a quick sting I knew in my arm. "You'd comfort me," I heard her cry, as the drug roared up into my head. "*You'd* comfort me—you *did* comfort me! You *did*, while you had planned this, you child-raping power-monger!" I sat down fast and laid my head back, so as not to break any bones falling, and hoped I'd wake up. Her curses went on in my ears long after my eyes failed.

I woke in Skorsas's arms, with Fifth and Kallijas leaning over me, in our guest room. The guards had carried me here without telling them anything except that I'd laid hands on the Imperator, and once I was recovered I was to await her summons.

It took my head some time to clear. Parched as a desert, I'd had several swallows of water from Kallijas's hand before it came to me I didn't know where it had come from. I dragged myself into the commode, and threw up, little trouble to induce it. My temples felt stabbed with two spikes. We emptied and cleaned two of the guest-gift phials of scent, and making a cut on the inside of my thigh filled them both with my blood. "Get these to two different Haians," I whispered in Skorsas's ear, "to analyze the drug. Tonight, right now, wake them up, pay them.

"Kall, you go to the Press, and Intharas Terren. Tell him you've got news if he'll put you up, but don't say or give him anything. If you don't hear from me in three beads, tell him *everything*. Do it all in ways I won't know." I gave him both letters—they were still in my shirt, though no doubt they'd been read—and as well my account of having been spring-darted, which I wrote right there, fast. "Fifth . . . stay with me." He was no safer anywhere else. "A lesson on politics this will be, for you."

Skorsas came back from the door in a moment. "Heart's sunrise, they wouldn't let me out."

"Yeolis?" I said. "They *will*." My body felt heavy as stone, but anger lightened it, as I pulled myself out of bed again. There were two guards, a hard-faced older one I'd seen among Inatalla's retinue, and a peach-chin. They stiffened, and the first was just saying, "We have orders to let no one—" when I grabbed him by the collar and threw him up against the wall. I left no pause in my stream of words, nor in shaking him. "I'm permitted to defend myself!" he shouted finally. "Go right ahead!" I shouted back. "We'll see what the Imperator thinks of you using your sword on a Yeoli who's unarmed, drugged and her brother!" The youngster was thinking to stop Kallijas, but that blue glare pinned him to the wall, and Skorsas sauntered by after him, nose in the air. Fifth started giggling.

I held the two; while they were wrestling me, they couldn't chase or call. Other guards came running, all Yeolis. When they saw who this pair had in hand, jaws dropped. That checked the pair long enough for me to shake my arms loose, spit indignantly, "I don't know where in the Garden Orbicular you two thought you were taking me," and stalk back into my room, pulling my snickering son by the hand. More grist for the rumor mill.

I lay down until the dizziness wore off. Then I changed my clothes—being spring-darted will rumple one's shirt—

and went out again, Fifth at my side. I couldn't know whether Artira's summons would take longer to come than three beads. "Should I keep quiet?" Fifth asked. Yes, I said, unless it was something he just *had* to let out, in which case he must find a way to say it civilly. The guards made a slight move to stop me this time, but no more.

It was not Kosai at the scrivener's desk, but another, who I knew; he'd moved here from Asinanai after the sack as a clerk. His face was pale, and hands trembling. "Ch-chevenga," he said, "she said she's not to be disturbed."

I took his hands between mine, pressed them still. "I know you can't tell me, Ancherasanga, but whatever's happening will all turn out well." I suppose I was past fear; Fifth patting his shoulder seemed to help, too, for he took a deep breath, and color came back into his cheeks. "May I borrow a slip of paper and a drop of wax?" I asked him. "I've got good reason to disturb her, which she'll understand." He passed them to me. As I wrote, saying in the least threatening way I could that I had someone at the Press and sealing it for her eyes only, Ancherasanga said, "It was all so simple and easy, when you were in office." Fifth signed chalk in agreement. I snorted.

It was late, near midnight. Artira looked as if she'd aged five years; at least I'd had sleep, after a fashion. "What do you want?" she said dully. "What do I have to do, to make you call off your dog on the Pages? No one's listening." So much I wanted to say, "I want nothing, Ardi. Nothing at all."

"I want to know one thing," I said. "Did someone's elbow slip onto the switch? Or is it Arkan politics and none of my business, how I became senseless?"

"How I hate telling you," she said, "you were right."

I saw it all, mostly by Ancherasanga's being where Kosai should have. My touch, the excuse: her moment of hatred, which he'd taken for her turning against me entirely, because he wished it, because his cast of mind saw it as possible. That was when the dart had come. I could imagine him rushing in, being indignant for her, snatching my letter, too soon, too fast, too much as if she truly believed me an enemy. I saw her looking up, sharp, and under narrow pale brows, her eyes seeing. Fearing me, he'd panicked, and leaned the finger-width too far that tips one off the cliff.

"It was Inatalla's elbow," I said. She just signed chalk. All this Fifth watched from my elbow, his great green eyes wide.

Whether she suspected Inatalla only of having it in too much for me, or had seen through everything, was not my business. Unless he could persuade the army to overthrow her, which I could not see, I was safe, and that should be my only concern. So I asked no more, but only said, "I'll call off my dog. The dart's between you and me. I came here to tell you face-to-face what I consented to, not to announce it; that's not for me or you. The letter about the statue I'll leave to you."

"I'm stopping work on it," she said. I felt my brows fly up; it was like finding the wall I'd beaten my head against melted away. "I had the coops checked. Your pigeon did come in." Had she reprimanded or dismissed Inatalla? None of my business.

"Then I've done all I came for," I said. "I'll leave tomorrow." She signed chalk, the motion like an old woman's. "You're overworking, Ardi," I said. "I know the signs. Listen to me, not *them*. They want to feather their nests; I love you."

"I love you too," she said softly. "But right now I can't stand you." A hint if ever I heard one; I quickly clasped her hands, and left her. All the way down the corridor, Fifth was silent as a ghost. I'm not sure I want to know, I thought, what he just learned.

Next day I woke at the Arkan cliff-dawn, a good way into morning, sluggish with the remnants of the drug. Both Haians were certain it was the standard brew; I need not fear. As I'd promised, I had my people make ready. Skorsas was clasping my greaves when a tap came on the door. It was a messenger summoning me to the Imperator; everything metal must come off me again.

I got as far as Ancherasanga. "She wished to inform you that a man of the Pages came early this morning, saying they'd got a courier yesterday evening from the Alliance Chevengani in Vae Arahi. The writers are waiting in the Jade Reclining Room." I tore my father's ivory comb through my hair as I ran through the corridors; then wondered why I was running. A politician again, I thought.

The world has more spawn-presses, I thought when I saw the crowd, a good fifty strong, with a Brahvnikian, a Lakan and three Enchians as well as Arkans and Yeolis. The buzz cut to silence as they saw me; I gathered by the first questions they'd expected her, and had not even known I was in Arko.

I told them the Bring Back Chevenga-ists had asked me and I had consented, but left out that I'd gone to them; when asked why now I said they had thought the time was ripe, which by Iyana's word was true. As is their calling they looked for the snide remark, the trick, the ulterior motive, even dared me to begin my campaign, since why else could I be here? It was those writing for foreign chronicles, I noticed, who were the most daring, unlike before. You need to ask, I wanted to say to the Arkans, why I'm here? When they did I answered only that the Marble Palace was treading a way I disagreed with, and would say no more until petitions were officially struck. When someone, bless her soul, asked was this really what I wished after all that had passed, I said, "What I wish is no matter in the face of the people's will." Half of those skittering pens, I'll wager, wrote that down as "Yes." Indeed I was a politician again.

I divided my time in half. In both nations I said I meant to see the two separated, a constitution enshrined in Arko and an Arkan Imperator chosen, by election, of course. In Yeola-e, I asked, "Are we oppressors? Shall we make them our slaves forever?" Too many for my taste roared back, "Yes!"; but I doubted they were a majority. I would tell them, "Shout at me with your old anger, then, but vote with the God-in-You." In Arko I said, "I set Arko free from Kurkas; I will set Arko free from Yeola-e." It was almost funny, to hear Inatalla declaim. "Don't believe him!" My letter to Artira on the statue was public knowledge now, as was how he'd intercepted it.

The hawks spared no expense, of course. Having little to say they made up plenty, as before; I was despot in my own right, my mind was soft, I was a fanatic, my objection to the statue was a play for power, I'd invented the letter to discredit Inatalla. All things I could make hash of with a few well-chosen words, half of them joking. As before, most of the writers were on my side, some for no other reason than that I was better for tales and quotes than Artira, but more, I think, because they knew I would set them free again too. (My own spawn-press, I should add, was never used in the debate; I'd sworn an oath to use none of my money or property to reinstate myself.)

Artira said very little, aside from, "The people will choose." The only time she ever called listeners to her was after Faraiko despised me in a speech for betraying my own sister; she did not take it as such, she said, and anyone claiming I'd meant it so lied. Once she announced the statue was being halted, it faded as an issue, a relief to all. The hawks could hardly champion the artwork while spitting on the model, vice versa for us. I should add, I suppose, that the head was completed: the artist, having already wrought its sections, begged us on his face not to undo his work. It is now in a room in the Marble Palace, public but not prominent, so that Arkans may see it if they wish, but don't have to. It is taller than I am.

It was a race to get the count done before snow closed the passes. By the time everything was tallied, the Lake was too cold for the Test; I'd have to do it in Arko alone for now, and come back to Vae Arahi in spring. As I'd expected, from the wind in the air, I got voted back. What I didn't foresee was by how much.

XVII

Artira stayed in Arko; I was in Hall when the numbers were read. I wept, letting myself take it too much to heart, I suppose; no one votes out of sheer love, at least no one with half a mind. Perhaps in Yeola-e it was love. In Arko: who can say, precisely? Many wanted to see the last of our sway, of course; others looked to keep their freedom; still others thought of me more as their own in the end, their Karas Raikas, who understood and was not shy of them. There were even those who just wanted to see another Imperator toppled, to feel their own power again, or wanted to see me move to their hand, banishing me, calling me back. All told, it came to some eight in ten, in both nations.

I stayed for a night of celebration in Vae Arahi, then went to the City Itself courier-style with Niku and Kallijas. The rest of my family followed by ship, everyone this time; the vote bespoke our safety.

It was twilight, the city quiet, when we came in. I made my greetings and sat to dinner with Artira. She, I knew, would also take the count to heart; yet she seemed cheerful, and said laughing, "Thank All-spirit for my big brother, who comes and takes these messes off my hands!" Then, when we'd barely finished, one of the butlers ran in, making the half-bow. "Imperator, there's a mad crowd at the doors, all shouting for the Imperator-elect!" She sprang up, paling, and had begun ordering the guard called out, when he made himself clearer: they were revellers, after my company, not my head.

Some will take anything as an excuse for a festival, I thought. Still, they are my people, however few; I shouldn't deny them. I went out into the moonlight with my single torch. There was a roar louder and deeper and longer than the sea; from near I could pick out the word it was made up of, my name. Gathered in the square, waving white scarves and banners, chalk-dusted black gloves, herb-pipes and flasks of wine, were a good thirty thousand Arkans.

We called you, they said in their myriad ways as I went out among them, touched by a hundred gloved hands while the guard all shook in their boots. We called you, and as we knew you would, you came. You are ours, spoke the blond-framed laughing faces, the shoulders I was lifted onto; you are here because we wanted you, you will do best for us, you will be our hand, our will. Chevenga, demarch-Imperator, you are our power, our will, our freedom. How could we not love you?

As after I'd killed Riji, they bore me all through the City; in a moment I was drunk just from the flying streams of wine I managed to catch in my mouth; I remember the Demarchic Guard pushing after me, trying for some semblance of formation, the writers chasing with pens, yelling "Shefen-kas, any comment?", Niku and Kallijas getting a grip on my ankles, then being lifted themselves. I had on a white linen shirt; feeling that was still not plain enough I threw it off; shortly thereafter I found myself naked but for crystal, wisdom tooth and Mana's arm-ring, and the people, Arkans, not caring a whit.

It lasted all night; I was still clasping hands, though I couldn't have walked if they'd put me down, when the east paled; as one we toasted the rising of the sun over the cliff. And thinking what it all meant, I wept out my heart. How many people are lucky enough to see all they have lived and worked and broken their hearts for so embraced, their faintest but fondest hopes answered tenfold, the pain and enmity they've dealt so forgiven, and answered with such love? "This is the greatest happiness I've ever known, or ever could know," I thought, then said, kneeling to kiss their hands, blind with tears. "All my questions are answered. There is no pain or doubt or grudge, none whatsoever, left in me. I will live out my life filled with this shining."

In that spirit, I did the Kiss of the Lake in the Palace Square fountain, took the robe and the seals, and began work with Artira. Now I learned what it was to be an Imperator with free hands, my wishes consecrated by the people. But as she laid the notes and records of her reign out before me, I thought, "The measure of my victory is the measure of her defeat. Or so she must feel."

She did the work left to her thoroughly and smoothly, having plainly prepared long in advance. She was as cheerful as before, and casual; but then so had I been, and there was a stiffness and a numbness, like a wooden doll's, and a rarity of her eyes meeting mine, that was too familiar.

On the last two days, as we finished up, I began asking her plans. To go home, she replied, and be with Kinishala. Pat answers; she said nothing of having children, as they so badly wanted. But when I spoke my concern, mentioning how it had been with me, she answered sharply, "Don't worry, Fourth Chevenga. As everyone says, I am not you."

Not knowing what else to do, the last night, I left her; then while Kallijas kept an eye on the bead-clock, since the sand-timer was coming by ship, I lay awake wondering whether I was killing her by inaction. A bead short of midnight it came to me what I must tell her that I had not.

I brushed through the gold chain curtain and padded blinking along the corridor in my robe, something I would not have felt entirely safe doing, in my first term. The guard at her door, an Arkan, said, "The late Imperator is not in, Imperator." He could think of no other title for her, I suppose; yet it set my heart racing and prickles spreading all over my skin. He didn't know where she'd been headed, only which way; I half ran as he pointed.

By the guards I traced her to one of the small offices; people weren't yet thinking, it seemed, to lock her out. "We're done, love," she said when I named myself; the words came out slurred; thinking of poisons I sized up the door for what it would take to break it open. But when I said there was one last thing, the desk cabinet door clicked quietly closed, and she said, "Come in." The door was unlocked.

A half-empty flask of wine stood on the marble plate, its smell filling the air. She was drunk, jelly-mouthed drunk, as I had never seen or imagined my sister could be. Does she mean to take a slower way, I thought, even as I wondered whether she'd had it tasted. I drew the cup and the bottle out of her reach, had strong coffee and a bowl of ice-water brought. "This has to do with death, love," I said. "Not yours: mine." That got her agreeing to sober herself as best she could.

Taking her hands in mine I told her my foreknowledge. She came to believe it, like most of those I told, by seeing so many things explained. "So you see, I won't be around to trouble you much longer," I said at the end. "I mean to find an Arkan Imperator by then, so you needn't worry about here; but Yeola-e will need you again."

She sat for a moment white in shock; then she let her head fall to the desk, and cried wholeheartedly as a baby, smashing her fists on the marble, sobs rising into keening. This isn't in grief for me, I thought—people swear to save that for my funeral—but some heartbreak of her own that my news has touched off. I waited, mute. Before she was done she tore open the desk cabinet, and thrust the paper from it before me. I read it only once, but I will never forget a word. It went thus:

Chevenga, my brother,

You of all people will understand why I have done this.

It all comes clear, what you were trying to tell me: I did fail, in a thousand ways. You were right, in every one of your points, as you always are.

You have done what you wished and planned, as you always do: you have taught Arko the lesson of the vote, that if they vote foolishly, they will pay. And now I see my part in it: I was the price they paid. You saw it from the beginning, as you always do: but you had

to think of your people before me or yourself or anything, as you always do.

All my life you overshadowed me, succeeded where I
would fail. Now this: and I find it more than I can
bear. I know you bore it, but as I said, I am not
you; you were always stronger. It is your destiny, your
nature, to burn so bright that those measured against
you cannot bear to live. I don't blame you, so don't
blame yourself, as I suspect you are inclined to do.

My brother, Chevenga called Beloved, you will never
fail at anything you set out to do, so I won't bother
wishing you success. I just wish you more of what you
were denied all too long: happiness. For marring it
with the grief my act has brought you, I am sorry.

I thought of you to the end. I love you. All-spirit
infuse you.

Your sister,

Artira Shae-Kaisa
Chiranyerai

I don't know how she meant to do it; she never told me,
and I never asked. She'd written the letter here, to leave it
where I and no one else would find it, and drank to nerve
herself up. I had barely come in time.

Having let me read it now, though, she'd clearly changed
her mind. She wouldn't want such a thing as a souvenir,
and neither did I, so to make sure no one ever found it, I
held it in the candleflame. No wonder the tears, I thought:
there is no pain purer than going on when one meant to
make an end. I knew.

We drew each other into our arms; she looked long into
my face, shaking away tears now and then, her hands warm
on my cheeks. "You see why I always hated your envy?" I
wanted to say; but it was too petty a thing, now. We were
grown up. She just said, "Poor Chevenga," and we clung a

long time, each being tender the first time ever, I think, sheerly for the sake of the other.

"Go home, love," I said. "Be with Kinishala, bear your children, drive away death with new life. I always wanted nieces and nephews. And when it comes time to be demarch—they'll reinstate you, there's precedent now— don't worry, you'll do well. I believe in you. I trust you, with my people."

She kissed my hand, thanking me for the blessing, I think, and said, "I won't fail you."

I am twenty-eight years old, as I write.

I know what those who love me, and know, are tempted to say to me. "This is the day you have lived for all your life, Chevenga. You could know no greater joy should you last another hundred years, only hardship. Die now, in the satin and the gold; die now and let your last taste be the wine of joy and the arms of love; die now, with Arko, Yeola-e and all the world singing your name."

So they are tempted, in their love. It would be the grandest ending to the story, one to leave the audience sighing. And who knows, it might yet end that way; someone could slide a knife through some crack in my armor tomorrow. But it would be maudlin, and to seek it, selfishness; the people didn't vote for a corpse, they look to the future. I will live my old lie to the end, it seems. I've promised too much to die yet.

This means no more time for writing memoirs, I'm afraid. From now on it will be fifteen-bead days in the Marble Palace for me, putting together the constitution, lobbying other heads of state on this matter of federation, seeking candidates for Imperator and doing all those things which supposedly keep the Imperator busy all day in between.

I've never been trained in constitution writing. The first lesson I have learned is this: there is no pleasing everyone, no matter how many audiences one holds. Knowing it will be graven in stone, they all want it worded precisely to suit their particular wishes. Between the *Fenjitzas* and the Enlightened Followers wanting to abolish all faiths but their own, women, men, low caste and high caste all objecting to the clause on equality, farmers wanting high tariffs, merchants wanting no tariffs, the one province demanding graven recognition as a distinct society and everyone wanting not to pay taxes, I have my hands full.

The federation dealing is slow, in truth, the others waiting to see what comes about in Arko, whether the new Imperator will want it, and be one they can deal with; I will not see it in my lifetime, it seems, for all it burns in my heart. As for Imperial candidates, a number of Arkans have leapt at the chance, all *Aitzas* of course, and not one whose spirit I like. The light of the path unconceived flashed the other day, though; I spoke of it with Kallijas.

"Tell me what you think of these traits, Kall," I said. "Arkan, of course, healthy, strong, brave, honest, just-minded, kind-hearted, utterly loyal to the Arkan people, charismatic, well-known, strict on himself, ascetic, altogether a great man."

"Marvellous, Sheng," he answered, "but if you don't mind me saying, this person seems fleshed out of your dreams, not reality."

"Well, I'm certain the idea of being Imperator has never crossed his mind—also a good sign, wouldn't you say?—and he's had no specific training; but I'd be willing to teach him all I could. Then I'd publicly recommend him." I'd promised to do that for only one, so they all wanted it; they imagined, probably rightly, it was the closest thing to certainty.

"Then you should put it to him," he said. "And *then* you should tell me who he is, because curiosity is killing me. If he exists, that is; he didn't yesterday. Or do you mean with your divine powers to fashion him out of clay, O Enlightening Leader?"

I put on the manner of an Arkan god, and mimed modelling his body, pinching here, squeezing there, until he squirmed, at which I declaimed, "He has life!" He fought me off, scolding me to be serious, and we wrestled all over the floor, ending up in an embrace.

"In truth, I do mean to put it to him, quite soon," I said, tickling his chin with my forelock. "And I imagine he'll accept, since, being a better prospect than any other, and loving his people, he is obliged to, isn't he?"

"Yes, I suppose he is. When I think of some of the others . . ."

"No doubt he will accept, then," I said; he agreed, with a nod. "Then I'll tell you who he is."

"Before asking him? Sheng, I shouldn't know before he does."

"*While* asking him." You'd think he'd have caught on faster; but as I'd said, the thought hadn't crossed his mind, to his credit. "You."

He turned many colors and spluttered many doubts, including "But I'm only *solas*!" until he remembered he wasn't, but, as we'd both predicted, he accepted in the end. Whether he will win the vote remains to be seen.

Perhaps not by me, after all. In Avritha's latest letter she writes that she prophesied this: "Chevenga. Finish thy work before summer." This paragraph, it seems, is farewell.

EPILOGUE

NORII MAZEIL

Month 3rd, day 35th, year 51st till the Close of the Present Age

Today in Vae Arahi, the village between two mountains that serves as the seat of state of Yeola-e, no one speaks his name. The pronoun, even neuter as it is in the Yeoli language, is enough. If it isn't, the negation or the past tense is.

The words hang like mist in the courtyard as people gather; weave through the offices, where the desks are all cleared off; burst out of the shocked silence over the village like blood spurting from a wound that had seemed healed. *He did, he was, he said, he would have wanted ...*

In the corridor, a long-time aide walking entirely calmly falls to his knees in mid-stride, flings up his arms, throws back his head, and wails like a child, in a middle-aged voice. "How *could* you?" he cries. "Chevenga, *how could you die?*"

I came to Vae Arahi with the Imperator out of curiosity, to see the place that bore and bred him, to see the ceremony that is most central to Yeoli political and spiritual life

313

done in the traditional place. Generous enough to do what most people would find impossible twice, once for each of his two nations, he had to wait to spring for the weather to get warm enough in Yeola-e. That I was prepared to report. Not this.

With some twenty thousand Yeolis, I witnessed him die the symbolic death which feels real to its sufferer, the only gesture of dedication deemed sufficient, in the Yeoli mind, to prove a fit head of state. I saw him reborn, to the ecstatic cheer of the crowd, redeemed fresh for four more years of service.

People near spoke to me in Enchian. The flavor of love Arkans have for Chevenga is remote, submissive, full of awe; here it's familial and hence familiar, he's everyone's son or little brother, the boy who left the village to do great things.

"Clear skies for Chevenga," they said to me. "No one can get in his way now. It's nothing but good for him, and will get nothing but better. For him, and us, and the world."

At this point, the public portion of the ceremony over, the demarch customarily dons the white robe of a Yeoli monk, and climbs to the heights of the mountain Haranin to meditate in solitude on what he has just felt, and the shape of the term of office to come. Though Chevenga protested, he was carried most of the way on joyful shoulders.

As the crowd dispersed, I wended my way up the Vae Arahi road towards Assembly Palace. On the distant slope I saw a tiny dark-headed figure in flowing white, ascending; finally, having convinced the last of the celebrants to cease dogging him, no doubt in gentler words, he was alone.

I went into the Palace to sip tea with the other scribes who awaited a word with him afterwards. Perhaps it was the wholly engrossing power of the ceremony, or the sense of brotherhood and goodwill inspiring the crowd, that lulled away any sense of hazard, so that it never occurred to me even to notice what to an Arkan Imperator would be unthinkable breaches in security. This is Yeola-e, after all. No one thinks anything of a king sitting alone, in trance, unguarded, in an open and unchanging place known to all, for several beads. Though from now on they will.

°　　°　　°

The first to know something was amiss were his wife Niku
Wahunai and his six-year-old daughter Vriah, who waited in
the glass-walled sunroom of his manor house on Haranin.
Both are empaths, gifted by the gods to feel the emotions
of others, even over distances.

Both cried out at once, in wordless horror. The guard was
shouted for; those present who counted themselves warriors,
including Kallijas Itrean and Krero Saranyera, seized arms
and ran to the place of meditation. Close behind were the
healer Kaninjer of Berit, and Skorsas Trinisas, who now
serves as his apprentice.

They found Chevenga lying on the stony ground, the robe
soaked scarlet now, three arrow-shafts standing up from his
body. One was in his chest, having passed through the base
of the right lung; the other two were below belt-height,
having pierced his intestines.

He was conscious, and had moved his feet onto a rock so
they were higher than his head, the first thing a soldier will
do for a wounded comrade, to offset shock. He was in tears,
witnesses say, and whispered the Yeoli holy words *kahara*
and *mahaiyana*, over and over, in horror, it seemed, as well
as physical agony. When asked who had done this, he could
not bring himself to answer.

A litter was improvised of spears and cloaks. Chevenga
refused anesthetic, feeling his wounds were mortal; "I have
to stay awake as long as I can," he said. "I have people to
speak to." Even a strong painkiller he would not accept,
fearing it would cloud his mind. He fainted from pain, once
as the arrow-shafts were broken off to allow him to be covered, and again as he was lifted onto the litter.

When word came to Assembly Palace and the Hearthstone Dependent, where celebrants had gathered and prep-
arations were being made for a night of revelry, everyone
at first refused to believe. Then the litter was sighted on
the mountain, and it was as if an axe had fallen through
every neck.

I have never witnessed the like in my life. In the Palace
courtyard stood two hundred people; yet it seemed empty
even of the whisper of breathing. Even the children were
stone-silent, for a good tenth of a bead. Under its festive
flowers and ribbons, every face, male, female, old, young,

wore the same expression, fixed as a statue's, of horror
beyond belief, as if its owner had felt his own death-blow.

Outside the manor house, where they had carried him, a
crowd gathered, keeping wordless vigil. The keystone shows
the Yeoli date it was built, to be Chevenga's reward and
refuge, 1554. Not even two years did he have to enjoy it.

As usual, the door was open. I waited with the scribes,
until Kallijas Itrean, looking pale and shaken, with a blood-
stain on one arm, invited us into the parlor.

"He told me to give you all one Saekrberk," he said, in
calm and even tones, drawing a flask and a set of tiny glass
cups from a cabinet. "*Korukai*, may your sorrows be softened. He's in the sun room, as comfortable as he can be.
They're doing all they can to keep him alive as long as
possible, but Kaninjer doesn't think he'll last past sundown.
He's speaking with Artira now, alone, state business he has
to pass on. They'll be a bead at least.

"Who did it, that is the worst of it. It was Yeolis, his own
people. Fanatics, who thought he was corrupting Yeoli, and
didn't like how much power he had, because they didn't
have it, I don't doubt. The woman who led them, I don't
know her name, though he knew her. That's one reason
why they got him; he didn't think they would. They were
Yeolis; he trusted them. The Demarchic Guard's been sent
out after them . . ."

A demarch assassinated in his traditional time of vulnera-
bility, having performed the supreme Yeoli ritual of political
dedication and trust, by Yeolis; in this land where politics
is so entwined with spirituality, it is in a sense the ultimate
blasphemy, an act that will echo in the Yeoli mind for centuries to come. Chevenga, to whom understanding of such
things is second nature, must have known that as he felt
the arrows go in.

Some two beads later, a servant signalled from within,
and Kallijas asked us to follow him. "His scrivener's with
him, to take questions and pass on his answers if you can't
hear; he can't speak louder than a whisper." Even now, he
would show himself face to face, let himself be grilled by
news-scribes. Everyone who could show Press or spawn-
press credentials was let in.

Chevenga lay on the sunroom divan, covered in blankets except for head and arms. He had allowed Kaninjer to do what was not intrusive to extend his time, the man who had always encouraged improved methods in medicine making full use of them in the end. A water-tube ran into one forearm, another tube ran from under the blankets to a hand-pump worked by an apprentice, drawing fluid from his chest to hold off the collapse of his lungs, while Kaninjer held a breath mask to his mouth and nose whenever he was not speaking. His kin were all around, stroking or clasping his hands, the young children gripping his legs under the blankets, Niku mopping sweat from his brow now and then, or dabbing his lips with water.

He was paper-pale, right to the ends of his fingers, and moved very little, even the constant Yeoli gestures, making the Imperial seals and demarchic signet flash on his hands, weak and tentative. Hard to believe, that this, and the white-robed hero who'd hugged and laughed his way through the crowd this morning, shining with joy and strength, in the prime of life and headed for nothing but good, were one and the same.

Yet even now, the familiar smile came, with its twinkle of gold, weak but not forced; then his usual greeting in four languages, given in a rasping whisper. He'd dictated his account; now the scrivener read it aloud. He'd given and signed his testimony, too, to be read at the trial of his murderers. Even now, he still directed everything, and smoothly.

"I was kneeling in the place of meditation on Haranin, as the ritual prescribes, when four people approached me. One I knew, Sharaini Anina, whose opinions are well-known to me. The other three were all men unfamiliar to me. All carried hunting bows and quivers.

"Thinking they were going hunting and had stopped on the way to watch me, I said nothing, but went on with my meditation. When they were perhaps seven paces off, Sharaini spoke a word, and the three men all drew arrows, nocked, and aimed at me. Then I made my last mistake, for which I beg forgiveness of all who have valued my life; I froze, and was still frozen, disbelieving, when they let fly.

"Seeing me lean back on my hands but not fall, Sharaina

commanded her friends to finish me, but I raised my arm and cried out that they'd done it in effect, for I knew they had; that I wanted a chance to say farewell to my family, and to know why this. Despite Sharaina's urgings, they stayed their hands.

"She said that my power had grown beyond that of the people's; that Yeola-e had exhausted every other means of getting rid of me, leaving those who wanted to save Yeola-e from foreign corruption, power-mongering, and the eventual coming of the Second Fire no alternative but to assassinate me; that I was worse than a foreigner, a Yeoli sold out to foreigners and foreign ways in a high position and with inhuman abilities to bend people to my will; that I therefore must be eliminated in whatever way necessary; that it was done as a sacred act in the people's name.

"I argued that my power and the people's were one, since I was in office by a majority vote both in Arko and, more to her point, Yeola-e; that never in my term had I done anything against its will, or anything important without its permission; that if any one person exercised their will in contempt of the people's, it was her, by assassinating a demarch not only approved but reinstated; that if anyone's action would draw the Second Fire closer, it was this, which would strike fear and horror into the heart of every Yeoli, that would make one less unthinkable act unthinkable, by committing it.

"She did not listen, but two of her friends did, and seemed to became deranged, out of remorse or whatever was in their hearts. One drew his hunting knife and thrust it into his own chest, and then as Sharaina begged him not to, the other did similar. They were out of my sight, but I knew by weapon-sense. Then she and the third fled northward towards Chegra.

"I knew climbing down to the Hearthstone was beyond me, so I waited and kept as still as possible, hoping I would live long enough to be found. The rest has been witnessed."

Sharaina Anina was until two years ago a Servant of Assembly of Yeola-e, representing county Aratai, and a founding member of Yeola's Children, a Yeoli nationalist group. She led the small radical faction that eventually split off, and was ousted from office by vote after proposing increasingly extreme actions. Who her younger male followers are is yet unclear. The corpses of two of them were indeed found near the place of meditation.

Once the scrivener had finished, silence fell, and lingered. Chevenga's faint whisper was heard loud and clear. "Just think . . . I have to go through *this* to find out what it takes to get a roomful of writers tongue-tied." There was a half-suppressed burst of laughter, twisted grins. Tension broken, the questions began.

Through the scrivener he told us that he was no longer in pain, so long as he kept still. "I don't mind dying," he said. "I expected it. I'm just glad not to be alone while it happens." He gave his blessings to Arko and Yeola-e, expressed his trust in Artira, who would again succeed him, recommended Kallijas as an Imperial candidate once more. He spoke of his hopes for a federation of nations, and a peace throughout the world that would last forever. All these words will be quoted in other accounts.

Asked what his death would mean in Yeola-e, he wept again. When he was a child, his father was assassinated while in office; the national grief that ensued was graven on his mind then. In his own case, he knew, it would be far worse. But he ended his answer thus:

"My life and my death don't matter so much as they seem to now, in their rawest moment. Yeola-e won't lose its spirit, fanaticism won't rule, we won't all suddenly start knifing each other. There are far greater things than the life of one person; the life of a country is a million times greater, the life of the Earthsphere a million times greater than that, the life of the endless sky around it yet another million times, or more, as no one can know. In all that I and my death matter nothing; it won't change much, and the last thing it will change is human nature. No one should lose sight of that, in their fear."

To Arko, he said, his death should make little difference politically. The constitution is nine-tenths written, the schedule for an Imperial election and the transition of power set, Artira sworn to honor it and continue his course.

He did not address how it might touch our hearts. Chevenga maintained to the end what he imposed on himself as a matter of principle from the beginning: silence on how he thought Arko would judge him. He feared it would be taken as how Arko *should* judge him, and that, he believed to his last breath, was not his business to say.

Yet he couldn't have imagined his death wouldn't touch our hearts. His presence in Arkan history, put in context, was momentary; I am reminded of a line from one of his favorite poems, "I came like water, and like wind I go." Minis Aan nicknamed him better than he knew, in the end. He was the briefest of flashes: but such a flash, bright and shattering, wide as the sky, bringing the storm that destroyed or washed clean, depending, as he would have it depend forever, on your view.

Eventually the questions dwindled and ran out, and it remained only to say the word that no one wanted to say, or hear: farewell. Tears flowed in plenty, as we lined up to clasp his hand or hug his head in our arms, disbelieving in our true hearts even as we did it, his grin and his jokes no remedy to that. Chevenga did have a sense of invincibility about him, and of eternity. Hard to remember, no one had heard of him a decade ago: hard to imagine, the world without him.

Catching my eye, Kallijas invited me to linger, since I had been close. I was alone with Chevenga for a time, and we spoke of personal things, reminiscing, praising each other's work. I did not stay long. Through the room's great windows, I saw the sun sinking near the mountainous horizon; he had become visibly weaker, moving less, leaving longer pauses between words. I should leave him to his loved ones, I saw.

In my last view of his living face, he was smiling, determined I should always remember him that way, I think, and ensuring I will.

The account that remains, I got from witnesses afterwards, mostly Kallijas. No surprise to those who knew him, Chevenga lived long past the time predicted.

Knowing he would never see another, he wanted to watch the sunset, for which they had to raise him to sitting. That taxed his strength; before it was over his mind began to wander, so they laid him flat again, this time on the hearthstone, where he had asked to be placed, his left side towards the fire, to die in its light and warmth.

His children pressed in around him, leaning their heads on his limbs, sometimes dozing. He whispered to each in turn, starting with Fifth Chevenga, his ten-year-old heir, giving them his blessings and praises and advice. He spoke to his spouses, his lovers, his brothers and sisters, his remaining parents, his grandmother, his aunts and uncles. "Yes," he answered, when asked if he heard the wings of Shininao. "And the silence in between, the silence in between all things. I can hardly hear anything else. This close it's very beautiful."

Though cut short—twenty-eight years old—he did not leave this life rancorous. Those present say as one that instead of saddening as the truth sank in, which they had feared, he seemed to grow happier as he weakened, as if forgetting all troubles, since he'd soon leave them behind. "It was as if the joy in him wanted to burn all of itself out while it could," Kallijas said, "and so shone very bright." His eight-year-old daughter Kima Imaye asked why it was so warm near him; "It is the life-force coming out of him," was Kaninjer's answer. "His was strong."

By his expression, and the words he occasionally mouthed, his dying dreams were full of marvels, of beauties inconceivable on this plain Earthsphere, more sublime than the living can know. An Arkan would say he saw through the open gate of Celestialis; a Yeoli, that he finally saw the God-in-Him in its entirety, and learned the ultimate truth, in all its wonder.

Two beads before midnight his hands ceased to move. One bead before midnight he breathed the words, "My senses are fading. I shouldn't cling any longer. Strip me, of everything." The seals and signet, his treasured Haian timepiece, the arm-ring that had belonged to Mana-lai Chereda, his crystal and his father's wisdom tooth were all removed. The healer's tubes were extracted, the mask put away; he even insisted the blankets be taken away, saying they were blankets, not shrouds, for warming the living, not wrapping a corpse.

He spoke his last words, asking those who listened to pass them on, but always leaving them to the end of the account. Niku and Skorsas caressed him, to let his final feeling be pleasure; he turned his head toward the fire, so his right ear faced upward, to let the beak of Shininao pluck out his soul. About a tenth short of midnight, while he gazed into the flames with the hint of a smile on his lips, life passed out of the body of Fourth Chevenga Shae-Arano-e. There was no sign, except that between one moment and the next his eyes became entirely still, and Kaninjer, feeling for his pulse, found none. Death took him without struggle, the witnesses agree, because he went embracing, not flinching, with whole courage, and hence no fear.

Chevenga, young though he was, prepared for his death in advance, carefully setting out who should get his belongings, leaving letters and instructions. Mana's arm-ring went to Krero, the Haian timepiece into his collection of clocks to be kept for Fifth, his father's wisdom tooth to his father's next nearest kin, his crystal back onto his corpse for the lying-in-state. Most Yeolis consent to having the four wisdom teeth extracted after death, to bequeath; Chevenga gave all his, leaving the gold ones to Niku, Skorsas and Kallijas. The seals and signet were wrapped in silk and locked in a box, to await Artira's ceremony of ascension.

As I write, arrangements are being made for the funeral. Assembly Palace is apparently trying to arrange that all his pall-bearers be heads of state: Artira has agreed, of course, and by law can name someone else Imperator for the day; that will most likely be Skorsas, Kallijas being far too prejudicial a choice. If Skorsas comes to himself by then, that is: once Chevenga was dead, he went deranged, and had to be restrained from killing himself. The other royalty will no doubt agree. In Yeoli style, his corpse will be cremated atop a pyre; as the flames catch, signal-fires will be lit all over Yeola-e, to signify the land's unity, in mourning.

This morning, the news came out that Sharaina and her remaining follower had been captured, and brought back to the palace before dawn. The secrecy was necessary, to keep them from being attacked by mobs. They will be truth-drugged, and tried. No one doubts the outcome. Ostensibly

Yeolis practice no death penalty; their gravest punishment
is *chiya sana koryala*, exile without safe conduct. That
means by law the criminal is no longer Yeoli, nor protected
by the law of any country, and must travel to the border
without guard. If the mob wishes to tear him to shreds,
nothing prevents them.

Now Chevenga lies in state, in the courtyard of the rebuilt
Hearthstone Dependent, in the shade of a linden tree. The
queue to pass the bier stretches through and past Terera.
As we wear mourning dye, the Yeolis wear black kerchiefs
over their heads; in some things, it seems, we and they are
not so different.

He wears a white robe, again. In his hair are twined the
tiny white flowers that grow on high Yeoli mountains; his
sword hand holds a bouquet of spring blooms of every color.
Under him is a bed of green ivy branches, the sign of peace.
His eyes are closed now, but on his lips the trace of a smile
remains, shy but content. The wind ruffles the black curls
of his forelock, a deceptive motion. He looks as if he were
asleep, having serene and pleasant dreams from which it
would be rude to disturb him. The tears of many of the
mourners seem to subside somewhat, as they see him close.
Even in death, he reassures, somehow.

Evening.
I did not mean to see the man, but I heard the voice, and
the thumping of fists on stone. Esora-e Mangu, Chevenga's
shadow-father, as Yeolis call the non-blood-father in a marriage of four, crouches on the floor of a small chamber,
whose door he has in his grief forgotten to close.
"*Arkai n'tye-ai m'andir? Arkai n'kra-ai tyena m'andir?*"
he cries, his voice high as a child's with anguish, but adult-
rough. *Why didn't you tell me? Why couldn't you tell me?*
On the floor is a paper, with his shadow-son's portrait, grave
and deep-eyed, that he strikes with his fists. The face, being
made of paper, does not change, and keeps its secrets.
"*Aemya si molarai?*" *Was I so evil?* Some family matter
Chevenga judged Esora-e unfit to hear, until after his death?
I cannot know.
He strikes the portrait until it is crinkled and dirtied, a
rend growing up the center, until his fists bleed, staining

the paper red too, his words turning inarticulate as pain turns to rage. He tears it in half, then in quarters, then shreds it as fine as a man tearing paper can, and scatters the scraps, and stamps on them.

A woman is standing beside me, also watching: Denaina Shae-Kaisa, Chevenga's shadow-mother, Esora-e's estranged wife, who has avoided him for some five years, until now, it seems. "*Dyanai*," she says; *fool*. But there is no contempt in it; only sympathy.

I watch, fidget with my noteboard, and think. When he comes to himself, I believe, he will regret doing this. When he sees, pain will strike, and hard tears fall, for his own senseless act; he will wonder, as those in grief are helpless not to, somehow, unjust as it is, whether this betrays the evil in him, whether as with this picture he had a hand in destroying Chevenga himself.

Regret nothing, Chevenga said; *do nothing you will regret*. Those words express both the ultimate ruthlessness and the ultimate morality, in endless and utter opposition—but to his mind, as his life-work attests, one entity. Yet who succeeds entirely in that? He didn't himself. Esora-e will regret, as his shadow-son did the sack of Arko; but for now his grief, his anger, the weakness in him that comes of being human, is his only truth. We can only see to the bounds of our strength this moment. We are mortals. That is the entire and only tragedy.

Chevenga's last words:
"Don't think I died too soon; we all do. Grieve for your own loss only, not mine; I had as much joy as anyone could ever ask of life, and I'm about to learn the one thing I could never know. This isn't an end, but a thousand beginnings. All-spirit and my love infuse you."

BUILDING A NEW FANTASY TRADITION

The Unlikely Ones by Mary Brown
Anne McCaffrey raved over *The Unlikely Ones*: "What a splendid, unusual and intriguing fantasy quest! You've got a winner here. . . ." Marion Zimmer Bradley called it "Really wonderful . . . I shall read and re-read this one." A traditional quest fantasy with quite an unconventional twist, we think you'll like it just as much as Anne McCaffrey and Marion Zimmer Bradley did.

Knight of Ghosts and Shadows
by Mercedes Lackey & Ellen Guon
Elves in L.A.? It would explain a lot, wouldn't it? In fact, half a millennium ago, when the elves were driven from Europe they came to—where else? —Southern California. Happy at first, they fell on hard times after one of their number tried to force the rest to be his vassals. Now it's up to one poor human to save them if he can. A knight in shining armor he's not, but he's one hell of a bard!

The Interior Life by Katherine Blake
Sue had three kids, one husband, a lovely home and a boring life. Sometimes, she just wanted to escape, to get out of her mundane world and *live* a little. So she did. And discovered that an active fantasy life can be a very dangerous thing—and very real. . . . Poul Anderson thought *The Interior Life* was "a breath of fresh air, bearing originality, exciting narrative, vividly realized characters— everything we have been waiting for for too long."

The Shadow Gate by Margaret Ball
The only good elf is a dead elf—or so the militant order of Durandine monks thought. And they planned on making sure that all the elves in their world (where an elvish Eleanor of Aquitaine ruled in Southern France) were very, very good. The elves of Three Realms have one last spell to bring help . . . and received it: in the form of the staff of the new Age Psychic Research Center of Austin, Texas. . . .

Hawk's Flight by Carol Chase

Taverik, a young merchant, just wanted to be left alone to make an honest living. Small chance of that though: after their caravan is ambushed Taverik discovers that his best friend Marko is the last living descendant of the ancient Vos dynasty. The man who murdered Marko's parents still wants to wipe the slate clean—with Marko's blood. They try running away, but Taverik and Marko realize that there is a fate worse than death . . . That sooner or later, you have to stand and fight.

A Bad Spell in Yurt by C. Dale Brittain

As a student in the wizards' college, young Daimbert had shown a distinct flair for getting himself in trouble. Now the newly appointed Royal Wizard to the backwater Kingdom of Yurt learns that his employer has been put under a fatal spell. Daimbert begins to realize that finding out who is responsible may require all the magic he'd never quite learned properly in the first place—with the kingdom's welfare and his life the price of failure. Good thing Daimbert knows how to improvise!

Trouble in a Tutti-Frutti Hat

It was half past my hangover and a quarter to the hair of the dog when *she* ankled into my life. I could smell trouble clinging to her like cheap perfume, but a man in my racket learns when to follow his nose and when to plug it. She was brunette, bouncy, beautiful. Also fruity. Also dead.

I watched her size up my cabin with brown eyes big as dinner plates, motioned her into the only other chair in the room. Her hips redefined the structure of DNA en route to a soft landing on the tatty cushion. Then they went right through the cushion. Like I said, dead. A crossover sister, which means my crack about smelling trouble was just figurative. You never get the scent-input off of what you civvies'd call a ghost. Never thought I'd meet one in the figurative flesh. Not on Space Station Three. Even the dead have taste.

What was Carmen Miranda doing on board Space Station Three?

CARMEN MIRANDA'S GHOST IS HAUNTING SPACE STATION THREE, edited by Don Sakers Featuring stories by Anne McCaffrey, C.J. Cherryh, Esther Friesner, Melissa Scott & Lisa Barnett and many more. Inspired by the song by Leslie Fish. 69864-8 * $3.95